Lynne Graham was born in Northern Ireland and has been a keen romance reader since her teens. She is very happily married to an understanding husband who has learned to cook since she started to write! Her five children keep her on her toes. She has a very large dog which knocks everything over, a very small terrier which barks a lot and two cats. When time allows, Lynne is a keen gardener.

Annie West has devoted her life to an intensive study of charismatic heroes who cause the best kind of trouble for their heroines. As a sideline she researches locations for romance whenever she can, from vibrant cities to desert encampments and fairytale castles. Annie lives in eastern Australia with her hero husband, between sandy beaches and gorgeous wine country. She finds writing the perfect excuse to postpone housework. To contact her, or join her newsletter, visit annie-west.com.

T0318065

PREGNANT THEN WED

LYNNE GRAHAM

ANNIE WEST

MILLS & BOON

First published in Great Britain 2025
by Mills & Boon, an imprint of HarperCollins*Publishers* Ltd,
1 London Bridge Street, London, SE1 9GF

www.harpercollins.co.uk

HarperCollins*Publishers*, Macken House, 39/40 Mayor Street Upper, Dublin 1, D01 C9W8, Ireland

Pregnant Then Wed © 2025 Harlequin Enterprises ULC

Greek's One-Night Babies © 2025 Lynne Graham

Ring for an Heir © 2025 Annie West

ISBN: 978-0-263-34446-2

01/25

This book contains FSC™ certified paper
and other controlled sources to ensure responsible forest management.

For more information visit www.harpercollins.co.uk/green.

Printed and Bound in the UK using 100% Renewable Electricity
at CPI Group (UK) Ltd, Croydon, CR0 4YY

GREEK'S
ONE-NIGHT BABIES

LYNNE GRAHAM

MILLS & BOON

CHAPTER ONE

THE GREEK TECH tycoon Nic Diamandis was deep in thought as he steered the SUV through what was increasingly looking like a blizzard. En route to his Yorkshire hideaway, he was only vaguely grateful that he was close to his destination. He was preoccupied with the infinitely more distressing family revelations that had been contained in the personal letter the executor had given him after his father's death.

Revelations that had plunged him into a devil's quandary.

In short, his father, Argus, had had an affair with his mother's closest friend, Rhea, and the young woman who was Nic's closest friend was actually his half-sister.

Six months ago, that truth might not have tasted quite so toxic. Indeed, Nic could have happily embraced it because he had always been fond of Angeliki Bouras, his childhood playmate, his adolescent wing woman. But then something had changed...for *her*, at least, if not for him. A month ago, Angeliki had got into his bed when he was half asleep and had made a pass at him. Awakening, he had rejected her in shock at her approach. And... Well, it had pretty much wrecked their friendship because he had not seen her since, and she wouldn't take his calls.

Telling Angeliki now that he was her brother would obviously only increase the fallout from that damaging incident. As for his mother? How could he possibly tell her such news when she was still so close and reliant on Angeliki's mother for emotional support? Hadn't Bianca Diamandis already suffered enough throughout her marriage to a monster? Nic's father, Argus, deserved no other label. He had repeatedly cheated on Nic's mother and humiliated her. He had also lied and conned his way through the business world, destroying those he disliked, bribing others, blackmailing the vulnerable. Argus had never been a father a son could respect and aspire to copy. He had been an abusive bully, securing his status through fear and intimidation. And Nic had always loathed him.

In fact, the only person likely to receive the news that Angeliki was a secret Diamandis without regret or prejudice was Nic's half-brother, Jace. Why? Argus had rejected Jace when his first marriage crashed and burned and Jace had been raised by his uncle instead. Jace had been the lucky *son who got away* and Nic could only envy his older brother for his escape from his own hellish childhood. That past was something he preferred not to think about, but his father's recent death had brought all that emotional stuff he abhorred to the surface again, unsettling him.

Nic slowed his speed as the falling snow grew ever more impenetrable and then sudden movement to the left seized his attention and he watched a tiny vehicle surge across his path and plunge into the field on the other side of the road. He blinked for a split second, fully aware now that he had just seen an accident, and was about to use his phone before common sense forced him to slow his pace and draw the SUV to a careful halt and climb out. After all, he was here on the spot and could possibly even save a life long before any emergency rescue could be enacted. He climbed out, a black-haired, six-foot-four-inch-tall wall of a man, warmly clad for the weather in sturdy boots and an overcoat. He walked back a few yards before spotting the car down the hill, lying on its side in the snow.

Clambering down the steep embankment, he cut across the straggling hedge and made it to the vehicle. It was resting on the driver's side. He opened the hatch at the back, very relieved that it wasn't locked. He yanked out the pink suitcase in his way and heard a woman's gasping sob.

'You're going to be all right. I'm planning to get you free. Are you hurt?' he asked, for it might not be safe for him to try and move her.

He heard her suck in air as though she was trying to get a grip on herself. 'Just bruised and shocked... I think. The car wouldn't stop. It just kept on going on down the hill and then it speeded up—'

'Doesn't matter. Do you want me to try and get you out? Or do you want me to call the emergency services and wait for them?' Nic asked.

'Oh, no, please just get me out, if you can,' she begged.

'Can you release your seat belt?'

'No, it's too far above me. I can't reach it,' she framed shakily.

'Stay calm. We'll get you out.' Nic swore, shedding his heavy coat as he tried to lever himself into what was surely the smallest car in existence. It was basically a city runabout and totally unsuited to the challenge of snowy and steep country roads.

'Without any jokes about women drivers,' she warned him.

And quite unexpectedly, Nic laughed, appreciating her snarky humour at such a moment. After all, he could tell that she was frightened by her shaky voice but she wasn't giving into the fear, she was fighting it.

'My name is Nic,' he told her. 'What's yours?'

'Lexy,' she mumbled as he stretched up to depress the seat-belt button and it released and she slumped fully against the door below her.

For the first time he saw the driver and no longer wondered why he had had no view of her even from the rear of the car, because she was absolutely tiny, almost child-sized and, on a positive note, she ought to be light enough for him to lift and extract. 'Grab my hand,' he urged, reaching down as close as he could get to her.

'Can I grab my handbag?'

'No.'

'But I can't do anything without my handbag!' she wailed in dismay.

'Right now, we're concentrating on getting *you* out.'

Lexy grabbed the big masculine hand and gasped as he literally hauled her up.

'Grip my shoulder,' he told her, and she complied as

he raised her up and she had a blurred vision of bronzed skin, black hair and very dark eyes.

With the muted venting of what sounded like a foreign curse word, he began to manoeuvre the two of them backwards out of the car.

'I can manage now.'

'You told me you weren't hurt and you are,' her rescuer complained, still carefully tugging her onward, his stubborn stubbled jawline prominent. 'There's blood on your face!'

'I think I scraped something when the car went airborne or when the airbags exploded,' she framed unevenly as she was lifted out and set on her feet. Her stiletto heels sank deep into the snow and she shivered, suddenly acutely aware of the thin shirt and smart tailored skirt she wore, garments quite useless in such weather. 'I was trying to get to the airport.' She checked her watch and winced. 'Too late now,' she said.

'At least you're alive and relatively unscathed,' Nic remarked as he grabbed his coat up and draped it round her shoulders to keep her warm. 'Do you really need that bag?'

She was like a miniature oil painting, Nic was thinking, even with the streak of blood from the small scrape on her cheek. She had tousled silky golden hair spilling round her shoulders, delicate little features and a mouth as naturally pink and luscious as a peach. Wide bluey green eyes. Beautiful, just a bit too much on the small side in every direction, he reasoned. Totally *not* his type. He had never gone for blondes. His mother was blonde. Angeliki was blonde. He reminded himself that neither was a natural blonde while wondering why he had to go to such lengths to avoid admitting that a woman attracted him even if she was standing bedraggled and in shock in heavy snow. Was it because she was an accident victim?

Lexy grimaced and groaned. 'No. I can't ask you to go back in there.'

But Nic wasn't listening. He was already halfway back in and he was so tall that with only a little ma-noeuvring he was able to vault back out again hold-ing the large purple workbag that held her phone, her wallet, her tablet and a hundred other items she didn't think she could live without, even temporarily.

'Thank you so much,' she told him sincerely. 'I have to ring the hire company and tell them I've had an ac-cident.'

'Where are you planning to go now, since the airport is out of reach? It's too far on roads this bad.'

In the back of her mind, the vague hope that *he* might have been able to drop her at the airport died. 'I've got nowhere to go,' she said, in consternation at that fact. 'And I don't know the area. I was at a busi-ness conference at a country-house hotel, but that's miles and miles behind me now.'

'There's no accommodation within easy reach around here. It's rather remote.' Nic reached for her case with a frown because he knew he had no choice but to take her back to his place, for the night at least. 'You can stay with me tonight and we'll see about mov-ing you elsewhere tomorrow.'

'With you...er, I don't know you.'

'Or ring the police or a friend, see if they're able to help you,' Nic continued with innate practicality and the simple desire to be gone. 'I'm afraid I can't hang around in this weather in case I can't make it to my place either.'

'I can understand that,' Lexy conceded, in a real tizz of indecision.

The guy had stopped in a blizzard at the scene of an accident and had taken the risk of getting her out of the car she was trapped in. Ostensibly, he was a decent man. Couldn't she take a risk on him? My goodness, was she turning into her excessively anxious and suspicious mother? Seeing threat behind the most innocent façades? For the first time she looked up at him. He was so tall, so broad and…so incredibly good-looking that all of a sudden she couldn't believe he could be a perv. Nobody that handsome needed to be, she thought foolishly, before getting embarrassed by that utterly stupid thought.

She dug shakily into her bag to extract her phone. 'I'll stay with you but, if you don't mind, I'll take a photo of you and your car registration and send it to my friend.'

Nic rolled his eyes and grinned. 'Whatever.'

She snapped a photo as he grabbed her case in one hand and began to stride back over the rough ground. Lexy followed at as close to a run as she could manage in her high heels, her feet already frozen blocks of ice. He paused on the other side of the hedge and stepped back to bodily lift her over it. Her shoes had no purchase on the slippery embankment, and he had to haul her up that as well, his coat trailing on the ground. Her cheeks were burning with mortification at her own lack of physical stamina as he urged her down the road and she saw a large black SUV parked.

'Registration photo,' he reminded her gently when the only thing on her mind was getting into his car and out of the cold.

Lexy laughed at that soothing encouragement for her to document him for her own safety. 'Right.' Chilled hands clumsy, she snapped the registration plate and, climbing into the passenger seat, she began to remove his coat until he told her to keep it on for warmth. She texted her friend and flatmate, Mel, with brief facts and attached the photos before heaving a sigh because suddenly she felt ridiculously sleepy.

'I'm so tired,' she framed.

'You're coming off an adrenalin high after the accident.

'My house is up here,' Nic intoned only a few miles further down the road, turning the car into a lane surrounded by what appeared to be a small forest. 'I like my privacy. I planted the trees before the foundations were dug.'

'You built your own house?' she asked in some surprise, because he had a smooth, polished edge that made it difficult for her to picture him doing anything that hands-on physical.

His facial muscles tensed. He hadn't meant he had actually planted the trees himself, but he didn't contradict her because an overnight unexpected guest did not require his life story.

Lexy's mouth ran dry in surprise as the driveway opened up to reveal a sizeable modern house that seemed to be mostly glass and wood. It was very elegant and clearly architect-designed. Her host, it seemed, lived at a much higher level than she did. Just as quickly her requiring shelter for the night seemed an even worse imposition.

'I'm really sorry that I'm putting you out like this,' she said awkwardly as she slid out of the car, head bowing in the wind blowing heavy snow at her.

'It's not a problem,' he assured her wryly. 'It's a spacious property.'

On the doorstep she turned aside as he disarmed some security alarm before he ushered her indoors to glorious heat. 'Take the shoes off. Your feet must be wet,' he urged her.

'And they hurt. Definitely not shoes made for walking in,' she quipped, bending down to remove the shoes and set them neatly by the wall before straightening again to take in her surroundings.

Wow, she thought at first glimpse of the metal sculpted starburst lights hanging far above, the sort of signature piece that only a designer created. Double wow, she thought as she noted a sleek bronze sculpture and the stone and metal staircase leading off the big limestone-tiled entrance hall. Triple wow, she thought, feeling the warmth of underfloor heating unfreeze the soles of her feet.

Thee mou, she literally shrank when she took off the heels. Nic stared down at her and realised that she reminded him of a fairy ornament on a Christmas tree.

Light, airy, insubstantial in some ethereal way. It made her incredibly feminine. Registering that he was staring, relieved that she hadn't noticed his absorption in her, he looked away, wondering just why he found her so fascinating.

'I'll stow your case in the guest room. It's second left down the corridor,' he advised, tugging open a door into a reception room. 'I suggest you go into the drawing room and warm up by the fire. The cloakroom's across the hall.'

Only rich people had drawing rooms, Lexy reflected uneasily as she tactfully took his advice, rather than follow him around like a tracker. Barefoot, she hurried over to the blaze in the log burner and defrosted in front of it before removing his coat and padding back out to the hall to enter the cloakroom and hang it up. Nothing else hung there and she assumed he lived alone. She freshened up at the sink, critically studying her wan, anxious expression in the mirror, dabbing away the streak of blood to note the tiny cut below her cheekbone. She had been lucky, really, really lucky, not to suffer a more serious injury, she reminded herself as she drove a brush through her long snarled-up hair and winced, reckoning that she had a bump at the side of her head.

Tugging out her phone, she made the necessary calls, one to the car-hire firm to report the accident and the location of the car and the second to her boss, Eileen, who ran the interpreter/translator company where she worked, to explain that she was currently marooned in the snow. There was a text from her friend, Julia, reminding her of her pick-up time in thirty-six hours for her lift down to Cornwall with Julia's mother. She winced, afraid she wouldn't make it back to London in time because of the weather. But she decided not to warn Julia of her current predicament and stress her out. A godmother had to turn up at a christening, after all, when it was such an honour to be chosen. Even so, Lexy was still surprised by her own selection for the role as she had only seen Julia once since university, after her friend had dropped out, married and moved to the country.

Warning her boss had been automatic even though her absence was unlikely to affect business, Lexy reflected wryly, as she received less work than some of her colleagues. The languages she specialised in, Korean and French, were not in as high demand as the likes of Spanish or Chinese would have been. Of course, it wasn't as though she had had much choice about the languages she had acquired through her own background, she conceded wryly.

Lexy had grown up in South Korea, where her banker father worked, and her French-speaking mother had provided her with her second language. Her decision to study languages had been purely practical. After her parents' contentious divorce and her mother's subsequent breakdown following their return to the UK, finding stable employment as soon as possible had been her sole motivation. She had studied for her language degree while working in an unofficial capacity whenever Eileen requested her services at the same time as working numerous jobs in the catering trade to make ends meet.

And at the end of the day, where had sacrificing her own choices got her? That unwelcome thought slunk in no matter how hard she tried to stifle it. Her mother had passed away in any case, unable to appreciate her daughter's efforts to sustain her, exhausted by the agonies of living without domestic staff and without a man to tell her what to do. Admittedly, Agathe Taylor had been a fragile personality. The most daring thing she had ever done had been to marry a much older man against her parents' wishes.

Lexy had never met her late mother's French family but had since learned that they too were dead. Her mother's sense of failure after the divorce had been strong enough to ensure that Agathe had not wished to get back in touch with her relatives. As for her father's family, they were now fully engaged with his much younger second wife and the son he had long craved. A son as opposed to a daughter, Lexy, whom he had never wanted. And he had not even attempted to hide those feelings from his daughter, ensuring that Lexy was always aware of his disappointment in her.

Suppressing those wounding memories, Lexy emerged into the hall to find her host waiting for her.

'I'll show you to your room. Like me, you probably want a shower, after your…experience,' he assumed.

Lexy simply assumed he wanted her out from under his feet in his own home, a reality she could easily understand. Her cheeks warmed with embarrassment as she questioned whether or not to make the offer she had already decided on.

'I was planning to offer to make dinner as a thank you for your help...that is, assuming there's food in the larder,' she admitted uncomfortably.

From his great height, Nic gazed down at her and paused. 'That would be very kind of you,' he told her, unable to suppress that generous response when he saw the anxious light in her clear ocean-coloured eyes. It wasn't the moment to tell her that he was a perfectly capable cook in his own right.

Geographical distance from his domineering father had given him a freedom he could never have enjoyed in Greece. As a business student in London, he had refused the large staffed apartment and the security that Argus had tried to force on him, protesting that he wanted a more normal experience than the Diamandis wealth had allowed him growing up. Argus had scoffed because he had always revelled in showing off his 'richer than King Midas' status and the bragging rights that went with it. Nic, on the other hand, didn't think he could have become half as successful as he had since been without that grounding understanding of how more ordinary people lived.

'I'll get changed first,' Lexy told him cheerfully, a huge smile transforming her formerly tense face. It reminded him of sunshine breaking out after rain and warmed him.

The big, elegant guest room was as impressive as the foyer and the drawing room. She opened her case and extracted what she needed to explore the private bathroom. Everything was the very last word in luxury. My word, who was this guy? A movie star with the bank account to match? If he was, she didn't recognise him. Certainly, he had the looks to follow such a career.

She had been close to mesmerised when she'd looked up at him in the hall because he was *that* good-looking. The stop-you-in-your-tracks-to-stare variety. Blue-black hair, flopping damply against his brow, showcasing perfect brows and a straight, equally perfect nose, not to mention the high cheekbones of a model and a full, superbly modelled mouth. Maybe he *was* a model, Lexy reasoned. Or just a random gorgeous guy!

For goodness' sake, why was she fangirling over him? Well, she could answer that with ease. He was definitely the most handsome man she had ever met, she conceded as she walked into the marble enclosed shower and sheepishly abandoned her own shampoo and conditioner to make use of the much fancier products on offer there for a guest.

It was not as though her life to date had allowed her to gain much experience with the opposite sex. Studying, working and looking after her depressed and distraught parent had consumed Lexy's life from the age of fifteen when her father had first dropped the bombshell that he'd wanted a divorce and immediately departed, leaving them marooned in London on what her mother had innocently believed was a holiday. And it *was* only a year since her late mother had passed away, leaving Lexy free of concern for the first time in years but also distinctly lonely. After all, she had deeply loved Agathe even while she was guiltily wishing her parent would grow a backbone in her dealings with her husband. Agathe had subscribed to the conviction that a husband was to be waited on hand and foot and never ever challenged. Unsurprisingly, she had received poor treatment in return for her near worship of her other half and that had included being ripped off in the divorce that had followed.

Lexy had become wary of men after growing up on the sidelines of her parents' dysfunctional relationship. Her father had been scary, cold and a strict disciplinarian. He might not have wanted a daughter but, once he'd had one, she'd had to be perfect in every way from her exam results to her appearance. She shuddered at the very thought of how he would have controlled her had she been a more challenging teenager before he'd departed their lives, but luckily he had been gone by the time she'd developed any rebellious tendencies and her mother had been too lost inside her own head to care what her daughter did, never mind what she wore.

But, even then, Lexy had had too many real-world problems to handle to act like a normal teenager. It had been Lexy who'd had to worry about how the rent was paid, food was bought or what school she attended because her mother might have been there in body, but she had never been there in spirit. Lexy hadn't had the time to crush on pop idols when by the age of fifteen she'd been an illegal kitchen worker in the back of a local restaurant, toiling all hours to pay bills her mother had ignored.

Only when Lexy had finally graduated to earn a decent wage had she had the time to date, and there just hadn't been anyone out there, give or take the occasional randy junior chef giving her the eye and making a move. So, it really wasn't any wonder that she was still inexperienced enough to be fangirling over her fanciable host, she decided ruefully.

After drying her hair, she pulled on the yoga pants and tee she had packed for the previous night but not got to wear because the business conference had run into overtime. Feeling fresh and reaching for her bag, which she went nowhere without, she walked back to the hall. It was already dark and through the glass she could see the snow piling up against the windows. She frowned.

'The snowfall is very heavy,' she remarked anxiously when she heard a sound behind her.

'Yes, it's quite a storm. Would you like a drink?' She flipped round to see Nic standing in the doorway of the drawing room. 'You might as well relax as there's nothing we can do about the weather.'

'You're right,' she conceded with a little nod of her head.

'Drink? I have pretty much everything,' he reminded her with a slanting smile that made her heart go bumpety-bumpety-bump straight away.

'White wine would be good,' Lexy responded, feeling the heat rise in her face and hoping he didn't notice.

Fortunately, he turned away and she followed him back into the very fancy big room, still barefoot because she had not thought to pack any other footwear for the hotel and no way was she forcing her feet back into the heels!

The wine came from a built-in chiller cabinet and she tried not to stare, but she felt as though she were visiting royalty because who else might have a disguised chiller in their drawing room? She accepted her wine glass with a tense smile and sank down on the edge of a plush armchair, knowing that if she sat back properly her feet would dangle like a kid's.

'So you were up here on a business trip,' he remarked casually.

'Yes. I was attending a conference as an interpreter for a South Korean tech firm,' she imparted with greater calm. 'I speak Korean and French. I spent the first fifteen years of my life in South Korea because my father worked in Seoul.'

'Interesting,' Nic commented, studying her with an intensity that made her feel slightly uncomfortable. *Thee mou*, she was gorgeous, he was thinking, scanning her pale perfect skin, her sparkling ocean-coloured eyes and her golden hair. There was something about her face that he found hard to look away from and she was reddening again like a traffic light. He focused on the drink in his hand instead, marvelling at his inept behaviour in such circumstances.

'Maybe you could show me out to the kitchen,' Lexy almost whispered.

'I apologise for staring,' Nic countered easily. 'You're impossibly pretty but I assure you that I am not about to do anything about it that could make you feel unsafe.'

Lexy laughed and said, without even thinking about it, 'I wish I could promise the same!'

Nic gazed back at her with stunned dark-as-night eyes, framed by lush velvet black lashes, narrowing.

Lexy turned hot pink and exclaimed, 'Because you're impossibly pretty too and I wouldn't want *you* to feel unsafe!'

'Kitchen,' Nic reminded her, thinking it was time to end this particular conversation.

CHAPTER TWO

NIC HAD EXPERIENCED every possible type of encouragement from women since he was around fourteen. But...

'Nobody has ever called me pretty before,' he heard himself say, regardless of his previous desire to conclude that dialogue. Lexy was now busily slamming through kitchen cupboards, checking the extensively stocked pantry and investigating the contents of the fridge in a sudden surging hive of industry.

'Well, they mustn't have taken a real good look at you, then,' Lexy mumbled, cheeks on fire as she established that Nic had a surprisingly refined spice rack and every possible tool in what was probably her dream kitchen.

Determining that he had no allergies, she pulled out vegetables, washed them and began to chop them up.

'I'm *not* pretty,' Nic informed her with huge conviction.

'Whatever you say.' He so *was*. She was mortified that she had said what she was thinking out loud, but she knew in her bones that she was safe with him because he had gone out of his way to ensure that she felt secure by allowing her to take those photographs with her phone.

She was ashamed that she didn't have any of the flirtatious chatter that women of her age usually had. She felt clumsy and unfeminine in his presence even though he had labelled her impossibly pretty. And that statement alone made her entire body sing a chorus of appreciation because compliments of that magnitude did not come her way. Not when she had grown up with a father who had once derided her because she lacked his height and, even though she had inherited his colouring, had failed to shine at maths or sports. Those criticisms had hurt like so many other of her father's little asides had done over the years, whittling away at her self-esteem, driving a need in her to support her loving mother in any way she could.

Nic stood in wonderment while she chopped at the speed of a professional chef and expertly threw together a beef stir fry flavoured with spices he had never used. Yes, he could cook, but not as it seemed *she* could.

'Did you learn to cook in South Korea?' he asked.

'No, I learned in the UK. You're seeing the results of seven years of part-time off-the-books employment in a restaurant kitchen. I started out washing dishes and peeling veg and by the time I left, I was good enough to function as a junior chef.'

'What age were you when you started?'

'Fifteen… Yeah, I know it was illegal, but my mum and I needed the money.'

'Didn't she work?' Nic was frowning.

Lexy shrugged a thin shoulder. 'She wasn't really able to. She was depressed after her divorce.'

Nic groaned. 'I know the damage a bad marriage does,' he surprised her by admitting. 'I used to urge my mother to divorce my father, but she thought divorce was a fate worse than death, so I can relate to some degree. But your mother was the adult, she shouldn't have left you to take care of the problems.'

'Why not? Mum had never worked a day in her life. She got married at eighteen and went straight into a set-up where a housekeeper did everything for her and my dad told her what to do the rest of the time. She couldn't cope without money... She didn't know how,' Lexy confessed as she drained the rice.

Seated at the kitchen island on a bar stool, Nic looked at the colourful plate of food set before him and accepted the implements she passed him. 'This looks amazing.'

'No need to over-egg the pudding,' she quipped. 'A guy like you living in a house like this...well, I bet you're not used to bad food.'

For the first time in his life, Nic wanted to deny that reality, wanted to be able to sincerely empathise with a woman, and yet he, a Diamandis from birth, couldn't. He had been born into a very wealthy Greek dynasty of high achievers. He had developed his first app at university and made a fortune out of it. He might have learned to cook as a student, but he had never in his life had to worry about paying for anything. Everything he had ever wanted was his...except a happy family, something he had longed for as a kid, growing up in a very tense and often hostile atmosphere, striving to avoid his perpetually angry and argumentative and violent father and his demands as best he could. But that was something he *could* share and at least it would get them off the controversial money topic.

'My father ruined my childhood by continually demanding that I compete against my half-brother from his first marriage. He was obsessed with me surpassing him and my brother is a clever guy and that wasn't easy,' he confided.

Her delicate brows pleated, blue-green eyes as wide and open as the Greek sky. She struck him as strangely blunt for a woman, unsophisticated, and yet she had a charm all of her own because he knew he was fascinated and he had always believed that it would take a very special woman to fascinate him. Yet here she was, the very first to do so and she appeared to have no womanly wiles whatsoever, which Nic considered even odder. He was accustomed to women who were only frank about sex but quite happy to lie, blur the truth and fake everything else in an effort to impress him. The name Diamandis was like a dramatic price tag wherever he went, signifying the riches his family had acquired over generations of inherited wealth.

'Why would he have wanted his two sons to compete with each other?' she asked in confusion.

'Because he didn't raise my brother and he didn't see him either. In fact, he acted like he hated him, yet it was very important to him that I performed better than my brother did, which was a serious challenge.'

'Parents can be weird,' she acknowledged as she

ate and sipped her water, having refused more wine. 'When my father divorced my mother, he tried to rid himself of responsibility for me as well, telling the judge that he shouldn't have to pay support for me because he had never had much of a relationship with me. Of course, that didn't fly, but the money he did have to pay was a drop in the ocean to him. It was as if, once he decided on the divorce, he wanted to put Mum and me *both* behind him as if we'd never existed.'

'How did we end up talking about deep stuff like this?' Nic enquired, elevating one ebony brow like a question mark. 'More wine?'

'No, thanks.' Lexy busied herself filling the dishwasher, wiping up.

'You cooked. I should clean up.'

'But you're still *sitting* there so you're not *that* keen to muck in!' Lexy shot back at him without hesitation.

His amused dark eyes danced like black diamonds in starlight and he grinned. 'Rumbled,' he conceded, wondering when a woman had last treated him like a regular man and indeed if it had ever happened before. Billionaires didn't get teased or mocked by women very often.

In fact, thinking about it, Nic could not recall a single woman treating him with anything less than deadly gravity when he spoke. He got special treatment. He didn't get called out on his quirks, his oversights, his short temper or his impatience. Everybody handled him with kid gloves as though he were a precious fifteen-carat diamond.

Lexy felt as though she was reeling from that wicked

grin of his. It wasn't just his striking good looks, she reasoned hesitantly, it was more something to do with that insanely compelling smile of his. It unleashed girlie butterflies in her tummy, left her strangely breathless and just about destroyed whatever brain power she possessed. Disconcerted by her own reaction, she turned away again and began to clean the counters, finding occupying her hands a great remedy for her increasing self-consciousness.

Her reactions made her feel like a stupid adolescent, too innocent for her own good. But she wasn't innocent, only in the most basic physical way, she thought ruefully. Being a virgin who had never even been on a proper date was humiliating. Sooner or later, she would have to move her life on in that line, but it would have to be with someone who was genuinely interested in her, someone with some even small degree of caring towards her. She had no plans to waste her time or her body on some guy looking only for a one-night stand. *Or had she?* Shooting a sidewise glance at Nic, she reckoned that if it were him, she could probably consider the idea, because she had never been so attracted to anyone before and opportunities didn't exactly come knocking on her door.

'Let's move upstairs. I have a cosier reception room up there with a terrific view.'

Lexy laughed. 'Is this your "come up and see my etchings" speech?' she joked.

'No, those immortal words have never passed my lips.' Nic grabbed the wine and a couple of glasses. 'More in the realms of Netflix and chill.'

'Well, it's not like your terrific view is likely to be visible in the dark,' she pointed out quietly.

'I don't tell lies,' Nic declared as they reached the top of the imposing staircase and she was shocked enough by the room that lay before her to gasp in delighted astonishment.

With only the flickering light of the log burner in one corner, the room was basically all glass, all view, and she could see the snow and the stars and the moon. It was absolutely beautiful, like some surreal dream. 'This is amazing.'

'I built it for the view.'

'Yet you don't live here the whole time, do you?' she said quite naturally.

Nic flashed shrewd dark eyes to her tranquil face. 'Why do you have that idea?'

Lexy shrugged, quite blind, it seemed, to his suspicion. 'It doesn't seem that lived in. It just doesn't have the vibe or any existing clutter. Initially I thought it could be a luxury let but then you had said you planted the trees, so I knew that wasn't right. So I thought maybe you travelled a lot for work.'

'I do,' Nic conceded, relaxing again as he hit a button to reveal the television screen and handed her the remote. 'Pick your own personal poison. I'm feeling generous.'

Nobody could have been more surprised than Nic when she put on an ancient episode of *Friends*. 'I thought for sure you'd put on a reality show... This is really old,' he complained.

'But this is more relatable than gorgeous chicks in

bikinis at exotic locations…or baking or fashion. I watched it growing up. It's my comfort choice.'

'I wasn't allowed to watch TV growing up. My father was convinced it would interfere with my studies.'

'Sounds like he was…a bit of a pain?'

'A lot of a pain,' Nic countered, sinking down on the sofa beside her.

Every so often, Lexy's attention strayed from the giant screen to the snow still falling heavily beyond the glass.

'Stop worrying. We're not trapped.'

'Your car is getting buried,' she contradicted.

'I'll leave next week regardless of how deep the snow is,' Nic murmured soothingly.

'Next week isn't tomorrow.'

'But you don't work at the weekend, do you? I assure you that you won't be trapped here for days,' he responded calmly.

'You don't freak out often, do you?'

Nic sent her another brash grin. 'How did you guess?'

His lack of concern soothed her. Her mother had fretted constantly about every little thing after the divorce and to some extent that habit had threatened to infiltrate Lexy as well.

'Is Lexy short for Alexandra or Alexandria?' he asked.

'Neither. It's Alexander on my birth certificate.'

'Assuming that you were born a girl—'

'I was. But my father was wanting and hoping for a boy and he wouldn't change the name he had chosen,' she admitted stiffly.

'This is actually quite funny,' Nic conceded of the programme, choosing not to comment on what he could see was a sore subject.

'I hate to say I told you so,' she teased.

And then Nic convulsed over one of Joey's lines and Lexy bounced on the seat and punched the air. 'Told you so…told you so!' she crowed like a kid.

Nic rested his hands on her slight shoulders as she turned to him. 'Smug, aren't you?'

Her eyes widened as she looked up at him. Even sitting beside him, she was still looking up and just as suddenly she was almost drowning in the velvet darkness of his spectacular eyes. There was nothing else in the world at that particular moment. It was as if time just stopped dead for her, freezing her in place.

Long brown fingers lifted to her cheekbone and spread at a slow cautious pace. 'Is this all right with you?'

A helpless giggle erupted from Lexy. 'Is this what happens when you tell a guy he's impossibly pretty?'

Nic's wicked smile flashed out. 'I think it must be…'

His mouth covered hers and his lips were unexpectedly soft. Not rough, not aggressive. But who was she kidding? It was only her third ever kiss. There would have been more had her mother not had hysterics when Lexy had tried to leave their little rental flat in male company. In the end men had proved to be too much hassle for her when she had already been struggling to cope with her mother. And why was she even thinking about such stuff when Nic was kissing her? Presumably he couldn't tell that it was only her third kiss.

'You taste amazing,' he said thickly against her parted lips.

Yes, amazing just about covered him as well, she thought helplessly as he pried her lips apart and went off on an exploration that made her shiver and sent a wave of heat she had never experienced before shooting up through her. His lips teased, his tongue stroked her lip line and then delved inside to provide more intense sensations. She was feeling way more than she had ever expected to feel from a single kiss. Her breasts felt heavy, swollen, her nipples prickling points and that wicked growing heat pooled in her pelvis.

'You're good at this…' she framed, struggling to catch her breath.

'I've been on a learning curve since I was fourteen.'

'That's young.'

'It wasn't in my circle,' Nic husked, gathering her slight body close, edging her carefully onto his lap, gripped by a seething desire as ironically new to him as it was to her and faintly spooked by it. In one strike, she hit every one of his sexual buttons, unleashing a craving that inflamed him, and it was infinitely more exciting than any female possibility he had met with in years.

But he was a playboy, like his big brother, Jace, he reminded himself. He did not have the yacht that his late father had dubbed 'the whorehouse on the seas' but he was far from being boyfriend material. And yet the appeal of those ocean eyes when she looked up at him? In a weird way it knocked him sideways. Even so, he was only twenty-seven and he had no plans to settle down for years and years… There, death of that worrying thought train of association.

He slid a hand below her loose tee shirt and discovered that she wore no bra. He cupped the warm, soft weight of her pouting breast and rubbed the pointed nipple greeting him. She gasped out loud and it was the sweetest sound he had ever heard. It turned him on so hard and fast he pushed against the zip of his jeans. He could barely credit the strength of his own response.

Lexy was being engulfed by a tangle of conflicting reactions. Her body was so on board with his every move that it was simply willing him on to the next step. Her brain was dimly echoing her mother's warnings about men, something crazy about why would a man buy a cow when the milk is free, a hangover from her mother's generation and out of step with current mores. But at the end of the day, it was simply sex, she reminded herself even though her emotions felt much more intense than that belief suggested. It was a bodily thing, not a mental thing.

She didn't need to tie herself up in knots about something so basic and naturally she was curious because the touch of his fingers on her breast was magically arousing. And when he used his mouth there as well, it was even better, like a hot wire tightening between her breasts and the juncture of her thighs. It made her squirm, it made her needy and she was entranced by those responses.

Her tee shirt glided over her head and vanished. He laid her down on the wide, soft sectional sofa and began to gently divest her of her remaining clothes. If it hadn't been so dark, she would have felt more exposed and shyer, but the only light in the room was the flickering flames of the log burner because he had switched off the TV. Outside the snow was falling in the most hypnotic style, big fluffy flakes drifting down beyond the glass, while all was cosy and warm and calm indoors. It felt magical to Lexy, absolutely magical, just as a dream would be with a gorgeous guy, a gorgeous house, and that gorgeous guy miraculously wanted *her*.

'This feels special,' Nic murmured softly, spectacular dark eyes locked to her. '*You* feel special. Do you want me right now? Or would you rather…wait?'

And Lexy stared up at him in wonderment, it being her conviction that no man would ever offer to defer his own pleasure to please a woman. She smiled, wide and bright then, at being proved wrong. 'I want you now,' she told him gently.

'Contraception?' he asked.

'No, I'm not on anything.' Lexy could feel her cheeks burning as he leant down to her. 'And I haven't done this before.'

His perfect ebony brows drew together. 'Haven't done what before?'

'Sex,' she said simply.

Comprehension tautened his lean bronzed features, followed by bewilderment.

'Don't look at me like that!' she said sharply. 'I just never had that freedom until Mum passed.'

Nic lowered himself down to her and kissed her breathless, struggling to slow the pace down to give her the treatment she deserved. 'I was surprised, not critical.'

That kiss connected Lexy again. She stretched up to him as he began to remove her last garments, hunger twisting through her, making her restless. He shimmied down over her body and spread her thighs and she just about had a heart attack when she realised what he planned to do. It was something she had read about in steamy books, not something she had ever fancied on her own behalf, and she went rigid.

'No,' she told him shakily.

'You'll like it,' Nic swore with sensual resolution. 'Please...'

It was the 'please' that seduced her. If he was willing to say that word in return for doing *that*, she couldn't say no. In any case, shouldn't she explore every possibility? This night was one night out of time between two strangers and it would never be repeated. Ten to one, during the night, the snow would vanish and he might drop her off somewhere and she would never see him again...*ever*. The prospect of never ever seeing Nic again left her chest feeling scarily hollow and she suppressed the thought of that scenario as soon as it appeared.

Breathtakingly exquisite sensations seized her. Yes, just as he had forecast, she liked every glide of his tongue, every lingering attention to the most sensually aware nub in her entire body. Her heart thundered in her ears and the cascade of feelings rose in a blinding wave and a climax shuddered through her, shaking her inside out.

'Don't you dare say I told you so,' she warned him breathlessly.

Nic grinned that smile that whipped her into the clouds and back with its charisma. 'I'm not stupid... I simply want to make this as good for you as it will be for me,' he murmured soft and low.

His sensual lips descended on hers again and a big hand curved over the pouting mound of her breast, skilful fingertips stimulating the beaded tip. The first spark of anticipation was rekindled at that moment. Lexy drew in a stark breath and surrendered to sensation.

When he slid between her slender thighs, she was on a high. His sensual attentions had provided her body with a slick welcome and he eased into her with care. Initially that feeling of fullness stretching her untried depths was both unnerving and stimulating and then he settled deeper and there was a sharp, tearing pang of pain that made her gasp in dismay. He stopped, gazed down at her with those incredibly warm dark eyes and leant back from her and shifted position to kiss her again, carrying her through that moment.

She felt his heartbeat. She felt him move inside her and the thrill of anticipation gripped her when she discovered that there was a wild hunger within her demanding more. It was a need, a desire she had never known before, and it was remorseless and overwhelming. His every potent thrust sent sensation shimmying through her taut body and a pool of liquid heat began to burn at her core. Her heart slammed inside her chest. She couldn't catch her breath as the wild tension built into a fierce, driving need. The excitement seething through her climbed to an almost unbearable level and then, with no warning, as it seemed to her, she was suddenly hurtling over the edge into wave after wave of glorious pleasure again. Nic shuddered in the circle of her arms and groaned.

In the silence of the aftermath, she couldn't quite credit what she had done or what she had just experienced. 'That was...' Words failed her.

'Wonderful,' Nic slotted in thickly, releasing her from his weight only to tug her back into his arms and drop a kiss on her brow that made her smile drowsily. 'You're about to fall asleep on me now.'

'Trying not to,' she mumbled. 'But it feels like it has been the longest day of my life...'

'You're sleeping in my bed with me tonight. I'm telling you now while you're still awake and capable of objecting.'

Lexy tried to lift eyelids that felt as though they had weights attached to them and swallowed back a yawn. 'Don't care where you put me,' she framed. 'As long as it's not out in the snow.'

Nic laughed but she was already going limp in his arms. He studied her tranquil face in helpless fascination because he was feeling things he had never felt before. Selfish though it would be, he was actually tempted to wake her up because he wanted to get to know her better. He wanted her company. When had that ever happened to him with a woman before? Or when had he ever felt so protective that he refused to wake up an exhausted woman? When, furthermore, had he ever cuddled one after sex? The more he thought about his own behaviour, the more bothered he was by it. What had happened to playing it cool? His normal approach? And why had it seemed so important to get her into *his* bed? After all, he always slept alone and never gave any woman the chance to assume that anything more than sex was on offer.

He stood upright, naked, tugged his jeans back on and then lifted her limp body up into his arms. He wanted her to sleep in comfort. Why did he care about that? Frowning, he headed through the connecting door into the master suite and carefully laid her on his giant luxurious bed, where he surveyed her from all angles with frowning curiosity. He didn't even want to leave her alone, which shook him even more. She was definitely making him feel weird.

Lexy woke up during the night and slid out of bed, pulled on Nic's discarded tee shirt and crept quiet as a mouse through the house to pour herself a glass of cold water. One glass of wine and tiredness had wiped her out very early in the evening, she thought in embarrassment. But she had no regrets, none at all. What if it wasn't to be *only* one night that he wanted? The thought slunk in and as quickly she squashed it again, afraid of being naïve. She was cautious in acknowledgement of her inexperience with men.

A sound behind her made her spin nervously. Clad in only his unbuttoned jeans, Nic lounged in the doorway. Her disconcerted gaze collided with liquid black enticement and she could feel her face burning as if it were on fire.

'You are *so* shy,' he breathed in amusement.

'I'm not… I'm not!' Lexy protested, throwing her head high, bringing up her chin as he slowly folded his arms round her and drew her close. The scent of him flared her nostrils. Clean, warm, masculine, already achingly familiar, as if he had somehow imprinted his being on her.

'I don't even know your surname!' she shot at him, discarding the cool front she would have preferred to show him.

'Diamandis.'

'Well, how do you spell that?' she asked huffily into his chest, knowing that it didn't really matter what his name was as long as he was there for her.

He spelt it out with precision. 'You sleep like the dead,' he informed her.

'I'm not going to argue about that,' she agreed with a flare of amusement driving off her previous drowning discomfort with him.

'Are you hungry?'

'No…but I'm not sleepy either. I must've slept for eight hours,' she pointed out.

Nic stared down at her with brooding intensity. 'Women don't usually fall asleep on me.'

'I can only suppose that's because they didn't have to get out of bed at four in the morning the day before yesterday to make a flight to work,' Lexy told him cheerfully. 'And then miss out on essential meals because my language skills were required during those hours as well, work late that night and present myself at seven a.m. for another shift yesterday. No, I'm not about to apologise for sleeping like the dead.'

Nic grinned in delight at that pithy comeback. 'I'm getting that message.'

'And *I'm* getting the message that you're one of those terrifying high-maintenance guys, who expects to be the centre of attention at any hour of the day.'

Faint colour darkened his sculpted cheekbones and his eyes narrowed. *High maintenance?* 'Of course I'm not.'

'Don't believe you,' she told him truthfully.

An involuntary grin slashed Nic's wide sensual mouth. Surprisingly he liked her sass, the insistence that she wasn't overly impressed by him, and not a flicker of recognition had crossed her face after he'd told her his name. 'I can see I'll have to get persuasive,' he teased, bending down to lift her off her feet.

'What on earth?' she exclaimed.

'I'm carrying you back to bed to prove that I'm *not* high maintenance.'

'All that proves is that you're bossy and you like your own way.'

His dark eyes glinted like molten honey and he frowned. 'No points for romance?'

'You're trying to be romantic?' she exclaimed in disbelief.

'For the very first time in my life and… *Thee mou,* you make it a challenge, *chriso mou.*'

'What language is that?' she prompted as he carried her up the stairs and he noticed that she wasn't objecting and that made him smile again.

'Greek. I'm half-Greek, half-Italian,' Nic imparted. 'But Greek comes most naturally to me.'

As he came down on the bed with her still gathered in his arms, she rested her cheek momentarily against his bare chest, revelling in the scent of his skin, the soft brush of the black curls of hair sprinkling his pectoral muscles. 'We have one small problem,' he divulged.

'What is it? Oh, my word, are you married or something?' she demanded in sudden horror, already striving to move off his lap.

Strong arms tightened round her to hold her in place. 'Don't be silly. I've never been married, engaged or committed to any woman.'

'Ever?' she stressed in stricken consternation at that admission.

'Not committed, but…' Nic shrugged a smooth brown shoulder, suddenly at a loss for words because it was way too soon to say anything even though he already knew that, come the dawn, he wouldn't be done with Lexy '…that could change at any time with the right woman.'

'The problem you mentioned,' she reminded him, relaxing a little more again, knowing in her bones, without knowing how, that he was referring to her.

'I only had one contraceptive in my wallet. I don't bring women here. You're the first. So, we will have to practise extreme caution when we get back into bed together again,' he warned her.

'Caution is fine,' Lexy told him sunnily. 'You get het up about the silliest things.'

'If you say so.'

And then he was sliding her into the bed while kissing her breathless and that fast, she wasn't thinking any more. It was the burn of his mouth on hers, the sizzling heat and growing ache at the heart of her and the wondrous caress of his hands that drove everything else out of her head. Although she had sworn she had had sufficient sleep, at some stage of their prolonged intimacy she drifted off again, comfortable and secure in his arms. The one thing she would later remember in detail, and loathe, was that at that moment she felt incredibly safe for the first time in years and quite ridiculously happy.

CHAPTER THREE

NIC SHOOK HER AWAKE, hauled up her pillows, physically lifted her up to rest back on them and murmured, 'Good morning…'

Lexy blinked before the unfamiliar surroundings locked into place and then centred on him: tall, dark, even more good-looking in harsh daylight than he had been in semi-darkness and the warmth of flickering flames. And she smiled, her heartbeat quickening as he slotted a tray onto her lap with the air of a man who had achieved something important to him.

'Breakfast in bed?' she gasped, not having to work at her stunned reaction at that much attention.

'To prove that I'm not only *not* high maintenance but also a reasonable cook,' he shot back at her with amusement glimmering in his honey-gold eyes, which were not quite as dark in bright light. Not quite so dark but still beautiful, quite spectacular in truth, framed with those outrageously lavish long black lashes. He still took her breath away.

Lexy examined her beautifully cooked omelette and toast and tea and grinned. 'I'm sensing that that expression "high maintenance" rankled last night. You do know that I've never had breakfast served to me in bed in my entire life?'

Nic frowned and sank down on the side of the bed beside her. 'Surely for a treat when you were a child at least?'

Lexy shook her head. 'Not once. If you weren't at the table on the dot of the hour, you didn't eat.'

'Sounds like I'm likely to be spoiling you rotten,' Nic said wryly of that strict childhood regime.

Lexy laughed as she tucked into her excellent omelette. 'You're not likely to get any objections from me.'

It was only as she finished actually eating and sipped her tea that she removed her mesmerised gaze from Nic and noticed that the snow had vanished from the trees outside. They were no longer white skeletons of winter trees clad in snow. 'The snow stopped, I see,' she muttered in surprise.

'Yes, it started raining in the middle of the night and it's mostly gone now.'

Pushing away the tray, she snatched up his discarded tee shirt again even though her brain told her that it was silly to be that modest with a guy she had spent the whole night in bed with. Cheeks pink, she emerged from its enveloping folds, catching the amusement in his gaze and lifting her chin in defiance of it because she couldn't change her inclinations in the matter of a few hours of an intimacy that was entirely new to her. She scrambled out of bed to stand at the tall windows and in the distance she could see the black ribbon of the road, clear of snow. In reality, her heart sank at that view because she knew she wanted to stay with him for the rest of the weekend, but she also knew that she could *not* stay.

'Can you drop me at the nearest railway station?' she asked him uncomfortably.

'Why on earth would I do that? I assumed you were staying on here with me,' he intoned tautly.

'I'm sorry. I would love to, but I can't. I've got to be in London by tonight because I'm being picked up very early to attend a christening tomorrow in Cornwall.'

'I'm sure your friends will understand that the vagaries of the weather have intervened,' Nic countered drily.

Lexy spun back to him, read the tension in his lean, darkly handsome face and almost bottled out. 'No, they won't. I've been chosen as a godmother and I agreed,' she pushed herself to declare.

'Is this for a very close friend?'

'I don't think that comes into it.' Lexy squared her slight shoulders and gazed back at him with a faint hint of reproach in her bearing. 'I said I'd do it and just because it doesn't suit me quite so much now isn't an excuse to let them down.'

His ebony brows flared. 'You didn't know that you would be stuck in the wilds of Yorkshire when you agreed.'

'A reasonable point, but I'm not stuck any more. I can see the road and it's clear.' Lexy could feel his annoyance and frustration with her and the irony was that she would have given almost anything to cave in and say that she would stay and forget her christening obligation. 'But the truth is that when I make a promise,

I keep it and I don't let people down at the last minute. And, Nic? That's not a bad trait to have, so don't make me feel bad about it.'

'I'm not trying to do…hell, pack up and I'll get the car warmed up,' he breathed curtly and she could literally see him accepting her argument and stifling his disappointment for her benefit and she relaxed again, as much as she was capable of relaxing when she was going against her own nature.

Clad in his tee shirt, she gathered up her discarded clothes in the room next door and hurried back downstairs to shower and pack as quickly as she could manage it. Was she crazy? she asked herself as she dried her hair. To leave a man whom she had just met but who had become outrageously important to her within a few hours? But that was life and if he wasn't interested in an ongoing relationship of any kind, staying on with him for one more day and night wouldn't be a guarantee either, she reminded herself doggedly. Either he was interested or he wasn't: it was that simple.

As she arrived back in the hall with her case and bag, Nic stepped forward, his overcoat and boots on now. 'You don't even have a coat!'

'It's still in the hire car,' she recalled belatedly.

'We'll stop on the way. I'm sure the car will still be there,' he said grimly.

'I can't ask you.'

'You're not asking. I'm telling you that you're not leaving in weather like this *without* a coat,' Nic told her fiercely as he opened the front door.

She felt as though a lifetime had passed since she

last climbed into his SUV. This time she was noticing that it was the very last word in opulence. She breathed in deep and slow to steady herself. 'I really am sorry that I have to leave.'

'My number is in your phone,' he told her, sharply disconcerting her. 'I put it in last night. What are you thinking of, not even having a password on your phone? I was so surprised that it opened for me that I just went ahead and added myself to your contacts.'

'That's okay.' Lexy bent her head but she was smiling like mad below her tumbling hair as he parked the car on the verge. Seconds later, she watched him break through the hedge and stride with innate impatience across the still snow-covered field towards the car she had crashed.

She wasn't falling for him, she assured herself, because nobody fell in love in a matter of eighteen hours, nobody normal or sensible anyway. It was just that she liked him, liked him an awful lot, she reasoned, and it wasn't only the sex, although that had been pretty spectacular. He was clever, he was kind, he was thoughtful and even though she suspected that it would come naturally to him to rap out orders like a domineering boss, he was controlling that tendency for her benefit. She laughed at herself as he reappeared at her side of the car and got her out to help her into her sensible winter coat. A full-bodied shiver ran through her as he carefully tugged her hair out from below the collar. He had yet to show her one thing about himself that she didn't like or appreciate.

He insisted on driving her all the way into Manchester, paid for the ticket when they arrived and he stayed with her until it was time for her to leave him. When he buttoned up her coat for her as though she were a child before she went through the barrier onto the platform, her eyes prickled with tears because nobody had taken that much care of her in more years than she cared to count. Armed with enough magazines to take on a world tour, she got on the train, still struggling to catch a last view of him, still struggling to credit that the whole encounter had not been some insane, wondrous dream...

Eighteen months later

Nic strode into his lawyer's office. Aubrey Harrison, a thin, sharp-featured man in his thirties, sprang upright to greet him.

'Sorry about this,' he said wryly. 'But I thought you should look at this paternity claim before it goes down the inevitable DNA route. It's a rather odd one.'

'Not another one,' Nic groaned in exasperation, because it seemed that no matter how careful he was, the false claims still came in.

Yet in years he had never had anything more than a one-night stand or, at most, a couple of nights with a woman. Obviously, he knew that accidental conception could occur and that such matters had to be checked out, but even so, they put him in a bad mood, regardless of how hard he tried to take them in his stride. It wasn't as though he had ever been a real playboy like his older brother, Jace. And in recent times, he pondered, his innate reserve locking down his lean, hard bone structure, there had been no play time included in his driven schedule. He had always been more into work than casual sex and only one woman had ever bucked that trend with him. As for her, she was long gone, lost in the wind along with her phone number.

Yes, he had made an elementary mistake and paid for it. Her number had simply vanished from his phone as though it had never been and at the same time as he had tried to check that mystery out, he had found a suspicious app on his phone that was tracking his calls and texts. That and the security concerns aroused by it had proved a major headache, he recalled grimly. Even so, in spite of the investigation he had had done, he had yet to discover the culprit.

'This claimant seems fanciful at the very least and the timing is all off. Why would she wait *this* long to claim child support?' Aubrey wondered, passing a document to Nic.

Nic took one cursory glance at the name and froze, not a muscle moving on his taut dark features while disbelief assailed him in a blinding surge. 'Lexy...' he almost whispered. Lexy Montgomery. Now that surname would have been very welcome had he known it, had he even thought to *ask* for it eighteen months earlier, only he hadn't. And he had had no success trying to find a Korean interpreter called Lexy in London.

'I take it that you actually know this woman,' Aubrey remarked in some surprise.

'Yes.' Nic had to clear his throat before he could speak. 'I know her but a lot of time has passed since we were together.'

'Our investigator wasn't able to discover a link between you and Miss Montgomery and she has no social media, which is strange in this day and age.'

Shaking his head as though to clear it, Nic forced his attention back to the document in his hold. 'There are *three* children,' he registered on an incredulous note.

'Triplets. Two boys and a girl. Even more unlikely, I surmised. The stats say only one in ten thousand births is a triplet one,' the lawyer maintained. 'And the chances of having triplets by a chance-met billionaire in the tech industry have to be even poorer.'

Nic was pale below his golden skin. 'My mother's mother was a triplet, one of three girls, and my mother is a twin. There have also been multiple births on my father's side of the family tree. It's not as unusual as you might think,' he commented flatly, thinking of how downright irresponsible he had been with Lexy that night and of how very possible it would be for her to have fallen pregnant. Guilt engulfed him in a crashing wave.

'What I don't understand is why she didn't phone me, when she had my number,' he confessed out loud.

'According to her solicitor innumerable efforts were made to contact you in person and by letter and phone and all of them failed. How do you want to proceed with this?'

Nic vaulted upright. 'I want to see her,' he said instantaneously.

'That's not on the table, Nic, and I would strongly advise you not to think along those lines before a DNA test establishes that these children are yours.'

'I'll do the DNA test immediately, but I'm more interested in knowing where she's living.'

'The information given is not current. I checked that out,' his lawyer informed him.

Resolving to find that out now that he was armed with Lexy's full name, Nic departed. Three babies, he found himself thinking in astonishment. Was that possible? He knew it was possible from his own family tree and he also knew that he had been reckless with her, reckless with a woman for the first time in his life, he reminded himself. But why hadn't she contacted him? Got pushy if she ran into some little difficulties? He couldn't imagine Lexy being pushy, didn't think she was the type. Not that she lacked backbone, he reasoned, just that she was sort of soft, gentle, not aggressive by nature and he had liked that about her, only not if that lack in her had kept them apart for more than eighteen months. While pondering that he was also working out how to get her address and a background report.

'It's the perfect night for a barbecue,' Angeliki declared, strolling into his office later that day as he sat at his desk, having been determined to work and put Lexy and the three babies he *might* suddenly have totally out of his mind. Only that hadn't worked. Two boys and a girl, born only seven months after that night, which meant that something had gone wrong with the pregnancy and the whole lot of them might have died. That horrified him and knocked him straight back into abstraction.

'I'm afraid I'm not in the mood,' Nic admitted, forcing a smile for her benefit. 'Sorry.'

Their estrangement hadn't lasted for long, he recalled. Angeliki had phoned and then come to see him. She had confessed that the breakdown of yet another of her fleeting relationships and a sense of insecurity had prompted her into that inadvisable straying into his bed. Of course, he had forgiven her, but he still hadn't told her that she was his half-sister, even though he had told his brother. And Jace? Jace had merely rolled his eyes without much perceptible interest in the news that he had a sister. Why? Probably because Jace was already dug deep into playing happy families with his wife, Gigi, and his little son, Nikolaos. A reformed rake, Jace was so into Gigi and their progeny that Nic was wholly glad to be heart whole and still fancy-free.

Nic, however, was feeling guilty that he still hadn't told anyone else, but he couldn't see that being given the news that she was a secret Diamandis would decrease Angeliki's general discontentment with life. Angeliki was an heiress because his father had made provision for her long ago, only that wealth, supposedly inherited from a distant relative, hadn't made her any happier. And unfortunately, she was still very much given to referring to that night Nic had rejected her, instead of just leaving that controversial topic alone, even though she had to see that it still made him uncomfortable to think of her in naked, seductive mode.

'You're not much fun today.' Heaving a sigh, Angeliki batted her eyelashes at him in annoyance as she leant back against his desk. 'What about tomorrow night?'

'I'm dealing with a bit of a crisis right now,' Nic told her with perfect truth.

'You should've said that first!' the beautiful blonde exclaimed in reproof. 'You can be so secretive about things that it worries me. Are you still seeing Mila Jetson?'

Nic shrugged. 'No, that's over.'

He recognised that he no longer confided in his friend as he once had but, having only recently registered her response to the women who passed through his life when Mila had complained, he wasn't unleashing her on the likes of Lexy. Angeliki could be bitchy and critical and very devious, and Lexy was none of those things, although if those babies were his, and he had to assume within the time frame that they *were*, she had some explaining to do about why she hadn't made tracking him down her priority months ago. He was angry about that. He was *very* angry about that omission, he reminded himself, and it took a great deal to make Nic angry.

'Good news, I hope,' Lexy's solicitor passed on during her first call in weeks. 'Mr Diamandis has already lodged his DNA sample with a private firm and has requested permission to send one of their lab techs out to your home to speed up this process.'

'My goodness…' Lexy murmured in genuine astonishment.

'I suspect he's keen to deal quickly and quietly with

the claim. Will you agree to me passing on your address and phone number for the collection of your sample?'

'Of course.' Lexy knew she didn't have much choice and would be grateful to avoid the stress and expense of a trip out. She hadn't worked full-time since she was five months pregnant. Eileen sent her occasional bits of translation work and she put the triplets in daycare one day a week to accomplish it. As she was living with the help of welfare, she received some free childcare, but nothing she was allowed to earn part-time in such circumstances was up to the challenge of keeping a decent roof over their heads.

That was why, as she moved back into the spacious living room to rejoin her friend Mel and share the contents of that call, she was beaming, because their current home was only a temporary one. She was house-sitting for Mel's parents while her father took up a year's placement on the faculty of a New York college. She looked after the family pets, Barney the Labrador and Chica the cat, and the house plants, keeping the lawn cut and the dust down. In return she received the use of their car and the glorious relief of having a comfortable place to live. But time was running out because the Fosters would be returning home in another few weeks and she would soon be homeless *again*.

'About time he stepped up to do something other than ignoring you!' Mel, a tall, lanky brunette exclaimed. 'Stop acting like your boat's finally come in. This is only his first move and, of course, he'll still be hoping the kids aren't *his* right now.'

Lexy compressed her lips. 'Well, I'm choosing to hope that he's finally come to his senses and accepted that he can't avoid his responsibilities any longer. I just wish I'd listened to you and gone straight to a solicitor as soon as they were born. I've wasted so much time with my phone calls and my letters and visits to that wretched office block of his. He truly is the most hateful man.'

Mel glanced at her watch and stood up. 'I'll have to run if I'm hoping to make dinner with Fergus tonight,' she confided. 'Sorry I can't stay longer.'

Lexy hugged her best friend with a lump in her throat because without that friendship, she honestly wasn't sure she could have made it through the horrendous challenges she had faced over the past eighteen months. Mel had been solid gold right from the start. She had never uttered a word of criticism over Lexy's very bad decision to spend the night with a gorgeous stranger. Nor had she said anything while, with hindsight, Lexy had waited with such foolish confidence for Nic Diamandis to phone her afterwards and had never heard from him again. And when Lexy had needed support and understanding, Mel had been there for her every time.

She went upstairs to lift her children from their nap. *Children!* Even when she wasn't consumed with worry about the future, she still marvelled at the wonder of her three babies. Ethan was already standing in his cot awaiting her arrival, which was par for the course. Ezra, his smaller twin, whose former health problems had meant his survival had been touch and go for a while, was lying back, eyes open but quite relaxed as usual. If Ethan was the boisterous one, Ezra was the quiet, more thoughtful one. And last, but far from being least, came her daughter, Lily, bouncing at the side of the cot in readiness to be lifted.

She grabbed two of them up and hurtled downstairs to place them in the playpen before returning to lift Ezra. He beamed up at her and she cuddled him. It struck her as particularly ironic that not one of her children looked remotely like her. They were a trio with unruly black hair, dark eyes and olive skin.

A call came from the DNA lab that afternoon and she agreed to a lab tech calling with her because it would save her a lot of hassle. Transporting three babies anywhere, even with the use of a car, was exhausting. The tech arrived within an hour of the phone call, which disconcerted her because she had expected to have to wait in at least the next day for the visit. The woman was barely in the house for ten minutes, taking a mouth swab with the minimum of fuss and promising speedy results. Lexy was tempted to say that she was in no doubt of what the results would be, but she said nothing.

She assumed that the triplets' father would be praying that the results were not a match. After all, he had gone to some trouble to avoid ever seeing her again. She had been informed that her phone calls to his office were unwelcome and once she had even been escorted back onto the street by two very embarrassed and apologetic security guards. Slowly but surely her mortification had become burnished by wounded pride and rage at the level his behaviour had reduced her dignity to. She owed Nic Diamandis nothing. However, she had become ever more determined that he should help to support his own children. She wanted nothing else from him and sincerely hoped that she would never have to actually lay eyes on him again.

That hope was plunged into disappointment two days later when the doorbell rang. Lexy was unprepared for a shock. It was her work day, and her children were at the nursery. She was clad in yoga pants and a tank top, spectacles firmly anchored on her nose and wearing not a scrap of make-up when she went to answer the door, expecting the postman. Only instead she found herself focusing in disbelief on the man she had spent months trying to see or contact, firmly, squarely planted on her doorstep. And she couldn't *believe* that Nic Diamandis was finally giving her the time of day, not after all her failed efforts and his established ghosting of her very existence.

'Nic…' Her greeting was weak and it swiftly died away, along with her voice.

'Lexy. We need to talk.'

Lexy tilted her chin. 'A bit late in the day for that, isn't it?' she heard herself quip, incredulity and bitter anger consuming her as he gazed back at her with apparently not even an ounce of decent discomfort.

And without another word, Lexy slammed the door shut in his face again, steaming with the recollection of all the many humiliations he had had heaped on her when he had evidently blocked her calls on the number he had given her and had then refused to recognise her name when she'd tried to see him, or even *speak* to him, at his precious giant office building in the city of London. No, no regrets, she reflected as she paced away from the door again, her arms folded in a defensive block. What sort of father figure would he be for her children anyway? There was no way that she would allow him to treat her kids the way her father had treated her, making her feel less, making her feel unwanted even within her own home.

Been there, done that, got the lesson in triplicate, not falling for the act again...*ever*!

CHAPTER FOUR

'YOU'VE GOT A huge problem here,' Jace Diamandis mused as he strolled across his sunlit office. 'No offence, but you've really screwed this up.'

'You think I don't know that?' Nic slung back at his older brother in a temper. 'Lexy has my kids and I doubt that she'll even let me see them!'

'Is it these kids or her you're really into?' Jace enquired lazily, watching his brother pace back and forth like a tiger in a too small cage.

'I can't be into children I've never even met,' Nic intoned grittily. 'But I *was* into her… Well, I was until she slammed that door in my face.'

'Nothing like an angry woman to knock you back to earth,' Jace opined unhelpfully, making Nic wonder why he had approached his elder brother for advice. 'But if you want to ace this, you're going to have to borrow a trait or two from our dear old, unlamented dad, Argus.'

Nic shot back a question for clarity in guttural Greek.

'You've got no rights as an unmarried father under British law. If she says it's detrimental to their interests to be in contact with you, her vote as their mother counts more than yours. What the hell did you do to her to make her that hostile?'

'I haven't *done* anything!' Nic proclaimed with pride.

'Doesn't sound like it,' Jace remarked gently. 'But if you want access to those babies, you're bound to bring in the big guns. It's your duty as their father. You need to marry her and then you'll have rights.'

Marriage! The concept was like a punch in the gut to Nic.

'Our father didn't think that way,' Nic breathed stiffly, striving not to feel uncomfortable about the reality that his path into the Diamandis family had not been as smooth or, indeed, as pristine as Jace's. He was the son of the mistress, raised in status only after his father was widowed and had rejected his firstborn son. He had always felt a little like a consolation prize, only brought into his father's public life to ease the stinging humiliation of an unfaithful first wife. And he knew that his mother, Bianca, had always felt the same...like an afterthought, a pretender to the Diamandis throne.

'No, but, sad to say, threats and intimidation work and you may need them to access those children.'

'I'm not that kind of man.'

'Just saying. Clean and upfront may not work but it *is* your job to bring those babies into our family, however low you may have to sink to achieve that,' Jace completed without apology. 'I'll put my legal team on it for you.'

'I have a lawyer of my own,' Nic protested.

'You need the big guns now,' his brother asserted. 'And family is family, Nic.'

'You certainly don't view Angeliki in that light,' Nic commented.

Jace grimaced. 'Our half-sister has an unpleasant reputation and she's not the nicest woman around. I'm in no hurry to claim her and that's why. How you can count her as a close friend escapes me. I know you grew up together but—'

'Nobody's twisting your arm to acknowledge her,' Nic broke in with the loyalty that was innate in him. 'But she's honestly not as mean as you seem to think or I wouldn't spend any time with her.'

Jace laughed. 'Because she plays nice with you. I suspect she still has plans to get you to the altar and you're the guy that *still* won't tell her what she needs to know to back off!'

Exasperated by his brother's sense of humour, Nic went to see his lawyer, Aubrey, only to discover that the Diamandis legal team had already been in touch with advice, none of which Nic wished to follow. Yes, he could play hardball with the best of them but not with the mother of his children, he reasoned grimly.

Coming to see you around eleven.

That was what the text announced at eight a.m.

Lexy worked through a mess of emotional reactions. No, she didn't owe Nic Diamandis the time of day but, at the same time, he was the father of her kids and simply ignoring him as he had long ignored her wasn't a good idea. Sooner or later, the triplets would inevitably decide that *they* wanted to know him. What was so very attractive about a billionaire? Well, inevitable was the exact right word, she had decided. He would be in a position to offer adventurous days out that were only a dream on her horizon. She couldn't shut him out of their lives, even if she wanted to in retribution. He *deserved* to be shut out of their lives but possibly his children would have a very different take on that outlook.

So, because he was like an inescapable blight on all their lives, she would accept *one* visit. She would let him satisfy his curiosity. And hopefully that would be the end of the whole drama. What single, very good-looking billionaire wanted to settle down to having triplet babies on the regular? She was safe. The first messy nappy would see him off, or a spit up or a meltdown. She had seen him on the Internet, with gorgeous, unattainable women clinging to his flawlessly groomed arm like magnets, the most recent a supermodel with the brain of a very tiny bird—proved by the telling interview she had given—but the body and face of a woman so perfect she looked unattainable to ordinary females. Lexy had only qualified for attention because she had been the only option available on a snowy night in the depths of Yorkshire. A man of Nic's ilk didn't do babies in the raw and there was nothing rawer than babies, wild and untrammelled and totally unpredictable as they could be.

Nic arrived, well primed for the challenge of babies, for young children had never been on his radar. His brother, however, was an experienced hand, able to fully convey the potential horrors that had enabled Nic to look now at any baby in much the way he might have regarded an unexploded bomb.

Lexy opened the door, confident in the conviction that she was decently dressed this time around.

Nic took one glance at the narrow skirt and shirt and suppressed a sigh. On his last very brief visit, he had never seen anything sexier than the yoga pants and the spectacles on Lexy with her hair all tousled and impossibly sexy, just the way it had looked when she'd got out of his bed following a night he had never forgotten. And then she'd spun round, her exquisite face out of view, to give him a glimpse of how she looked from behind and that fast the yoga pants had vanished from his memory as he'd measured instead the perfection of her slender hips and surprisingly plump derrière in the fine fabric. He had breathed in deep and slow, striving to stave off the swell in his groin, genuinely embarrassed by his own reaction because, *Thee mou*, he wasn't a teenager any more when such responses were inevitable.

Lexy was priding herself on her essential decency. She could have let the babies get overtired and treated him to their worst but instead she had let them have that early morning nap as usual and get up again, once more restored to good humour. The trio of babies on the rug all looked up as she reappeared and they, every one of them, smiled. She supposed it was just as well that her kids had no idea whatsoever that their foolish mother had just been slaughtered in the mental stakes by their father. Truth was, Nic was still impossibly pretty. She had rationalised him in photos online, reduced his appeal, fought off the effect of his sexy sizzle.

Only all of that didn't work in the flesh. Here he was in person, as flamboyantly gorgeous as a tropical sunset and raining all over her parade of indifference. Black designer jeans outlining every powerful line of his narrow waist, lean hips and long, strong legs, a simple tee shirt framing what had to be the muscular chest definition of a pin-up. He was a study in raw masculinity and sensuality.

She wished that Mel were there to bring her down to earth again with a necessary bump and remind her that Nic Diamandis might look like a dream in face and body, but in character he was the very definition of a rat or some far less presentable word. He wasn't the man she had believed he was the night they had first met. She had been naïve, and he had been deceptive in everything he said and did with her.

'So, here they are. The reason I assume that you were so keen to come here in person and finally acknowledge my existence,' Lexy remarked brittly, unable to resist inserting that last little provocative reminder.

Nic stared down at a rug containing a virtual scrum of babies. The littlest one gave him a huge smile and, that fast, Nic was dropping down on his knees to try and reach their level and not be scary to them. The little one crawled on hands and knees straight over to him with the most charming air of acceptance and clambered up onto his lap.

'And this is…?' He had been meaning to pick Lexy up about that crack about his failing to acknowledge her existence, but the approaching baby had trumped that urge.

'Ezra. That's Ezra.' In truth, Lexy was disconcerted

by Ezra's attitude because he was usually the wariest of her trio. 'Ethan's twin.'

'Why's he so much smaller than his twin?' Nic asked straight off.

'He wasn't thriving in the womb like Ethan and Lily, which is why they all had to be delivered early, and initially he had breathing problems,' Lexy confided reluctantly. 'But he's slowly catching up by growing faster than his big brother.'

'So kind of you to keep me informed,' Nic voiced between gritted teeth while smiling because Ethan, the larger twin, was coming his way, but his daughter, Lily, was still staring, undecided, from the other side of the rug.

'I made every possible effort under the sun to keep you informed but I met with a blank brick wall,' Lexy framed very politely.

'You're lying and you know you are,' Nic murmured softly.

And that fast, in the wake of that toxic exchange, Lexy wanted to kill him stone dead, all her recollections of being pregnant and alone and a mother and alone piling up inside her like a threatening avalanche. 'I hate you,' she said equally softly. 'I hate you so much I can't stand having you here but I'm trying very hard indeed to be civilised.'

'Civilised is not always what it appears to be,' Nic quipped as Ethan clambered onto his lap, trying to stand up, failing, trying again, grabbing at Nic's hands to show him how to play the game he wanted. Reminded of Jace and his indomitable spirit, Nic smiled down at his son and let him jump up and down happily with the support of his hands. *This*, he decided, was what was truly important, *not* her and her poor attitude.

Lily was sidling closer to him, big brown eyes fixed to him as though he might bite and, in her, he saw her mother, more anxious, more scared than any Diamandis had ever been, and it annoyed him. His daughter was afraid of him and that *was* unmistakeably Lexy's fault.

He freed Ethan to the toy that was stealing his attention and reached for Lily. She came to him with huge, troubled eyes and he judged Lexy even harder for that distrust. On his lap, she settled and kept on gazing up at him with a growing steadiness that entranced his cynical soul. Then, without the smallest warning, she clawed her way up the front of his tee shirt and wrapped both arms round him. It was unexpected but very welcome and he hugged her close with gratitude that she was still sufficiently trusting to offer a stranger that affection. Even so, Lexy's outright hostility took him aback. Why was she lying to him? She hadn't got in touch with him, indeed hadn't made the smallest attempt to contact him.

Tense silence reigned while Nic engaged the babies with the toys on the rug. Lexy could feel her own face growing stiffer and stiffer because she was so angry with him and she couldn't express it.

'Would you like coffee?' she asked curtly.

'No, thank you. I won't be staying much longer,' Nic murmured flatly.

'Good. I have to give them lunch soon and that's a very messy deal,' she declared, striving to lighten the atmosphere a little for the sake of good manners.

Lexy could not recognise the man in front of her as the man she had met and shared a bed with, which she supposed was her warning that she had mistaken his character from the outset. He was cool and guarded and irredeemably superior, very much a posh, sophisticated Diamandis male. He hadn't been any of that when they had met, not even at first and not later either, she recalled with lingering pain.

'We could leave the kitchen door open and have a word in there,' she proffered, very keen to ensure that he did not have an excuse to make a second visit.

Nic vaulted upright with easy athletic grace and scanned her where she stood in the doorway. 'Whose house is this?' he asked.

'My best friend, Mel's parents own it,' Lexy divulged reluctantly. 'They're abroad. I'm the house-sitter. I look after their pets, plants and try to keep the lawn down.'

'You don't rent or own it, then. You have a home elsewhere?'

Lexy was wondering why he was being so nosy. 'No, I don't. Between having three young children and being unable to work full-time for more than a year now, my options are few.'

'You're virtually homeless,' Nic informed her, as if she mightn't already have grasped that fact.

'And that could be because the father of my children has paid nothing whatsoever towards their support!' Lexy fired back at him without hesitation.

'*Skase!*' Nic shot down at her, because she had almost shouted that response.

'And what does that command mean in English?'

'Keep quiet,' Nic translated the politer term frigidly, because all he could see was the three babies who had crawled over to join them, all three faces raised and brimming with curiosity and possibly even a little annoyance that they had been abandoned as the centre of attention. He scolded himself for that fanciful thought, not even convinced that babies that young had much in the way of thought.

And then to his horror all three faces crumpled and they burst into tears. Lexy brushed past him and got down on the floor to comfort them and they swarmed her like little vultures, nestling, clutching, grabbing, howling.

'It's *my* fault. I raised my voice to you and it frightened them,' Lexy framed as the howling subsided to more manageable levels.

'I'll leave you to feed them,' Nic said levelly. 'I'll come back tonight at eight and we'll talk then.'

'Fight, you mean.'

'I have no intention of fighting with you,' Nic asserted with glacial bite. 'You are the mother of my children and I respect that status even if I'm a little dubious about you as a person.'

'Thanks, but no, thanks,' Lexy muttered as he vanished out of the front door and she shut it firmly behind him.

'Well, how did it go?' Mel demanded on the phone an hour later.

'Not very well. We argued through it as best we could with the triplets there and he's coming back this evening to argue some more. Nic really doesn't like being told that he fell down on his responsibilities.'

'And that's catnip for you at the minute,' her friend guessed. 'But maybe give the aggro a rest until you can get some kind of adult arrangement ironed out between you.'

'I was hoping he would just pay up and go away.'

'I don't think you know him well enough to decide how he may react to being a father,' Mel countered with tact.

Unwelcome though they were, Mel's shrewd comments cooled Lexy's anger with Nic. Did she really want to drive him away so totally that her babies lost out on the possibility of a father figure? And the answer to that was…no, she didn't. In other words, she couldn't afford to be short-sighted. Literally and figuratively, she reflected wryly as she studied her little trio striving to feed themselves and dropping food everywhere round their battered mismatched highchairs. If Nic was capable of loving her babies, his interest in them would be invaluable.

Right now, Lexy was broke, totally broke, and it was like that every week, stretching the pennies to go further, adding up the groceries at the supermarket before she went to pay, getting in first at the charity shop to search the rails. She was poor, she was so poor she had given up make-up and all sorts of stuff she had once naively taken for granted. And that was the world she lived in when her kids deserved so much better from their rich father. If he could offer more, then it was her duty to accept it and be polite about it. Taking potshots at him wasn't going to fill the kitty or put food on the table.

* * *

Unaware of Lexy's resolve to be less incendiary, Nic was brooding. He was angry, so angry with her for subjecting them both and their children to what promised to be chaos and bad publicity. But for all he knew, Lexy would enjoy that kind of attention because she wasn't the woman he remembered. Yes, she was still attractive to him to the most annoying degree but everything that he had admired inside her seemed to have vanished. There was nothing sweet or gentle about that waspish tongue of hers or the angry dislike flashing in her eyes.

In truth, Nic had never dealt with an angry woman in his life. Jace had seemed much more seasoned in that line. Nic had handled Angeliki's angry flouncing and dirty glares but she had never got verbal with him or insulted him and he did not think their friendship would have survived had she done so. Why? Nic had a low threshold for insults because he reckoned that every day from birth until his demise, his father, Argus, had hurt, humiliated or outraged him in some way. Even adult status hadn't protected him. Argus had liked to get on the phone to critique his business choices, his performance, his choice of friends. In fact, Argus had been his horrible abusive self, right up until the very day he died. To both Nic *and* his unhappy, derided mother.

Lexy had to change before Nic's second visit. A dressy shirt did not long survive triplet proximity. She didn't have many clothes. When she was pregnant, she had traded in good stuff in return for anything that could fit a small woman with a physically large pregnant belly. All she had left were the items nobody had wanted and she knew it was time to get on with the lawn again, a never-ending duty in summer time, so on went her denim shorts and a tee. Probably the same tee he had once taken *off* her all too willing body, she reflected morosely as she brushed her hair and left it loose.

The ride-on mower was an unpredictable horror that didn't always work and visits from the local mechanic were a regular feature. As soon as the triplets were down, she went out to tackle the mower and when, glory of glories, it worked, nothing would have removed her bottom from that seat until she had done the whole lawn. She was near the end of the back lawn when she saw Nic standing below the rear porch watching her and looking a bit like the Grim Reaper in a dark suit, faithfully cut to make the most of every line and muscle in his long, lean physique. He looked maddeningly stupendous, and she was stricken that she had lost sight of time and hadn't contrived to get indoors again and change into something more appropriate for his benefit. Even so, mindful of her new attitude, she lifted her hand in as friendly a wave of acknowledgement as she could fake and pointed at the corner to let him know she would be stopping when she finished the grass. One last strip to go.

The ear-splitting decibels of the mower stopped and Lexy removed the headphones she had been using and manoeuvred off the machine with all the awkwardness of her unfortunately short legs. Tugging self-consciously at the hem of the denim shorts, she hurried up the slope and onto the rear patio to greet him.

'I'm sorry to have kept you waiting but once I get the mower going, I stay on it until I'm finished,' she confided, anxiously fixing her gaze on his lean, strong, utterly expressionless face.

'Why are you not angry any more?' Nic enquired disconcertingly.

Lexy grimaced, feeling more uncomfortable than ever as she led the way indoors through the kitchen into the living room. 'It's not that I'm not angry, just that anger isn't a good idea right now with you only just meeting the triplets. I need to stop letting it get in the way,' she muttered.

Nic was astonished that she had done exactly what he had been hoping she would do to ponder and reach the same conclusions he had. There was no profit in an angry resentment that kept them at daggers drawn. Together they were parents to three children and the children were what mattered most.

'Coffee? A drink?' Lexy proffered.

Nic was studying her legs, very shapely legs, he had to admit. 'Coffee…black, no sugar.'

'I remember.'

'The less we remember now from our first meeting, the better,' Nic startled her by proclaiming. 'The situation has changed radically and time has moved on without…well, without me. I want to correct that.'

'And how do you think it best to do that?' Lexy called out from the kitchen as she poured the coffee she had brewed in readiness, grateful that the larder was so well stocked, although she had rarely used anything from her hosts' cupboards for the food was not hers.

'I think we should get married,' Nic drawled, almost in a chatty tone, as if what he was saying were not anything like as shocking as it was.

'I beg your pardon?' she murmured, the hand holding the jug shaking.

Nic sprang upright and walked back to the doorway to look at her with grave dark brown eyes. 'Marriage will fix everything—'

'Nothing's broken,' she just about whispered in her disbelief.

'It is in my world,' Nic contradicted. 'My children are illegitimate, which will very much upset my whole family and make it almost impossible for them to inherit anything from us. I owe them *and* you more than some paltry monthly payment towards their support. You're homeless and penniless and none of you should be living like that. If we were to marry, you would all be properly taken care of.'

'Maybe I don't need to be taken care of,' Lexy framed, cheeks hot with shame from being called 'homeless and penniless' in one sentence, even if it was true.

Staring down at her, Nic was reading everything in her aquamarine eyes. Mortification, resentment, hurt. It shook him inside out to see those feelings in her face because it knocked him right back to their one and only night together. 'Everyone needs taking care of occasionally,' he pointed out.

Lexy winced and passed him his coffee. 'You don't

understand. I've been living on handouts and other people's kindness since even before the babies were born,' she admitted chokily. 'My friend Mel and her parents have been unbelievably good to me.'

'If you marry me, you'll never have to worry about money or where you live ever again,' Nic murmured like a snake charmer.

Lexy vented a choking laugh that was a partial sob because she was fighting to hold the tears back. The very last thing she had expected from Nic Diamandis was a marriage proposal. It was so old-fashioned, so wildly unexpected from the man who had ignored her and their babies' needs while it evidently had suited him to do so. 'I'm not sure I can believe that you are sincere with this…or that you could suggest that I marry you for your money,' she muttered. 'I mean, I would never ever even consider marrying a man for his money. I'm not a gold-digger or a—'

Nic caught one of the hands she was waving dismissively in the air between them and held it to steady her. She was all over the place, like a tree rocking in a storm, and he could see the tears glimmering in her beautiful eyes. He hadn't intended to upset her. He had intended to soothe her, offer her options, and marriage had not been his first choice of those options, even if it was only matrimony that would satisfy his family, end the drama and give him unalienable rights over their three children.

'I would be happy for you to marry me for my wealth.'

'But clearly you're not talking about a n-normal marriage,' she stammered, sneaking a questioning look up at him.

'A marriage on paper, obviously,' he conceded, while striving not to notice the pert shimmy of her clearly unbound breasts below the tee shirt and monitor his own very, very hungry body. She was dynamite in a tiny package, his personal kryptonite, it seemed. 'But you'd have to fake being a real bride for my family's benefit because that will integrate our triplets into the group and make everything smooth again.'

Lexy's lower lip had long since parted with the upper as sheer disbelief gripped her hard. 'So, you're serious about this marriage idea. It seems like you've thought it through and you like things…er, smooth.'

'Call it crisis management. It's my strength,' Nic told her in a very businesslike tone. 'We marry for a while. You acquire a proper home, in this country or wherever else you wish to live. The children get to know their father. All the complications melt away. When we have had enough of the pretence we go for a divorce and co-parent.'

Marry *for a while*. That put the proposal in a much clearer perspective, she acknowledged ruefully. It would be a temporary arrangement, not the usual life commitment. And she could see his point. Like whitewashing a dirty wall, the end result would be very visible. She and her children would have recognised importance in his world and evidently that meant a lot to Nic Diamandis. As a wife or even an ex-wife, she would have a position and nobody would pity her or look down on her. Their children would be recognised as family members while all her money worries would go away.

'Why are you willing to do this? I mean…it's more of a big thing for you with your lifestyle than it would be for me,' Lexy pointed out with as much tact as she could employ, because a playboy faking a marriage could hardly engage in his normal pursuits. Unless, of course, and again she was being naïve, his cheating outside marriage could provide the reason for an eventual divorce? She decided not to ask any more awkward questions and was beginning to turn away.

'I'm willing to do it because my mother was my father's mistress before he married her. A *married* man's mistress.' Nic spelt out that reluctant admission between compressed lips and Lexy stopped dead in her tracks. 'I was three years old before my father married my mother after he was widowed by an unfaithful wife. Pulling us forward into his life officially was a face-saving gesture, no more.'

Lexy slowly turned back, cut to the bone by that sudden unexpected confession that sliced away all that Diamandis gloss and revealed the truth of the ordinary humans behind the billionaire façade. 'Oh…' was all she felt able to say about such a very personal and private thing.

Nic expelled his breath in a sharp exhalation. 'And all the years I was growing up I felt that my mother and I were looked down on within the family as being something less than his first wife and my elder brother. I don't want that happening to my children.'

Lexy nodded jerkily, finally fully understanding that

motivation and trying not to be touched that he had confided in her. After all, that motive was absolutely understandable in his position, considering his own more humble beginnings. Nic hadn't started out as a Diamandis with a silver spoon in his mouth. No, he had been the son of his father's lover on the side and disregarded while his father was still married to another woman. That knowledge shook her rigid, taught her afresh that appearances were often misleading and that she too had judged Nic to be an absolute four-letter word of a man because of his privilege in life and his treatment of her.

For the first time, as well, it occurred to her that his treatment of her did not line up with the man wishing to marry her to prevent his children from enduring that sense of insecurity that he had suffered as a young boy. He was more sensitive than she had appreciated, under that surface gloss, that flaring, oh, so attractive confidence.

Amazingly, it took very little thought at all for her to decide that, yes, now that he had talked the talk, she would give him her trust and marry him. Ethan, Ezra and Lily would profit from that move in every way possible. She understood why he was making the offer and she understood that it would not be a real marriage. And really, what did she have to lose? Homeless, penniless. Those weren't only words. They didn't express the daily fears and anxieties that grabbed her and strangled her with stress. She put on a front for Mel, who had already done so much for them, but the concept of being no longer poor shone like a brilliant, inviting sun on Lexy's horizon.

She wanted to buy her babies decent clothes, feed them the best food, put them to bed in comfortable cots. And she wanted to feel that they were safe. It crossed her mind that she would be willing to marry the devil himself to achieve those ends. Tears burned the backs of her eyes because she knew that, over the past eighteen months, she had sunk so very low in her expectations of life. If Nic was willing to sacrifice so much for his children's benefit, then it was highly probable that he would also be able to love them. And that mattered, mattered so much more than the material benefits because Lexy knew what it was like to grow up without a father's love.

'Okay,' she said stiffly. 'I'll marry you.'

CHAPTER FIVE

'GOOD HEAVENS…' Mel hissed when the cars that had met them off the helicopter drove them along a paved lane towards the giant villa studded with fancy pillars. It towered like a monolith on the heights of the hill on the island of Faros. It was Nic's home on the island, not the even larger house at the other end of it, which belonged to his elder half-brother, Jace, and their grandmother. The house Nic had inherited had only been built in the first place because their father, Argus, had fallen out with his mother, Electra.

'Prepare yourself for a very extravagant setting,' Nic had advised humorously on the phone. 'It's my house now but it's all grand Roman splendour. My father didn't do good taste.'

The two cars came to a halt. Yes, *two* cars. Nic had hired three nannies, *three*, he explained because he didn't want any nanny to feel overworked taking care of their children and he wanted every one of their babies to receive the very best care. Lexy's head was still spinning at all the changes that had taken place in her world over the past two weeks. Yes, only two weeks, not only to refill her skeletal wardrobe and buy all the bridal finery, but also to organise what had sounded like a very big wedding. Luckily her input had not been much required aside from a couple of phone calls to establish the food she liked and the colours and flowers she preferred.

'It's like being on another planet,' Mel had said at one point of Lexy's rags-to-riches transformation.

Even better, she had told herself often, Nic had achieved all the arrangements with her by phone. A much safer way to maintain their tenuous at best relationship, she reasoned, keeping it like a straightforward business arrangement, an agreement, a *deal*. His money in exchange for what he deemed to be respectability, which was marriage and fakery. He had warned her on that score too that she would have to pretend that they were keen on each other.

And how difficult could that possibly be when he looked the way he did and she was challenged to take her attention off him when he was in the same room? Nor did it take into account the number of times when, purely for reference purposes, she had looked up some of those photos of Nic online and learned stuff about him that she hadn't bothered to access when he had ghosted her eighteen months earlier. Like his name at birth had been the Italian Domenico and his mother, Bianca, had been a minor socialite in Rome when she'd first met his father. Little stuff, she consoled herself in explanation, that she had needed to know for the wedding and the people she would meet.

As the car drew up, she glimpsed an entire group of people waiting and her backbone melted like snow in summer. All those people, all those rich, important people, who had to believe that she was something she was not in Nic's eyes. She smoothed damp palms down over her designer dress, a muted shade of green teamed with wedge heels, and began to climb out as the door opened. And then she glanced up and realised that it was Nic opening the door and her sense of relief at seeing him was so intense after so many days that it left her dizzy.

'Nic...' she muttered as she stepped away from the door.

'Lexy,' he said, a literal five seconds before he swept her into his arms, whereupon he lifted her up to him to overcome their difference in height and kissed her.

And it was everything she had tried to forget, everything she had refused to relive. It was as though he lit a torch inside her and it blazed out of control. It had been so long since she had been touched that way that she dropped into that kiss with all the self-preservation of a drowning swimmer. His lips moved over hers, soft and firm and so erotic her toes curled inside her shoes and they fell off without her noticing. She grabbed his head, rediscovering the luxuriant depths of black hair she had previously sunk her hands into with pleasure. His tongue twined with hers and breathtaking heat swept up through her, a slow-burn effect pooling warmth between her thighs. Her head fell back as she gasped in oxygen.

'Get a room,' an unfamiliar voice said nearby.

Sudden awareness flooded back to Lexy and she blinked, registering belatedly that she and Nic had a sizeable audience. Embarrassment swallowed her alive. 'Put me down,' she mumbled.

'You lost your shoes,' Nic dared to remind her, and as soon as he set her down she scrabbled at his feet to relocate them.

How had he noticed the shoes when she hadn't even registered the wretched things falling off? She was mortified beyond belief. What a way to greet the in-laws! She understood, however, why Nic had gone in for the display. It was only part of the faking that he had mentioned would be part and parcel of the whole charade of marrying him. He expected them to look like a convincing couple and how else could he achieve that? Even so, had he had to fall on her like a ravenous beast the instant she appeared? Wasn't that overkill?

'Lexy, meet my brother, Jace...and his wife, Gigi.'

'Welcome to your own home,' the slender young woman told her with a big, warm smile of apology. 'I can't wait for the wedding tomorrow.'

'By the looks of it, neither can they,' Jace quipped, and Lexy's face turned an even hotter pink. 'I was wait-ing for the movie cameras to start rolling.'

'Yes, it was so romantic,' the little silver-haired older lady who had joined them said brightly and Lexy found herself enfolded in a hug. 'I'm Electra, Nic's grand-mother, but you can call me Yaya like my grandsons do.'

Nic led the way upstairs through a splendid marble foyer ornamented with grand and very large pieces of gilded furniture, a backdrop that would have looked more at home in a museum or a palace than on a small Greek island. Imposing and impressive it certainly was, but nothing about the ambience was comfortable or welcoming.

He paused at the door of an upstairs room and ushered her in. 'For the children,' he said with quiet satisfaction.

And there it was in front of her: the nursery of her dreams, complete with beautiful cots and all the pretty pieces of baby paraphernalia she had not been able to afford. Lexy gasped, fingering the edge of a polished wood cot, stroking a soft, smooth cotton cover. 'Was this where you grew up?' she couldn't help asking.

'No, I had this done specially for the triplets. This house wasn't built until I was an adolescent. I've already made arrangements to have three separate bedrooms prepared for Ethan, Ezra and Lily for when or if you choose to divide them.'

'My goodness, you've really been busy,' she framed unevenly, taken aback that he was already thinking ahead into their babies' futures.

'I'll show you our rooms,' Nic murmured, a hand closing over hers as the nannies began piling in with the baggage carried by a uniformed staff member.

'It's all very formal here,' she remarked.

'My father's preference, not mine. While we're here, feel free to change anything. On previous visits, I preferred to stay with Jace and Electra in the other house,' he admitted wryly. 'This was never a happy place for me.'

'Oh…' And she wanted to ask questions and know more but was that really appropriate in a fake marriage? Just at that moment, her mouth still tingling from his, and gripped by embarrassment at how she had surrendered into that kiss with more enthusiasm than strictly necessary, she decided it was better *not* to ask and to respect boundaries.

'This is you...' As her luggage was trekked in past them by more uniformed staff, Lexy gazed wide-eyed at the vast bedroom, decked out in gold, and the extreme grandeur of the gilded four-poster, and she giggled. 'Well, it's not really me,' she almost whispered. 'I feel a little ordinary looking at this.'

'My mother said she liked it, but then she was required to like it to please my father,' Nic told her. 'But she was a farm girl from a country town and I would suspect she must've felt a little overpowered as well.'

'A *farm* girl?' Lexy questioned in surprise before she could bite back the query. 'But I read that she was a socialite—'

'No, no. That was a face-saving fiction dreamt up by my father and aired because he could not have said that *he* had stooped to marry a farm girl, whom he met at a market.'

'And obviously he fell for her there,' Lexy completed.

'He was married and supposedly crazy about Jace's mother, so I suppose it depends on your viewpoint.'

'I think you're...' Lexy hesitated.

Nic studied her expectantly. 'I'm what?'

Lexy winced. 'Possibly a little too overly negative about your father, but maybe he *was* an all-round horror of a man—'

'That is how I see him. He was a man who did terrible things to a lot of people,' Nic said tightly, sinking her stomach with that admission about his parent. 'I operate very differently in business and in my own life.'

Lexy nodded, grateful to have not offended him. 'On that note, I shall be comfortable in this bedroom even if the décor is a touch overwhelming.'

'My room is through the communicating door but it's locked. I'm afraid I can't conserve your privacy tomorrow night because there is no way Yaya will put a bride and groom into separate bedrooms and as they're holding the wedding for us—'

'It's fine. We'll survive,' Lexy hastened to soothe even though her brain was exploding with confused questions.

This was the guy she had first met. Considerate, thoughtful and kind. Where had that guy gone during her barrage of phone calls, letters and office visits over eighteen months? Had Nic Diamandis simply *panicked* at the news of her pregnancy? Had he blocked her calls and dumped her letters because he couldn't face the problems her pregnancy would create? What else was she supposed to think if she was no longer able to think of him as an inherently bad, irresponsible man who thought only of himself?

Of course, he couldn't defend himself for such reprehensible behaviour, but if he was trying to make good now and make up for it, shouldn't she at least recognise the effort he was making to redress the damage he had done?

'It's a family dinner this evening hosted by Jace and my grandmother at their place.'

'What do I wear?'

'Something long and glam,' Nic advised as he departed again. 'I'll send in some jewellery for you to choose…a couple of things to use. My mother sent it here. Bang a ring on your engagement finger. It will look better.'

'Your mother knows we're fake?'

'No, my mother thinks we're real and that we ran out of time, choosing to skip the engagement phase,' Nic murmured ruefully. 'She's a romantic.'

And I was as well, until I met you and then you let me down, Lexy reflected in suppressed anguish.

She had fallen in love in the space of an evening. Who did that? Which sane, intelligent woman would do that? But she had paid the price for that foolishness, hadn't she? She had had many months to agonise over her disillusionment.

She went back to the nursery to spend time with her babies and get to know the nannies a little better. Beth, Susie and Indira were young, active and chatty and Ethan, Ezra and Lily were calm and content in their care, which was fortunate when it was the wedding tomorrow and they would see little of her, she reminded herself. For a while she strolled around the house, getting acquainted with rooms, and when she had wasted enough time, she went back to her room to dress for dinner.

A large handsome jewellery box sat on the dresser awaiting her. From Nic's mother, she assumed, thinking that it was a very generous woman who just offered her own possessions to a future daughter-in-law she had yet to meet. A farm girl, fancy that. But possibly Bianca Diamandis mightn't like to be reminded of her more humble beginnings and Nic should have kept that info to himself.

Thinking such thoughts, Lexy picked out a kind of blingy diamond and emerald ring and threaded it on her ring finger to try before setting it aside to wear. Evidently, Nic had told his mother that she didn't own any jewellery. What a very kind gesture! She picked a slender diamond necklace for the neckline of the dress she planned to wear before heading for a shower and a thorough grooming.

Finding her babies already sleeping in their cots, she sighed, wishing she had made it in time for a goodnight cuddle, but she would be up very early the next morning to attend to them all. Fully gowned and feeling incredibly opulent but ill at ease in a long silvery blue dress with its mermaid skirt, which made it impossible to take anything other than very small steps, she descended the sweeping staircase to where Nic awaited her in a dinner jacket and bow tie, looking exactly as he looked in all those online photos.

Except just for once he lacked that recurring arm ornament, Angeliki Bouras, a woman who in normal circumstances Lexy would have asked a lot about. What was so special about the exquisite blonde apart from the obvious? Why did Nic's relationship with her appear to survive when other women seemed to last mere weeks in his company? Unfortunately, Lexy was aware that she had no right to ask such nosy, personal questions of a man about to make a fake marriage to her.

Nic was enthralled by the vision of Lexy in that dress with diamonds glittering at her throat and on her hand. 'You look amazing,' he said.

'I look like a gold-digger,' his future bride told him tartly. 'All got up in a designer dress sporting all this bling.'

Nic grinned, that breath-stealing grin she remembered, and her heart hammered. 'Maybe I've got a thing for sexy little gold-diggers…who knew?'

'Stop it or I'll laugh and I'm trying so hard to be refined and serene,' she admitted.

'They're only people, good and bad, friendly or unfriendly. Wealth doesn't make them one whit better than you and that's the only difference,' he said soothingly as he tucked her into a low-slung scarlet sports car and drove off.

The massive villa at the other end of the island had an elegance that his father's house did not. Nic parked outside it and handed her out. 'Show's on now. Fake it until you make it.'

'But you haven't even told me what our story's supposed to be.'

'I kept it simple. Lost your phone number, lost touch, turned the city upside down trying to find you and then, bullseye, here you are with my children,' Nic proffered lightly. 'The love of my life.'

'Do we have to exaggerate?'

'The only people here who matter are my immediate family. Jace and Gigi. My mother, Yaya. Oh, yes, and my best friend, Angeliki.'

Wow, *best* friend, well, she hadn't guessed that likelihood very well, had she? Relieved by that news, Lexy smiled. 'I'll do my best.'

But from the first frozen glance from Angeliki's fine dark eyes, Lexy registered that the beautiful blonde might be her bridegroom's best friend, but she was never going to be equally chummy with his bride-to-be. Clad in a fabulous bronze evening gown, the Greek heiress outshone every other female present and Lexy was relieved to be warmly hugged by Nic's mother, Bianca, a diminutive brunette with a bubbly, positive personality and a bunch of chatter.

Bianca refused to be thanked for the loan of her jewellery. 'I remembered how overpowered I felt by the Diamandis tribe just after Argus married me and I couldn't have my daughter-in-law feeling the same way,' she chattered cheerfully with an openness that was utterly unexpected in such a glittering array of high-society guests. 'I'm relieved that my son saw through the façade of the often spoiled, entitled little madams he meets and married a young woman with a job and independence.'

'That's great,' Lexy said weakly as she was enthusiastically grabbed into a hug, thinking that it was not the time to mention that independence and a proper job were a long way behind her since the birth of her sons and her daughter.

'And if I promise to come really early and not interfere in anything bridal, can I please come and see my grandchildren tomorrow morning?' Bianca continued winningly. 'I'm just gasping to meet them, but I didn't want to be too pushy and wait at Nic's house today for the opportunity.'

'You're not being pushy at all,' Lexy assured her. 'You will be very welcome.

'I like your mum,' she murmured to Nic as they took their seats at the formal dining table.

'She's lovely, isn't she?' Jace's wife, Gigi, volunteered cheerfully. 'Next to Yaya, she's a favourite. Neither of them judge or criticise or bitch.'

'Electra Diamandis is a lady from head to toe. She has bred-in-the-bone class,' Angeliki interposed crushingly from across the table.

Gigi rolled speaking eyes at Lexy and she almost giggled at the blonde's snobbish intercession. The foolish woman didn't seem to grasp that it was an insult to exclude Nic's mother from such a compliment. 'And Bianca is simply pure charm and warmth,' Lexy commented.

The meal proceeded at a stately pace and Lexy noted that Angeliki rarely removed her attention from Nic, regularly addressing little witty comments in excluding Greek to him while studiously ignoring Lexy's existence. No, definitely not friendship material.

It was a longish evening. There was a lot of meeting and greeting after the food was eaten. Lexy was flagging by the time Nic intimated that it was time to leave and she had gone out to the hall to retrieve her evening wrap when Angeliki approached her. 'It won't last—you and Nic,' she spelt out thinly.

'And I want your opinion because...?' Lexy countered.

'He only wants those children. I'm warning you that

you'll lose them if you go ahead tomorrow,' Angeliki announced with the sweetness of a viper.

Lexy merely nodded and turned away to unfurl her evening wrap and cloak her bare shoulders. But her tummy had turned over at that warning and she told herself off for being affected by a woman who very obviously wanted Nic for herself. So much for this particular female best friend, a relationship that could only work if there was a lack of attraction on both sides.

'You seem troubled,' Nic commented as he tucked her back into the car after a long trail of goodbyes.

'Not at all,' Lexy said stoically, resolved not to run telling tales, which would likely be poorly received. Unlike Angeliki, Lexy could read people, and Angeliki might want Nic but she could see that Nic did not want her back, in spite of her beauty and her lithe, shapely sexiness. 'It's just been a long day and I'm very tired.'

The next morning was Lexy's wedding day and she was still tired because she had lain awake a long time worrying that there was truth in Angeliki's nasty suggestion. How far could she trust Nic in believing that he would not try to remove her children from her care in their eventual divorce? And in truth, that was not yet an answer she could give. Yet, bearing in mind her financial struggles over the past eighteen months, she did not believe she had a choice because it was her duty, just as much as it was *his*, to ensure that their children had a more stable, secure home. But she could not credit that Nic would want to risk hurting his children by depriving them in any way of their mother.

She found Bianca Diamandis down on her knees in the nursery playing with the triplets and sensibly clad for the occasion, so she wasn't too bothered about wearing a dressing robe herself. Sitting down on the rug with Bianca, she helped Ethan, Ezra and Lily get to know their grandmother. As she returned to her room, she met Nic in the corridor, tall and darkly handsome in a cotton sweater and tight jeans.

He held a finger to his wide firm lips in a silencing gesture. 'Bride and groom aren't supposed to see each other before the church,' he told her.

Lexy flushed and disappeared into her bedroom again, deciding that so far she wasn't doing very well in the 'faking it' stakes because until now the concept of such traditions had passed her by. Mel awaited her, having ducked out of the dinner the night before because she had said she wouldn't be comfortable in such lofty company. But Lexy was tempted to tell her that she had felt perfectly comfortable, with the single exception of Angeliki's shrewish approach.

Her beautiful gown hung awaiting her but a small procession of professionals was due first to do her hair, her make-up and her nails.

'So, how do you feel about this now?' Mel prompted, for her best friend was not entirely sure she should trust Nic enough to believe that he would only do right by her and his children.

'Moderately hopeful,' Lexy confided. 'He's making an effort and I can see it. It may be happening a bit late in the day, but you can only applaud a guy brave enough to say that he's quite happy for me to marry him for his money.'

'Either that or he's a very devious character,' Mel remarked, predictably less tolerant as a lawyer, having stood by Lexy during her worst experiences during the crucial eighteen months of Nic's absence.

The bridal preparation team arrived then and there was no time for further personal conversation. Within a couple of hours, Lexy was viewing herself with Bianca's diamond tiara anchoring the short veil she wore to the back of her head, letting her dress, which she loved, do its thing without further embellishment. She had reasoned that it might well be her only wedding gown ever and, with cost no object, she had shopped for her fantasy. Fashioned of sequinned silk tulle and delicate embroidery, it had the slender silhouette of an Edwardian tea dress with a fitted boat-shaped bodice and long tight sleeves, shaping her figure without burying her in loads of fabric that would only accentuate her lack of height.

'You look stupendous,' Mel told her dreamily.

As Lexy paused at the foot of the aisle in the large village church, she viewed the packed pews and lifted her head high. One of Jace's uncles had offered to fill in for her absent father, whom she had not bothered to invite, but Lexy had politely declined the offer because she was giving herself away, not depending on some male figure to take charge of her.

But as Nic turned his proud dark head to look at her, she felt a reaction she knew she shouldn't feel to the seemingly stunned appraisal he was dealing her. Gosh, he was good at faking it, she thought in admiration. Really, *really* good…

CHAPTER SIX

THE WEDDING CEREMONY was formal and relatively brief.

'You look very beautiful,' Nic murmured in the sunlight on the steps afterwards while the photographer snapped pictures.

'You don't need to fake it in private,' she assured him out of the corner of her smiling lips.

'You can't accept a compliment like any other woman?'

'Not when I'm wracked with nerves, no,' she conceded in apologetic afterthought.

He steered her through the crush into the beribboned car that would take them back to the house and the reception. 'I don't say stuff I don't mean, not even to fake it,' Nic censured.

Lexy breathed in deep and slow and scrutinised the platinum wedding ring on her finger because she *still* felt as though she were figuring in a daydream and that she couldn't possibly be legally wed to the tall, absolutely gorgeous and very wealthy man beside her.

'Nothing feels real to me today,' she said truthfully. 'I've lived a very quiet life and all this—the hype, the fuss, the glitz—it's totally alien to me.'

'I only want you to feel comfortable. I can promise you that after today, there will be no hype, no fuss.'

Calming down then, she allowed him to guide her into the house where they had dined the night before, where they greeted guests as they arrived before entering a room the size of a ballroom where the meal was being staged. Caterers were everywhere.

'Did you invite your father?' Nic enquired over the first course of their meal.

Lexy froze. 'No. I contacted him shortly after I had the triplets and he wasn't interested. In fact, he gave me a lecture about irresponsibility and even though Ezra was still in the special care baby unit, he didn't want to visit him or even meet his first grandchildren. So, no, I didn't want to invite him…even though he would probably be very impressed by you because you have status and wealth,' she completed uncomfortably.

Lean, strong features taut, Nic nodded. 'I agree with your decision.'

Relieved by that response, she relaxed more. 'I've only got Mel here as a guest and I asked her parents if they wanted to come, but her father doesn't have any leave left. Really, over the past couple of years, there's been nobody else close enough to warrant a wedding invitation.'

Nic breathed in deep, carefully choosing his words, although there was a storm brewing inside him that he was holding back. 'You've had a tough time without backup.'

The silence simmered and screamed between them and neither of them attempted to break it with adverse comments. Lexy wanted to ask him what had possessed him when he'd chosen to ignore and deny her situation. Nic wanted to ask her why she hadn't given him a chance to help her and, even worse, had chosen to lie about having given him that chance when he knew for a fact that she had not.

The wedding speeches were short and soon over. The cake was cut and served and the dancing began. They spent ages socialising before Nic closed his hand over hers and whirled her onto the floor to dance. Initially Lexy was as stiff as a tree trunk in his arms, but he eased her closer until the warmth and strength of him bled through the layers of their clothing and melted the cold knot of indecision inside her. Heat pooled at the heart of her as he moved against her, powerful thighs and narrow hips flexing. Her nipples prickled and tightened and she swallowed hard as her body went off on a wonderland of rediscovery about Nic's body without any prompting from her. In embarrassment, she tried to suppress her natural reaction to his proximity.

'Relax,' he urged huskily as she tensed again. 'This performance is almost over.'

Yes, it *was* a performance, she reminded herself grimly, not a real wedding day and she shouldn't be responding to Nic as if he were a genuine husband or as if they were a couple in love.

Angeliki Bouras slid with a subtle sidewise movement between them. 'I need a word with you in private,' she informed Nic without embarrassment, as if it weren't the slightest bit strange to part the bride and groom on the dance floor.

Irritation assailed Nic. Sometimes, Angeliki had the worst sense of timing, he thought as she urged him out of the ballroom and into Jace's library across the hall.

'What is it?' Nic asked with an impatience he tried to mask out of politeness.

Angeliki smiled wide and bright, tossing her long blonde tresses back over one slim shoulder, dark eyes intent. 'I felt it was time to give you some advice... now that you're married without having *wanted* to get married.'

That latter statement was truer than he wished and Angeliki actually voicing the fact set his teeth on edge. 'I don't need advice.'

'Obviously you got married to secure your children. Three of them—*Theos mou*, couldn't she have been less productive?' Angeliki mocked with a wince of distaste as though fertility were a vulgar topic. 'So what now? If you're wondering, I can help.'

'I'm not in need of any help,' Nic cut in firmly.

'If you live with your bride, you'll be *stuck* with her,' Angeliki pointed out. 'That's not what you want.'

'You don't know what I want,' Nic sliced in with finality, already swinging round to return to the door and leave her.

'I'm thinking of what will make you happy,' Angeliki declared, impressively enough that he turned his head back, warm dark eyes seeking his with sympathy. 'I advise you to stash your unwanted bride in one of your many houses—say that lovely chateau in

France—and leave her there to be Mrs Diamandis on her own. And then you continue with your life just as you like it, your freedom reclaimed.'

Nic frowned, exasperated by her interfering advice. 'My plans with my wife and children are none of your business, Angeliki. However, your outlook is ridiculously limited. For a start, I have three children who will *always* be my children and I must act as their father. That's my role in life. My father didn't do it for me, but I will not be found lacking in the parental role when it comes to my children,' he asserted grimly, ignoring her angry glower of dissatisfaction. 'Excuse me… I should be with my bride.'

Nic appeared beside Lexy again and drew her straight back onto the dance floor. 'Sorry about that. Angeliki was being a drama queen.'

'Does she make a habit of that?'

'More often than I find comfortable. I can still recall her screaming tantrums when we were kids,' he confided with a chuckle. 'She prefers to be the centre of attention.'

'And she's not likely to get that at our wedding,' Lexy remarked, wishing he weren't quite so fond of the beautiful blonde, who could only treat his bride like wallpaper.

Nic drew her close and the ripples of heat filtered through her, relaxing her body again. No matter how hard she tried to stifle her response, it deepened in strength. She stole a glance up at him and his dark eyes were a stunning blaze of gold between dense black lashes and her mouth ran dry, her breath shortening in her tight throat.

With a muttered phrase that could have been an imprecation in his own language, Nic lowered his head. 'When you look at me like this...'

With scant warning, his mouth crushed hers and she quivered in the shelter of his arms, instinctively pressing closer, shaken to appreciate that he appeared to be as aroused as she was. The press of his long thickness against her abdomen sent a faint shiver rippling through her because it had been so long since she had been touched, so long since that night when she had discovered that she was a much more sexual being than she had ever dreamt. Recollections lingered no matter how hard she tried to shut them down and forget them.

Nic steered her off the floor into the shelter of one of pillars that edged the big room, providing quieter seating areas and shadowy spaces. He spread her back against the pillar and kissed her with a depth of hunger that she was utterly unprepared to meet. Desire melted her like a hot pool of honey spreading in her pelvis.

Nic lifted his head, black hair messily tousled by her roaming fingers. 'I want you,' he admitted thickly.

The tension and insecurity she had fought off all day took fire from that blunt admission. It felt really good that he wanted her to such an extent. At that moment, it seemed as though it validated her, made their marriage truly human and more real. The connection that had linked them the night that she had conceived their children was still there in spades and she couldn't fight it off.

'Escape is only twenty feet away,' a familiar voice murmured without any expression at all.

'I beg your pardon?' Lexy almost whispered as she jerked her mouth free of Nic's addictive taste.

From a couple of feet away, his brother, Jace, dealt her a wide smile. 'You two can leave. You've ticked every box. The bride and groom are free to slip away now.'

Her face now hot as hellfire, Lexy swallowed hard. '*Seriously,* Jace?' Nic quipped.

'Rear staircase behind that door at the foot,' Jace informed his brother. 'Thought you might not be aware of that exit as you didn't spend much time here as a boy.'

Nic said something in Greek and grinned wickedly down at her. He bent down and, before she could even guess what he intended to do, he scooped her up into his arms.

'So discreet,' Jace teased with sincere amusement.

'He doesn't know we're fake,' Lexy muttered helplessly as Jace strode down the room like a man on a mission.

'Doesn't need to know. He only knows that we've had enough of the festivities. And possibly that we can't keep our hands off each other.'

Speak for yourself, she almost said in disagreement, but he set her down on her feet again on a small landing up a narrow staircase, and while she was striving to muster a sensible thought with which to prop up her sinking dignity, Nic dragged her back into his arms for another hungry, driving kiss that splintered through her trembling length like a bolt of lightning, burning and racing through every nerve ending in her body. His long fingers, his big strong hands ranged over her curves as he bent down to her, and her heart was hammering so hard she was scared that it might pound right out of her chest.

'Do you want me?' he breathed raggedly.

And there it was: the opportunity to call a halt. But Lexy was no hypocrite, no liar. 'I want you,' she muttered unsteadily, wondering how she could still be that vulnerable, questioning whether a retreat into cold dignity would somehow magically persuade her otherwise. Unfortunately for her, a stronger urge was warring for dominance inside her. It was a crazy *what the hell?* feeling, absolutely new to her sane and sensible self.

Unmistakeable satisfaction slashed Nic's wide sensual mouth and his dark golden eyes glimmered bright with admiration. 'You didn't lie, play games—'

'I *don't*,' she cut in as he urged her up the stairs.

As she paused at the top of the steps to catch her breath, he captured her parted lips afresh and her temperature rocketed, desire coiled up tight within her, urging her to reach up and frame his lean, dark face with her hands. He lifted her off her feet and into his arms again, striding down a wide, imposing hallway full of paintings. 'Yaya's art gallery,' he proffered with humorous brevity as he thrust wide a door into a bedroom.

It contained a massive bed decked out in pristine white sheets. Rice and almonds and flower buds were scattered across it.

'Rice and almonds for happiness and prosperity,'

Nic informed her as he shook the sheet clear of the offerings. 'Yaya likes the ancient traditions.'

'Well, you don't really need to be hoping for the prosperity,' Lexy pointed out.

Nic flung back his darkly handsome head and laughed outright at that truth. Heavens, he was breathtaking in that moment, so gorgeous, she couldn't credit that he was now her husband. But her husband for how long? Lexy squashed that thought, all of a quiver with conflicting emotions and feelings, her body taut. There was a little voice in the back of her head warning her that, married or otherwise, she should not be even considering sharing a bed again with the father of her children. Lifting her chin, she glanced across the room at him, and common sense wasn't worth anything when he was *still* her fantasy, she conceded ruefully.

There had been little to celebrate beyond the health and happiness of her children in the months since they had last been together. All that time she had felt as though she were simply running to keep up and by the end of it, after infinite months empty of the smallest adult fun, she had felt as old as the hills. And there Nic Diamandis stood, jerking loose his bow tie, toeing off his shoes, with the kind of confident insouciance that should have set her on fire with rage and resentment...only it didn't. Everything about Nic Diamandis set her on fire sexually. That calm, innate assurance, that cool, sophisticated edge, that deep-pitched sonorous drawl of his, the devastating good looks, not even to mention the unexpected kindness and understanding he could give. She told herself that she was doing something for *her*, not for him, not for the children, something just purely for her.

After all, why would she care about how he felt? This guy who had used her to provide him with entertainment on a snowy, forgotten night in Yorkshire? That was all 'they' had been, no matter how hard she had tried to believe otherwise in the disillusioning months that had followed. She could use him as well to fill the emptiness inside her chest, the loneliness that sometimes bit very deep. He didn't need to know that *she* needed more, *cared* more than that. And in addition, she was far from stupid, well aware that an unconsummated marriage could be legally deemed to be no marriage at all when it came to severing those ties. Lawyers for rich people were paid to be very clever and only a foolish woman would ignore that reality with a divorce on the horizon.

'You're a thousand miles away...' Nic's reflection appeared behind her in the cheval mirror she had moved towards and he looked like a tall, strong, shirt-clad monolith in the dimness of the shaded windows. Tall enough to touch the sky, she would've thought as a child. But she was no longer a child and the sheer size and breadth, the inherent strength of him sent a sensual shiver through her taut frame. 'Do you need help to get out of the dress?'

'What do you think?' Lexy almost whispered, her mouth drying up again as he glanced back at the complex lacing and hook arrangements that had fitted her into her fantasy gown. She didn't know whether it was a curse or a blessing that it had not crossed her mind once that her bridegroom would have to help her get out of her dress again. It was that platonic arrangement they had agreed and where was that now?

Nic laughed again. 'I think you'd have to be a contortionist to get out of it alone.'

The first few hooks began to loosen the fit of the gown. He might have big hands, but he had precise fingers, she recognised as the lacing tightness round her ribcage eased, fingertips swiped smoothly across her shoulders, and without warning the whole dress was dropping, pooling round her feet like a statement, leaving her clad in the tasteful bits of nothing much that were all the dress design had allowed.

'A garter.'

Nic knelt down behind her, making her ludicrously aware of her wispy lace strapless bra and knickers and the pull-up pale stockings, over one of which was layered a 'something blue garter', a gift from Mel, even though her friend was aware that she was not a real bride. Mel, as Lexy had become, was a cynic and had agreed that this might be Lexy's only ever wedding.

'I didn't think you'd even be wearing one.'

'You don't know that much about me,' Lexy said, enjoying that truth, enjoying that he didn't know how much tougher she had got, how much she had changed from that gentle, forgiving person she had once been.

'I'm willing to learn,' Nic husked, trailing the garter down to a dainty ankle, freeing her foot from her shoe to thread it off, pausing only to gently extract her other foot from its shoe. Had she been the kind of woman who still believed in her fairy-tale prince she would have been swooning, weak at the knees from his aplomb and smooth words. Only now she wasn't that naïve.

He vaulted upright again, snapped loose her bra and it fell away. His hands rose to cup her breasts, her nipples straining in the cooler air…and from his touch. She realised that as she had stood there thinking ever more bitter thoughts, on one level she had been trying to talk herself out of getting intimate with him again. He filled her with indecision and she was not an indecisive woman. Yet still her body hummed and throbbed that close to him, pulsing with a hunger she could not suppress, and that *was* a humbling acknowledgement.

Slowly, *very* slowly, as though he knew what was inside her head, Nic turned her round and claimed her parted lips again, swallowing what she might have said, utterly silencing whatever indecisive thoughts she might still have been feeling in his radius. When he kissed her, when he held her close, there was only him and the wild, insane attraction of him, and he drew her down on the bed with gentle hands. In that instant she was lost because he didn't push, he didn't demand, he was everything that she remembered…the guy who *cared* about how she felt.

The span of his hands over her breasts, which were fuller and rather less pert than they had once been, turned her inside out with anticipation. She was all woman, all in the control of desire in an instant, wanting, needing what he could offer. Her nipples tingled and prickled, hunger like a dam burst threatening to break penned up within her, so that her spine arched to deepen that pressure and a faint moan escaped her.

'I've never wanted any woman the way I've wanted you,' Nic husked.

And she didn't believe him, didn't care because she wanted him more than her next meal, which in times gone by, when she had gone hungry for her children, meant more than he could ever have appreciated in his gilded world of privilege and excess. He was laying her down on the bed and she almost felt like telling him that subtlety of the type he was offering was unnecessary because she was definitely a sure thing. He was the guy that had taught her, that very first night they had been together, that even when she was sore and exhausted, she could still want him with the fire of a thousand suns. And he hadn't been careful and, fool that she had been in her innocence of what a disaster an unplanned pregnancy could be, she had acquiesced. In reality, Nic Diamandis was only reaping the seeds he had sown.

'I want you too,' she admitted without the smallest embarrassment, watching him peel off his shirt, revealing a chest that belonged in a sculpture gallery, lean, honed abs and tight, taut musculature of the type rarely seen in ordinary men. No, there was nothing ordinary about Nic Diamandis, he was absolutely the dream and the fantasy she remembered, and no longer did she marvel that she had succumbed to all that pure, bronzed temptation. So what if she was looking at him as a sex object? Hadn't that only been how he must have viewed her that long ago night?

'I wasn't expecting you to be so…open,' he muttered unevenly.

'I'm not the same woman you met eighteen months ago,' she warned him.

'I see that,' he conceded, an uneasiness to the admission that pulled at her, making her wonder what he was thinking until she reminded herself that she really shouldn't care at all what he was thinking. After all, he was her husband now and where his thoughts or his heart went now was no business of hers because she wasn't looking for him to love her or essentially *care* for her. She was expecting him only to help care for their children and ensure a secure future for her and the kids. All that romantic stuff? She was done with that. The romance stuff had burned her down to the bone because she had fallen in love with a guy who truly didn't exist, not a guy who would have shied away from her and turned his back when she'd turned up inconveniently pregnant and desperate.

He unbelted his narrow-cut trousers and she rejoiced in his masculine beauty like a groupie, ashamed of herself and yet still wanting him so much. Bitterness and resentment didn't provide the barrier she had expected, she conceded ruefully, heat pulsing at the heart of her, because surely no woman had ever reasonably wanted a man as much as she still wanted him? The trousers dropped, so did the boxers and she was enthralled, because these views were what she had not seen that first time in the shadows and the darkness of the bedroom.

'I love the way you look at me,' Nic confided

hoarsely, his glittering golden eyes holding her fast. 'Like you want me as much as I want you.'

'I *do*,' she confided without self-consciousness, because that wasn't a weakness, not the way she had learned to consider it. She was merely separating wanting from love and that was easy after the battles she had lived through.

'It bridges our separation,' he breathed, coming down to her, all husky, muscular, supremely aroused male, and she was mesmerised by him, no longer marvelling at the manner in which she had succumbed to him before. He was something else in terms of looks and charisma, the perfect ten if such a list of male attributes existed.

He claimed her mouth with erotic expertise, parting her lips, skating along them, only finally delving deep, and she fell into that kiss as if there were nothing beneath her, only a swirling, ever heightening world of pure sensuality. Yes, he was unbelievable in bed, she told herself, lying prone on the bed as he dallied over the swollen buds of her breasts, kissing a line down from that area to the next. Playboys didn't get to be what they were without lots of practice, she reasoned absently, struggling now to stay in touch with her brain.

'I dreamt of doing this again. Your body, it's so perfect,' he groaned.

'It's not perfect any more,' she heard herself say, wondering if he hadn't picked up on the stretchmarks on her abdomen and her breasts and even her thighs, because her body had behaved badly when she'd been

pregnant with the triplets. There wasn't a part of her
that hadn't swollen up way beyond perfection.

'But it's *you*,' he emphasised, as though she were
still the hottest female on earth that had ever been seen.

'And it's you,' she whispered, small hands lifting
to frame his high cheekbones, fingertips drifting off
into the lushness of his black hair. Heavens, he was
gorgeous.

Skilled fingers traced the heart of her then, probing,
exploring, and he followed with the heat and expertise
of his mouth. Within seconds she was lost in what he
was doing to her, lost in sensation and need. Hunger
burned in her pelvis like a flaming torch and she was
arching and gasping and moaning and racing into climax without any input of her own.

'I want you to enjoy this,' Nic husked thickly. 'I want
you to be like this with me...*always*.'

Chance would be a fine thing, she thought, struggling to get her brain back because, really, he was *that*
good in bed. Not that she had anyone to compare him
with but, even so, honour where it was due. She was
sure there were plenty of men who left women wanting and unsatisfied, because she had listened to Mel,
a veteran of several failed relationships, and she knew
that the brand of sexual joy she was receiving was not
universal. She knew exactly why she was putty in his
expert hands: Nic knew what he was doing in bed with
a woman.

He slid over her and even her sated body reacted to
that provocative move, the buds on her breasts tightening again, the burn at her core reawakening, be-

cause she already knew that he could deliver... Oh, boy, could he deliver.

He lifted her legs over his shoulders and a kind of blissful anticipation enfolded her, damp heat turning her inner spaces to liquid welcome. Her heart picked up pace, the blood in her veins racing in concert, and he entered her, and there was a slight burn and a stretch. Even so, he felt amazing. Her body gave way to his as though such an intrusion was welcomed and it *was*, it was everything she had recalled in the dark of the night in private, because nobody policed her dreams.

And the substance of her dreams only got better as he moved, withdrawing and then entering again, pushing hard to the very centre of her being. Delight encased her body, a slow roll of delight she couldn't resist, no matter how hard she tried. Her hands closed over his shoulders, fingers digging in. When the next thrust came, she was so into it, she moaned, and he looked down at her with those glittering golden eyes and she was lost in the sensation, her hips shifting as though to accommodate him although he was managing fine without her input. He was going slow and she wanted more.

'Speed up,' she urged without thinking about it.

And he did and it was as amazing as everything else he had ever done with her. Mind-blowing pleasure engulfed her as her level of excitement built and built. With every fibre her body was surging to a peak, and he took her there with effortless perfection. She cried out at the height of a heart-stopping climax and he followed her with a raw male groan of completion.

'You are so unbelievably sexy,' he told her.

'It's you…as long as I don't look for anything more,' she mumbled, her body limp and sated in that aftermath of satisfaction, every defence down.

A moment after relieving Lexy of his weight, Nic slowly levered himself up and gazed down at her with scorching dark golden eyes. 'And what does that mean…exactly?' he prompted dangerously.

'Well, you already *know* what it means,' Lexy contributed, struggling to get her brain working again in the wake of that gigantic physical rush of pleasure. 'You're useless at the long haul. You're more about the short, non-committal stuff.'

The gold in his dark eyes flared to a brilliant blaze. 'That's not really what you think about me,' he assured her, seemingly impregnable in his ego.

Lexy leapt out of the bed, driven by pride and nothing else, for she could not abide allowing him to believe that, because he didn't deserve it after what he had done to her: he had deserted her when she'd needed him most. She yanked the sheet off the bed with an almighty tug and wrapped it round her because she refused to stand there naked and seemingly vulnerable—she refused to be vulnerable around Nic Diamandis again.

She lifted her chin, eyes the colour of tropical seas striking back at him in challenge. 'It *is*,' she confirmed with near pleasure, because in the moment after all that physical stuff she felt happy to be fighting him again. Indeed it felt good and made her feel better. 'You let me down when I most needed your help. I had nobody but Mel and, eventually, her parents. But I was alone, struggling through a very difficult pregnancy and unable to work from quite early on. I needed support and you weren't there for me in *any* way!'

'You didn't contact me,' Nic informed her afresh, every syllable one of biting clarity. 'You didn't give me the chance! I was not aware that you had ever tried to contact me.'

Lexy's teeth gritted. 'That argument doesn't wash,' she told him frankly. 'I phoned your office. I even tried to make appointments with you there and the closest I got to seeing you was getting out of the lift on the top floor before I was discreetly removed by your security guards and taken back downstairs and shown back onto the street. I was very pregnant at the time. It wasn't the warmest welcome to your workplace.'

'My security staff would *not* manhandle a pregnant woman,' Nic declared with the utmost confidence.

'Oh, there was no manhandling involved,' Lexy agreed. 'The guards were respectful and polite and, I suspect, very embarrassed, but it was made quite clear to me that I must not return to the premises. And I *didn't*. That was the day I gave up on you showing some spine.'

'I beg your pardon?' At that offensive charge, Nic vaulted out of bed in a colossal surge of temper, dark golden eyes now burning like flames, lean, dark features rigid with incredulity.

'You heard me,' Lexy said, her mouth running dry but that didn't silence her. 'I'm finally being honest with you about how I feel. I was six months pregnant and the size of a house. I was supposed to be on bed-rest, but I gave it up that day to make one last attempt to reach you, and you know how that turned out, so please stop trying to pretend that the guy who rejected me and ignored me was a nice guy...because you're *not*.'

Nic was studying her with fixed intensity. 'I cannot believe I'm even listening to this nonsense.'

'Right,' Lexy murmured, noticeably unimpressed by that rejoinder. 'You want me to put all that in the past and bury it because now you've changed your mind, but life doesn't work like that, Nic. People don't work like that either. You blocked my phone calls, and you ignored my letters and my requests to see you at work—because I didn't know where you lived in London. You *ghosted* me, and, no matter how reasonable or kind you are now, it'll take a long time for me to forget being treated like I was a nobody, a nuisance and a burden you *couldn't* accept!'

Nic breathed in so deep in a visible effort to maintain self-control that she was frozen to the spot watching that struggle. Beneath her stressed-out gaze, he retrieved his boxers and his dress trousers, pulling them on in quick economic movements, lean bronzed muscles flexing as he dressed and reached for his shirt. 'That's not what happened and you know it,' he told her flatly. 'You didn't try to contact me. If you'd come to my office even once, I would have been told about it.'

Silenced by that protest but unimpressed, Lexy shrugged a dismissive shoulder.

Nic's mouth compressed. 'I'll use another room to-night,' he spelt out in a raw undertone, fighting the incendiary urge to call her a liar again. 'I refuse to exchange words with you when you're in this mood.'

'It's not a mood. It's an actual sense of bitterness and you made me like this,' Lexy declared, wincing when her voice almost hit a note of apology because no way was she taking back anything that she had claimed. 'But perhaps it's best you sleep somewhere else… Won't someone notice that the bridal couple are sleeping apart?'

'What do you care?' Nic fired back at her, bristling like a panther someone had had the nerve to try and stroke like a pet.

Lexy's complexion switched from flushed to very pale and she straightened her already stiff spine even more. 'I'm sorry I haven't been better at pretending to be a real bride,' she muttered truthfully. 'But I have feelings like everyone else and right now I'd prefer to be with my children.'

'*My* children as well!' Nic exhaled audibly, surveying her with hard, dark eyes and a tight mouth, his jawline tight as a bowstring and as hard as a rock. 'In half an hour a car will collect you at the rear exit. I will send a maid up to escort you there and you can make a discreet return to our children for what remains of the night. But be warned, we all have a *very* early start in the morning. We're flying to South Korea for a week. I have business there.'

Thrown into disbelief by that sudden string of disclosures, Lexy merely watched as he departed. *South Korea?* Her birthplace and her home for years? What was that about?

Nic hadn't said one word that she'd expected him to say, which both infuriated and frustrated her because she wanted him to frankly admit why he had behaved as he had during her pregnancy. But possibly she was being naïve again. They might have just set the bed on fire together but theirs was not a real relationship. It was a marriage of convenience, not a marriage of true love. Why would he strip himself bare of his pride and admit that he had made mistakes and ignored her when she'd needed him?

Yet only honesty could bridge the gulf of bitter resentment between them. She knew he wasn't a superhero, and she wasn't hoping for him to turn into one either but, at the very least, she deserved better than what he had so far given her, she told herself heavily.

She began to look for clothing to put on beyond her discarded bridal regalia. With a grimace, she made use of one of the robes hanging in the sumptuous bathroom. It would do fine for sneaking out some rear exit late at night, she told herself ruefully.

CHAPTER SEVEN

LEXY WAS HALF asleep when she boarded the private jet for the very long flight to South Korea. The nannies were like walking zombies and the triplets were all asleep.

Lexy had spent what remained of her wedding night in the gilded four-poster alone and wide awake and she blamed Nic for that unfortunate fact. Nic Diamandis, her *husband*, strange as that truth still was to accept, was, even now, set on concrete denial of his past misdeeds. How could she possibly work with that? In reality, there was no way. But at the same time, Lexy was awash with self-loathing and impatience over the part she had played. The last thing she should have done with her fake husband was stage a giant confrontation on their wedding night. That had definitely been a badly timed and poorly executed move.

What had possessed her?

Unhappily, Lexy was well aware of why she had lost control of her tongue. Nic had dared to behave as though everything were normal between them when it was anything but! She had been spread paper thin in the moments after she had retrieved her wits following their renewed intimacy. All right, she had been upset, torn apart by the awareness that she had succumbed yet again to Nic's sexual charisma. A woman abandoned to give birth alone to triplets the first time could not have an excuse for voluntarily signing up for more of the same casual sex. What else could it be with a guy like that? Nor did the fact that they were now legally married somehow justify her self-destructive behaviour.

There she had been making all those excuses to herself when, quite clearly, she had merely fallen yet again for Nic's irresistible quality. How could she still find him irresistible? That alone was unforgivable. Where was her pride? Her dignity?

Lexy shot a narrow-eyed glance across the aisle to where Nic sat working at his laptop. They had all had breakfast as a party, with the conference room onboard his private jet serving as a dining room. Casually dressed in designer jeans and shirt, Nic had got down on the floor there to play with his sons and daughter afterwards and, later, had even borrowed Lily from a nanny to help feed them. Yes, he was definitely aiming at the Daddy of the Year award, Lexy conceded. Even though she felt mean having that thought she was unable to stifle it after the manner in which they had parted the night before.

After all, aside from polite and unavoidable acknowledgements, the new bride was now being ignored. Perhaps he liked to remind her that she was only a bride in other people's eyes. Just as when she got the chance she would remind Nic that the only reason she had slept with him was to ensure that their marital ties were fully legal in terms of a later divorce. That was the sole way that she could save face, she told herself angrily. If he couldn't admit the truth of his own faults to her, why should *she* be honest?

Why would she admit that when she took even a glance at his strong, perfect profile or his shimmering dark eyes it virtually stopped her brain in its tracks? Or that she was a particular fan of his physique clad in form-fitting jeans that enhanced and outlined every lean, muscular line of his compelling masculinity? Or that she didn't have to think very long to recall the hard, erotic surge of him inside her the night before and that even the memory of that intimacy made her feel hot and damp all over and sex-obsessed? Those were matters that she had to keep private for the sake of her own sanity.

A fleet of limousines met them off the runway and they all piled in to speed down the motorway to Seoul. 'Aside from business, why did you choose to bring us here?' she heard herself ask, because she just could not contain her curiosity.

'Originally this was intended as a pleasure trip. It's your birthplace and the culture in which you grew up. I believed you would enjoy rediscovering it.'

'That was a very kind thought,' Lexy said stiltedly and kicked herself for asking because, really, he was always determined to portray himself as a nice, decent guy even if he wasn't.

'And then a tech company in which I'm particularly interested came up as a possibility and the business angle took over.' Nic shot her a glance from level dark golden eyes. 'You see, I didn't have to be truthful about that, but please note that I *was*. I'm not a liar, Lexy. I never have been and I never will be because my father lied at the drop of a hat to my mother, to me, to friends and employees and I have a strong distaste for those who choose to go through life fooling and deceiving others.'

The atmosphere was so tense as he made that little speech that Lexy tried and failed to swallow. His level, hard gaze burned into hers and she looked away hurriedly. Colour washed up over her face because what could she possibly say in response to *that*?

From the first night they'd met and he'd pretended that she meant more to him than she actually did, Nic Diamandis had been lying to her in one way or another. According to him, he had never received her letters or her calls, nor had he blocked her visits. And possibly he was *never* planning to tell the truth on that score, she reflected with a sinking stomach. He was a billionaire, highly successful in every field. Why would he strip himself bare of his pride and arrogance for her sake? Why on earth would he ever admit that he had panicked like a teenager at the prospect of a sickly pregnant woman he had never expected to hear from again? And a woman carrying children he had not planned to have?

It was equally possible that he hadn't panicked, she conceded. Perhaps there had been some other secret reason why he'd been determined to keep her out of his life and if that were true, would she ever be told? Her triangular face tightening, she sat very still and continued to say nothing.

Nic compressed his wide sensual mouth and said

smoothly, 'So, have you got friends to look up while you're here?'

He was holding onto his temper by a hair's breadth, weary of her refusal to concede that she had not made any attempt to contact him after that night in Yorkshire. He reminded himself that he had lost the means to contact *her* and that it was highly likely that she had made the worst possible deductions from his silence. But why the hell, if she was suffering through what sounded like a very difficult pregnancy, wouldn't she have still approached him for help? For the first time it occurred to him that that just didn't compute because, right from the start, Lexy had impressed him as a rather practical young woman with sound common sense.

'It's a bit late for that. I left Seoul when I was fifteen,' she reminded him wryly. 'I didn't have a best friend here. My father wouldn't let me even go out shopping with other girls and my mother only accepted visitors at home when Dad needed her to host his business dinners. It was quite a restricted upbringing, off to school and then back home to do my homework and study. I wasn't very good at maths, so there was a *lot* of studying and tutors and extra classes and all the rest of it. The school day is long in Seoul.'

Lexy was not exaggerating. Her father had taken the smallest sign of her failing to excel in any subject to heart and she still broke out in a cold sweat remembering him telling her over and over again what a stupid girl she was when it came to algebra. His expectations of her had never been met, no matter how hard she'd worked.

'To be fair though,' she added, because she hated to sound weak, 'top academic results are very much a thing here with parents, and children are expected to study hard.'

'I will need you to work as an interpreter here for me,' Nic admitted grudgingly because, really, at that moment, he didn't wish to be beholden to her for any assistance, but at least they were talking again, which was preferable to the reverse. He had no desire to live with Lexy in a state of sustained hostility. That would scarcely aid his resolve to act as a proper father to his children. And that was where his relationship with Lexy would begin and end, he promised himself fiercely. The wedding-night passion had been a crucial error, a case of both of them messing up what should have remained a platonic marriage.

It was dark and the night sky was already lighting up with the approach to Seoul, a city that rejoiced in a great number of skyscrapers because it was ringed in mountains and land was at a premium. The limo sped along city streets. There were neon-lit advertisements and bright lights everywhere and occasional glimpses into packed shopping streets. But most of all, Lexy felt the busy buzz and hum of an Asian city that literally never slept.

'Where are we staying?' she asked abruptly as she recognised the exclusive streets of Gangnam. It was the wealthiest district in Seoul.

'I hired a house large enough to cope with the size of entourage we require travelling,' Nic told her with an amused quirk to his sculpted mouth. 'And live-in staff to keep the household running. Not a hotel, but it should be close enough to offer you some pampering.'

Lexy stiffened. 'I don't need pampering.'

'You've been living hand to mouth for a long time. Of course you do. I appreciate that you put our children first in everything but that does not leave me ignorant of what you must've gone without.'

'How on earth do you even know that?' Lexy shot at him furiously and then comprehension sank in as she recalled seeing him chatting to her friend at the wedding. 'Mel told you, didn't she?'

'I think it was supposed to shame me, but how anyone could credit that I could come to your aid without even knowing where to find you is the mystery.'

'So back to square one again,' Lexy gathered in exasperation. 'You had my phone number—'

'I lost it. I don't know how.' Nic threw up his hands as she stared back at him with wide eyes, questioning such a well-worn excuse. 'But it *does* happen and unfortunately, *very* unfortunately in our case, it happened to me and I never got your surname or the name of the company you worked for or anything else which could have identified you.'

Lexy glanced away from his lean, darkly handsome features again. Now that she considered it, she could not recall giving him her full name or any other details. They had both been very laid-back in that line and she still remembered asking for his name and it was only because of that and his status that she had easily contrived to identify him and his workplace.

His dark eyes were suddenly serious. 'I had every intention of seeing you again.'

Oh, how she wanted to believe his excuse and that claim, like every other woman who had ever spent days and weeks waiting and totally expecting a call from a man because she had believed in him when she'd first met him. What kind of idiot would she be if she tried to believe in him again now? Or would faking trust she didn't feel be the gateway to peace between them?

'I'll *try* to believe that,' she breathed stiffly, stepping back from the brink of an endless tussle between them about who was lying about the past. Well, she already knew it wasn't her! But she didn't want to live in daily hostile exchanges with the man she had married. For wealth and security in the future, she reminded herself stubbornly, refusing to admit that she could have made a mistake marrying a stubborn-as-a-pig male who wouldn't tell the truth at the point of a gun! What other choices did she have?

None. No home, no job, no money. The daily struggle of poverty had meant that her children got less and she couldn't return to that with Ethan, Ezra and Lily when Nic had offered her the alternative. The seemingly *easy* alternative—the marriage—that was not quite so easy in practice.

The limo had left the road to pull up in front of a ginormous ultra-modern house. 'This is it?' she gasped, gaping at the black angled roof and the curvy walls.

'Yes.'

Without any warning, Nic waved a hand at the driver

hovering to open the door beside her. 'Before we go into the house, is an agreement possible?'

'About...er...what?' she pressed anxiously, her smooth brow furrowing.

'Clearly, we have to leave the past behind us to share even the children,' Nic intoned gravely. 'Let's not make this marriage more difficult than it needs to be and risk subjecting our children to a bad atmosphere. For their benefit we should fake being together and acting happy and relaxed. I don't want my new relationship with them getting poisoned by *our* problems.'

Lexy went pink. 'I agree that would be a good idea, *but—*'

'Look on this as a holiday and on me as a friend and I will attempt to facilitate that view to the best of my ability.' Intense dark golden eyes held hers fast. The faint hint of cologne and male flared her nostrils. She loved the scent of him and her tummy danced with butterflies. This close to Nic she could barely think straight, and the label of friend was the very last one that she would have attached to her reaction to him.

'All right,' she agreed, amazed that after his denials he could turn everything on its head, think outside the box and come up with the suggestion of a truce, however temporary it might prove to be.

Was she only playing into his hands with her agreement? Papering over the cracks? But he was right, successfully sharing the house and the children, never mind their lives, entailed a certain harmony and right now they weren't anywhere near achieving that. How could he be so sensible and yet persist in acting as though she were the one lying about the past? That too was a question she deemed more wisely buried for the present. He had come up with a solution and she wasn't too proud to grasp an olive branch, particularly not when she had to think of the welfare of their three children.

Just as she was thinking that she noticed that Nic was stepping into the house, nodding to the housekeeper, bowing low. With a spurt of speed, she grabbed his elbow to hold him back. 'Take off your shoes,' she whispered as he bent his head down in turning round to find out what she was doing. 'Wearing them indoors is a big no-no here.'

'I forgot.' He bent down and removed them, following her example of using the shoe rack provided at the lower level of the entrance hallway.

Relieved by his acceptance, Lexy moved into the house to speak to the housekeeper and introduce her to Nic. 'Nic, this is Kang Ji-Rae...' And she laughed. 'I think she's more excited about our kids than us. Triplets are popular here and more common.'

'You're going to be very useful here,' Nic told her.

Lexy laughed again as one of the nannies came in holding Lily and her daughter held out her arms to her father for the first time. His smile was huge as he lifted her, delighted by the invitation. Lexy grabbed Ethan, and Ezra started crying, and it was a little while then until they got the babies settled again with a selection of toys and snacks. The babies had been incredibly good for babies whose whole routine had been disrupted by travel, Lexy informed Nic defensively.

'I thought they were marvellous during the flight,' he opined with a shrug.

'Only because they were in a private jet and they weren't restricted to a seat for most of the journey. We were very lucky.'

'Lucky to have them,' Nic chipped in as he rearranged Ezra's bricks for his son to knock down again. 'They're happy babies. Considering that you were alone coping with them, you've done a terrific job.'

An uncertain smile of surprise curved Lexy's tense lips. 'Thanks.'

Reaching out, he closed his hand over her curled fingers. 'Relax, *chriso mou*,' he urged.

Feeling a prickling sensation spreading from her wrist with only that casual touch, she gently tugged her hand free again. 'Where are we sleeping?' she asked as the babies were pretty settled in and quite content.

'I'm afraid that didn't work out quite as I planned,' Nic murmured flatly, evidently having already established that reality while she was occupied with their children, faint colour flaring over his high cheekbones, accentuating the brilliance of his dark-as-night eyes.

'Meaning?' she prompted with assurance because she could tell embarrassment when she saw it.

'I assumed there would be enough rooms here for us to sleep separately but that is apparently not the case,' Nic breathed stiffly. 'This nursery has been set up in the room I expected you to occupy. It has a communicating door with the master suite, where we have been placed together.'

'We can manage,' she conceded grudgingly, belatedly foreseeing the intimacies she had expected to avoid with him. 'Let's hope it's a big bed.'

It was an enormous bed. Even for a male of Nic's imposing physique, it would be a challenge to accidentally bump into him in that amount of space, Lexy thought with relief. Because here he was, not doing a single thing to attract her, neither verbally nor physically, and the attraction still looked like a wall she couldn't bust down. That was life, she told herself, swings and roundabouts, and she had to learn how to handle life in close proximity with Nic Diamandis. Yes, and act like a platonic friend, so easy to say, so hard in reality if you were as fiercely attracted to someone as she was to him. She couldn't explain the source of that continuing attraction. No matter how hard she reminded herself of his transgressions, it was simply there as the air was there and the ground beneath her feet: always present, impossible to ignore.

'Dinner is at nine because the housekeeper didn't know when we would like to eat, but evening meals are generally scheduled at a much earlier hour here,' Lexy told him.

'Evidently, you promise to be an invaluable resource,' Nic remarked as he removed his suit jacket. 'What do I wear tomorrow to this first business meeting?'

'A black suit if you've brought one, accent on formal,' she told him a little breathless at the sight of the biceps moving below the fine fabric, only drawing her attention to the narrow cut of his waist and the lean flare of his hips and long, strong legs.

They parted into separate bathrooms. There might be only one master suite, but it was of lavish proportions. Lexy's clothing had already been hung in an equally separate dressing room and she selected a short, soft blue dress that was her version of casual formal.

Platonic—it was Nic's new inner placard for marital harmony, and she appeared from the bathroom as he was about to leave their room, slender and lithe as some sort of woodland sprite, he reflected abstractedly. And totally lovely in that weird female way where very little make-up and a brush through the hair could still make her look like a million dollars. Averting his attention, he went down to dinner.

Over dinner they made very polite conversation because both of them were tired, jet lag kicking in. Lexy excused herself first after enjoying only a light meal, the abundance of what they were offered more than her tummy could handle after such a long journey. She donned silky pyjamas from her huge collection of couture clothing, gifted by Nic prior to their marriage. Sliding into the vast bed, she rested her weary head down on a soft pillow.

And then the light by the bed flicked on again and she lowered her eyelids, determined not to react to Nic's proximity, because she was a big girl in terms of age and maturity and she wasn't about to make a fuss about the necessity of sharing a bedroom when they were a married couple. The bed shifted and gave a little with Nic's arrival. He doused the light. He was very quiet, very considerate of her presence, and for some reason it annoyed her, rather than soothing her.

'Are you exhausted?' she heard herself ask without any awareness that she was about to speak to him, which seemed impossible, but his existence in the same bed with her, even if she couldn't feel it, struck her just then as utterly unforgivable. He was this guy she had dared to marry, who had sex without really thinking about it and she couldn't forgive him for that. For the night before, the wedding night of her dreams, had turned into a fight instead.

'Not really. I dozed during the flight,' he admitted.

Gosh, wasn't it great to be a seasoned long-haul private-jet traveller? she thought nastily, and she knew she was being snippy and couldn't quell her tongue. 'Great not to be looking after three babies, wasn't it?'

'You weren't exclusively looking after our brood of babies either,' Nic pointed out smoothly as she sat up in a sudden movement to look down at him in the moonlight. 'That's why I hired three nannies.'

'I want to slap you right now,' Lexy confided shakily.

Nic slowly, gracefully, with a fluidity of motion that set her teeth even more on edge, sat up as well, the sheet dropping to his lean waist, shadow glimmering over his hard, muscular chest, picking out the swells and the hollows, every one of them in exactly the right place to drive a woman to madness. 'I get that, but I don't understand why,' he countered levelly.

'You don't understand why?' Lexy gasped in a rage with knotted fists. 'Last night you were in bed with me—'

'I'm not about to forget that.'

'Telling me that you dreamt of being with me like

this, telling me that I was unbelievably sexy!' she whipped back fiercely.

'And it was all true,' Nic delivered like a man with a death wish, and she wanted to kill him stone-dead where he sat. 'One thing doesn't change…no matter *what* you say or do, I *still* want you.'

'How dare you?' she exclaimed, piling up his sins inside her brain like an avalanche ready to drown them both.

'I always dare,' Nic countered, stretching out a hand to smooth the tumbled hair from her cheekbone, to tuck it neatly behind one small ear, the brush of his very fingers setting up a chain of reaction through her body.

Her nipples strained and prickled under her light camisole, goose flesh sprang up on her exposed skin and her tummy danced with butterflies again while her lower regions, well, she didn't even want to think about the receptive warmth gathering there. That she could be that weak, *that* susceptible to him, inflamed her.

'*I* dare because you don't even try,' he murmured sibilantly.

And somehow it was either slap him or kiss him, and later she wouldn't comprehend what made her lean forward and seek his wide, sensual, thoroughly annoying mouth for herself. Nonetheless, she *did*. Warm lips brushing, a hand closing over her elbow to ease her closer, and she fell into that kiss like a snowflake on a summer day. Her anger melted into something else entirely, something that really didn't seem to matter in the height of her overwhelming response of that moment.

He could kiss. Every time he kissed her, she forgot

how good it was, even if only the night before had been the last time. And that wasn't an excuse, because she was past making excuses when every fibre of her being urged her simply to connect with him again as though it had been months when it had been only hours. As his tongue took a subtle dance across the roof of her mouth before connecting with her own, she grabbed him with both hands and he closed both arms round her, tugging her closer until her breasts were crushed against his broad chest.

And then, in the midst of that passion, Nic pushed her back and gazed down at her with his stunning dark eyes glittering. 'I need to be certain that this is what *you* want.'

And that was it because all of a sudden she was back in her own head and body and just then it felt as though it would be yet another massive betrayal of pride and dignity to allow such closeness.

'It's not what I want,' she lied without hesitation.

Lexy lay back down, her body humming and pulsing like an engine that had geared up for a race. She didn't want to think, she refused to think beyond the reality that in the nicest possible way her husband had rejected her and she was back to wishing she could strike him stone dead.

Only that wasn't what she truly wanted either, she registered in growing dismay. She really didn't want anything bad to happen to Nic Diamandis. And why was that? As she mulled over that final thought, only exhaustion sent her to sleep.

CHAPTER EIGHT

As Nic and Lexy emerged from the lengthy business meeting, Nic was in a better mood with his bride. She had been a professional and businesslike interpreter for the duration and, while once or twice seeking clarity on some technical term from him, she had been confident and impressive. As they entered the lift together, he turned to her. 'What were you chatting about to the chairman at the end? He seemed very pleased.'

'I told him that we would be visiting Bongeun-sa Temple this afternoon and he was delighted that you are taking interest in culture here,' she explained lightly.

'And are we truly planning to make this trip?' Nic enquired, angling up one sardonic brow.

'Obviously.' Her eyes assailed his, her lovely face serious. 'It wouldn't do not to go as you'll probably be asked for your impression of the site at your next meeting. I've been before on several school outings and it's a lovely relaxing place, right in the heart of the city.'

'Did you also mention that this is our honeymoon?'

Lexy went pink. 'That would be too personal for sharing but I would imagine that the chairman is already aware. This company is his life's work and although he does not have a family to pass it on to, he wants to sell to a businessman he regards as good, and the "traditional family man with children" image will serve you well here.'

Nic nodded, appreciating how astute she was, how efficient. How that bled into her less presentable flaws he had yet to discover, he brooded.

They returned to the house for lunch and spent some time with their children before heading back out to the Buddhist temple, which had an amazing location, set as it was in the very heart of the towering glass city sky-scrapers, perfectly preserved on a hillside filled with vast and ancient trees.

'I would have brought the children but there's too many steps for the pram,' she explained rather guiltily.

'The house has a massive garden. Easier to entertain three babies on the spot,' Nic quipped, staring down at her as she stood in the shade, her silky hair catching a flickering strand of sunlight and gleaming gold, her eyes translucent in colour. His hand came down on her shoulder and he felt her tense as he bent his dark head.

In a sudden movement, Lexy twisted away just as an elderly monk came down the steps with a wooden staff, studying them as he passed with a frown. 'I'm sorry,' she said, her lips tingling as though he had ac-tually touched them with his. He hadn't, but there had been a certain heat in his gaze that had spelled out his intention.

Nic had straightened, strong tension etched in his strong jawline. Dismayed, Lexy reached for his hand and laced her fingers through his. 'Out of respect, *this* is as close to friendly as we can get as this is a sacred site,' she proffered apologetically while wondering why she was bothering to explain, because surely he should not even be *trying* to kiss her! She fell off that mental high horse as soon as she recalled kissing him the night before in their bed and her face turned red as fire.

An unexpected laugh of understanding was wrenched from Nic and he glanced at her. 'Relax, *glykia mou...* you're as red as a traffic light but I'm not on the brink of dragging you into the bushes *yet*. Who knows what condition or mood I'll be in within another couple of days?' he teased.

As she attempted to release his hand, his fingers merely tightened their hold and she gave up before an unseemly tussle could occur. Nic definitely didn't appreciate being told what he could and could not do with a woman, she registered, particularly one to whom he was married. And she supposed that, even in a slightly twisty way, she could understand his reasoning.

After all, what had *he* gained from their marriage? Full access to Ethan, Ezra and Lily and legal rights over them. Mel, ever the lawyer, had ensured that Lexy was well acquainted with those facts before she'd reached the altar. Even so, Nic had given up far more than Lexy. He had enjoyed total freedom, unfettered by anyone or anything, and he had surrendered that freedom to marry her.

Lexy, on the other hand, had gone from rags to riches and had escaped much of the daily slog of raising three demanding babies. In short, prior to their marriage, she had had *no* freedom to lose. So how did Nic feel now, stuck with a platonic partner in his bed? He was a man who was probably accustomed to enjoying sex whenever or wherever that desire took him. He was not used to sudden celibacy being forced on him.

'I have a question,' Nic murmured as they slowly climbed the steep steps of the temple.

'What do you want to know?' she asked, removing her footwear to enter the shrine.

'Why did you sleep with me on our wedding night?' Nic enquired, smooth as glass.

In the act of bowing to the custodian greeting them, Lexy winced, gritted her teeth and flushed miserably while wishing that he had chosen a more private moment for such an inquiry.

But then Nic could be very impatient. It had been a struggle for him to talk at the slow, measured pace of the elderly chairman and show that deference for age that was expected in Korea. Now a thought had occurred to him and he had plunged impulsively right in with it, even though the surroundings were inappropriate. Annoyed by his candid question and put on the spot, Lexy simply ignored it while inside the temple cymbals clashed, small bells rang and soft chanting began. He dealt her a fulminating appraisal and she ignored that as well, watching while he paced restively back and forth through the vacant space behind her.

Lexy's temper raced up through her like a rocket ship. He only listened when he wanted to listen, only talked when he wished to, and had pushed her away when she had given him considerable encouragement the night before. It didn't matter what she did, somehow he *always* found fault! Her teeth ground together and her chin came up, anger darkening her more usually calm gaze.

Without a word she joined him again to walk back to the car.

'You've got nothing to say to me...*at all*?' Nic shot at her in a decidedly scornful undertone.

Lexy felt like a pot on a stove ready to boil over and she couldn't contain that indignation. Whipping round on a quiet curve of the path, she breathed, 'I slept with you because an unconsummated marriage can be set aside as invalid in some circumstances. And naturally, when we're going for a divorce, it wouldn't be in *my* best interests to risk that. Happy now? Gold-digger wife right here!'

As she stared defiantly up at him, Nic's darkly handsome features froze and he lost colour below his olive skin. Sudden shame and mortification engulfed Lexy as they walked back in tense silence. What a thing to say to him when they were supposed to be doing the mature thing and sticking to a civilised truce! Why did Nic Diamandis make her act like a volatile teenager? It took a great deal to make Lexy lose her temper and he kept on bringing out that side of her and she hated it! She had lied to make a point, to save her pride, to pretend that she was cunning and mercenary. She had preferred him to believe that rather than the unlovely truth that she was simply a pushover for him.

'Did your best friend of a lawyer tell you that you had to sleep with me at least *once*?'

'No, Mel didn't, actually. I read it some place a year or two back,' she admitted wearily, relieved to tell the truth about something. 'I don't even know if it's still a legal requirement these days.'

She stepped into the luxury vehicle that glided next to the kerb to pick them up and sidled along to the far end of the rear seat. Chagrin held her fast and then just as suddenly as she had lost her temper, the anger was gone and she breathed out slowly. 'I was lying,' she told him reluctantly. 'I was annoyed with you and so I lied. That was wrong, particularly when we're trying to work out how to navigate this marriage peaceably.'

Nic was stunned by that wholly unexpected speech, that fierce quality of sincerity that powered her and the sheer honesty it carried. Brilliant dark eyes locked to her flushed and unhappy profile. 'You're admitting that you were lying?'

'Why wouldn't I? The reason I gave—about an un-consummated marriage—was untrue and hurtful as a motivation and I shouldn't have said it,' Lexy conceded heavily. 'I slept with you because I wanted you and for no other reason.'

'You still want me?'

'Haven't I admitted that already?' she exclaimed in extreme self-consciousness.

'I only pushed you away last night because I wasn't sure you knew what you wanted from me,' Nic confessed, disconcerting Lexy as well with his frankness. 'And I didn't want to risk screwing things up with you again.'

'Oh…' Lexy felt hot and uncomfortable, probably, she reflected ruefully, because she wasn't used to discussing anything to do with sex. And the law of averages being what it was, she had landed the guy who would say anything and talk about it even in the equivalent of a church!

Nic muttered a Greek curse under his breath. He felt weirdly light-headed for an instant. Lexy *still* wanted him. No doubt it was pleasing him to hear that so much because he burned for her every time he looked at her. And he reckoned that he looked at her and thought about sex at least sixty times an hour. No woman had ever had that effect on him before and he was seriously hoping that that fixated hunger died away soon because it wasn't easy to tolerate in a relationship as fractured as theirs was. It had been even less easy to tolerate when he had been unable to find her, he reminded himself darkly. He *needed* to get that sexual infatuation out of his system before the divorce happened. Of course, getting a divorce didn't need to be set in stone, he reasoned. That was something that could only be decided between the two of them and who knew how their marriage would develop in the coming months?

All of a quiver, literally, because Lexy couldn't get that disturbingly intimate conversation out of her head, she returned to the house with him and they spent time with the children in the nursery on the floor. Ezra adored Nic, crawling straight to him, grabbing at his hands to play his favourite game of standing up, because Ezra was desperate to stand and walk. Ethan came more slowly to him, wary, grasping his hands and then bouncing with all his exuberant energy and laughing out loud with sweet baby vigour. Lily came to Lexy, a calmer personality like her mother, and rested on her lap sleepily. She was always quicker to tire than her brothers. Lexy cuddled her daughter with a heart full to overflowing.

'Dinner is set for six-thirty because I said we don't mind eating earlier,' she told him softly. 'I didn't consult you—'

'No, that's fine with me. It's been a long day,' Nic conceded, tugging loose his tie and undoing his collar, sculpted stubbled jawline clenching to throw his flawlessly chiselled features into prominence, accentuating his high cheekbones, his straight ebony brows, his aristocratic nose and wide, perfect mouth.

And she thought, how do I handle this, this unbearable longing, this hunger that comes out of nowhere and just seizes hold of me? He looked as delicious as a long cold drink on a too hot day. Swallowing hard, she turned away as they entered their room, heading straight for the dressing room to choose a fresh outfit. She chose a slim pink sheath dress and changed inside the dressing room, not wishing to hand out signals she wasn't sure she wished to follow up.

Returning to the bedroom, she learned that Nic suffered from no such inhibitions. Naked, bronzed and muscular, Nic was getting dressed too and she drifted straight back out of the bedroom and downstairs to wait for him. How did she traverse such intimacies now? Certainly, she shouldn't be watching him the way she did, *unless*… Why shouldn't she want him when she was married to him? Would a man think twice about watching his wife undress?

They ate a meal of so many dishes and courses, arranged across the tabletop in Korean banquet style, that she had to name it all for Nic. He sampled *bulgogi*, thin beef marinated in sweet soy sauce, *ssam*, grilled meat wrapped in vegetable leaves, *samgyetang*, ginseng chicken soup, *gimbap*, round rolls of rice with savoury extras, fish, rice and noodles. *Kimchi*, pickled vegetables, she explained, appeared at every meal. She suggested that she take him out to sample street food some evening and offered him hints for how he should behave when he dined out later in the week with the chairman at a renowned restaurant.

As she finished the cookie provided for dessert, Nic stood up and closed a hand over hers. 'Let's go to bed,' he murmured lazily.

Lexy reddened because it was still very early. 'It's only—'

'And this is our honeymoon,' he reminded her smoothly.

As he pressed her upstairs, she shed her insecurity. He wanted her and she wanted him. There was absolutely no reason why they should not explore that connection more. He was kissing her long before they reached their bedroom and she was grabbing handfuls of his shirtfront in her eagerness to reach actual skin.

'You're wearing far too many clothes,' she told him.

'So are you,' he said, closing the bedroom door, peeling off his jacket, ripping off his tie and his shirt with an urgency that thrilled her.

'It wasn't supposed to be like this,' she framed without much vigour.

Nic spun her round, ran down her zip and the dress fell to her feet. 'But it *is*...'

While she kicked off her shoes, Nic stripped off his clothes and she couldn't take her eyes off that lean, muscular physique of his and the heated ache at the core of her merely gathered strength. With new decisiveness, Lexy reached behind herself to undo her bra and cast it off, wriggling her hips to shed her knickers. Even while she was doing such things, she was marvelling at the new confidence he gave her. But then a guy viewing her body with the same appreciation he might have awarded a goddess *was* pretty encouraging, she thought, helpless to resist such silent flattery.

He came down on the bed with her, all urgent and aroused and reaching for her, and her heart was hammering so hard she was out of breath, losing herself in the allure of his hungry kiss, the crushing of her lips by his, the sensual exploration of his tongue that sent sensation winging through her whole body.

'I've never wanted anyone the way I want you,' Nic growled, spreading her across the bed to work a slow steady passage down over her slender curves, long fingers touching, teasing, penetrating, watching as her spine rose and a gasp escaped her. 'And I really couldn't wait any longer tonight.'

He made her feel like the most beautiful woman in the world and when she looked at him his sheer gorgeousness almost overpowered her because, realistically, Nic Diamandis had been her fantasy from the first moment she saw him. She ran admiring fingers through his thick black hair, moaned as he found a raspberry-pink straining nipple with his devouring mouth and moaned even louder when he traced the most sensitive spot of all and shifted his attention there with keen concentration. Her first orgasm hit her like a train roaring down a hill and, moments later, he tilted her up and thrust into her slow and deep.

'Ah…' she sighed because as her body so welcomed the invasion of his, it felt impossibly good and little quivers of response eddied through her pelvis.

He flexed his hips and changed speed with a grunt of pleasure as she lifted up to him. From that point, self-control fled Lexy, if it had ever existed. Excitement vanquished discipline and drove every thought out of her head. Sensation was cascading through her willing body in a dam burst of elation. Breath caught in her throat, her heart racing, she was flying higher and higher, particularly after he slid off her, flipped her over and grabbed her hips to raise her again and drove back into her in that new position. She hit an explosive climax right then again, pleasure surging afresh when he kept going, jolting her with ever deeper thrusts. A shriek she muffled in the pillows erupted from her as she reached the plateau again and finally flopped down, convinced she would never move again.

'That was…' Words escaped her.

'Wild. You like it fast and hard…as do I,' Nic informed her, words not evading him.

Lexy grimaced into the pillows and flipped over again. 'Just don't ask me to comment afterwards,' she mumbled awkwardly. 'This is all still too new to me for me to feel comfy talking about it.'

'Still?' he queried.

'Well, when on earth could I have had the freedom to do this with anyone else?' she shot at him irritably.

Nic pulled her close, tossing the rumpled sheet over her, leaning back, feeling fairly pleased with the world in general because she was simply amazing in bed. And she was his wife, something of a sobering recollection, he registered. His wife for at least a year, maybe even longer. Well, there was no reason why they shouldn't enjoy their time together. Temporary truce for a temporary marriage.

But a thought crept in… A divorce would mean Lexy and his children moving into their own accommodation. Like that chateau in France Angeliki had had the bad taste to mention. He wondered what he was going to do about his half-sister. At the wedding she had behaved a little like a jealous girlfriend and he didn't want Lexy to end up in Angeliki's line of fire. It would have been so much easier if Angeliki hadn't tried to seduce him that night. If that hadn't happened, he would have felt able to tell her immediately that they shared a father. At least if he told her the truth about their blood relationship, she would back off and stop acting so possessive, he reasoned, resolving to move ahead with telling his best friend the truth to stop her interfering in his life.

He pictured Lexy as lady of the chateau in France. She wouldn't be on the single shelf for very long, he ruminated, growing increasingly less relaxed as that reality sank in on him hard. He was appalled by the idea of her with another man. In fact, the concept almost made him feel sick. As for the children moving out from under his roof and a potential stepfather pushing his way in? Well, those possibilities held no appeal either. He released his breath in a pent-up rush. There was no need to think about all that stuff now. Presumably a few months down the road he would feel differently.

After all, there wasn't any way he would tie himself down for any longer to a liar, was there? No guy in his right mind would do that.

'I suppose I should get up. It's only half eight,' Lexy lamented.

Nic locked both arms round her, trapping her without even thinking about it. 'No. I have plans for you.'

'Really?' Looking at him upside down, Lexy's eyes widened.

'Yes, we stay in bed and use the opportunity,' he murmured, moving her onto the bed beside him and claiming her swollen mouth with his again.

CHAPTER NINE

NIC SUPPRESSED A SIGH, reluctant to move as he eased back from his wife's sleeping body. Obviously, the honeymoon idyll had to end, and he had to get back to work. For the first time in twenty-nine years he had been lazy. More than three weeks of sheer unpardonable sloth, the fast-track week in Korea, followed by two weeks on the island of Faros, living in his late father's monstrous gilded palace.

Sightseeing followed by sun, sea, sand. *And sex*. He covered Lexy's slender thigh with a large towel because he didn't want her to burn when the sun moved. Vaulting upright, he adjusted the overhead canopy to ensure that she remained in the shade. Below the giant lounger the sand was churned up, awash with buckets, spades and Nic's first attempt since childhood at a sandcastle, all the evidence of the triplets' presence earlier. Tears and tiredness had sent them back up to the house with their nannies for a nap.

Lexy's sheaf of golden hair was tangled, her face composed, her slender little body relaxed. Something tugged hard in his chest and he breathed out heavily. He told himself that it was good that he was leaving her for a day. They needed a break, they needed to let the rest of the world in, only it wouldn't help him to reach a decision about what to do about her and his marriage. Keeping the truce they had agreed, but not confronting her afresh, was *killing* him because Nic was like a dog with a bone when anything angered him and he couldn't let it go, no matter how hard he tried.

His lean, strong features were tense, his frown darkening in tenor. The marriage that was never supposed to be a proper marriage and the honeymoon that happened purely by accident. By accident? *Theos mou*, wasn't he a little too mature to be choosing an excuse of that kind? Lexy was the wife he had never planned to have, who had somehow become a real wife. She was thicker than thieves with his mother and his sister-in-law, Gigi. As for his grandmother, Electra, who rarely complimented any woman, his yaya had told him he had done exceptionally well in choosing Lexy as a life partner. And his brother, Jace, loved the fact that their wives got on like a house on fire.

But this afternoon he had to fly into Athens and discover the nature of the 'urgent personal matter' that had prompted his London office manager, Leigh, to fly to Greece for a confidential meeting. Leigh didn't fuss over the small stuff. Leigh was level-headed. Someone on his staff must have screwed up very badly and Leigh was blaming herself, he surmised, or perhaps Leigh had developed some ghastly serious illness, which she wanted kept secret. What else could it be?

He was fond of the older woman, who had once worked for his father and who was more efficient than anyone else in either office in London or Athens. She managed his staff with quiet assurance, managed *him* to some degree too, he conceded with wry amusement, prompting him to take a break when he worked too many hours, sending in food to sustain him, and she guarded him from unwelcome callers like a Rottweiler.

'You should have woken me up!' Lexy scolded, catching up with him on the path up from the beach, panting slightly at the gradient. 'You're leaving, aren't you?'

'I hope to make it back for dinner,' Nic admitted, grabbing her hand to physically pull her up the last few feet. 'But don't wait up for me if I'm late.'

He strode into the echoing hall where a litter of tiny sandy sandals almost tripped him up. The triplets were walking but some better than others. Ethan still wobbled like a tiny drunk. Lily was the most sure-footed, but she had taken a vehement dislike to sand. Ezra was full of glee at his own prowess and loved to get his feet wet.

Nic smiled, loving the lack of order that was gradually invading his father's once very grand property. Lexy had changed things. The staff were more relaxed, the structure of the household less rigid, the meals more casual and everybody was happier, including himself. He, however, was no less rigid in his moral outlook than he had always been, he acknowledged uneasily as he stepped into the shower. He could not abide dishonesty. He could not commit to a woman who had lied to him. How could he ever trust her?

The most likely scenario, he had decided, was that Lexy had met another man after that night in Yorkshire.

Perhaps she had doubted the paternity of her children at that point and very probably she had not wished to contact Nic and pull him back into her life just then. What else was he supposed to think when he was continually seeking justification for her long silence and even more dubious claims? After all, he knew that she could never have visited his office without him being informed of the fact, even if it was after the event. Phone calls? Leigh would've consulted him. Letters? They would have arrived on his desk.

Nic was in a dark mood, Lexy thought, emerging from her own shower, for once blessing the separate facilities of the huge master bedroom suite they occupied together. But he wouldn't talk about what was on his mind, even if she was convinced that she already knew.

After all, wasn't she worrying too? Here they were, married and with three kids, and the 'faking the marriage' idea had never even got off the ground in reality. Somehow their relationship had become genuine, the scorching physical chemistry between them too powerful to overcome or ignore. That had been their first mistake, the mistake of total intimacy, she recognised, but the biggest mistake of all was that she had fallen for him again. Absolutely, totally and for ever fallen in love with Nic Diamandis for the second time. And why not? Wasn't he still her fantasy guy? Her perfect guy with one major drawback: he didn't trust her, didn't believe in her and as a result he never talked about anything with her that might be happening more than two days in advance.

She sensed that he was almost always right on the edge of walking out of their messy relationship. And why did he stay? Oh, that was a very easy question to answer. He stayed because he adored Ethan, Ezra and Lily. Once he ended their marriage, he would be deprived of daily access to his sons and his daughter.

Nic emerged from his dressing room, fully clad in a sharply cut black suit teamed with a silver-grey shirt and tie. As always, he looked amazing. He was every inch the tech billionaire who had recently acquired a legendary South Korean computer firm that would ensure his empire maintained an even sharper edge in the development stakes.

'I've been thinking that I may stay on for a few days in Athens,' Nic told her quietly. 'It's time I caught up with work. We'll be returning to London soon anyway.'

Her tummy shifted queasily, a hollow opening inside her heart. 'I could come with you,' she pointed out and hated herself for stating the obvious.

'I take too many breaks when you're around,' he parried drily. 'But I'll miss the kids.'

Only he would not miss her, that obvious qualification of his coming to her mind and wounding. He hadn't said that he would miss *her*. Maybe all she was to Nic Diamandis was convenient sex on tap and, when required, a mother to his children. Well, tough cookie, she thought in sudden defiance. She was worth more than that!

As her husband strode on downstairs, she watched him head for the helipad where his pilot was awaiting his arrival. Just as quickly and noisily he was gone in the helicopter with its distinctive Diamandis logo, up into the air and en route to Athens. And was she planning to be here waiting obediently for his now unspecified date of return? No, to hell with that idea!

She had to be proactive when it came to her own life. She lived in a fake marriage that already had a specified end date. But Nic wasn't happy and neither was she. Returning to London, asserting her independence, made sense because he wasn't going to be part of her life for ever anyway. She needed to move on, make plans for the future, lay down some solid foundations. For the past month, all she had done, she conceded with squirming reluctance, was lay down for *him*. And romanticise absolutely everything they had shared, which, in the circumstances, was unforgivable. Her fingers worked nervously at the gold necklace she wore, a designer piece he had bought her on Corfu on one of their days out on Jace's yacht.

She remembered the look in his eyes as he'd clasped it round her throat, that way he had of looking at her as if she were the only woman in the world, the hundred per cent attention always focused on her. It was a kind of charisma Nic Diamantis had, she reasoned, that ability to make a woman feel special even if she wasn't, but ultimately it *hurt*. Every hour he spent with her hurt because no gesture, no act of passion, no tender words ultimately meant anything to him. He was only keeping the stupid truce, keeping her content because a contented woman didn't make waves.

That awareness in mind, she rang Jace's wife, Gigi,

conscious that they were flying back to London that very afternoon, to ask if she could accompany them.

'Didn't Nic ask you to go with him to Athens?' her sister-in-law asked in surprise.

Lexy's cheeks burned red as the heart of a fire in mortification. 'No, and he's not sure when he's coming back either so I thought I might as well head to London now in advance. I know you're leaving today and I was hoping you could give us a lift...all of us, the kids and the nannies.'

'Of course we can, but I'll check with Jace first,' Gigi completed more slowly, clearly thinking through to try and guess what was motivating Lexy.

'Do you think he'll say no?' Lexy asked before she could bite back the nervous question.

'No, Jace keeps his own counsel, but I assume you have your reasons,' Gigi responded calmly. 'And in any case, if you want to head to London today you could make your own arrangements, but you might as well travel with company. We can wrangle kids together.'

While Lexy was planning her departure from the island, Nic was entering his Athens head office, lifting his hand to greet familiar faces without pausing while being assured that Leigh awaited him upstairs in his office. He strode into the sunlit room, apprehension tensing his muscles as he scanned the older woman with her dark hair worn in an elegant chignon and her steady blue eyes.

'Firstly,' Leigh began in an anxious undertone, 'I want to tender my resignation, sir—'

'What on earth…?' Nic breathed with a frown, wrong-footed by that startling opening to their meeting.

'I made a bad decision because I chose to trust someone close to you and when I've finished explaining myself and my actions, you will be very angry with me,' she assured him unhappily. Moving forward, she laid a slender folder down on his desk. 'I kept records of everything though.'

'Someone close to me?' Nic was already prompting, ebony brows pleated, because very few people were close to him outside his family. He had long conserved his independence and ensured that his judgement was unaffected by others. It was probably, he conceded, the only preference he had copied from his father's chosen operational secretive mode in business.

'Miss Bouras,' Leigh declared, disconcerting him even more as she stepped forward.

'Angeliki has nothing to do with any aspect of my business,' he said defensively.

'This is personal, confidential,' Leigh reminded him sadly. 'And I was the fool who listened to her and followed her advice. Look at this first…'

Nic froze and grasped the phone she was extending to study the photograph showing on the screen and disbelief assailed him. It was a picture of Lexy chopping vegetables in his kitchen in Yorkshire that long ago night. A photo he had believed that he had taken when she was unawares and had later searched for but failed to find on his phone—he had assumed that he had done it too quickly and it hadn't taken. 'Where did you get this photo from?'

'Miss Bouras gave it to me for identification purposes,' the older woman explained.

A sinking sensation hit Nic's stomach. 'Why would she do that? *Identification?*'

'Miss Bouras came to see me. Almost two years ago. She explained that you had a very persistent female stalker causing you an awful lot of grief.'

'A…a stalker?' Nic exclaimed in disbelief. 'I've never had a stalker in my life… This woman… Lexy is my wife!'

'Yes, and I'm afraid I only realised that she was an official part of your life when I saw the pictures of your wedding online,' Leigh admitted with a grimace. 'But I believed what Miss Bouras told me and I did as she asked.'

'What did she ask you to do?' Nic shot at her in a harsh undertone.

'To protect you from this woman, this supposedly obnoxious stranger trying to force herself into your life. She said that you were greatly embarrassed by the situation and trying to handle the problem discreetly. I could imagine you reacting that way to a female stalker…' Leigh muttered ruefully. 'You wouldn't want a fuss or any scenes at the office.'

'Leigh… I've never *had* a stalker!' Nic repeated forcefully. 'I can't credit that Angeliki approached you with this ridiculous story.'

Leigh looked grave. 'She did, sir, and she was very specific in her advice and instructions. She told me to destroy any letters that arrived, but I kept them as I assumed there would be a court case eventually and that you would need them as evidence. I noted down the phone calls and any visits that the young lady made.'

'The young lady being my *wife*?' Nic almost whispered, his stomach turning over sickly. Letters, *visits*, exactly as Lexy had claimed.

'It wasn't until I saw the wedding photos that I understood that I had made a very grave error in listening to Miss Bouras and trusting her word, rather than approaching you direct to discuss her instructions with you. You would scarcely marry a stalker.'

'Thank you for that understanding at least,' Nic muttered, raking an abstracted hand through his thick black hair while true comprehension began to sink in hard as a hammer blow to the head. Indeed, he felt as though he had been body-slammed against a brick wall and the stuffing had been knocked out of him. He was in shock.

He was already thinking back to the phone number that had disappeared from his phone. He hadn't thought much about the photo, only that he had taken it in haste while she had been unaware and that perhaps it hadn't taken, after all. But only one person ever knew the current password he had on his phone, his friend from childhood, Angeliki. Only one person had ever had free access to his phone and she had evidently used it to ensure that he couldn't contact Lexy.

And lo and behold, that was the same person, the *only* person, he had innocently told about Lexy. He had returned from Yorkshire the same day that Angeliki had finally decided to take his calls and he had been so high on that time with Lexy that he had mentioned to his half-sister that he had met 'someone', an important *someone*, whom he had named and described and waxed lyrical about.

Theos mou, what an idiot he had been! Thinking back to that period, he knew that only a complete fool would have talked about another woman to a woman he had recently rejected. Only by then he had already been thinking of his best friend as his half-sister, a safe confidante to his mind, if not hers.

'My worst recollection is of instructing the security men to show your pregnant wife-to-be down to the street,' Leigh almost whispered, her blue eyes shining with tears of regret. 'I felt dreadful about that even at the time but I thought... I thought it was my duty, my job to protect you from annoyance and unnecessary drama. I believed Miss Bouras. I knew you trusted her and I trusted her as well until I saw those pictures of your wedding. Then I realised that I had to come forward and speak up. Look, I've already taken up enough of your time and I can see that you're rather taken aback by all this—'

'Try...shocked speechless,' Nic corrected in a roughened undertone. 'But it's not your fault. I trusted Miss Bouras too. You cannot resign over this matter. I will explain all this...*somehow* to my wife. I will deal with the consequences. It is my responsibility.'

'Every call your wife made to our London office was logged and every letter is contained in the file, sir. The letters are unopened, of course,' the older woman proffered uncomfortably, indicating the file lying on his desk. 'I'm sorry about all this stuff. I know you don't like it.'

But Angeliki did, Nic reflected darkly. Angeliki thrived on drama, would have enjoyed coming into his office, telling her lies, ensuring that not a single person on his staff would give credence to Lexy, indeed would instead treat her like a stalker, a woman trying to force herself into his life where she was unwanted and unwelcome. And he felt seriously nauseous again when he recalled how very badly he had wanted to hear from Lexy twenty-odd months ago. It was as though his life had suddenly been rolled back in time and he was reliving what he would have felt then. Furious anger filled him. He knew that he had to see Angeliki first, had to confront her and finally tell her that they were siblings.

Once more refusing to accept Leigh's resignation, telling her that she had been as deceived in her trust of Angeliki as he had long been, Nic left the office to visit Angeliki's penthouse apartment.

Angeliki's housekeeper answered the door and ushered him into the airy reception room where her mistress was lying along a couch with a magazine, wearing a silk teddy below a sheer robe that she didn't bother to close as she sprang up, a huge smile lifting her beautiful face. 'Nic…always a welcome visitor.'

'Put something on,' he urged brusquely. 'You're not going to like me much after I've finished talking to you.'

In an exaggerated movement, Angeliki tied the sash on the robe, too proud of her long, shapely body to be pleased about hiding it.

'This is about Lexy, my wife.' Nic felt the need to

attach that possessive label, noting how the blonde's face tightened. 'The moment I told you about her, you conducted a campaign to prevent her from coming back into my life.'

Angeliki raised a pencilled brow. 'Of course I did. I had to prevent you from doing something stupid because you were acting like a teenager about her. I've never seen you like that over a woman.'

'And clearly it was very stupid of me to confide in you. You broke into my phone, didn't you? Stole the photo, blocked her number, did every rotten thing you could to ensure I *couldn't* see her again!'

'Because you were about to make a *huge* mistake! I'm your best friend. I protected you from yourself.'

'I didn't need protecting. I'm an adult and far from innocent.'

'You were infatuated for the first time in your life!' Angeliki sliced in with a cutting edge of venom. 'You didn't know what you were doing. *Theos mou*, you had only parted from her a couple of hours and you were already agonising over whether or not you would look desperate if you phoned her!'

'You cut off someone who was important to me and, even worse, you left her no means to contact me when she needed my support because she was pregnant. So, no, Angeliki, I have nothing to thank you for. You deprived me of seeing my children coming into this world, you deprived me of times with the four of them that I will never get back!' Nic raged at her, out of all patience with her drivel. 'My office manager has told me that you gave her Lexy's photo and said that she was a stalker.'

His half-sister backed off a few steps and grimaced. 'Oh, she's told you about that. I was hoping that my intervention wouldn't come out for a while.'

'You don't screw up other people's lives like this,' Nic breathed rawly. 'It's unpardonable. Why did you do it? Were you jealous that I wanted her and not you?'

'Oh, don't be silly. I don't *do* jealousy.' Angeliki actually snorted with scornful laughter at that accusation. 'I've never cared about any of the women you've been with! But she got in my way and I don't let anyone do that to me.'

Nic lifted a lean brown hand. 'News update, Angeliki. Now I'm *in your way* too and if you ever get in hers again, I will ruin you! I don't know why you think Lexy was in your way when you and I weren't even seeing each other.'

'Because you *married* her!' Angeliki launched back at him in angry interruption, her dark eyes hard and cold. 'That was *my* place you gave her, not hers! Together we could be the new power couple in Greece. You were always meant to be mine, Nic, but I had to wait for you to grow up and see that we *belong* together—'

'We don't, and never could be together,' Nic incised with the icy bite of finality. 'Not only do I not want you in that way, but you are my half-sister. We share the same father.'

Angeliki backed off several feet, shock etched in her fine features. 'That's not possible. My mother always hated your father for the way he bullied mine.'

'It happened between them and you are the result, accept it.' Nic shrugged, not in a sympathetic mood. 'The legacy that made you an unexpected heiress came from my father's private coffers, not from some distant relative. Argus paid his dues in that line.'

Angeliki stared back at him in horror, as if her whole world were falling down on top of her. 'That's not possible…because that means that when I got into *your* bed—'

'Nothing happened,' Nic reminded her shortly.

'And how long have you known about this?'

'Since a letter was given to me after my father's will was read. I was going to tell you then, but the bedroom episode had recently occurred and I didn't want to make the announcement until the dust had settled on that.'

'You're my brother,' Angeliki said queasily. 'That toad, Jace, who won't give me the time of day, is my brother too.'

'And you and I are not friends any more and never will be again,' Nic framed coldly. 'Not after what you did to Lexy. Are you even aware that your lies about her being a stalker led to her being thrown out of my office building when she was heavily pregnant? I suspect you don't care.'

'You're right there!' Angeliki lashed back at him bitterly, dark eyes hard and hollow, reminding him unpleasantly of his late father. 'I don't give a damn. The blasted Diamandis family looks after itself and nobody else. I wish you'd had sex with me that night because it would have made you feel dirty and you're such a clean, decent guy. You were *never* for me!'

'That's good.' Turning on his heel, Nic strode out of her apartment with a sense of relief. He still had to see his mother, bring her up to date with the Angeliki situation, but he had had enough emotional drama for one day.

He had, he accepted, wrecked his relationship with Lexy from day one of their reunion. His principles had got the better of him. He had been blind, judgemental and intolerant. He had wanted Lexy to be that one perfect ideal woman without flaws. And fancy this, she truly *was*. He was the one with all the flaws, the guy who had learned he couldn't trust anyone at a very young age.

Not his father, who had once rammed him head first into a wall for irritating him as a toddler and put him into hospital. Not his mother, who had always put his father first and made excuses or lied for Argus, regardless of what he did. Not the string of women chasing him for his wealth, his status or even the right to stand beside him in a photo and reap that fleeting fame. And not even the one close friend he had ever had, Angeliki, who had clearly been determined to marry him from early on right up until she discovered that she was a blood relation. He also saw in her that, of all three Diamandis siblings, she resembled Argus the most with her cold, calculating, unscrupulous nature. What she wanted, she got, and she didn't care how she had to go about getting it. He had been learning to trust his older brother, but they had only got to know each other after their father's death, and he had retained his wariness about letting anyone come close.

By the time Jace phoned him to tell him that he was taking Lexy and the triplets to London with him, Nic was hitting a bottle of whiskey hard and hating himself. He had hurt his wife *again* and she was leaving him. It was exactly what he deserved…to lose her and his children.

CHAPTER TEN

'MY FATHER COULDN'T leave the London town house to Nic because it was mine according to the terms of the Diamandis trust. So, shortly before he died, he bought one directly across the street in the same square to leave to your husband.'

'How very convenient,' Lexy remarked, her cheeks warm, looking out of the windows at the leafy square, adorned with a well-kept garden in the centre. 'I imagine it's as imposing inside as everything else your father furnished.'

'I've never been inside it. You'll have to invite us over for me to offer an opinion,' Jace quipped.

'You're welcome to visit any time,' Lexy told him warmly, cheered by the knowledge that they lived only across the square, although she supposed she could hardly confide in Gigi if her marriage was in as much trouble as she believed it was. No, she needed Mel and had already texted her friend to let her know when she would be arriving and where she would be staying.

'Nic didn't sound too enthusiastic about you travelling without him. You're not thinking of ditching him, are you?' Jace asked. 'You make him happy. He only smiles and laughs since you came into his life. I swear he's the most serious Diamandis ever born.'

Lexy's face flamed. 'Of course I'm not,' she declared with as much assurance as she could gather, when in truth she didn't know what she was doing.

And she was no wiser after she and the kids and the nannies piled into the tall town house across the street to be greeted by an honest-to-goodness butler, who introduced himself as Dexter, and a housekeeper called Agnes. Lexy had phoned ahead of their arrival and had been assured that there was a large nursery already prepared for her children and rooms in the staff quarters to house the nanny trio.

The front hall was timeless, from the original Georgian tiles below her feet to the decorative painted panelling on the walls. The furniture was antique, but nothing was gilded or ornate or too large for its place. It was surprisingly plain and fresh, the gracious ambience almost contemporary.

Nic didn't phone her that night and she didn't bother phoning him, having decided that her days of running after Nic Diamandis were over. Perhaps they could separate now but keep it quiet for a few months to keep his family happy, she thought sadly, fighting against her own instincts with all her might. If they broke up, it could be done with dignity and no great drama. After all, love had never been a component of their arrangement. An arrangement, an agreement, were more apt labels than that word 'marriage'. Just because she had chosen to share a bed with Nic and fall back in love with him didn't magically change their arrangement into a real marriage.

It was dinner time two days later before Nic appeared and he hadn't phoned in the interim. She looked up from settling Ezra into his cot because he had been very restless and there Nic stood in the doorway. And her first anxious thought was what had happened to him since she had last seen him? Shadows were etched under his dark eyes, a heavy cloud of stubble darkly outlining his jaw and tense mouth, his tie loose round his unbuttoned shirt collar.

'You look tired,' she said tautly.

'It's been a rough few days since I last saw you,' he conceded heavily, walking over to join her by the cot, clasping Ezra's tiny hand as it immediately reached up to grasp his father's fingers.

A shout sounded from Lily's cot and, moments later, Lily's tousled head appeared above the cot rail. Nic lifted her, gave her a hug and laid her down gently into the cot again while she babbled her nonsense at him, only the occasional syllables sounding as if they could be part of a word. He peered down hopefully into Ethan's cot, but their second son was dead to the world as usual. Nothing woke Ethan up after a busy day.

Lexy studied Nic, wondering what was wrong. Sheathed in a silvery grey suit that fitted his big powerful physique with the designer precision of Italian tailoring, he took her breath away as he always did. He had a smoulderingly sexy vibe even when he was travel-weary.

He raked long fingers through his cropped black hair. 'I need a shower, a shave—'

'Maybe some sleep?' Lexy suggested.

'No. I have a lot to tell you,' he muttered heavily. 'I'll tell you most of it over dinner.'

Lexy winced. 'Can't you just spill it now?'

'No, I owe you far too much to trot it all out like it's trivial stuff.'

Although she didn't intend to, Lexy found herself following him into the bedroom, a tranquil, beautifully furnished space the very opposite of the gilded grandeur of his father's palatial home on the island. 'Why's this house so different from the one on Faros if it belonged to your father first?' she asked.

He was halfway out of his shirt, his lean brown muscular torso twisting as he swung back to look at her, a wry smile briefly crossing his lips. 'He purchased it just before he died. I renovated it. I hired an interior designer and asked her to respect the house's history. My father didn't appreciate any history but his own.'

Nic scrutinised his wife, a small, slender figure clad in jeans and a tee shirt. She liked plain clothes: he had learned that shopping with her. She had conservative tastes, didn't like anything that screamed high fashion or showed too much of her body. And yet she was beautiful, show-stopping in her own way, with her soft silky golden hair, her delicate curves and glorious aquamarine eyes.

He disappeared into the bathroom and Lexy sank down at the foot of the bed. She relived the depth of pain she had seen in his stunning dark eyes as he'd looked at her and her heart sank. The backs of her eyes burned. Was it simply that he was so unhappy with her that he couldn't hide it? It was ironic that she simply wanted him to be happy, and she had believed he was while they were in Korea and on his family's island. Only, when her happiness depended on having *him* in her life, she was scarcely a disinterested observer. She didn't know how Nic felt when she wasn't around. She didn't think he had missed her because he hadn't phoned since they'd parted in Greece, and she didn't think he was an emotional guy, unless he lost his temper out of impatience and even then he didn't say much, certainly would never be abusive. It was possible that he was emotional deep down inside but that he kept that side of himself buried around her.

Hey, this is the guy who knows that you married him for wealth and security, she reminded herself as she tugged out a dress to change into. She didn't need to fuss over herself when she was never ever going to be competition for Angeliki, but then he didn't seem to find the blonde heiress attractive. She couldn't sit down to eat with him in a stained tee shirt, not unless she was a total lazy slob. Finding the bathroom empty when she emerged, she went for a quick shower to freshen up before she dressed again.

Nic's hair was damp, a fresh shirt hanging open as he pulled on jeans.

'It's funny,' Lexy said ruefully. 'I get dressed up for dinner, you get dressed *down*. It shows what a bad match we are.'

'We're not.' Nic watched her perch at the foot of the

bed, her hands linking together in a tight grip that told him she was very tense and anxious. He breathed in deep and strong. 'You know, I missed you—'

'You could've taken me with you,' she reminded him.

'It's just as well that I didn't. I got very, very drunk the night before last and I'm still feeling the effects. I found out a whole lot of distressing things over the past two days and I didn't handle it well.'

Her smooth brow furrowed. 'Distressing?'

'Very distressing and very much a blueprint of my own flaws, so I probably wouldn't have been good at trying to explain it all to you in the frame of mind I was in. I'm not saying that I'll do it any better tonight but at least I'm desperate enough to *try*,' he completed grimly.

'I've been wondering if maybe we should be thinking of…of a er…friendly separation…even if we're living under the same roof,' Lexy proposed shakily. 'I don't want to deprive you of the kids and it's not like I hate you or anything…or you hate me.'

Nic lost all the colour in his bronzed complexion and stared back at her as if she had punched him. 'I don't want a separation—'

'But perhaps it's what we both *need*,' Lexy qualified. 'You're not happy right now and I can see that—'

'Shelve this discussion for now but let me say first that that's not true. I will explain why. Obviously you're unhappy and I don't blame you,' Nic declared flatly. 'But that could change if other things changed—'

'People don't change,' Lexy sighed.

'That depends on their motivation. Let's eat and I'll

tell you about Angeliki,' he urged, grasping her hand to tug her up and head her downstairs.

'*Angeliki?*' she questioned in bewilderment.

'Yes, and my office manager, Leigh, and my mother. I've been talking to all of them in the last couple of days and it was an eye-opening, very unpleasant experience.'

A maid delivered the starter beneath Dexter, the butler's watchful gaze. Lexy lifted her wine glass while Nic pushed his glass away and poured himself some water.

'Angeliki…' Lexy prompted uneasily.

'We grew up together. Her mother, Rhea, is my mother's best friend. It was inevitable that I saw a great deal of Angeliki. She was like a little sister to me. She's a couple of years younger than I am. I…' He hesitated, his lean dark features tightening. 'I loved her as a part of my family. As a teenager, I was quiet, good-living and a disappointment to my father, who would've been delighted if I'd gone wild like Jace did but that was never me. Angeliki was colourful, adventurous and everything I was not, an entertaining companion for the adolescent years.'

'But the friendship remained—'

'Yes, until she tried to get into bed with me a couple of months before I met you and I rejected her. I was shocked by her approach, totally unprepared for that.'

Lexy almost winced because, in some ways, he was still innocent, certainly not always good when it came to reading the room. 'Angeliki has always wanted you for herself. I saw that in her the very first time I met her. So,' she pressed, helpless not to ask. 'Did you sleep with her?'

Nic studied her in wonderment. 'Of course I didn't. It was always platonic on my side of the fence, and she reacted badly to rejection.'

'I can imagine,' Lexy muttered in relief that her own reading of that relationship had been correct.

'For weeks, she wouldn't answer my calls and I felt bad about it. Then my father died and, being Argus, he left a bombshell letter for me, which I received after the will reading. A letter telling me that Angeliki was my half-sister.'

'Good grief!' Lexy gasped, unprepared for that revelation.

'I couldn't face telling her straight after that getting-into-my-bed episode, so I thought I'd let the memory of that fade before I told her the truth.'

Lexy nodded, following that reasoning but shaken too by the sudden awareness that Angeliki, the shrew, was actually a member of Nic's family.

'And then I met *you*,' Nic informed her. 'And that was like casting a stone in a very deep pond because Angeliki got in touch with me again and I told her about meeting you.'

'You told *her* about me?' Lexy repeated in surprise at that admission.

'Yes. Total idiot about women here,' Nic quipped with a curled lip. 'I raved about you like a teenager, according to her, and she realised that I'd finally met what she saw as competition.'

Lexy winced. 'I could never be competition to a woman as gorgeous as Angeliki Bouras.'

'Beauty is in the eye of the beholder, and I saw you

as a beauty from the first moment I saw you,' Nic disagreed. 'A beauty with ten times Angeliki's appeal.'

Lexy studied him in astonishment and recognised
that he absolutely believed that, believed that she was
way more attractive than his half-sister. Of course she
was, *now* that he knew Angeliki was family. After all,
Nic was laying it on a bit thick because how good could
she have looked after that car accident in Yorkshire?
Nose and ears red, face white with shock in the cold?

Nic lifted a folder onto the table and pushed it in
her direction. 'This is the file that my office manager
gave me the day before yesterday. It lists your every
phone call and includes your letters…read only by *me*,'
he specified with care. 'And that's why I got drunk.
After reading those and understanding how alone you
felt coping with so much, I was devastated.'

'I don't understand. You're saying that you never received my letters back when I posted them? How can
that be? Your office manager? Why would she hold
back confidential letters?'

'Angeliki told her that you were a stalker.'

'A…*what*?' Lexy gasped in disbelief.

'She persuaded Leigh that you were a stalker by
showing her your photo and told many lies that indi-
cated that you were a woman causing me embarrassment. Leigh only smelt a rat when she saw photos of
our wedding.'

'Naïve,' Lexy muttered weakly, thinking of the icily
polite lady she had had to speak to when she had been
futilely seeking a meeting with Nic at his office. Leigh
had never ever been rude or dismissive but had always

remained professional and courteous even if she hadn't given an inch.

'No, I think the real problem was that Leigh is kind of motherly with me.' Nic frowned. 'She's known me since I was a little boy coming into my father's office. When Angeliki told her that a stalker was targeting me, Leigh would have gone into super drive to protect me because she saw that as her job.'

'Right…' Lexy's voice was fading away as the main course was laid in front of her. It looked amazing but her appetite had gone. She sipped her wine instead.

'So, after Leigh had brought me up to date on what had been happening behind my back, I sat down that night and read your unopened letters,' Nic admitted.

Lexy blinked, said nothing, but how *could* she feel when those letters had been written so long ago when she was in a certain frame of mind, a *desperate* frame of mind? In short, she cringed, gulped more wine, sat silent.

'I felt like a four-letter word of a guy reading those letters. I… I was heartbroken. I drank a lot that night. I tried to find solace in something but there was nothing there to comfort me. I let you down. I *failed*. I took the risk and got you pregnant and then I wasn't *there* for you to help, to support,' Nic recounted in a raw undertone. 'Nothing I can do or say can make up for those months you were alone. You did *all* the right things. You tried to get in touch with me, but Angeliki's ploys foiled us both. It didn't occur to me that she had always had access to my phone and had blocked your number. I spent a fortune trying to trace you, trying to find out where you worked, and I failed there as well because

I didn't know something as simple as your surname. That says it all.'

'That you weren't thinking any more clearly than I was when we first met,' Lexy chipped in helplessly, thinking back. 'I left you to attend that christening and I lived to regret that.'

'Why?' he asked in surprise. 'You had made a commitment and I respected that.'

'My godchild's parents had a huge fight during the christening party and split up a few weeks after that,' Lexy revealed ruefully. 'And in spite of my texts, I haven't heard from my friend since then, so, yes, with hindsight I was a fool to insist on attending that event.'

'But I respected that...your loyalty to your friend. I accepted it because it was the sort of thing I would have done,' he confessed ruefully.

'Even though it cost us so much?' she almost whispered.

'Yes, because you wouldn't be the woman I fell in love with if you had behaved any differently.'

'Think dinner's over,' Lexy muttered, her entire attention locked to Nic's taut, darkly handsome face, because she was barely able to credit that he could speak so casually about *loving* her. 'How can you just say that?'

Nic tossed his napkin on the table. 'I fell for you the same night I met you.'

As he rose from the table, he signalled Dexter and the older man headed for the exit door. Nic searched her troubled face. 'No pretending now, not any longer,' he breathed. 'You're my ideal woman and I almost lost you. Not once but *twice*.'

Lexy was only emerging from her shock. 'You're saying that you fell for me that night?'

'Yeah, I was as seriously uncool and excited about meeting you as Angeliki accused me of being. I was exactly like a dazzled teenager. Apparently, that's how I was talking about you the day after I met you.'

'Me too,' Lexy admitted as he rounded the table. 'I talked you up to the sky with Mel and then you didn't phone and I cringed at all the stuff I'd said about you.'

Nic gazed down at her, dark eyes glittering and full of longing. 'Do you think I could bring those feelings back?'

Feeling cornered, not quite sure how she should feel after that declaration of love, Lexy frowned, only to be startled when Nic dropped down to his knees beside her. 'I'll do just about anything. I'm so sorry I trusted Angeliki and lost you. It's something that I can never make up for.'

Lexy's hands rose from her lap, unclasped and framed his strong cheekbones, small fingers stretching. 'But perhaps I can consider forgiving you,' she said breathlessly, utterly mesmerised by the dark golden, black-lashed eyes claiming hers.

'Truthfully?' he exclaimed.

'Jury's still out,' she warned him.

'If you will only agree to stay with me as my wife, I promise to be the best husband ever,' he assured her, still on his knees.

'Oh, I'm gonna stay,' Lexy told him with confidence, fingers delving into the luxuriant depths of his black hair. 'I mean, you've got a lot going for you. Honesty, that's a plus…especially when you mess up.'

His dark head bent as he grimaced. 'Yes, I lost the plot. Jace warned me way back that Angeliki was toxic and I didn't listen. That side of her never bothered me because, until recently, it wasn't aimed at me. She won't be a part of our lives in the future.'

'But she's your sister.'

'And far from happy about the fact. After confronting her, I went to see my mother to break the bad news that her best friend had given birth to her husband's child,' he told her tautly. 'And that was anything but fun.'

'I can't imagine,' she murmured, thinking of Bianca's soft, affectionate heart. 'That must've hurt her.'

'Not at all,' Nic disconcerted her by responding. 'She already knew the whole story, had *always* known, which explains why she was constantly careful to remind me that Angeliki was the little sister I had to look after when we were kids. Apparently, it wasn't an affair between Argus and Rhea. He had information about Rhea's husband which would have financially ruined the family…he virtually blackmailed her into bed.'

Lexy winced. 'Oh?'

'He threatened Rhea that he would reveal that bombshell unless she acquiesced,' Nic revealed with strong distaste. 'She gave in and Angeliki was the surprise result. It wrecked Rhea's marriage and there was a divorce.'

Lexy was frowning. 'And your mother actually *knew* that he did that to her best friend?' she exclaimed in bewilderment.

Nic vaulted upright again. 'Yes, we talked and I didn't understand. That's the thing about my mother. She forgave my father no matter what he did. She says he wasn't a good man but that she loved him anyway. He beat her, he beat me and it still didn't change anything.'

'He got physical?' Lexy stood up with a grimace. 'I didn't realise.'

'It's not something you talk about. I learned to stay out of reach when I was quite young. He would fly off the handle if you annoyed him. Mum tried to distract or interrupt him and if that didn't work, she would tell me that my father was in a bad mood and that I had to understand that he was a very busy man.' Nic shrugged in dismissal. 'But that's how I grew up, being bullied and beaten, and I learned fast that if I showed any emotion, he saw that as a weakness.'

Lexy stretched up on tiptoe, her small hand stroking his jawline soothingly. 'I'm sorry. I didn't know.'

'When I met you, I was still living with that conditioning. I knew that I wanted you more than any woman I'd ever met straight away but I couldn't process it. I fell for you that night—it was crazy, but I did. I liked everything about you. You were down to earth and frank and that impressed me. Then...' Nic spread eloquent hands and a wicked grin slashed his lips. 'The sex was incredible and all I wanted was more and more of you and that's what we would have had, had Angeliki not intervened.'

'But she did, and I had the triplets alone but for Mel,'

Lexy completed with regret. 'We can't change that but I learned to hate you for that.'

'Could you learn to unlearn it?' Nic prompted very seriously. 'I'm not planning to keep anything from you any more. Perhaps I should've been more honest from the start. Our wedding night wasn't planned... I genuinely was not expecting that to happen.'

'You *made* it happen!' Lexy tossed back at him as he swept her off her feet at the foot of the stairs. 'What happened to the rest of dinner?'

'We gave up on it. I didn't make it happen,' Nic protested as he carried her upstairs like a parcel. 'I guess, I was just overexcited.'

'Yeah, no short memory here...you and all the supermodels you entertained yourself with while we were apart. I saw you on the Internet with them.'

'But I didn't have sex with a single one of those dates.'

'You expect me to believe that you didn't sleep with any of those gorgeous ladies?' Lexy asked incredulously as he laid her down on the big bed in their bedroom.

'Yes. Since the night I met you, there hasn't been anyone else.'

'But...?'

'At first, I was expecting to find you and I was being faithful,' Nic contended, faint colour edging his high cheekbones. 'And then when I couldn't find you, I was so into *you* that I wasn't attracted to anyone else. I've never slept around. You and I were special and I couldn't move past that. And I was glad I hadn't given way to lust when I finally found you again.'

'Only because I put a solicitor on your trail,' Lexy broke in, but she was thinking about that. About Nic Diamandis with his many options choosing not to have sex with anyone else after her. And she liked that, she liked that so much that she felt light-headed in receipt of that confession. He had been loyal to her even after he had lost hope of seeing her again. He had valued what they had found together. All of a sudden, she could think back to that passionate wedding night and forgive herself for being part of it.

'There wasn't anyone else for me either...although I can't pretend I had many opportunities to stray,' she whispered. 'Is there a reason why you brought me straight to bed?'

A boyish grin skimmed Nic's mobile mouth. 'The obvious.'

'I like that you're not pretending.'

'I'm done with pretending. I grew up having to pretend that I lived in a perfect family, but the truth is that it was dysfunctional...and violent,' Nic framed tautly. 'And at times, I despised my mother even though I always loved her too. But she took everything my father threw at her and when I talked to her yesterday and she told me that she'd always known about Angeliki being my sister, I felt out of all patience with her.'

'I think I might have been as well,' Lexy said uncertainly. 'But Bianca was very young when she met your father.'

'She told me that she still loved him until the day he died, but she also told me that she stayed with him for *my* benefit,' he admitted with a sardonic twist of his wide sensual mouth. 'She said that if she had tried to divorce him, he would have fought to keep me as his all-important son. He had the power and he would've won, but I didn't like being blamed for her choices.'

'Of course you didn't,' Lexy agreed, linking her fingers with his to tug him down on the bed beside her. 'But maybe you could stop being so judgemental.'

'I need to,' he agreed grimly. 'I wanted you back a month ago. I wanted you on any terms the moment I saw you again.'

'Enough to take me on as a gold-digging wife?'

Nic laughed. 'I wanted you any way I could get you!'

'Me and the kids,' she qualified.

'You're my family,' he said simply. 'My fatal error was wanting you to be perfect and holding all those months we were apart against you. I see in black and white. No shades of grey. I assumed that you were lying to me about having tried to contact me while you were pregnant and I couldn't get past that. I should've given you a clean page and let it go but I wasn't capable of that.'

'Neither was I. I couldn't forgive you either for not coming to my rescue,' Lexy confided gently. 'I thought you were lying too, unable to face up to the situation at the time and unable to admit that either. I still fell back in love with you…'

'Seriously?' Nic prompted in astonishment.

'Oh, totally.' Lexy looked up at him with wry blue-green eyes. 'Don't know what it is about you, but you've got that vibe I can't resist—'

'I love you so much.'

'I'm starting to believe that,' Lexy said, sitting up to begin unbuttoning his shirt. 'You're wearing too many clothes again, Mr Diamandis.'

Never slow to take a hint, Nic straightened, stepping away to remove the shirt and follow with the jeans and the boxers. Lexy wriggled her shoulders and began to try and undo the zip of her dress but Nic got there first, running it down and gently easing the dress up over her head while she kicked off her shoes, peeling down the hold-up stockings she wore.

'Leave those on…they're sexy,' Nic murmured.

Lexy just laughed, watching him come down to her, bronzed and sleek and breathtaking, and her heart stopped inside her for an instant. 'Do you think it's possible to fall in love at first sight?'

'I did.'

He looped her tousled hair back from her brow and leant down to claim her lips with his. 'I fell for you like a ton of bricks. The instant I saw you and you started talking and then you cooked—'

'Major selling point from the guy who can afford a personal chef!' Lexy quipped.

'Everything about you is a major selling point. Your face, your smile, your honesty, loyalty, kindness. Your ability to accept a less than perfect guy.'

'But he's *trying*!'

'I want to deserve you and our children. I need to do a better job than our parents did,' he admitted in a raw undertone.

'And we'll be all the better for it because we know we're not perfect,' she told him soothingly, smoothing a tender hand down over his hard jawline. 'I will never stop loving you, flaws and all.'

'So, you weren't leaving me after all when you came here?'

'Maybe I finally wanted you to sit up and take notice. I was miffed that you didn't want me in Athens with you. But no, I didn't want to leave you. It was more about trying to protect myself from being hurt.'

'I will strive to never hurt you again. I love you. I will always be here for you, from now until the end.' His dark golden eyes were molten with love and tenderness as he claimed her parted lips with his and silence fell as they luxuriated in being together again. Intimacy entwined them heart and body, passion and need zinging through them, joyful pleasure and security entangling them as Nic held her close in the drowsy aftermath. In the middle of the night, they got up to raid the kitchen and recalled that long ago night in Yorkshire.

'No triplets this time,' she warned him when they finally fell back into bed.

'But maybe some day *one* more baby?' he proposed.

'It would take an act of God to persuade me to go through that again,' she warned him ruefully. 'And you can't tell if it will be one baby or more than one.'

'Let's talk about it some other time,' Nic murmured sensibly. 'Did I tell you how much I love you?'

Lexy smiled happily. 'You can tell me again. Over and over and *over* again.'

EPILOGUE

Five years later

LEXY STROLLED OUT onto the bedroom terrace of her brother-in-law's yacht and lifted her binoculars to scrutinise her home on the island of Faros. There had been big changes to the property, which had required a major redesign. It no longer resembled a palace. It was more of a sprawling and comfortable beach house, and it was much better suited to a family with young, active children.

Five children, she reflected in wonderment, marvelling that she was the mother of so many. She had allowed Nic to persuade her to try for another baby and, instead of one baby, they had been blessed with twin girls. So that was that now, they were content that their family was complete. Madison and Ella were non-identical and even as toddlers both had burned with high-octane energy. Madison was blonde like her mother and Ella was dark, but they both had Lexy's aquamarine eye colour. Ezra was very much their babysitter on the beach.

As she squinted through the binoculars, she could see her eldest son standing, hands on hips just like his father, telling the little girls to stop doing something he saw as dangerous. He was very protective of his little sisters. Ethan, meanwhile, a risk-taker to the core, was climbing the steep rocky outcrop at the end of the beach and Lily was sitting far below him with her nose deep in a book, staying well clear of the noise and chaos created by her siblings.

Lexy's mother-in-law, Bianca, was sitting on a rug above the beach, her husband, grey-haired Matteo Rossi, by her side. They were supervising the kids for the weekend while Lexy and Nic took off to Corfu to celebrate Lexy's twenty-seventh birthday with dinner and a night at a club.

A step sounded behind her and her binoculars were tweaked from her grasp.

'You promised that you would relax,' Nic censured, making a nonsense of the stricture when he took the opportunity to lift the binoculars to his own eyes to spy on their family. 'Why did we ever think that a broken leg would put Ethan off climbing?'

'Well, at least we've got a retired doctor on site in case of emergencies,' Lexy quipped, referring to Matteo, the laid-back older man Bianca had married during her sojourn in the country of her birth.

'Yes. I like my stepfather. My mother seems much happier.'

Four years earlier, Bianca had announced that she was tired of being a Diamandis and needed a change. She had bought an old farmhouse near the village where she had been born in Italy and had pretty much left the trappings of her wealth behind her, with the exception of her frequent flights back to London and Greece to see her grandchildren. Lexy was very fond of her mother-in-law and had interceded with Nic, who had been rather overprotective and suspicious when his mother had first met Matteo.

A childless widower, Matteo was a cheerful man with a terrific sense of humour and a great love for both his second wife and her grandchildren. They took occasional trips back to Italy but had based themselves in Greece since their marriage. Although Bianca still regularly saw her friend, Rhea, Rhea's daughter, Angeliki, carefully avoided the Diamandis tribe for neither of her half-brothers trusted her around their families or friends.

During term-time, Lexy and Nic lived in London, where the children went to school, and summers were always spent on the island, but in between times, they travelled widely. Jace and Gigi and sometimes Matteo and Bianca stepped in to take the children and allow Lexy to go off on occasional business trips with Nic. They had returned to South Korea several times together, exploring and enjoying the freedom of being childfree, however briefly.

Lexy was looking forward to seeing Mel and her husband, Fergus, at the party on Corfu that evening. They were staying there on their vacation and Lexy would introduce her friends to those of the Diamandis family attending. She couldn't wait to catch up on gossip with Mel.

Lexy stilled as she felt Nic's fingers brush her shoulders and something cold and heavy settled round her throat. 'What on earth?' she gasped, fingers fluttering up to touch the jewel suspended between her breasts. She hurried into the bedroom to look in the mirror and study the large teardrop diamond pendant on a platinum and diamond collar. 'Wow! Snazzy.'

'Happy birthday,' he murmured huskily as he closed both arms round her and eased her slight body back into the solid heat of his. 'I told Jace we'd be late for dinner.'

'Is that so?' Lexy gave a shameless little wriggle of encouragement as she spun in his arms and stretched up to connect her mouth to his.

As he kissed her with hungry intensity, he was also in the act of sliding down the straps on her sun dress and divesting her of it and she laughed, feeling it fall round her bare feet. Her hands slid under his tee shirt to smooth up over his muscular torso. 'I like my gift,' she told him softly. 'It'll go amazingly well with the silver dress I'm wearing tonight.'

'I know. I made Gigi tell me what colour it was.' Nic flung off his tee shirt as Lexy stroked her hands slowly over every part of him within reach, teasing the zip straining at his groin and running it down to release him. 'So forward now, Mrs Diamandis.'

'You have no idea,' she said, pushing him back in the direction of the bed. 'You were in California for a whole week.'

'And you missed me,' Nic gathered with a wicked grin as he hauled off his jeans with enthusiasm.

'I always miss you.'

'I was on the phone so much I didn't think you'd have

the chance to miss me,' he teased, hauling her down to him and whisking off her lingerie to seal his mouth to a prominent pink nipple.

'Every time I turned over in bed and you weren't there,' she complained with a faint moan.

And then the conversation died away and the passion took over, their bodies straining together as he drove into her with an urgent groan.

'So I think you're getting something fluffy and four-legged from Gigi...just warning you,' he told her breathlessly as he sprawled back against the tumbled sheets.

Lexy beamed. 'She's been looking for a dog for us for months. The children are at just the right age now to be more responsible and Gigi will have tested him out living with their kids,' she said, her body heavy with relaxation and happiness bubbling through her because Nic was home again and she hated it when he was away.

'Act surprised when she shows you before we get off on Corfu. He's rather big though and lively.'

'Perfect for Ethan.'

'Just like you're perfect for me,' Nic quipped, resting back with a smouldering smile of satisfaction. 'You smoothed away my rough edges.'

'Put you in touch with your inner man,' Lexy slotted in, trying to imitate Jace's deep sardonic drawl while thinking about how much more open Nic had become with his emotions now that he no longer felt that he had to suppress or hide them.

Nic rolled her over and closed both arms round her. 'I love you madly, desperately and for ever, *agapoula mou.*'

'And I love you,' she told him, resting her cheek down on his shoulder. 'Perhaps because you're still impossibly pretty.'

Lexy laughed like a drain as he tickled her in retribution, and they never made dinner at all.

* * * * *

If Greek's One-Night Babies *left you wanting more, then be sure to check out the first instalment in The Diamandis Heirs duet,* Greek's Shotgun Wedding

And why not explore these other stories from Lynne Graham?

The Baby the Desert King Must Claim
The Maid Married to the Billionaire
The Maid's Pregnancy Bombshell
Two Secrets to Shock the Italian
Baby Worth Billions

Available now!

RING
FOR AN HEIR

ANNIE WEST

MILLS & BOON

For Malvina.

Thank you so much for your friendship and support
through the years.

CHAPTER ONE

PORTIA SAT AT the end of the row, hands folded over the catalogue in her lap as the auctioneer discussed the finer points of the next item in the sale.

Even though she worked here, she felt out of place today at the famous London auction house.

Usually she was in a back room at a desk, dealing with paperwork. It was only occasionally that she helped in reception or brought refreshments into the hushed, refined rooms where experts met clients.

It wasn't the wealth of the people around her that made her nervous. It was the fact that there were only a few more items until hers.

Her knee jigged up and down until she forced herself to still, drawing a deep breath. But she couldn't be calm. So much rode on the sale. *If* it sold.

Of course it will sell.

It might not be a 'significant' painting, much less a masterpiece, but as the valuer said, there was a market for well-painted English landscapes. She'd get something for it.

Would it be enough?

After years of low-paid jobs, always worrying about money, this was her opportunity. With her hard-won savings, and a decent sale price, she'd take the plunge and get herself that university place she'd worked towards.

A degree in art history was hardly a guarantee of a secure career but Portia knew what she wanted.

Fate could steal all your happiness in a moment. She refused to give up this dream at least. It was the one thing that had kept her going.

Instead of being cowed by heartbreaking loss and her father's vengeful fury, she'd grown more determined to fight for her dreams. Pursue what she felt passionate about.

Portia grimaced. Passion was something she'd left behind long ago. Except for art. That had brought some solace in the dark times.

So it was fitting that a painting might be the means to turn her life around.

Her hands clenched. It was one of fate's typically nasty tricks that the one painting she'd inherited—presumably because her father had been advised he had to leave her something in his will—was the one painting she'd keep if she could.

The artist had captured the afternoon glow of sunset on old stone, the sparkle of mullioned windows and the froth of pale pink roses that made Cropley Hall look like an illustration from a storybook. Her mother had redesigned the old garden and planted those roses.

During Portia's childhood it had been a magical place, full of joy and adventure. In those days her mother had been there, and Portia had rarely had much to do with her father.

Now the painting was her only possession that linked her to her mother.

'And now we come to our last item.'

Adrenaline shot through Portia, her heart kicking so hard she started and the glossy catalogue slid to the floor.

This was it. No time for regrets.

She bent down and retrieved the booklet. By the time she settled back in her seat, bidding had begun. She saw a woman in green raise her hand. Then the auctioneer looked to someone further back and the price crept higher.

There was no bidding frenzy but there were two buyers, then a third. Portia craned her neck to see them. The white-haired man in the loud jacket was one of them, but the bidder at the back of the room remained elusive.

What does it matter who buys it? You can't vet them to make sure it goes to a good home. You just want the money.

And yet... Her gaze returned to the painting displayed at the front of the room. She felt a tug of regret, a longing for what she'd once had and what might have been.

The sense of loss was so sudden and profound it overwhelmed her. She blinked down at the catalogue with hot eyes.

Memories whirled through her head. Snippets of the past. And with them, a host of emotions, making her heart ache and her stomach churn.

Portia kept her head bowed, struggling against the maelstrom.

It had been years since she'd felt distress this consuming. She couldn't remember the last time she'd cried. Yet that prickling at the back of her nose and the thickening in her throat belied her composure.

By the time she had control of herself it was over. Women reached for handbags. Catalogues were tucked under arms and the noise in the room increased as people chatted and rose from their seats.

She jumped up, about to ask the man beside her about the winning bid on the last item, but he turned to talk to someone on his other side.

Portia stepped out of the row. Phil, the porter, caught her eye and smiled. She hurried over, just in time to catch him before he carried the painting away.

'How much, Phil? I missed it.'

'Missed it? With Mr Tomaras buying it? That was a bit of excitement. I didn't think it would be his sort of thing.'

Her eyes widened at the idea of an ubersuccessful Greek tycoon being interested in her painting. But then Phil mentioned the final bid and that wiped everything else from her mind.

There'd be enough to support her through a degree, or most of it, so long as she worked part-time and was careful with her cash.

Relief buoyed her as she exited into the back rooms and made her way to her desk. Her supervisor had told her to leave early to make up for some recent long days. Even so, it took a while before she was ready to go.

This windfall would change her life. Yet nerves vied with elation. Some sixth sense warned her not to take her good fortune for granted.

Portia shook her head, pushing away that premonition of trouble. She didn't believe in premonitions. She believed in working hard and pursuing opportunities.

She walked through the elegant front rooms with their exquisitely curated displays of jewellery and fine art. Her steps slowed. Not because she cared about the palpable air of luxury, but because of the remarkable pieces on display. One day maybe, she might work here as an art expert. Or in a gallery or museum.

Excitement burst through the strange wariness that had engulfed her.

It's going to be all right. Better than all right.

Its going to be wonderful.

She lengthened her stride, clutching her shoulder bag close. She smiled at her colleagues on the reception desk and headed out. The auction house sat back from the street, and she entered the long entrance corridor with landscaped courtyards on either side.

Ahead cars passed, their lights on against the fading December afternoon. She'd almost reached the footpath when a figure stepped out, blocking her way.

The man stood with the light behind him, tall, broad-shouldered, with curling hair that brushed the collar of his short leather jacket. Jeans covered his long legs.

Portia's heart seemed to stop.

Not out of fear. She was still in one of the world's most prestigious auction houses, and the chances of being mugged in Mayfair at this time of day were low.

What slammed her to a halt was the overwhelming sense of déjà vu.

But she didn't know him. He was broader across the shoulders, taller too, and those thighs…

She looked sharply away, rather than peer up at him in the dim light.

The boy she'd known had been all whipcord strength but lanky by comparison with this man. It was just the hair and the jacket that made her think of him. She blamed the painting of Cropley for bringing the past back to life again.

She hitched a shaky breath and stepped to one side, ignoring her rocketing pulse.

He sidestepped too.

'Pardon.' She moved to the other side of the corridor just as he moved that way.

Portia paused, deciding it was better to stand and let him enter rather than try dancing around him.

Except he didn't move, just stood, stopping her exit.

'Well, well, well. Imagine meeting you here, Princess.'

Heat doused her in a rush that made her cheeks burn. A second later the burn became a chill so absolute it felt like she'd turned to ice.

That voice. Once familiar. But she'd never heard it sound like this. So harsh.

Only one person had ever called her Princess. It had been their secret joke. He'd likened her to Sleeping Beauty, trapped in a castle surrounded by roses, waiting to be woken.

You woke all right. You lost your naïveté quickly.

In the end she'd rescued herself from her thorny prison.

Slowly, reluctantly, she lifted her head while her heart beat a sickening tattoo high in her throat.

The clouds that had blocked the daylight filtering through the courtyards must have lifted. Or the staff had noticed how dim the lights were in the walkway and brightened them.

Whatever the reason she saw him clearly now.

Denim blue eyes against olive skin and glossy black hair. The unusual combination had always been incredibly captivating. His remarkable bone structure didn't hurt either, all honed, spare lines and strong, almost arrogant features. All except for his mouth which was wide and beautifully sculpted.

And incredibly soft.

She remembered the feel of it against hers.

It took every scintilla of self-possession not to press her hand to her chest. She struggled to breathe.

She felt winded. Like on the day after her mother's funeral when she'd saddled her mother's horse to escape across the fields and taken a bad tumble at a high gate.

A voice came from far away. It was so reedy it took a moment to recognise it as her own. 'Lex? What are you doing here?'

The stern lines of his features didn't soften. The only change was the slight rise of slashing black eyebrows.

As if surprised she'd question him?

Once they'd been…

No, don't go there.

Because now as her lungs and her brain started working again, she remembered he'd feel no pleasure at seeing her.

Instead of answering he stooped to pick something up.

'You should take more care of your purse.'

Portia looked down to see her bag in his broad hand. She hadn't even noticed it drop.

'As for what I'm doing here.' Now he smiled, his mouth curling slowly. But it wasn't a smile of welcome or approval. It looked...sharp. Razor-sharp. 'I was buying some artwork, what else?'

Of course he's not here to see you. He didn't even know you were here.

A man spoke from behind her shoulder. 'Mr Tomaras, I thought you'd left.' Portia turned to see Piers Jameson, the director of the auction house. 'Can I help you with something...?'

She didn't hear the rest because she was too busy grappling with what he'd said.

Tomaras.

But his name wasn't Tomaras! It was Moran. Lex Moran.

'...old acquaintances.'

Portia only caught the last couple of words when both men turned to look at her. Piers Jamieson with an expression of mixed delight and surprise. Lex with an unreadable stare that nevertheless told her that after all this time he hadn't forgotten. Or forgiven.

'Well, what a coincidence.' Jameson gave her an assessing look. 'I won't hold up your reunion. But I'll send you that modern sculpture catalogue, Mr Tomaras.'

The catalogue Portia was in the process of proofreading before publication.

Alone now with this grim stranger, she was tempted to spin around and go back to her desk, using that as an excuse to avoid further conversation.

Except this was her only chance to see Lex, talk to him. They had unfinished business.

The thought made her throat constrict and her stomach quiver. So much had changed since then.

'You look as wide-eyed as a rabbit in the spotlight.'

There was no humour in his expression, only a piercing yet distant curiosity, as if she were a specimen ready for dissection. Suddenly she wished they hadn't met. Even though she'd wished, prayed for this opportunity for years.

Of course he doesn't care. The past is just that, over and done with.

She shrugged. 'It's a surprise, seeing you again.'

'Don't you mean, seeing me *here*? A working-class lout among the well-heeled?'

Her cheeks turned fiery at his sarcastic tone. But who could blame him? It was a direct quote, after all. Her father hadn't kept his prejudices to himself.

Suddenly Portia was too bone weary to face this.

'You look like you need reviving. Come on.'

He tucked his hand beneath her elbow and turned towards the street. Instantly her blood fizzed and her pulse leapt. His fingers tightened convulsively around her as if he felt it too, before he eased his grip. She was aware of a swift, sideways glance, so intense it scorched.

So it's still there, after all this time.

She'd told herself the attraction was no more than a memory. She couldn't believe the man beside her felt anything but cold curiosity. As for her own feelings… They were too confused to decipher.

Liar.

Portia found herself walking beside him, incredibly aware of his size, his heat, and a tantalising hint of cologne that made her think of white sand beaches in the sunshine and toned male flesh.

A shiver ripped through her and again his hand tightened. Holding her captive or supporting her?

A bubble of laughter rose in her throat and she wondered if it was hysteria. She felt strange, the street and the other pedestrians blurring as if unreal. The only reality was the man beside her and the queasy mix of excitement and distress roiling in her stomach.

They entered a bar, a famous, exorbitantly priced place that Portia had never visited. The furnishings were opulent and the service discreet as they were led to an alcove booth upholstered in smoky grey velvet.

'What would you like to drink?'

Lex didn't use her name, she noticed. 'Water's fine.'

He turned to the waiter, asking for a glass of wine that she knew by reputation alone. It seemed he'd developed a taste for fine wine in the years since she'd known him. And deep pockets.

Could it be true, what Phil had said? 'Tomaras? Is that really what you call yourself now?'

Something flashed in his eyes. Something hard and dangerous.

But Portia wasn't scared of him. What did she have to be scared about? He had never hurt her. Yet that coolly assessing stare felt like a honed blade scraping her skin.

'It's my name.'

His voice was deeper than she remembered, burring across her skin and raising goosebumps. Making her aware, at a cellular level, of him as a *man*. Despite the circumstances, she felt a softening deep inside. The liquid warmth of a woman reacting to a desirable man.

If she were going to be totally honest, she'd felt it from the first, even in that moment of shocked disbelief.

She sat straighter, her voice unintentionally harsh as she fought her own body. 'Alexandros Tomaras? That's who you really are?'

It didn't make sense. She'd *known* him. Known everything about him. He wasn't Greek. He was English, with Irish ancestry.

'That's who I really am.' When she didn't respond he continued with more than a touch of impatience. 'Shall I show you my passport?'

The waiter arrived with a glass of red, a glass of sparkling iced water with a slice of lime, and some snacks.

Portia almost wished she'd ordered alcohol, something to soothe her strung-out nerves. But she needed all her faculties.

She reached for her glass. 'If you say it's your name, then it is. But how?'

'So you're interested *now*?'

Portia stiffened, hearing his emphasis on the last word. As if she wouldn't have been interested in the past. It shouldn't surprise her, yet she wasn't ready for the blast of distress and regret.

The glass paused halfway to her lips and her eyes sought his. They were narrowed, gleaming slits of… No, she couldn't read his expression.

Or you don't want to.

She lifted her shoulders as if his disapproval didn't matter, then sipped her water, forcing it down her tight throat. Ignoring the pain that bloomed in response to what she knew must be scorn.

He lifted his wineglass, swirled it slightly and inhaled before drinking. Portia tugged her gaze away from that sensuous mouth and the way his throat moved as he swallowed.

With the utmost care, she placed her glass on its silver coaster, her hand reaching for her bag.

'I found my father.'

Her head jerked up, eyes widening. 'Your father? Really?'

Excitement made her smile. Lex had never known his father and his mother had been evasive on the subject. She remembered how frustrated that had made him. But her smile faded as she met his unblinking stare. He didn't look pleased.

'You didn't like him?'

'On the contrary, he was one of the first truly decent people I knew.'

Lex's gaze drifted to a plate of snacks and he took his time selecting one before popping it into his mouth.

Which gave her time to consider his expression and his words. The implication was clear. That there was no one in his life when they knew each other that he'd call *decent*.

Including you.

Intellectually Portia had known he might feel that way. Yet his disdain was hard to bear.

'He was delighted to meet me. It was the best day of my life, discovering him. I have a family now.'

Despite her pain, she couldn't begrudge him that. Though he'd always been stoic, she'd witnessed what life was like with his difficult mother and knew how he'd yearned to discover the truth about his father.

She'd heard the taunts, not just from her father, who'd claimed he was shifty and idle, inheriting bad ways from an unknown traveller father. Taking their lead from her father, half the locals had been prejudiced against the precocious boy with dark olive skin and a mother who refused to comply with village expectations.

'I'm glad for you both.' Was that a flicker of surprise? 'So you took his name.'

'Actually, I always had it. It turns out my mother lied. She was married when she had me.'

Portia felt her eyes widen. Lex had grown up with a single mother, using her surname when all the time he was entitled to another. They'd lived in straightened circumstances, sharing a tiny cottage belonging to his mother's ageing uncle by marriage who worked in the stables at Cropley Hall.

'I don't understand.'

He shrugged, the fluid movement dragging her gaze to those imposing shoulders.

'She left my father without warning. He searched for us for years, mainly in Ireland where she came from and America where she had relatives. He wondered if she'd run away because of postnatal depression and an inability to adjust to a new life in a foreign country.' He paused. 'We'll never know now she's dead. But she lied and caused us both tremendous pain. Some people are like that.'

Bright eyes bored into hers. There it was, the contempt she expected.

She opened her mouth to explain but words wouldn't come. How could she explain to this judgemental stranger, this man who'd been so hurt because of her?

Portia had been strong for so long, but the reality of Lex's disdain punctured something inside her. She felt unbearably weary. What was the point, anyway? He wouldn't believe her and even if he did it wouldn't change anything.

But one thing she had to know. 'Did you come to the auction because you knew I'd be there?'

His grimace answered her. 'I had no idea you'd be there. I saw the painting of Cropley Hall and decided to buy it.'

She swallowed, the movement jerky. Maybe, after all, he had some fond memories of that time. 'Why?'

Another shrug. This time the movement looked somehow Mediterranean. As if the boy she'd known had never existed and Alexandros Tomaras had lived all his life in the Greek sunshine.

'A whim.' He held her gaze for a long moment. 'But I'm having second thoughts. I won't keep it. I never did like the place. Maybe I'll burn it.'

His tone was soft and even, the look in his eyes deliberately cruel. He knew how much she'd always loved the place, even in those last years under her father's increasingly stern rule. He understood her love of art too, and how the idea of destroying it horrified her.

Realisation swamped her. Coming here was a mistake. Talking with him would bring no closure, only hurt.

Portia understood his anger but refused to be a whipping boy. She'd had enough of cruel men.

She blotted her lips with a linen napkin and slid from her seat. 'Thanks for the drink, Alexandros.' Lex, the boy she'd known, was long gone. 'I'm glad things worked out well for you.'

She turned and threaded her way through the tables towards the exit, back straight, chin up and without daring to look back.

CHAPTER TWO

LEX STOOD AT the windows that lined one side of the conference room. From here he could see the dark blue Aegean Sea beyond Athens.

He shoved his hands in his pockets and rocked back on his heels, annoyed at his inability to concentrate. The meeting had gone well and he should be following up with his staff, confirming their next steps. There was so much to do, given his expansion plans.

But it wasn't business on his mind. It was a pair of dark, pansy-brown eyes, wide with hurt. A narrow jaw clenched as if to hold in a spill of emotion.

The moment he'd seen Portia hurry from the auction room, exiting via a back door, everything had changed. Slid off track. As if the world he knew abruptly shifted sideways so that even the most familiar things looked different.

Felt different.

He shook his head. Even viewing her from behind, with her partly obscured by the crowd, recognition had been instantaneous. Like a slamming fist to the gut.

Seeing her after all these years shouldn't have altered anything. Their time together was ancient history. She'd made a fool of him. He should have known, given her background, not to believe in her.

But you did. And you almost wanted to again.

Because just for a few moments when they met again, she'd

looked lost and distressed. As if the past had meant some-thing to her. As if *he'd* meant something to her.

She took you in once and she was trying to play you again. Of course she was distressed, coming face-to-face with you out of the blue.

But Lex couldn't dismiss the nagging feeling of unfinished business. There were things he wanted to know.

He'd never been vengeful, and even at the time when his world crumpled, he hadn't completely blamed Portia. She'd only just turned seventeen to his nineteen. Lex had told him-self he shouldn't have been surprised that she'd turned out more like her awful father than he'd believed possible.

Yet her betrayal, and more—her scorn—had hurt.

Almost as much as discovering how his mother had lied to him all his life. So many wasted years…

Logic told him Portia's betrayal had been ultimately a good thing. He was better off without her. And yet…

He shook his head. It didn't matter what she'd done, he shouldn't have lost his temper. He'd learnt in business that revealing emotion was a weakness an opponent could use against you. He'd let anger take over in London.

Did she guess how hurt he'd been? Had she silently laughed at him?

Or had she regretted their parting, now she saw he'd be-come a man of wealth and power?

The Oakhursts had always valued prestige and money.

Lex raked short fingernails across his scalp, trying to break the cycle of fruitless thoughts.

He shouldn't have threatened to destroy the painting. He wasn't into empty threats. But at the time it had been im-perative that she not guess the rush of emotion that had led to his bidding.

He'd seen the painting in the catalogue and been deter-mined to own it. If old man Oakhurst was in such financial difficulty he had to sell off his precious possessions, how fitting if Lex acquired one of those once closely guarded treasures. The supposed ne'er-do-well bastard son of a shiftless gypsy, the old man had called him.

But Lex hadn't bought it merely from a sense of one-upmanship. It had been a little over a decade, yet something in him had softened, yearning, when he saw that painting.

Because it had taken him back to that halcyon time with Portia, brief but oh-so-sweet.

That was why he'd told her he intended to destroy it. Because he couldn't let her guess he'd acquired it out of sentimentality.

He no longer believed in youthful dreams. Looking back now, it was remarkable he ever had. It was only with Portia...

Lex turned and strode from the room. He had work to do. He needed to focus on the present not the past, and on his plans for the future.

Three weeks later he returned to Mayfair.

Ostensibly he was here to view the sculptures in an upcoming auction. But the tingle of anticipation at the base of his spine as he strode into the hushed, plush reception area had nothing to do with art and everything to do with the prospect of seeing Portia.

He'd resisted, just, hiring someone to investigate her. There must have been significant changes in her family if her father was selling off possessions. But pride halted him. He wasn't interested enough in the Oakhursts to spend good money researching them.

A phone call from his PA to the auction house, confirming Portia worked there, didn't count as an investigation.

A job in a prestigious art auction house was exactly the sort of work young aristocrats dabbled in. Whatever changes there'd been, her father was still pulling strings, getting his girl a job where she wouldn't get her hands dirty. Where she'd be bound to meet the *right* sort of people.

Lex's lips drew back in a sneer. Funny how the right sort of people were only too ready to welcome him these days. Money talked.

But his derision couldn't cloak a singular, disturbing truth. That three weeks ago, seeing Portia for the first time in over ten years, Lex had felt something he hadn't experienced in years.

He'd refused to find a name for it, choosing to tell himself it was simply a lingering remnant of old emotions, dredged up in the surprise of meeting her again. But it had unsettled him, so he'd made his way back to London to prove that this time when he saw her he'd feel nothing.

Then he'd walk away and never see her again.

'Mr Tomaras, it's a pleasure to welcome you back. You're here to view some pieces?'

Lex paused to shake hands with Piers Jameson who ran the place. 'I found myself in the vicinity and thought I'd stop by. And I might follow up an old acquaintance while I'm here. Portia Oakhurst.'

'Of course, I remember.' He saw the other man's glint of speculation. 'I'll ask her to come out now.'

'I'd prefer to surprise her when she finishes for the day. Meanwhile I'll check out the pieces on display.'

'Excellent, excellent.' Jameson led him towards a large gallery room where items for the next sale were on display. 'I'll make sure she finishes up in…half an hour?'

Lex thanked him and entered the gallery.

Who do you think you're fooling? Even Jameson guessed your priority was to see her.

Only because then he could wash his hands of her. Once past the initial surprise, it would be like seeing a casual acquaintance. Nothing more. No…feelings.

Lex took a catalogue from an eager staff member and

strolled into the gallery space, artfully lit to display the sculptures to best effect.

There were a few pieces he might be interested in, including a small Cycladic figure, primitive yet powerful. He could imagine it in his home.

Or thought he could. Once more Portia interfered with his decision-making, distracting him so he found himself paying more attention to the view of the reception area, waiting for her to emerge, than to the display.

He checked the time. It had been half an hour and more by the time he saw a slim figure in blue-grey walking towards the exit.

His pulse kicked. Not with excitement but satisfaction that this was almost over.

One more short meeting and he could cut her adrift. Portia Oakhurst would be no more than a distant memory, a salutary lesson in the dangers of excess emotion and trusting the wrong person.

Lex sauntered out into the reception area and followed his target.

He mightn't have any interest in Portia anymore but that didn't stop him appreciating the way she moved. She'd always had an athletic grace, particularly in the saddle, and that translated now into a wholly feminine poise. The fitted jacket and straight skirt outlined slender curves that he might have found alluring in another woman. The sway of her hips was enticing but not exaggerated. Her blonde hair was pulled up in some neat arrangement that accentuated the slimness of her neck.

Yes, if she were anyone but Portia Oakhurst, he might have been tempted.

Towards the end of the corridor she shrugged into a dark coat.

He lengthened his stride, catching her up on the pavement.

'What a coincidence,' he murmured and watched her start. Satisfaction was a tiny but discernible glow in his belly. He'd hated the way she'd made him feel last time they met. Struggling to get control of himself. 'Years go by and suddenly I see you twice in a month.'

Slowly she turned, revealing first her profile—that almost straight nose with just the tiniest bump near the bridge, neatly angled chin and soft, slightly pouting lips. Lex focused quickly on long dark lashes and the elegant arch of one eyebrow.

Then she was facing him, eyes wide, lips parted in surprise and face pale against her red lipstick.

There goes that theory.

You were supposed to meet her and feel nothing.

Lex dragged his attention away from those pillow-soft lips and back to her eyes. In this light and against that blue suit they seemed to shimmer between amethyst and deep brown.

He cleared his throat. Then surprised himself by saying, 'I wasn't really going to destroy the painting.'

He stiffened. He wasn't given to blurting out information. If anything he tended to be reticent, keeping his thoughts to himself. He'd grown up a loner and he'd found that trait an asset in business. He couldn't remember the last time he'd spoken without thinking.

Emotion rippled across her face. Shock? Relief? Whatever it was, her features no longer looked frozen.

Lex tried not to notice how the wash of colour across her cheeks became her. But that was impossible because despite what he'd told himself, he wasn't immune to Portia after all.

He looked down into those velvety eyes and discovered a yearning so deep no amount of logical argument could eradicate it. He felt it in his chest where his lungs grew tight and heavy. It was a tingle in hands that wanted to reach out and reacquaint themselves with her soft skin. Above all it was a weighted fullness in his groin, a physical hunger that banished any thought of walking away.

'I'm glad,' she said and for one delicious instant he thought she meant she was glad to see him. Until his brain clicked into gear and he realised she was talking about the picture being safe from harm.

How the mighty have fallen. The voice in his head was smugly mocking. *You've grown used to women hanging on your every word and trying to get your attention.*

Her gaze skated away as if she were suddenly uncomfortable. 'You're here to view the items for the next auction?'

Lex nodded, registering how her voice had turned breathless. Relief eased tensed muscles. She wasn't immune either. That darting sideways glance under her lashes and the husky edge to her words betrayed sexual awareness.

An interest Portia seemed determined to ignore. She looked past him as if searching for a bus as raindrops began to sprinkle.

'That's right.' He paused, deciding not to admit he'd already discovered she worked there. 'You?'

He watched emotions flicker across her features as if she wasn't sure whether to admit she was on the staff. Was she ashamed of working for a living? Once he'd have laughed at the idea. But then he hadn't known her as well as he thought he had. Portia Oakhurst wasn't the girl he'd once believed her to be.

'It's where I work.'

'You always were interested in art.'

Her eyes rounded as if in surprise that he remembered.

He was tempted to tell her he remembered everything. Including every word of that final, appalling text.

The memory hardened his jaw and he saw her take a half step back.

How was it possible to dislike and distrust a woman yet at the same time desire her?

Her head tilted and she regarded him. 'I don't remember art being one of your interests.'

Lex shrugged. 'I came to it later.'

His father's impressive art collection had been a catalyst for his own interest. That and the fact he was no longer trying to make ends meet by holding down three jobs for substandard wages. Admittedly he was too busy to have a lot of leisure time, but that was his choice. He could afford time off to enjoy the luxuries of life when he chose.

Was Portia a luxury he intended to enjoy?

It would be madness. He never made the same mistake twice. Yet something deep inside decreed that he'd regret walking away from her now.

Because you want to be the one to walk away this time and leave her wanting?

He told himself it would be understandable to want payback after the way she'd treated him. But Lex knew it wasn't that.

The gentle patter of rain became a steady drumming, wetting his hair. Yet instead of hurrying away as she'd looked ready to do a few moments before, Portia stood looking up at him, her scrutiny intense.

He reached out and touched her elbow. 'Come on, there's no point standing out here getting wet. You never did stay for that drink.'

Still he waited. It had to be her choice to come with him. He discovered his lungs had tightened as he waited for her reply. What was it about her that ignited such a visceral response?

He'd spent years working hard to make something of himself even before the challenge of building up his own business. Yet waiting for her response made him feel like that callow youth he'd once been, so eager, foolishly trusting.

One way or another he needed to get this woman out of his system.

Finally she nodded. 'Why not?'

But the look she gave him belied her flippant answer. Her eyes were serious, her mouth firm as he led her around the corner to his hotel.

They crossed the black-and-white-tiled lobby with its high domed ceiling, making for the bar. They garnered a few curious stares but he ignored them. Public curiosity was part of his life now.

Instead Lex was minutely aware of Portia beside him. Her scent, that familiar perfume of bluebells, teased his nostrils, reminding him of spring at Cropley.

The memory shattered when they reached the bar. Usually quiet and discreet, today it was filled with a throng of loud young people, dressed to the nines and celebrating at the top of their voices. Their accents spoke of inbred privilege and their shouts proclaimed their total lack of care for anyone but themselves.

'Change of plan. There's a lounge upstairs that won't be full of Hooray Henrys.'

A tiny frown formed on Portia's forehead and for a moment he feared she had second thoughts. Then she nodded and he led her to the lift. In his belly satisfaction and anticipation coalesced.

Portia shouldn't be doing this. She should have turned back when they stepped out of the lift into a hushed corridor that led, not to public rooms but to private suites. But she'd stood mute as Lex used a swipe card to let them into a magnificently appointed suite.

Because she needed to do this. Needed to set the record straight. *And then walk away.*

But as she watched Lex's long-legged stride across the room, the sharp, achingly familiar angle of his temple and jaw, her breath hitched in her chest before finally escaping on a long sigh.

She didn't want to walk away.

Even though she'd managed it a few weeks ago, she wasn't sure she could do it now. Then his barely disguised anger had simmered between them, and her guilt.

But today it felt different between them.

It felt as it had that summer when she turned seventeen. The spark between them. The communication that went beyond words. The flare of heat. The breathless passion that opened a whole new world to her.

You're kidding yourself. There's no going back, even if you wanted to.

But she could at least set the record straight. Didn't they both deserve that?

'What will you have?'

Lex turned towards her, phone to his ear, and even from a distance the intensity of that stare made her shiver. She told herself it was because she was cold and damp.

'Hot chocolate, please.' She caught his flash of surprise before he turned back to the phone, placing the order. Maybe these days he only drank champagne and expensive wine.

Too wired to sit, she paced the length of the room. It was large, superbly furnished and with multi-million-dollar views over the park. It had all the elegance of a grand country home where exquisite taste blended with comfort. Luxurious rather than brazenly opulent.

Like Cropley Hall had been in its heyday. How completely circumstances had changed. This world was Lex's now while she struggled to make ends meet, living in a tiny shared flat.

But she was proud of making it on her own. Her father had expected her to return home with her tail between her legs.

Portia's skin prickled with awareness. She sensed Lex approach though his footsteps were silent on the plush carpet.

It was one of the few things about him she'd forgotten. The fact that even though he wasn't in her line of sight she could pinpoint exactly where he was, as if some internal radar were attuned precisely to his presence.

Right now he stood less than an arm's length behind her left shoulder as she looked out at the dripping green park.

Heat sang in her veins and she found herself rubbing her hands up her arms, disturbed by her reaction.

'You're cold? I'll turn the heating up.'

'No, I'm fine.' She felt her cheeks burn and busied herself removing her rather shabby, old coat.

'Let me take that.'

She shook her head and moved away, draping it over the arm of a chesterfield lounge. 'It's okay.'

That way she could grab it if she needed to make a quick exit. Whenever he got close she felt jumpy. Aware.

Maybe this was a bad idea after all. But she was no coward and she'd wanted, for so long, to clear the air between them.

'So you don't live in London?'

Obviously not, since he was staying in a hotel. But she needed to break the gathering silence.

'My home is in Greece.' His voice was deeper than she remembered but still had the ability to make her nerves twitch and her insides tighten. 'But there was something that needed my attention in London.'

He doesn't mean you. He's a businessman. He's probably here for commercial reasons and happened to stop by the saleroom. He didn't even know you'd be there.

That was a relief. Portia could tell him the truth about that long ago night and then they'd go their separate ways. This would be the last time she'd see him and, she told herself, it would finally lay the ghost of their doomed relationship.

Then, at last, she'd be able to move on.

Wasn't that what she'd wanted all these years?

She drew a sustaining breath and swung around, discovering him closer than she'd thought.

Had he always been this tall?

Tall and broad across the shoulders and chest. She had an overwhelming impression of lean, hard strength, of implacability.

She'd never been nervous around Lex, despite the whispered mistrust of many locals. They'd been wary because he was different with his swarthy looks, unknown background and reclusive mother. But to Portia he'd been a friend, confidant and then finally...

But he'd changed since then. Even those remarkable blue eyes looked different. Once she'd been just as likely to see laughter there as anything else. Now they were guarded.

And that's none of your business. Say what you have to then go.

'Lex, I—'

Movement on the other side of the room caught her eye. A man in a dark suit entered from the back of the suite, carrying a large tray.

'Over here, sir?'

'Yes, thanks, Mason. We'll look after ourselves from here. I'll see you in the morning.'

'Very well. Good night, sir, madam.'

He inclined his head and left the suite.

'You have a butler with you?' She supposed it was what billionaires did, yet still she was surprised.

Lex gestured for her to sit before handing her a bone china mug that smelled enticingly of rich chocolate and was topped with whipped cream.

'Mason's employed by the hotel. One of the perks of staying in the presidential suite. Can you really see me travelling with a butler?'

Portia shook her head. 'I don't know you anymore.'

Something flared in those blue eyes that she couldn't read, then he inclined his head. 'It's been a long time.'

He offered her the food the butler had brought. Dainty blinis with smoked salmon and dill, and fragrant quiches so tiny they'd be a mere mouthful. But she was too tense to eat. She shook her head and sipped her drink.

The rich but not overly sweet chocolate was balm to her stretched nerves. She sipped again, wrapping her hands around the mug, soaking up its comforting warmth.

Lex poured a small glass of red wine and took a nearby armchair. He lifted his glass. 'To old acquaintances.'

Portia raised the mug and sipped but she couldn't relax. She was caught in a web of old memories and sharp, new sensations. This wasn't the boy she'd given her heart to so long ago, despite the powerful drag of physical attraction.

But they had unresolved issues. Now she understood why she'd been so on edge these past few weeks. She wouldn't be able to rest until she set the record straight between them.

'Do you—?'

'That night—'

Both stopped, waiting for the other. She felt her heart pound too high and fast. Saw his eyes narrow.

'What about that night, Portia?'

There it was again, that silken undercurrent in his tone when he said her name. An insidiously strong undercurrent that tugged at the defences she'd built so painstakingly over the years.

She licked her lips and clutched her mug tight.

'You thought I deserted you that night, didn't you?'

He stilled so completely it was hard to believe he breathed. 'You made it clear you'd changed your mind about us.'

Portia shook her head. 'I didn't. I was planning to come to you but he stopped me.'

Over the years she'd seen many expressions in Lex's eyes. Laughter, sympathy, desire, even rapture. She'd seen him angry but never with her. She saw it now, a cold fury that was more daunting for the way he controlled it. Only the tick of his pulse and that searing fire in his eyes betrayed him.

'You don't believe me.'

Those straight shoulders shrugged with such insouciance she could almost believe it no longer mattered to him. Except she'd read the ire he held in check.

'You mean your father? You told me yourself he had no idea about us. What are you saying he did to you?' Lex drawled. 'Locked you up in a tower? This is the twenty-first century, Portia, not the Middle Ages.'

Portia slammed her drink down on the low table between them and shot to her feet. She'd expected anger yet his sneering disbelief caught her on the raw.

'You know Cropley Hall doesn't have a tower. He used the dungeon.'

CHAPTER THREE

LEX SAW HER wrap her arms around her middle, shoulders curving protectively.

Even then it was impossible to believe. The very idea was pure fantasy. It had to be, because if what she'd said were true… That didn't bear thinking about.

Portia turned away. 'Whatever you were told wasn't right, Lex. I *wanted* to come to you that night but I couldn't.'

He put down his glass carefully. It was easier to concentrate on that than the riot of emotions her declaration unleashed.

'You're seriously saying your father locked you away in a dungeon?' The man was bombastic and prejudiced but he was too fond of his own reputation to do anything so outrageous. 'Apart from anything else, Cropley Hall is a house, not a castle with a handy dungeon.'

Portia let out a shuddering sigh, dropping her arms and pushing her shoulders back. Then she walked to the end of the chesterfield and scooped up her coat.

'Forget it. It doesn't matter now. It was a mistake to come here.'

Already she was walking away from him. Only this time, instead of saying goodbye by text she simply turned her back, dismissing him.

Lex wasn't aware of moving, but the next instant his hand was on her upper arm as he turned her to face him.

What he saw hit him like a physical blow.

He'd only seen Portia cry once, the day her mother died. Even then she'd pulled free of his arms, not wanting to wallow in tears, and concentrated on grooming the horses and mucking out stables until hours later, exhausted, she let him lead her away.

Now he looked down into eyes glazed with unshed tears. Eyes shadowed by hurt. She blinked and looked away, shaking her hand free.

Leaving him with a sharp ache slicing from his chest to his gut.

Then he remembered. Whatever her faults, Portia wasn't a liar. That last text from her had been brutal. It had devastated him, spurring him to leave not only Cropley but Britain too. But it had at least been honest. She'd left him in no doubt about their relationship ending.

Lex looked at her averted face, the tight downward crimp of her mouth, and felt a tiny sliver of doubt puncture over a decade of resentment.

'Talk to me, Portia.'

'There's no point. It was so long ago. A whole lifetime ago.' Those lush lips crumpled for a second and then she turned back to him.

Her pale face was composed now. Her eyes were still bright but no longer brimming. Her gaze met his but it was unreadable, as if she'd blanked out all emotion.

That made him more than ever determined to get to the bottom of this. He'd always been able to read her but now she shut him out as if he were a total stranger.

Let her. You are strangers. You lost your chance for a future years ago. You're different people now.

And yet...

'It's getting late.' Her voice was flat. 'I've got a long commute so it's best if I—'

'Tell me, Portia. I promise to listen.'

He was no longer a reckless teenager, driven by hormones and emotion, thrilled that the girl he'd loved returned his feelings.

Maybe, despite the sizzle of physical attraction that had brought him back to London, it wasn't sex that would finally break their thread of connection. Maybe hearing her excuses would do it instead.

Either way, Lex knew that one way or another, their lives were headed in separate directions.

She gave him an assessing look then picked up the coat that had fallen to the floor and moved away. But instead of going to the door, she perched on the broad arm of the chair near the window, arms folded under the coat. As if ready to leave at any moment.

Lex strolled across to stand on the opposite side of the window. He propped a shoulder to the wall, hands in his pockets.

'Tell me.'

'My dad found out about us that morning. Raine saw us coming out of one of the outbuildings and heard enough to know I planned to elope with you that night.'

Something caught Lex under the ribs. They'd been found out?

Lex remembered Raine. The woman who'd started coming to Cropley Hall mere months after the death of Portia's mother. Old man Oakhurst was besotted with her and there had been rumours of an impending wedding.

There was no love lost between Portia and her father's lover.

'He went ballistic. I've never seen him like that.'

He'd have been apoplectic at the idea of his daughter eloping with the youth he'd always despised, despite Lex's hard work and ability with the horses.

'His roars would have brought the house down.'

Yet none of the staff had mentioned it while he and his great-uncle worked that afternoon at the stables. Lex had even seen Portia's father late that day. The man had been brusque but no more than usual.

'That's just it. He didn't shout. He went quiet and cold. It was eerie, seeing him so furious he shook with it, but bottling it up inside. It wasn't like him at all.'

Lex tried to imagine it and couldn't. The man was a loud-mouthed bully. His rages were renowned.

'He grabbed me by the arm and marched me into the library, then told me he had plans for me that didn't include me throwing away my future on you.'

That Lex *could* imagine. The man was a snob and would want his daughter to marry an aristocrat, or at least a wealthy man.

'He refused to listen. Every time I tried to speak he kept going as if he didn't hear me, until finally...'

Portia hesitated, one hand lifting to her cheek, and despite his doubts, Lex felt his blood run cold.

'Finally, what?'

'He slapped me.' Her face turned to his and Lex read a shadow of his own shock there. 'So hard he knocked me right off my feet.'

'What?' Lex straightened, hands fisting by his sides. 'He *hit* you?'

The man was known for his abominable temper. Even the horses grew nervous when he came near. But according to Portia he'd never physically lashed out.

'I couldn't believe it either. Maybe that's why I was woozy afterwards. I couldn't seem to get my balance back. He frog-marched me out of the room and down the stairs. By the time I realised where I was, the door was locked and he'd taken my phone.' She paused. 'There *is* a dungeon, you know. Just the remnants of one at the far end of what's now the wine cellar. Cropley was built on the ruins of an old castle.'

As if that were the most important thing out of everything she'd said!

'He *hit* you! And locked you up?'

Nausea swamped Lex. He'd put her at risk and hadn't been there when she needed him. He wanted to reach for her but the look on her face stopped him.

'How badly were you hurt?'

'Just bruising and shock.'

'There's no *just* about it. Nothing excuses that.'

She nodded, her expression sombre. 'I knew he'd be furious if he found out about us, which is why I wanted to sneak away. But I never expected he'd react the way he did.'

Portia drew a deep breath. 'It turned out he had money worries I didn't know anything about. Apparently we'd been living beyond our means for years.'

'Don't you mean *he* had been?'

It was true Portia had had the advantage of living in a stately home with private stables. Despite that she'd been unspoiled and down-to-earth, mainly he suspected because of her mother's influence. Her father, on the other hand, lived lavishly, entertaining and holidaying frequently and at great expense. His costly tastes were only surpassed by his avid interest in horse racing. Had his downfall been gambling or bad investments?

Portia shrugged. 'I suspect that was one of the reasons he pursued Raine, for her money. He'd hatched a scheme for me to marry someone rich too, to keep him afloat.'

'So having you run off with a penniless yokel didn't fit his plans.' Lex gritted his teeth, horrified that he'd known nothing about this. Guilt crawled through his belly. He'd left believing Portia had dumped him at the last minute, leading him on while laughing behind his back. 'What happened? I got a text.'

'It wasn't from me. I never got my phone back. I spent that night and all the next day locked away downstairs. Then he told me you'd packed up and left.'

Lex still reeled at the revelation she really had been a prisoner. It didn't seem possible. It shouldn't have been!

It was no help to recall this had all happened years ago. To him it was fresh news. How could she sound matter-of-fact about it?

All this time he'd thought…

'That text was so convincing. It *sounded* like you. Until it got to the bit about not tying yourself to a hopeless case and about the joke having gone on long enough.'

It was easier to stare at the pitiless rain visible in the glow of the lights than look at Portia.

'You said I'd been good for a summer romance—a bit of rough on the side—but wasn't *suitable* long-term.'

He remembered every word. They were engraved in flaming letters in his brain. He'd even imagined Portia saying them in that crisp accent of hers.

Now his tortured mind conjured the memory of how her clear voice became endearingly hoarse in passion. His nape prickled, the fine hairs there standing up as sexual hunger stirred.

Some things had changed, but not everything.

There was still something about Portia that drew him at an elemental level.

'*I* never said any of those things! It was my father, or him with Raine's help. She had a knack for cutting people down to size.'

'I'm sorry, Portia. Sorry that you had to face that. If I'd known—'

'You weren't to know. There's no point now talking about *if only.*'

Lex supposed it was easy for her to be sanguine after all this time. But it would take him time to process this. Adrenaline beat through his blood, and the need to take action. To make things right.

He turned to see her watching him closely. What did she see? Anger? Resolve? Or was she seeing that summer long ago when love had seemed as natural as breathing, when nothing else had mattered.

She was right. Everything had changed. *They* had. Their hopes and plans. Even their personalities. He was no longer an impulsive youth who believed in soulmates and happy-ever-afters.

He saw shadows of pain in Portia's eyes and knew she too had left behind that innocent belief in the power of romance.

'I take it your father's plan didn't work out.' It can't have since he was auctioning off paintings.

Why don't you ask straight out whether she married the man her father had chosen?

Because he didn't want to hear about Portia being with someone else.

He'd told himself that because she still used her maiden name and didn't wear a ring, she was single. Available. Besides, if she'd married the man her father had wanted, she wouldn't be working in an office job. She'd be living a more glamorous life.

'You thought I'd meekly marry to please him? After what he'd done to *us*?' She tilted her chin up in a way that was pure Portia, eyes flashing. 'I thought you knew me better than that.'

Lex felt a strange frisson of emotion at the way she said *us*. An echo of the past when there'd been nothing more important than him and Portia together.

'I expressed that badly. I meant—'

'It doesn't matter.' She made a slicing gesture. 'I don't want to talk about my father or the past anymore. You know the main points. That's all that matters.'

She rose and stood before him. 'I came because I promised myself if I had the chance I'd let you know I didn't stand you up. There's no going back, of course. We're not the people we once were. But you deserved the truth and I wanted to clear my name. You must have hated me.'

Lex paused before replying. There was no point in telling her she was right. He *had* despised her, for using then discarding him.

All this time he'd been wrong about her.

He grappled to absorb that.

Finally he said, 'Thank you for telling me. It's good finally to know the truth.'

Though it appalled him. He wanted to confront her father. It might have happened years ago but the man couldn't be allowed to get away with his actions.

'Why didn't you contact me sooner?' he asked belatedly. If he'd known...

'He took my phone, remember?' He heard something steely in her voice. 'And when I finally got somewhere I could call, you didn't pick up. I tried multiple times.'

In the state he'd been in, if he'd received calls from a number he didn't know he'd have ignored them. Then he'd left the country almost immediately and had been determined to leave his old life behind. 'I ditched my British SIM when I went to Greece.'

So she'd have had no way of contacting him. Lex felt like he'd taken a step on a staircase only to discover thin air beneath his foot. It was an unpleasant sensation that made his stomach knot.

'So, now you know. I'll be on my way.'

She turned but Lex stepped in front of her. She couldn't

just walk out after dropping that bombshell. He wasn't ready for her to leave.

'It's pouring out there. Why not stay and share some wine with me? I'll order a meal then take you home.'

Her eyes locked on his and heat flared under his skin.

The same heat that had fired his blood these past three weeks, fracturing his concentration and breaking his sleep.

The same heat he'd experienced as a teenager, lusting after the lovely girl who'd been the centre of his hopes and dreams.

Their joint future might be dead and buried but the physical dynamic, that searing attraction, was stronger than ever. Just standing this close to her made his pulse race and his hormones try to wrangle control of his brain.

'Thanks, Lex.' Her smile was wistful. 'But it's probably better not to.'

'Why not? You hate me because of the rift between you and your father?'

Portia's eyes rounded, her mouth gaping. 'I don't hate you. I never hated you.'

Lex didn't know why her words affected him so deeply but they did. He felt something turn over in his chest, a hard, tight knot that was part pleasure, part pain.

She may not blame him but he blamed himself.

All this time he'd pictured her laughing at him, thinking herself better than him. Blaming her for his heartbreak. Instead she'd suffered because he hadn't been careful enough, hadn't managed to spirit her safely away from her dreadful father. He'd swallowed her father's lies and walked away without a backward glance.

'I'm sorry, Portia. I should have stayed and looked for you. I should have known you'd never send a message like that.'

He'd loved her. He should have trusted her. Guilt was a sharp blade, slashing through his ribs.

Now he understood that beneath his bravado there must

have been an undercurrent of self-doubt, fed by years of contempt and suspicion from the local squire and many of the villagers. Had their doubts insidiously undermined his own conviction?

When he'd got that poisonous text it had seemed like confirmation that Portia's love for him had never been real. That the very idea of it was too good to be true.

'It's over, Lex.' Her mouth turned into a flatline 'It's in the past.'

He hated the way she kept saying that. She was right, they were no longer in love. But there was something still between them, apart from the weight of guilt in his belly. Something he couldn't ignore. It had dragged him back to the UK in the depths of a dreary winter. More, it had disrupted his work schedule, something unheard of.

'But is it really in the past?'

Her eyes narrowed. 'What do you mean? We don't have a relationship anymore. We don't even know each other now.'

Lex nodded. 'I agree. We have our own lives, our separate futures. We're not destined for a romantic happy ending, even if we believed in it anymore.' He paused, waiting to be sure she wouldn't contradict him. She didn't. 'But you feel this too.' He knew she did.

She didn't answer straight away. Was that trepidation in her expression? 'Feel what?'

Her chin was high, her face giving nothing away, but he didn't miss the slight tremble in her voice or the way her breathing shallowed.

'This connection.'

He lifted his hand and let his fingertip skim her cheekbone, down to the corner of her mouth where her lips parted on a gasp that made the smouldering heat in his groin ignite.

Her pupils dilated, turning those velvety eyes into dark pools of longing.

'It's real, isn't it, Portia? Still there after all this time.'

He needed her to admit it. Despite her lust-darkened gaze, he needed absolute confirmation he wasn't alone in this.

Lex's pulse jumped as warm fingers closed around his wrist. He stiffened, guessing she was about to drag his hand away and deny the powerful tug between them.

She held his hand steady, then unexpectedly turned her face to kiss the centre of his palm.

Lightning struck, bolts of it sheering through his body, turning muscle and sinew to white-hot metal, making his blood thunder.

He moved instinctively, looping an arm around her waist and pulling her hard against him.

Instantly sensations bombarded him. He felt her against him from chest to thigh. He hadn't held her for years yet his body remembered and revelled in her proximity.

Arousal stirred and he knew she must feel it.

He tried and failed to remember any other woman who'd affected him so instantaneously.

She curled her free hand around the back of his neck. Her other hand still held his, bringing it close again for another kiss. Anticipation was an effervescent tide in his blood, a streak of tingling awareness shooting straight to his groin.

But instead of pressing her lips to his palm, Portia nipped the flesh at the base of his thumb, sending his whole body into overdrive.

Dark eyes surveyed him from under long lashes. 'If you're talking about sex, the answer is yes. The attraction's still there.'

CHAPTER FOUR

OF COURSE HE'S talking about sex!

Love is long gone. He spelt that out just now, careful that there not be any misunderstanding.

If he'd really loved her he'd have trusted in her all those years ago instead of believing father's lie so easily.

Portia cut off that train of thought. Regrets and what-ifs were luxuries she couldn't afford. But right here, now, was some consolation for the pain she'd borne.

Mutual hunger, strong and cleansing. Surely enough to wipe away past hurt, if only temporarily.

She craved Lex with every bone in her body. Walking away from him weeks ago had solved nothing and the wanting was as strong as ever. She *needed* the fiery rapture, the incandescent joy he'd share with her.

Her battered, guarded heart swelled as she read Lex's glittering gaze. Felt the push of his erection against her abdomen and the answering yearning that had been absent from her life so long. The emptiness.

He didn't try to disguise his arousal.

His sexual honesty had always excited her. For all his tenderness and care of her, there had always been something elemental, earthy and essential about Lex. Something that called to the wild side of her nature, the part of her that had wanted to run free, away from family rules and expectations.

But Portia wasn't that young girl. 'What do you want,

Lex?' He wasn't the only one who needed to lay out param-
eters.

His slow-curling smile cut through her emotional boundaries like a hot blade through butter. She felt the loosening
inside, not just of muscles and tendons. It felt like a layer of
the tension she carried, that had cushioned her for so long
from too-close connection, melted away.

'I want you, Portia. That's why I came back from Greece,
to see you again.'

His honesty stole her breath. That he'd come here for her
seemed impossible yet, given her own reaction, utterly right.

Portia lifted one eyebrow, playing for time. She needed to
shore up the tiniest bit of self-possession. Because her body
clamoured desperately to have this man without thought or
caution.

'Quick sex on the sofa?'

'I was thinking more of thorough sex on a very wide bed.
But if you prefer the sofa we could start there.'

His wolfish smile was like a match to dry tinder. She felt
heat saturate her skin all over. Between her legs moisture
bloomed.

'And you're leaving tomorrow?'

He frowned. 'The day after. But I don't—'

'Good. I'm not after a relationship.'

She couldn't think that way. Caring led to pain. She'd
spent the last decade trying to avoid emotional attachments.
Besides, she'd just got to a point in her life where she had
a real shot at pursuing her career goals. There'd be no side-
tracking now.

Even for the first man who'd made her fully aware of herself as a woman in years.

Slowly Lex inclined his head. 'Nor am I. I have other priorities at the moment.'

Portia wondered what they were. Family? Business? Once

they'd shared their dreams and hopes for the future, believing those dreams would be twined together. How long ago that seemed, like a different life.

It *was* a different life. The day it ended was still branded in her memory, every detail vivid.

'Portia?' His narrow-eyed stare made her wonder if she'd missed something. He seemed to be waiting. 'So you're happy with no strings?'

'Absolutely. I have my own priorities and they don't include a partner.'

For a moment she thought Lex was going to probe further. But maybe she'd imagined that fleeting frown, for soon enough he was smiling again and she felt the impact deep inside. It was a quickening in her womb. A swirling heat in her blood and a softening of her knees, making her clutch him tight.

He took her weight easily, shuffling his legs a little wider to encompass hers, drawing her in against all that lovely body heat.

Portia felt his chest rise hard against hers. His soft groan of approval teased her nipples, drawing them tight.

His voice was rough and she revelled in the sound of his hunger. 'So we have an understanding.'

It wasn't a question but she answered anyway. 'We do. No strings, no expectations. Just—'

'Pleasure.'

His hand cupped her eager breast and she sighed her relief. She'd forgotten how good that felt. And when his thumb and index finger closed unerringly around her nipple, darts of fire zigzagged through her.

'Pleasure.' It sounded like a promise, and suddenly her humdrum world of hard work and scrimping her pennies turned into something glorious and golden.

'Show me, Lex. Make me feel...'

His head lowered, his mouth brushing hers, light as the caress of silk on skin. Yet his touch, his nearness, undid her.

Portia had an instant of trepidation, realising how much he made her feel, even with that tiny caress. After so many barren years it shook her foundations.

But she refused to pull back. Her need was so intense it might scare her if she took time to think about it. So she didn't. Instead she flung herself into the flames, determined, just for one night, to live to the full.

Besides, she'd lost so much, she refused to lose this opportunity for rare delight. No other man in all those years had made her feel this way.

She grabbed his shoulders, straining up on her toes, bringing her mouth fully against his, demanding a proper kiss.

There was an instant of stillness as their lips joined and then her world took fire.

Something broke within her, a constriction, a barrier. Suddenly she was all molten heat and urgent responsiveness. She moulded herself to his tall frame, a sigh escaping as he lifted her higher, his sure strength only adding to her excitement.

Mouths melded, tongues sliding and exploring, rediscovering tastes and sensations that should have been distant memories, but somehow were achingly familiar.

The beauty of their kiss made the backs of her closed eyes prickle. Not with regret, but because she'd forgotten how wonderful a kiss could be.

'Portia.' His voice was gravel and velvet, a trail of arousal that spilled from his lips into hers to wind through her needy body.

She shivered and burrowed closer, wrapping her arms around his neck, pressing into him as if he were the one solid thing in her world. Perhaps he was. Everything else reeled away from her.

'I need you.' Lex lifted away from her questing lips until

she opened her eyes and met his stormy gaze. She shivered again, reading a carnal excitement there that matched her own. 'Now.'

It took her dazed mind a second to realise he was asking permission. 'Yes, now.'

Maturity must have changed her, or her memory was faulty. Avid as she'd been for his attention as a teenager, she couldn't remember ever feeling this desperate.

She clung on tight as Lex swept her up high against his chest and turned to carry her across the room. Just as well. She wasn't sure her legs worked.

They passed glowing lamps and walls with exquisite artworks but the furnishings were blurred because her attention was fixed on Lex. The taut, masculine angles of that shadowed jaw. The strong, tanned column of his throat. Those lips, slightly reddened from their kiss. Jewel-bright eyes that tracked from her face to wherever he was carrying her, then back again.

Each sweep of his gaze undid another knot inside her.

They reached a bedroom lit by lamps either side of a vast bed with a counterpane of blue and gold. Blue for his eyes. Gold for the bliss that beckoned.

Portia stifled a shaky laugh at the flight of fancy as Lex lowered her to her feet. She didn't do flights of fancy anymore.

But tonight is an exception. You can let go, just this once.

Her stockinged feet landed on thick carpet. She must have lost her shoes on the way.

The way he looked at her made her feel…precious. Unique.

A jagged breath snagged in her chest and she wrestled the idea away, shoving it into the same locked place in her mind where she'd relegated painful, dangerous memories. She couldn't afford to read too much into this.

It's sex. Purely physical. Nothing else.

'Tell me you've got condoms. Because I haven't got contraception.'

If she'd thought to ease the fraught expectancy of the moment she failed. Because Lex nodded, his eyes aglow with a promise that notched her need even higher.

He opened a nearby drawer, pulled out a box and put it on the bedside table.

Her eyes widened. Either Lex believed in saving money by buying in bulk or...

'Take your clothes off, Portia.'

Disappointment surprised her. 'You don't want to do it?' She'd imagined his hands on her.

His nostrils flared on a deep breath. 'You don't know how much. But I don't trust myself.' He shrugged off his jacket and tossed it onto a nearby chair. 'It's better that you do it.'

The thought of him teetering on the edge of control only made her need flare brighter. She followed his lead, slipping out of her jacket and draping it carefully over the back of the chair. In a few hours she'd leave here and she refused to do it looking crumpled and thoroughly debauched, even though she suspected that's exactly how she'd feel.

Excitement skidded through her, making her fumble as she struggled with the zip of her skirt. By the time she'd laid her skirt across the chair, Lex was shirtless, his feet bare.

Portia couldn't stop a gasp of appreciation. He'd always been handsome, and charismatic with his quicksilver energy. Now he'd filled out, taller, broader, more potently masculine than she remembered. The sight of his leanly muscled torso dried her mouth and drew her touch.

His rich olive skin was hot, the sprinkle of dark hair across his pectoral muscles teased her palms. His brown nipples were tight buds, almost as tight as her own that pushed hard and swollen against her bra.

Her hands trembled as she slipped them across his hot chest, yet her touch was sure and possessive.

She wanted him so badly, needed to claim him.

She leaned in, pressing a kiss to the hollow at the centre of his collarbone, then following his sternum down. His chest rose massively, his indrawn breath a hiss. Elation filled her, knowing he was so susceptible to her touch.

Portia nuzzled his skin, peppering tiny kisses over him, exulting in the way his hands tightened on her hips, anchoring her to him. She reached a nipple, laved it and felt the ripple of his response under his skin. She closed her teeth around him, nipping delicately.

'Enough!'

Strong hands moved to her shoulders, putting some distance between them. 'You need to be naked.'

His deep voice was a growl that seemed to have a direct connection to her womb. Internal muscles clenched convulsively at the sound of his voice.

'You first.'

She reached for the fastening of his trousers but he beat her to it, whipping it undone with satisfying speed. A moment later, as he stepped free of his clothes, Portia gawked at the most stunning form she'd ever seen. His torso tapered down to narrow hips, his musculature impressive, with only an appendix scar to mar what looked like perfection.

His erection proudly defied gravity, as solid and strong as the rest of him.

Dark hair dusted powerful thighs, his legs long and even his bare feet somehow sexy.

It had been years since she'd let herself remember Lex's body in any detail. Now she felt awed.

'Your turn.'

Without giving herself time to think, Portia hooked her thumbs through the waistband of her pantyhose and dragged it down, catching her underwear on the way. She slid the fabric down her thighs, past her knees and finally off her feet.

Lex watched with absolute concentration, his gaze tracking the movement. Then, when she straightened, she saw his attention fix on the hemline of her white blouse that hung just low enough to preserve her modesty.

If there'd been any moisture in her mouth she'd have laughed at the idea of modesty. She felt daring and free for the first time in years.

It turned out sexual arousal could block out mundane concerns about making ends meet.

She loved the way he swallowed convulsively, the twitch of his hands as if he wanted to reach for her. His erection bobbed as if eager for her.

Portia reached out but before she could touch, Lex took a step back and sat down abruptly on the bed, reaching for the box of condoms without once taking his eyes off her. 'Time for protection.'

She watched him tear open a packet, then roll on the condom, wishing it was her touching him.

Suddenly she couldn't wait. Her hands went to the buttons of her blouse. Surely there were more buttons than usual? She fumbled a little but finally got it undone, turning to drape it with shaking hands over her jacket.

When she turned back her heart leapt. Lex sat on the side of the bed, knees open, eyes so hot she felt tiny ignition points under her skin as fire erupted. He beckoned. 'Let me, golden girl.'

Golden girl.

It was what he'd called her all those years ago when they'd met secretly in the stables or the old summerhouse, surrounded by its concealing tangle of roses.

He'd called her that the first time they made love, when she'd been full of wonderment. And the last time too, when she'd been fervent with excitement, knowing that from that night they'd be together forever.

They'd been soulmates, or so she'd believed. Lex was the one person apart from her mother who'd accepted her for who she was. The tomboy, horse-mad and romantic. Portia had seen beyond Lex's taciturn demeanour. He was clever and driven but generous and caring.

'Portia?'

His eyes bore the glaze of arousal. There were no shadows. No doubts. No what-ifs.

That was what she needed, complete absorption in the moment. No more of the past. No more if-onlys. She closed the distance between them, stopping only when she stood between his thighs.

Lex smiled, his hands finding her bra's fastening, then smoothing the straps off her shoulders so it fell to the floor. Admiration flared in his eyes and something that might have been awe.

His expression had her arching her back, thrusting her breasts out and into his waiting hands.

Her eyes fluttered shut as he cupped them, his murmured praise a silky ribbon that wove around her body and deep inside, tighter and tighter, making her need escalate.

Portia planted her hands on his shoulders, feeling the rigid muscle and bone and that glorious heat.

'I need you, Lex.'

'Soon,' he crooned against her breast as one hand trailed down her abdomen to the damp nest of curls between her thighs.

A lightning spark shuddered through her and she tried to open her legs wider, only to be trapped by his thighs.

'No!' She saw his heavy-lidded eyes snap wide open as she spoke. 'Now. I don't have time for foreplay.' The need was too urgent. She craved the relief of his body with hers.

His mouth hooked up at one corner, his voice a lazy drawl. 'What do you think we've been doing?'

But then he lifted his gaze to meet hers and his expression changed. Understanding pulsed between them and for a second it felt more than sexual.

But that wasn't possible. They didn't know each other anymore. They were simply strangers who shared a past.

'Poor Portia,' he crooned, as he skimmed his hands along her sides, thumbs brushing the underside of her breasts and stealing her breath. Then he opened his imprisoning legs and slid his hands to her hips. 'Ride me, then.'

It was the work of the moment to step over his thighs and straddle him, her knees either side of his hips.

His attention dropped to her breasts, bobbing before him and he leaned in to suckle one, drawing slow then hard, making her body hum with arousal. Portia buried her hands in his thick hair, clamping his mouth to her breast as he drove her to the edge of reason.

Eyes the colour of a summer storm cloud looked up at her as he released her breast and nuzzled the other, making her hips shift restlessly. 'Ride me, Portia. Let me have all of you.'

Then he closed his mouth on her other breast and drew hard.

She bit her lip against the sob of need rising in her throat, and reached down to hold him.

He was heavy between her thighs, hot where he nudged her, and when she sank onto him there was nothing but the sensation of oneness. The stroke of hard maleness against sensitive femininity. The friction that turned anticipation into pleasure and pleasure into desperation.

Eyes closed, Portia rocked against him, driving them together, feeling the unstoppable spark grow and grow.

Lex's hands were tight around her hips, encouraging yet

slowing her too, not letting her race too fast towards oblivion, making her work for each morsel of pleasure.

His mouth was on hers now, murmuring words of encouragement interspersed with groans of delight. They rocked together, moving in tandem, drawing out the gratification with complete sureness as if their bodies remembered every detail of their past loving.

Finally Lex pushed even higher, even harder, biting her earlobe and telling her the other things he wanted to do with her.

She felt the gathering rush at the base of her spine and deep inside. Felt the spasms begin.

Her eyes snapped open and there he was, watching her, joining her, sharing the shock of too-sudden ecstasy. Bliss beckoned, consuming her, so profound she would have been scared but for Lex there with her, looking as stunned as she felt.

Portia heard herself cry out something, heard him whisper her name in a voice that didn't sound like his. Then there was nothing but his frantic pulsing inside her, the shuddering, wonderful release of her body and rapture engulfed her.

CHAPTER FIVE

'HELLO, PORTIA OAKHURST SPEAKING.'

There was a brief silence on the other end of the line, a pause just long enough for instinct to tighten her skin and snag her breath.

Then a smooth, deep voice purred in her ear. 'Portia. I'm pleased to catch you at your desk.'

She sagged back in her chair, trying and failing to control her galloping pulse.

It had been three weeks almost to the day since she'd seen Lex. She'd walked out of his hotel late that Saturday morning without a backward glance, telling herself there'd be no regrets. That night of fantastic sex had finally burnt out the last remnants of her feelings for him.

She'd told him the truth about the day they'd parted, that she hadn't deserted him, and he'd accepted it easily. Because the feelings they'd once shared were long dead. Now, she'd told herself, she could move on and fully put the past behind her.

But for three weeks she'd started every time the telephone rang. Every time she saw a tall man in a leather jacket. Every time she glimpsed unruly dark curls and a squared jaw. The thought of running into Lex kept her on edge, half fearing and half wishing he'd seek her out.

And here he was, calling her at work. 'Lex, what a surprise.' She waited but he didn't fill the silence. Her hand tightened around the phone. 'Are you ringing about an up-coming auction?'

This time his silence had a sizzling quality to it. As of an-noyance barely held in check.

'Don't insult our intelligence by even pretending to think that, Portia.'

Did he deliberately drop his voice as he said her name, making it drawl so low she felt it scrape through her pelvis?

She sighed and tugged her earlobe. So much for pretence. He knew too much about her.

And you know a lot about him. Especially how he likes his sex.

The needy clench of her body reminded her she was no-where near immune.

Portia looked towards the open door but there was no one nearby. 'Why did you ring, Lex?'

'Why do you think?'

She chewed her bottom lip and reminded herself it wasn't for the pleasure of her company.

'I don't have time for a game of twenty questions. I have work to do.'

'But not on the weekend.'

The silence thrummed with the heavy beat of her pulse. It was Thursday. Was he asking her to spend time with him this weekend?

'No, I have other things planned.' Like grocery shopping and cleaning the oven in her small shared flat.

Boring things said a voice in her head.

But sensible and safe.

'I'm flying to London soon. Can I tempt you to spend the weekend with me? I know a place outside London I think you'll like.'

Portia put her hand to her chest, trying to still her racing heart. He was right, it *was* tempting.

That night three weeks ago would, she knew, be emblazoned on her memory for life. The sort of memory she'd take out and dream over when her bones grew arthritic and her body bent. Or probably long before that, because she suspected whatever her future held, there'd be little to compare with the ecstasy, the sheer vibrant joy, she'd experienced with Lex.

That's because you've never let another man into your life the way you let him in. Now that part of your life is over.

Portia grimaced. That was why she had to say no.

Over the years she'd met attractive men but never been tempted to risk herself in another serious relationship. It scared her sometimes, her inability to put herself out there. To trust her heart, even a little, to someone else.

Because she'd spent so long relying only on herself that independence was her default position, a defence against hurt?

Because she couldn't forget the pain of his desertion?

Or because no other man had made her feel a tenth of what he had?

Fury sizzled under her skin. Could she be that weak?

'I'm afraid that's impossible. But thanks for the offer.' Her mother had brought her up to be polite.

'You don't want to spend time with me? You're saying you didn't enjoy our night together?' His tone challenged her to deny it.

'Oh, I enjoyed it. You're a very accomplished lover.'

She paused, searching for words that would end this quickly. Because his invitation was far too tempting. The scary fact was she *wanted* to spend the weekend with him. Her blood fizzed with anticipation at the very idea.

But it would be a mistake. That night together was supposed to have marked the end of the relationship that had haunted her for years. She needed to make a clean break.

'Well, then—'

'But I'm not in the market for a sexual relationship right

now. That night we were prompted by ghosts of the past. All that emotion around how our affair ended.'

It hadn't been an affair. For her it had been far more. But that was all she'd admit to.

She hurried on before he could interrupt. 'It was a…relief to let go of all those feelings. And the remnants of our old physical attraction. But it's over, Lex. I don't want to go back.'

'I'm not talking about going back. I'm just proposing a weekend together.' His voice dropped low. 'I guarantee you'd enjoy it.'

That was the trouble. Portia was sure he could. But where would that leave her? Pining for him all over again?

'Again, thanks for the offer, but you'll have to look elsewhere for a weekend companion.'

She ended the connection.

Portia sank back in her chair, staring at her computer screen but seeing instead Lex as she'd left him in the hotel. He'd been sprawled, naked, one arm reaching across the bed from where he'd roped it around her waist while they slept. His jaw was darkened with stubble that had left red patches across her throat, breasts and inner thighs. Her sated body had hummed with a sense of well-being, filled with a sweet warmth that belied the need to leave.

She'd stood there on wobbly legs, half hoping he'd wake and stop her going.

That was what had finally given her the impetus to walk out the door—knowing that if she weren't careful, she'd find herself in thrall again to the only man she'd ever loved.

Lex hadn't planned on returning to the auction house after she'd refused his suggestion of a weekend together, yet here he was, once more surveying the sculptures coming up for auction.

He'd told himself he'd cancel the trip to London. It had

been a spur of the moment decision anyway. True, he'd spent a useful afternoon in meetings, but the impetus for the visit was Portia. Despite her rejection. He just hadn't been able to keep away.

He'd told himself he needed to forget her.

Six weeks ago he'd woken in his hotel suite, looking forward to a lazy Saturday in bed with her, only to discover she'd abandoned him.

Just like old times.

Except she hadn't abandoned him that first time. All those years believing she'd made a fool of him, using him for her own amusement, and she'd been a victim of her father's brutality.

That had to be why Lex's reaction to her now was so confused. Why he couldn't just walk away as she had.

Something lingered, some shred of…

He shook his head. There *was* no connection between them. Whatever emotional bond they'd once shared had been severed. The only thing left was sexual attraction.

That was why he was here, because he still wanted her, physically. Instead of his need abating after they'd been to bed together, the craving had grown stronger.

That was why he'd returned to London. He wasn't a man habitually driven by hormonal impulses. Portia was the sole exception. It must be something to do with imprinting on her as his first love. Or their affair being cut short so abruptly.

And the fact that she's a fine woman.

Portia had an allure that even her severe business suits couldn't dim.

Lex stared at the little white figurine before him. A piece of prehistoric, Cycladic sculpture. The female figure was stylised, its face almost smooth, breasts and hips rounded, arms crossed. But there was something about the figure, something powerful and enigmatic that drew him.

A grunt of laughter escaped. Powerful and enigmatic, that was how he'd describe Portia's allure.

It wasn't just her slim body, her feminine shape now more rounded than in her teens. It wasn't only her passion, her un-bridled hunger for him that had met and matched something raw and untamed in himself.

There was something *else* about Portia, something that had sunk its claws deep inside him and wouldn't let go.

He didn't know what it was and he didn't want to know. He just wanted to sate it so he could move on with his life.

Except she'd refused him.

His lips curved in a reluctantly appreciative smile. It wasn't often anyone said no to him these days. He'd striven to get where he was, initially with backing from his father, but his success was due mainly to hard work, strategic vision and the ability to negotiate to get what he wanted.

Clearly his negotiation skills were rusty. Portia had been so definite when she turned him down.

He'd withstood temptation for three weeks but then he'd caved and booked a flight to London.

He needed this done. Complete. Then he'd move on.

This being his rampant sexual hunger for her.

'Mr Tomaras.' The husky voice tightened his belly. 'You've seen something you like?'

He turned and met familiar velvety eyes that drew him back to that night in bed with her. All that softness. All that eagerness. He'd been so aroused he'd worried he might come on too strong. But Portia had met him with a wild hunger that matched his own.

He couldn't believe she didn't want him anymore. Surely he saw a flicker of interest, her colour deepening?

'Ms Oakhurst. Is that how it's going to be? No more first names?'

She shrugged. 'This is my workplace.'

Yet she'd sought him out. She could have slipped past without saying a word while his attention was elsewhere. But then Portia had never been one to shy from a challenge or what she believed to be right.

Something dropped hard inside him. Had she come to tell him face-to-face that she didn't want to see him again?

'Ah. Discretion.' He nodded as if it made sense, when the only thing that made sense to him right now was the need to gather her close and kiss her until neither of them could remember their names. 'To answer your question, yes.' Deliberately, he lowered his voice. 'I see something I want.'

She blinked, pupils dilating, and there it was. Desire.

He saw it in her parted lips. In the sharp rise of her breasts, betraying her breathlessness. In that now smouldering look that didn't belong in a workplace. She might protest, but she couldn't hide her response to him.

If he'd doubted, even for an instant, his continuing need for Portia Oakhurst, the leaping arc of heat between them proved him wrong.

Breathing deep through flared nostrils she turned to survey the spotlit figurine. 'You're a collector?' She frowned. 'It doesn't really fit with the oil painting you bought here. They're very different styles.'

Lex shrugged. Was she really so interested in his taste in art? Or was she finding words to fill the silence?

'That was a spur of the moment decision.'

He'd regretted it soon after, for he didn't have space in his life for sentiment. The painting had taken him back to a time when he'd been young and vulnerable. When he believed in...

But Lex didn't do regrets. Especially when that purchase had led him directly back to Portia.

'As for the figurine, I can see that in my home.' It was easier to talk about it as a furnishing than a piece of art that resonated with him at a primal level. His emotional response to the ancient artefact was something he preferred not to admit. 'I might loan it out for a while to a museum in Athens. If I buy it.'

From the corner of his eye he saw Portia turn and tilt her head, as if to view him better. 'So you're a philanthropist as well as a collector?'

He shrugged. 'I think those with the money to own significant art should share their good fortune.'

'Unlike my father.'

'He *is* very possessive.'

Once his wife died, Portia's father had refused to open his home for any charitable functions or for the village fair that had been held in the grounds for as long as Lex could recall. The man had broken with centuries of tradition, jealously guarding his property for himself.

'He *was* possessive. He's dead.' Her voice was toneless.

Lex swung around to face her, shocked. Her father wouldn't have been that old.

He tried to read her expression. But she didn't meet his eyes, staring instead at the sculpture behind the toughened glass. Her blank expression deliberately concealed her emotions.

'I'm sorry.' Lex had hated the man but he'd been the last of her family. He remembered how devastated she'd been when her mother died. 'That's why the painting was auctioned? The estate's being sold?'

She shook her head and turned away from the display. 'No. Most of the estate is entailed. It's gone to my father's second cousin. That painting was my inheritance and I sold it.'

Lex scrutinised her taut features, knowing there was more here that he wanted to understand. Her words made it sound as if she'd inherited only the painting, which made no sense.

Surely not all the contents of her home had been entailed? And why sell the picture? He knew how much it meant to her.

She'd spoken of it when she was young, calling it the perfect view of her home, the first thing she'd save if Cropley Hall went up in flames.

Maybe she needs money.

Lex frowned, testing the idea. He'd assumed she was a wealthy woman, inheriting money from her mother. Then, surely there'd have been something from her father, something more than a painting.

He realised there was so much about Portia that he didn't know. Things he wanted to understand.

'I'll leave you to your art,' she said, turning away.

'You're leaving? But you came to me.'

He glanced at his watch, realising it was after the gallery's official closing time though no one had come to hurry him on his way. One of the perks of being wealthy.

'It's late, Lex.' Her tone, or maybe it was the serious expression she wore, imbued the words with extra weight. 'I assume I won't see you again. I wanted to wish you…well.'

She was saying goodbye. A permanent goodbye.

Lex's stomach knotted and he was surprised to feel pain catch under his ribs. Surprised at the abrupt feeling of loss.

'Wait!'

His hand shot out, snagging hers. Instantly he felt that jolt of physical connection, like an electrical charge. He pulled his hand back, flexing his fingers and saw her do the same, eyes widening.

He breathed deep, centring himself.

'It's still there, Portia.' Slowly she shook her head, whether in disagreement or in disbelief, he didn't know. 'You feel it too, don't try to pretend you don't.'

Her head jerked up, eyes flashing, but when she spoke her voice was low, reminding him they weren't totally alone. One of her colleagues might appear at any moment. 'I'm not pretending anything. I'm just being sensible.'

In her neat jacket and trousers of dark forest green and her hair up in some neat bun arrangement, she did look sensible. Except for the flush climbing her throat and the light in her eyes.

'Sensible because you see no future for us.'

She inclined her head. 'We agreed that we lead completely separate lives now.'

'And yet there's still this.'

Deliberately he stroked his finger down the side of her hand, watching her flinch and bite her lip. He knew what she was feeling because he felt it too, the sizzling tingle spreading from that point of contact, radiating through his body.

'It doesn't mean anything.'

'Stop pretending, Portia. Of course it means something. It means that, whatever the rights and wrongs, we still have unfinished business.'

She shook her head. 'No. If we ignore it, it will go away.'

Lex shoved his hands in his trouser pockets, watching the way her gaze followed the movement then lingered at his groin before slowly climbing. Just that look, and the realisation she shared this preternatural awareness, had his body hardening.

'How's that working for you, Portia? You're more on edge now than you were before. It's getting worse, isn't it? Not better. I can read the signs.'

He stepped closer, lowering his voice to a whisper, suppressing his own shudder of longing as he caught a drift of her scent, bluebells and intriguing woman. 'Your lips are parted. You're flushed. Did you know you're leaning towards me?' He watched her straighten and his mouth curled in a too-tight smile.

'You're trembling, Portia and—' he touched her again, this time lightly clasping her wrist '—your pulse is racing.' He watched her swallow. 'Your skin's tingling, isn't it? Your breath is quickening. You want me to touch you. Not just your hand but—'

'Stop!' Her voice sounded strangled. Yet she didn't immediately pull her hand away.

She closed her eyes, drawing a breath that lifted her breasts against her jacket. At the open neck of her shirt he saw her pulse throb, matching the frantic beat he felt at her wrist.

'I can't do this here.' Her voice was raw, her eyes huge and he felt—almost—like a brute for forcing the issue. But he was only acknowledging the truth, something she tried to avoid.

Lex released her hand and stepped back, ignoring the silent howl of protest as he denied himself. He half turned away, catching sight of someone down the corridor switching off an office light.

She was right, this wasn't the place.

About to invite her somewhere quiet to talk, he stopped. The first time he'd bought her a drink she'd walked out on him. The second time they'd spent the night in his bed, and still she'd walked away the next day.

His breath stuck in his lungs, his chest seizing.

Maybe she's right.

Maybe the only sensible action is to separate.

Every instinct screamed against the idea. He wanted more. He wanted to slake his thirst for her, have her again and again until the unrelenting need finally faded.

But it was Portia's choice too. If she said no, and she had, that was her right. He'd have to live with it.

Suddenly his boundless certainty faded.

Lex refused to become a man who'd pursue a woman against her wishes.

He'd intended to make her admit the truth—that she wanted him as much as he wanted her. He'd planned a weekend that would allow them time to give in to every erotic impulse until there was nothing left.

A weekend of pure indulgence, where you got everything you wanted.

But Portia said no. Suck it up and walk away.

There was a metallic taste on Lex's tongue and a sick feeling in his belly.

'You're right. This is your workplace. I shouldn't have come.'

He inclined his head, stiff neck muscles straining. One last look into those beautiful eyes and he dragged his gaze towards the exit.

In the distance two people stood in the reception area, studiously not looking this way. Too studiously. He'd drawn unwanted attention to Portia, making no secret of his interest. She deserved better.

'If I decide to bid at future auctions I'll do it online. You won't have to worry about me turning up here again.' He half turned towards her but didn't meet her gaze. 'I wish you well, Portia. Goodbye.'

He'd taken three steps when something touched his hand. Warm fingers slid over his then pulled away.

He halted, turning and there she was, heart-stoppingly sexy in her plain business clothes and neat earrings. He recognised them, he realised. They were tiny golden roses, the last gift she'd ever received from her mother.

The sight reminded him that while he'd known her long ago, they were strangers now.

She opened her mouth and he fixed his own in a slight smile ready to acknowledge her farewell.

But his smile solidified when she spoke. 'You're right, Lex. We can't go on like this.' She breathed deep. 'I need time to pack and I need to be back to London on Sunday evening.'

It was so unexpected it took a second to understand.

'I'm accepting your invitation, Lex. I'll spend the weekend with you.'

CHAPTER SIX

THE END OF winter had brought a freeze and the view beyond the deep-set window was stunning. The rolling countryside shone white with snow, topped by a rare blue sky that seemed to go on forever.

When Portia suggested a walk before lunch, he'd agreed automatically. Because what pleased her brought him pleasure too. Besides, logic decreed that after two nights at this exclusive retreat they should finally venture further than their suite.

But they'd got sidetracked and the vision before him was so much better than any bucolic view.

Portia's hair glowed like dark honey in the sunlight streaming across the bed. Her hair curtained her upper back, except at her spine where he'd kissed his way down from her nape to a spot between her shoulder blades.

He lowered his mouth again, nipping this time and feeling her naked body twitch beneath his, her rump sliding against his erection.

Lex paused, telling himself that *this time* he wouldn't rush. This time he'd conquer the driving need to have her as soon and as thoroughly as possible.

He drew back on his knees, clenching his teeth at the loss of contact. He concentrated instead on the taste of her as he kissed his way lower, and the incredible softness of her flesh beneath his palms. Her murmurs of wordless encouragement and delight made him want to take her to the stars again.

Lower he went, hands shaping her waist, mouth nipping and kissing each vertebra. She twisted beneath him, breathing ragged, and he knew she wouldn't last long. Soon she'd beg for completion. He loved the husky sound of her saying his name, urging, demanding or crying out in triumph or even shock as ecstasy took them.

He couldn't get enough of it. Of her.

Today was Sunday and they had to return to London later. His scheme to incinerate this all-consuming lust by stoking the fire until it turned to ashes hadn't worked.

They needed more time. They needed—

Below him she gave a sinuous wriggle, making his hands tighten on the swell of her hips. The shape of her, those devastatingly feminine curves, even the narrow splay of her shoulders, gleaming beneath her rumpled hair, sidetracked his thoughts.

Then she lifted herself up on her knees, her buttocks circling against his engorged penis. It all felt so perfect he feared he'd explode there and then.

He pulled back a little, at the same time smoothing his hands along the downward tilt of her body towards her shoulders, detouring to sweep out and brush the sides of her plump breasts.

'Lex.'

His skin tightened at the sound. His name on her lips was voluptuous, a sensual promise and a sigh of gratification melded into one.

The remaining blood pumping in his arteries surged south. She pushed back again and suddenly he was the one on the edge of control when moments ago she'd been lax and sleepy while he'd led the erotic interplay.

Every time, she turned the tables.

Not making sex a contest, but simply undoing him.

Portia lifted her upper body, grasping the headboard, and he took the opportunity to capture her breasts fully, kneading and stroking them, torturing himself and her with how magnificent that felt.

Gently he pinched her nipples and she hissed a breath, shifting against his groin.

Stars sprinkled the edges of his vision as everything grew tighter, harder.

'Are you ready, *Chrysi mou*?'

He heard muffled laughter, quickly stifled. 'Can't you tell?'

She was amused? While he was racked with pleasure-pain at the effort it took to control himself?

He released one breast, tracing a line all the way down her body to the cleft between her legs. His fingers found slick, wet heat and she pushed convulsively into his touch.

'Lex!'

He heard the strain in her voice and knew they were equals in this, had been from the start. Yet he wasn't used to feeling so completely at the mercy of impulses he couldn't control.

'Tell me you've already got that condom on.'

'I'm always prepared.'

Sex was too important for carelessness. He was meticulous about that and, he dimly realised, so was Portia.

'I can't imagine you as a Scout.' He heard a gurgle of laughter and this time he found himself smiling despite the way his body strained.

Lex nudged her knees wider, lifting her hips, and let himself slide between her legs. He shuddered, close to physical overload.

'They wouldn't have let me join the Scouts.' He clenched his teeth as he positioned himself against her. 'They met on your father's land.'

'He couldn't have stopped…oh!'

Yes, oh. It never ceased to amaze him how perfect their union was. Every time. Whether rushed and desperate or more considered, at least in the beginning. Each time it felt like the world stopped turning.

Sensation juddered through him as he guided himself home. For the longest moment they both held still, absorbing the wonder of it. Then Lex had to move. Because he was only human and his need for Portia was too strong.

Gripping her hips, he eased back then drove hard, relishing the way she met him, creating a rhythm of surge and retreat that tantalised and heightened their need.

The way they moved together made his brain blank so that all he could think of was Portia and their incredible, tantalising journey towards completion.

Knowing how she responded to his touch, he leaned forward to cup one bobbing breast.

Okay, you like it too. That soft weight, just the perfect size for your palm.

Their rhythm sped up, smooth movements becoming staccato. Breaths growing choppy. Friction impossibly arousing. Until he felt the tight tickle of sensation around his lower body and knew he couldn't last.

Lex leaned in, his chest to her back, finding the place at the side of her neck that made her shiver. Gently he nipped her there. Grabbing the bed head with one hand, he slid the other down her body, tracing each undulation of torso and belly before delving between her thighs again.

There. That gasp of breath. The shiver across her skin that became a clenching shudder of internal muscles, greedily claiming him.

For a moment Lex hovered on the brink of smugness. Because he'd lasted long enough to bring Portia undone. Then a climax hit them both, a single wave crashing over the pair of them, catching them up and hurling them into another dimension.

Pleasure was too mild a word for what he felt. It was everything. Fire. Bliss. Pure ecstasy. Possessiveness too. Satisfaction. Joy at her rapture. And shock at how perfect the moment. Lex squeezed his eyes shut against the final, phantom shudders.

As the blaze of golden light finally receded and he came back to himself, he knew a hint of disquiet.

Far from satisfying his hunger, this weekend had done nothing to diminish his need for Portia.

The suspicion of disquiet grew. He felt like a swimmer who'd overestimated his abilities as deep water closed overhead. As if he'd ventured out of his depth.

Lex dragged diamond-sharp air into his lungs, feeling the cold clear his head. 'You were right. It would have been a shame, returning to the city without getting out into the fresh air.'

Portia slanted him a sideways look from dark eyes. 'Do you miss it? The countryside?'

'Greece has countryside too, you know.'

'You know what I mean. The *English* countryside.'

The way she said it reminded him of how much she'd loved Cropley Hall. She'd been a country girl at heart.

Their footsteps crunched loud on the frozen ground as he let the silence lengthen, considering.

He'd been a country boy. He'd been just a toddler when he and his mother had moved in with her uncle. As a child, Lex had loved the place. The adventures to be had. The animals and birds. The freedom.

It was only as he grew older and bore the brunt of disapproval and suspicion for being different that things changed. He'd chafed at the restrictions of living in such a small community, longing for opportunities that beckoned elsewhere. Longing for a chance to prove himself.

He would have left earlier, but for Portia.

They stopped at a summerhouse overlooking a small lake and he felt a tug of pleasure.

They'd grown up several counties away from here but the rolling hills, frost-edged forest and view across the water towards a nearby village held both beauty and familiarity.

Yet it had been easy to turn his back on England, believing it had nothing to offer him.

'I've been too busy to feel homesick. Besides, Greece is my home now.' It still surprised him, how easily he'd adjusted to life there. How Greek he felt.

As if reading his thoughts, Portia said, 'I think it's remarkable. You didn't even speak the language. How did you even *know* your father was there? You said your mother never spoke about him.'

He shoved his hands deep in his pockets. 'She didn't. She refused to discuss him. As I grew older I wondered if he'd treated her badly and that's why she wouldn't talk about him. Or if she'd even known who he was.'

Portia moved closer, slipping her arm through his and staring at the scene. Their breaths were visible plumes in the frigid air that mingled before disappearing.

Being with her after all this time, talking with her, was far easier than he'd believed possible in the days when he'd thought she'd betrayed him.

It was incredibly easy being with Portia like this. No strings, no expectations.

This was supposed to be nothing more than sex yet it felt like there *was* something more. He supposed it was their shared past, their knowledge of each other.

For whatever reason, Lex found himself revealing what he'd told no one apart from his father.

'I went to Greece on a hunch.'

It hadn't been his original plan. When he'd thought he'd have Portia with him the idea had been to stay in the UK, find somewhere they could both find work.

'It must have been based on something.'

Lex shrugged. 'I found something a long time ago, at the back of a cupboard. Just a paper bag, printed with what I thought at first were mathematical equations, because I'd just started learning algebra. Then I realised I was looking at Greek letters making words, not maths.'

He'd stood there puzzling over the letters until his mother discovered him and snatched the bag away. He'd never seen it again. She'd blustered about him prying but refused to meet his eyes and her mood had been bad for weeks afterwards.

'My mother's reaction made it obvious it was something she didn't want me to know about. So I set about trying to learn more.'

Most people he'd known then would have made some comment about him always seeking out trouble. Portia simply nodded. Had she guessed how incomplete he'd felt, not knowing who his father was? How deeply he'd felt the sneers and jibes about his mother and himself, though he'd taken pride in never showing weakness?

'I'd memorised some of the symbols and researched them with a bit of help at the library. I remembered just enough to translate one word. Athens. I'd assumed she, or someone she knew, had bought something at a shop in Athens.'

'And you thought that someone might have been your father.'

'It was an incredibly long shot.' But as a kid he'd been desperate to find out the truth about himself. To find his father. 'But it was the only possible lead I had.'

He cleared his throat. 'One of the library branches had an old teach yourself Greek book. I borrowed it so often over the years that when it grew too tatty to stay in circulation, the librarian gave it to me. I used to read it at night in bed.'

Portia's hand squeezed his arm. 'You never said.'

He nodded. This was the one secret he'd kept from her. Because giving voice to his hopes would have shown how faint they really were? Was he, even then, trying to be a macho male, impervious to weakness?

'What was there to say? I knew I was probably building something out of nothing.'

She leaned close, her breasts against his arm. 'But it gave you purpose and hope.'

Lex turned to look down into eyes of deepest purple-brown. He'd shared so much with her, all those years ago. But he thought he'd concealed the feeling that a vital part of himself was missing.

He was surprised at how easy it was to accept her understanding. He'd spent so long keeping his emotions to himself.

'So that's why you went to Greece.'

He nodded. 'There was nothing to keep me in Britain.' He felt her minute flinch and almost regretted his words. But it was true. He'd felt betrayed and alone. His huff of laughter was forced. 'It turns out I'd learnt a lot of useful grammar but my pronunciation was woeful and my words very stilted and old-fashioned.'

'But you *did* it. You taught yourself. And you found your father. All because you followed your instinct. I'm so happy everything worked out for you, Lex.'

Automatically he nodded. He had a wonderful life. Challenging work. Friends. Family. A beautiful home as well as wealth. Yet…

'How did you find him? There are millions of people in Athens.'

'You give me too much credit. I'd never have found him. It was sheer luck. I was working a couple of jobs. I finished each evening doing a shift as a kitchen hand in a restaurant. One night the owner's father came into the kitchen. He made a fuss about how I looked like his old friend when he was younger. We thought he was exaggerating. But then weeks later he brought his friend to the restaurant and the pair of them were convinced the resemblance was no coincidence.'

Warmth filled him at the memory. It had taken a while to sort out the details but from the first his father had accepted him.

That implicit trust had been rare in Lex's life. He'd only had it twice before. From his mother's uncle who recognised Lex's way with animals, and from Portia.

'Tell me about *your* father.'

She flinched and would have pulled away except he held her arm close to his side.

'I don't like talking about him.'

'Give me the abridged version then.'

'He's dead. What else do you want to know?'

Lex stifled the knowledge that he was pushing into territory that was painful for her. He didn't enjoy talking about his mother who'd been difficult and moody. But surely he deserved to know what happened to the man who'd destroyed their plans.

'His actions impacted me too, remember.'

Portia slipped her arm from his and turned to face him, her expression hard to read. 'You know that because of what he did you went to Greece and eventually found your father. He'd have hated knowing he'd done you a good turn, however backhanded.'

Lex nodded. The irony hadn't escaped him. But his curiosity wasn't spiteful. It wasn't for himself he wanted to know but because he had a growing suspicion that locking his daughter up wasn't the worst Portia's father had done to her.

Finally Portia sighed. 'You're so stubborn. Come on, I'll

tell you while we walk back. It's time we packed, ready to leave.'

The reminder that their weekend was almost over punctured Lex's satisfaction. But he nodded and turned.

Her father still had the power to drive a wedge between them. She didn't take his arm as they walked and his pleasure in the landscape dimmed. Amazing how their good mood had been wrecked by the mere mention of the man.

When she spoke her voice was crisp. 'I can't really tell you much. I gather he and Raine stayed together for several years but didn't marry.'

'You gather? You're not sure?'

Portia kept her gaze fixed on the country house hotel before them. 'I never saw him after that night.'

'You what?'

Lex slammed to a stop. After a couple steps she turned, eyebrows raised. 'What? You thought I'd have anything to do with him after what he'd done to me? To us? That I'd meekly sit at home and let him tell me how to live my life?'

She turned and started walking, leaving Lex to follow. He caught up in three strides as she spoke again. 'My father had done his best to make my mother miserable. He would have succeeded if she hadn't been strong enough to stand up to him. I had no intention of letting him try to run my life so I left.'

'He wouldn't have liked that.' Lex frowned, imagining the older man's fury. 'He must have made your life hell. Presumably he tried to get you to go back?'

'He would have had to find me first.'

'You ran away?'

She shot him a sideways stare from under bunched eyebrows. 'Of course I ran away. That was always the plan.'

'To elope with me, not *alone*!'

She'd been barely seventeen and despite their affair, Portia had been in many ways an innocent. She'd been protected from a lot of life's harsh realities. Lex's gut crawled at the idea of her naïve and vulnerable, out on her own.

It wasn't as if she had a lot of friends or relatives she could go to. Most if not all wouldn't stand up to pressure from her father.

'Well, you weren't there, so I had no choice but to go alone. Anyway, I survived. I don't know why you're looking at me like that. I didn't sell myself on the street.'

Lex swallowed hard, tasting fear. He knew how difficult it could be, fending for yourself without a support network. He'd done it himself but he'd been two years older, more experienced and not a pretty young woman.

His skin crawled, thinking about the dangers she'd faced.

He wished her father wasn't dead. Lex would have enjoyed making him pay for his actions.

'How did you support yourself? You didn't have much money.' Her father had controlled her finances.

'I worked as a stablehand for a friend of a friend. Several hundred miles away. I did that for a long time, as well as juggling casual jobs. The pay was never good with my lack of formal qualifications but I got by. The last few years I've worked in London. I didn't bother trying to hide my identity by then.'

Lex could only guess at the effort it had taken to build a CV that took her from mucking out stables to working with the elite of Mayfair.

The stable work made sense. Portia had escaped to the stables and woodland whenever she could. It was her safe place. Where she'd gone after her mother died, stressed not just from grief but, he'd always suspected, from dealing with her bombastic father.

'If my father had wanted to find me he could have but he'd washed his hands of me.'

The man had rarely had time for his daughter, except to show her off to his fancy guests. *Then* he'd been proud of her looks, her equestrian skill and her engaging personality that was such an asset when he had visitors.

'Tell me about the painting, Portia.'

She swung her head around and this time he read emotion stamped on her features, her mouth tightening. Would she tell him it was none of his business?

Instead she shrugged as if humouring him. 'It was all he left me. That's why I sold it. There's an art history course I want to do and the money will give me the freedom to study.'

He was curious and wanted to know her plans. But she was only telling him so much under sufferance.

Despite physical intimacy, over the weekend Portia had only talked about her life in general terms. Movies she'd seen, books she read or the latest world news. Or art, they'd talked about art a lot.

They'd set boundaries around their personal lives. That made sense because this interlude was fleeting, designed to leave them free to move on with their lives.

Yet Lex had begun to chafe at those boundaries.

He hauled his attention back to the conversation. 'Surely, even if the estate is entailed, your father had personal possessions he could bequeath?'

'It's questionable how much he still owned. Money flowed through his hands like water.'

'What about your mother's money?' She'd been wealthy. 'And her jewellery?'

Portia's mouth tightened, as if impatient at his persistent questions. 'I suppose he inherited her money when she died. As for the jewels, last time I saw any, Raine was wearing them.'

Lex opened his mouth then shut it, refusing to release a

stream of useless invective against her father. But it was difficult to hold in his fury.

Portia slanted another sideways glance at him as they stood before the exclusive hotel. She reached out, threading her fingers through his.

'It doesn't matter, Lex. I didn't expect anything from him. That night he threatened all sorts of things, including to disinherit me if I didn't do as he wanted. So it came as no surprise when he did just that. You know he didn't have a forgiving temperament.'

Forgiving temperament! The man had been a narcissist. Totally greedy, self-indulgent and temperamental. It was a wonder his daughter had grown up the way she had, but then Lex's memories of her mother were all positive.

'He still had a duty of care. And surely a legal obligation to leave you something. You were his only child.'

'I think that's why I inherited the painting. To show I hadn't been left out completely, in case I tried to challenge the will.'

'But you didn't challenge it.' He didn't bother to make it a question. He knew the answer.

She looked down at their joined hands. 'There were a few things I'd have liked, some mementos of my mother for instance. But I've got by without them all this time. It would just be sentiment. He probably withheld any trinkets of my mother's, knowing I'd like them.'

Suddenly she smiled. 'But he did me a favour. The money from the sale of the painting is a game changer. Until now I've been busy making ends meet and putting a little money away, but now I've got a financial cushion that means I can work fewer hours and focus on study.'

The double doors before them opened and a staff member emerged, carrying designer luggage down the broad steps towards a waiting car. Behind him in the foyer guests stood talking.

Impatience stirred. This wasn't the place for a private conversation. It also reminded him that their time together was up. Soon they'd leave for the city too.

Holding Portia's hand, he guided her away from curious eyes, towards a side entrance.

It was clear now to Lex that a brief, passionate weekend wouldn't obliterate his need for her.

The feel of her hand against his undid his resolve. Or perhaps it was the proud angle of her chin, making it clear that the details of her past and her future were private. Despite her exuberant, breathless physical hunger for him.

Adrenaline shot through his blood as her hand twitched in his.

He didn't want her emotionally dependent on him.

An emotionally barren childhood with a distant mother had made him wary of relationships. He hadn't known love or been close to anyone. *Until Portia.* Their debacle of a relationship had gutted him, destroying any fragile belief that he was cut out for romantic love.

Business had been his salvation. His thirst to succeed was as strong as ever, fuelled by the need to prove himself, including to his new family. Work and his family were enough for him.

Yet at the same time this, with Portia, wasn't over.

'We—'

'Lex, I—'

'You first,' he invited.

They'd reached the side entrance and Portia slipped her hand from his, shoving it deep into her coat pocket.

A moment ago she'd looked almost regal in her determination, as if bestowing a favour in talking about her father. Suddenly she looked less sure of herself. Her glance darted around before settling near his mouth.

Instantly heat coiled in his groin. He wanted to kiss her again until her hair was mussed, her breathing heavy as she clung to him, eager for more. They'd go to their suite and—

'It's been a fantastic weekend, Lex.' Her voice was low and husky. He felt it like suede stroking his skin. Anticipation stirred. 'I've enjoyed every minute of it.'

He hoped his smile wasn't too smug. 'So have I.'

'I'm glad things have worked out for you and I wish you well in the future.' She drew a deep breath. 'The sex has been...amazing. But there's no future in it. It's better if we don't meet again.'

Suddenly those dark eyes fixed on his. He couldn't believe what he was hearing. He *knew* she felt the current of attraction as strongly as he did. It was there in her face, in her straining body as she leaned closer then shifted back half a step as if afraid to get too near.

'We need to go our separate ways from here. I know you have a flight to Athens later and I can get a lift to the railway station to save you coming all the way into London.'

He was still gathering his stunned thoughts when she went on. 'So thank you, Lex. And goodbye.'

CHAPTER SEVEN

PORTIA POURED HOT water over the teabag, carefully putting the tea canister away then getting milk from the fridge. She paused, drawing a slow breath, before grabbing a cloth and wiping down the already clean kitchen bench. Cloth in hand, she looked around for something else to clean.

Stop being a coward. It's time.

Another slow breath, deeper this time, as she tried to settle the butterflies that felt more like fire-breathing dragons, swooping and diving in her stomach.

Dropping the cloth, she took the three steps needed to reach the end of the bench. To the small plastic item resting there so innocuously.

She didn't touch it. There was no need. The result was clearly visible.

Positive.

She swallowed and it felt like the hardest thing she'd ever done.

That foolishness made her laugh, the sound somewhere between a giggle and a sob. There'd been much harder things in her life than this.

Before she could stop them, memories seeped through the barrier she'd erected against them. Darkness and pain. Grief and raw despair.

She stiffened, forcing them away, focusing on the present.

Riding out the quiver of emotion and shock until her shaky knees strengthened.

She was pregnant. With Lex's baby.

After all these years, to be carrying *his* child.

They weren't even in a relationship! For a brief time they'd come together again, spurred by whispers of the past and a combustible passion that surely stemmed from a sense of matters not resolved between them. But in reality they were strangers now. No matter how amazing their physical compatibility, they both understood their lives no longer intersected.

Lex had taken her at her word. She'd said she didn't want to see him again and he hadn't argued. That confirmed what she'd already told herself, that their relationship lacked depth or meaning. He wanted the sex but that was *all*. The liaison could lead nowhere.

She hadn't seen or heard from him since. He'd dropped her at the station that day, waiting to ensure she made the connection into the city before driving himself to the airport.

Portia hadn't kissed him goodbye, too fearful that any physical contact might weaken her resolution.

Because she'd wanted, badly, to see him again. To prolong the affair. But spending more time with him would only make her weak and dangerously needy for a man who could never be hers.

Her gaze strayed again to the test result.

It was as if fate enjoyed throwing them together, making her confront her weakness.

She was tempted to get out the other kit she'd bought. But this was the second positive result. Did she really need a third? In her heart of hearts she'd known the truth. She'd suspected when she'd first noticed her tender breasts. Had been fatalistically unsurprised when her period was late, even though they'd taken precautions.

She couldn't remember Lex being careless with protection. Which meant theirs had to be one of those few cases that defied probability.

Reaching for her tea, she sank onto a nearby chair. She might have expected the positive result, yet she couldn't get her head around the enormity of it.

Or maybe you're too scared to think about what this means. About what the future might hold.

She raised the mug to her lips, sipping and hoping the routine act of drinking tea would restore a sense of normality to a world that had suddenly turned upside down.

Her laugh was strained in the quiet room. She had the feeling her world would never be *normal* in the way she'd known it again.

But what would it be like, the future? She had some serious thinking to do. She took another sip of tea and found her other hand had slipped down to cover her abdomen.

We need to go our separate ways. Thank you, Lex, and goodbye.

It had been over a month since he'd heard Portia's voice but her words, her tone, were as clear in his head now as they'd been that weekend when she'd dismissed him.

Dismissed him!

Lex ground his teeth as he remembered her matter-of-fact words. As if she had no regrets, no yearning for more.

Was it true? Had she found it easy to turn her back?

Ego whispered it wasn't possible. Not when *he* was still mired in a tangle of frustrated desire.

Or maybe it wasn't that at all. They lived in separate worlds these days. Perhaps she was just better at accepting that. Maybe her willpower and self-control were stronger than his now.

In recent years he'd grown used to getting his own way.

From the little Portia had mentioned about her life after Cropley Hall, there'd been few chances for self-indulgence.

Whatever the reason, it had been a matter of pride that he stay away from her. He refused to pursue a woman who didn't want to be pursued. Which was why he'd resolved not to come to London for the auction.

Except now business brought him to the UK. The reason he'd been at the auction house in the first place was because he'd been meeting researchers in Britain who sought a manufacturing partner for their breakthrough technology.

He turned into a familiar Mayfair street and stifled a grim smile.

Back in the UK again, his decision not to attend the auction in person had seemed ridiculous. He wasn't here to see Portia. She'd be working in a back office. Since his trip coincided with the auction, it made sense to attend. It would be ludicrous to stay away.

He wouldn't seek her out. He'd learnt as an unloved child to accept rejection and move on. If they met, well, they were both adults. She needn't fear he'd try to weasel his way back into her life.

In fact, it would be good if they *did* meet. After the frustrating weeks he'd spent recently, there'd be some satisfaction in showing her he'd moved on.

A sarcastic inner voice disagreed but Lex shut it down. He'd attend the auction, secure the pieces he wanted and walk away.

Easy.

And it was. He was made flatteringly welcome and enjoyed a conversation with a collector he'd met previously, an American interested in more modern pieces but with some fascinating insights. The auction held no major surprises and Lex acquired the pieces he wanted.

He was considering accepting the American's suggestion

that they go for a drink when he felt his nape prickle and his pulse quicken.

Lex inhaled sharply and let his gaze rove the people still clustered, chatting.

Portia wore another skirt and jacket, this time in a deep colour somewhere between blue and purple.

Instantly every sense went on alert. There was a buzz in his ears and a quickening deep in his belly.

How did she do it? Look so alluring and at the same time so buttoned up? Was he the only one aware of her incredible sensual draw? It seemed impossible.

His gaze ate her up. The sweet curves and shapely legs. The way the deep colour of her clothes complemented her blonde hair and dark eyes. The contrast with her porcelain skin, her cheeks blush warm and—

Lex frowned, reading tiredness around eyes that looked bruised.

He didn't owe her sympathy after she'd pushed him away. He'd had his own share of sleepless nights, because of her.

But his chagrin and frustration melted as he really took her in, her body taut as she searched the crowd. She looked… fragile.

Then her gaze met his and he felt that familiar wallop of sensation, like a fist to the chest.

Like homecoming.

Rubbish. They'd once known each other well, that was all. She was, he realised abruptly, the person who'd known him longest. His mother and her uncle were dead and he wasn't in contact with anyone else from childhood. That was all this was. The familiarity of a shared past.

Yet a warning bell jangled in his ears. He turned away, determined to accept the American's invitation to a drink.

Except he heard himself say, 'I'd enjoy that, but another time. I've just seen someone I need to talk with. Perhaps we'll meet at the Copenhagen auction?' He barely registered her response. 'If you'll excuse me?'

Portia wasn't needed in the auction room. She'd come specifically to see him. Yet as he approached she stepped back, half turning as if to leave before halting, eyes fixed on her clasped hands.

Concern scraped his breastbone. 'You wanted to see me, Portia?'

She looked up, her expression veiled. But he'd been right about the tiredness. There were dark shadows beneath her eyes. 'I do. If you're free.'

Portia looked past him, her mouth pursing. Turning, he saw the American looking their way before picking up her bag and leaving. The woman was eye-catching and glamorously chic with her tumble of flame-red hair, slender frame and flamboyant clothes.

But, he realised, he'd only been interested in her knowledge of art, not in her as a woman.

Lex surveyed Portia's expression and felt a fillip of satisfaction. Could that be jealousy she tried to hide?

It shouldn't matter. But concern overrode logic. 'I have a little time.'

For a long moment she was silent. Regretting the impulse that had brought her to him? When she spoke her tone was hard to read. 'Thank you. But we can't talk here. Shall we walk?'

Which is how he found himself, ten minutes later, strolling through a Mayfair park. The sky was pale blue and drifts of daffodils brightened the scene but the air was chilly, a contrast to the warmer weather he'd left in Athens.

Beside him, Portia walked with her arms crossed, yet something about her posture told him it wasn't from cold. That flash of concern he'd felt for her was back.

'What is it, Portia?'

His first thought, when she looked so fragile, was that she'd had bad news. But perhaps it was something different. Perhaps she'd struggled these past weeks too. Maybe she wanted to extend their liaison but wasn't sure how he'd react to the suggestion.

She looked around as if making sure they couldn't be overheard, then nodded towards a nearby seat. 'Let's sit.'

Intrigued, Lex sat beside her on the park bench.

'There's something I need to tell you.'

He waited, but there was no admission that she'd changed her mind. No suggestion that they get back together. Her words seemed to have dried up and with them, his sanguine hope that she wanted to pick up where they'd left off.

Despite the brisk breeze, her cheeks were pale and in the sunlight, the shadows under her eyes darker than he'd thought.

Premonition curdled his belly. Something was wrong. Something major, otherwise she wouldn't have contacted him. Was she ill? His mind rebelled at the thought.

Unable to sit still, he shrugged out of his winter coat and rose to drape it around her shoulders.

Startled eyes met his. 'What's that for?' As if she hadn't even noticed the cold.

Lex lifted his hand from the coat collar, letting the back of his fingers brush her cheek. It was chilled.

But that didn't stop heat igniting when he touched her. His fingers tingled with it and he saw warm colour rise in her face as if that fleeting contact affected her the same way.

It was still there, the attraction, the bond.

He shook his head and sank onto the seat beside her, closer this time.

'You'll be cold. You're not used to this wintry weather.' Yet she didn't take the jacket off.

'You forget the years I spent mucking out stables at dawn,

come rain, hail or snow.' Not to mention the fact that a Greek winter could be cold, especially in the mountains. He'd even learnt to ski there. 'I'm listening, Portia.'

She nodded, twisting on the seat to face him. 'I had some news recently. Unexpected news.'

Lex's heart dived. She looked so sombre. All he could think of was some catastrophic health condition.

He nodded encouragingly though he knew he didn't want to hear this.

Portia looked at the seat between them. Following her gaze he realised he'd reached out to hold her hand. He hadn't even realised he'd done it.

'I'm pregnant, Lex. Pregnant with your child.'

There was no mistaking the words. The sound of them still echoed in his ears. But it was so unexpected he had trouble processing it.

He frowned, trying to make sense of it when he'd expected to hear something quite different. 'Pregnant? But we took precautions, every time.'

He'd left nothing to chance and Portia had always been just as cautious as he, making it clear she didn't want an un-planned pregnancy.

'We did, but nevertheless…' Dark eyes surveyed him se-riously. 'It's a lot to take in, I know. But I'm sure. I've seen a doctor who confirmed it. There's no doubt at all.'

'Pregnant!'

Lex looked as stunned as she'd felt when she got the posi-tive test result.

So that's one thing you've got in common. Apart from sex.

Portia squashed the sarcastic voice. This was hard enough without the reminder of how little they really shared.

As if to confirm that, Lex moved away. The comforting warmth of his encompassing fingers lifted from her hand as he shot to his feet and strode a couple of paces away to pause, one hand raking his scalp, leaving his hair tousled. His other hand shoved deep in his pocket, pulling his trousers tight to mould the curve of his buttocks.

Her mouth dried. Not this time with nerves but with awareness. For a second she squeezed her eyes shut. When, she wondered, would that be over? When would she be able to look at Lex and not want him?

What if it's never? whispered that voice in her head. But she refused to heed it. She couldn't allow that to be possible.

He swung around and she read the harsh lines furrowing his brow and clamping his mouth. He didn't look happy.

She told herself it would be unfair to judge his response when he was obviously in shock. She hadn't smiled at the news either, too overcome by surprise and the weight of worry for the future. If they'd been in a loving relationship, or if she'd decided she wanted to be a single mother, things would be different.

Portia *was* excited. Even though she knew it was early days.

Life had taught her that while joy could be found, just as often there were obstacles and challenges. Like what a millionaire father-to-be would expect.

She studied Lex's stern profile. Would he want to be a hands-off father, only providing financial support? She couldn't imagine he'd wash his hands of the baby totally, though who knew how a baby would fit his plans. Maybe he had some sophisticated Greek woman in mind for when he decided to settle down. Another woman's baby wouldn't be welcome then.

Or maybe when the news sank in he'd be thrilled. Would he want to spend time with his child? Visiting the UK regularly?

He turned, denim-blue eyes meeting hers. 'Pregnant with my child.'

It sounded like a statement rather than a question but Portia sat straighter. 'It's definitely yours. I haven't been with anyone else.'

She bit her lip before she said anymore. Better to let him think she meant there'd been no one else since he came to the auction house. There was no need for him to know she'd never had another lover.

At first she'd been too heartbroken and too busy working long hours to support herself to think about a boyfriend. And somehow over time it had become natural to keep her distance.

Life was easier alone. Better to think that than let herself admit she'd never met another man who tempted her the way Lex did.

His eyes narrowed, his gaze boring into her as if trying to read her very soul and every secret she possessed. It took everything to sit there and meet that penetrating stare.

'I wasn't questioning it, Portia. I was just…coming to terms. Are you keeping it?'

She stiffened. 'Yes.'

He nodded. Did that signify acceptance or pleasure? But what did it matter? Either way, she was committed to this pregnancy. And glad she didn't have to argue about paternity with him. One of the benefits, she supposed, of their shared past. He knew she was truthful.

'Thank you,' he murmured.

Portia blinked. She wasn't sure what she'd expected but it wasn't thanks for not wanting to terminate the pregnancy. Some of the tension bled from her shoulders and spine. She felt herself slump lower on the seat.

'Have you thought about where you want to have it?'

Again he surprised her. 'A hospital in London, I suppose. I hadn't got that far.'

It was still a long way away.

She remembered her mother saying she hadn't wanted to

buy a pram until just before Portia was born, superstitiously fearing to tempt fate. Portia understood that fear. There were too many things that could go wrong in a pregnancy.

'Why do you ask?'

'You could have excellent medical care in Athens.'

Her gaze shot to his. 'Athens?'

Too many half-formed thoughts shot through her brain. Did he want his child born there to get Greek citizenship? Did he want to raise it there without her? Her heart hammered. It was a crazy idea. Lex would never try to do such a thing.

But he wasn't the boy she'd once known, was he? For all their shared memories and passion, he was Lex Tomaras now, a rich man living and working in a foreign land with phenomenal resources at his disposal. A virtual stranger, except in bed.

'Why would I have the baby in Athens?'

He spread his hands and lifted his straight shoulders in a gesture that seemed at once totally Mediterranean and surprisingly enticing.

'It would make sense. If you married me.'

CHAPTER EIGHT

'MARRY?'

The word escaped as a yelp so loud a couple of pigeons strutting in hopes of a feed took off in a whir of wings. A woman approaching with a pram stared hard then took a turning onto another path.

Portia noticed all that even though her gaze was fixed on the man before her. For something strange had happened, time slowing, the air around them thickening while she became aware of so many sensations she'd never noticed before. The weight of her eyelids as she blinked. The frenetic rush of her pulse. The effort it took to fill her lungs.

'It seems a sensible solution.'

Solution. Did he see their child as a problem? Her mouth flattened as she processed that. She hadn't missed his frown when she told him the news, but she'd put that down to surprise. Now she wondered.

'Sensible? It sounds completely Victorian.'

Now his frown was back, edging towards a scowl, and still he was the most compelling, attractive man she'd ever known.

Pregnancy hormones had a lot to answer for. This was the man who'd left her without a second thought. Who'd broken her heart.

'Victorian?' He faced her full on now, feet planted wide, hands deep in his pockets in a stance that accentuated the breadth of his shoulders and the strength in his long frame.

At nineteen he'd been slender and rangy, tough from working in the stables. Now he'd filled out to the lean strength of a powerful man in his prime. 'You think it's old-fashioned to want to raise my child? To give it a family?'

The tight knot beneath her ribs pulled loose and suddenly her breath came more easily. His intentions were good. He was thinking of their child.

Their child. Even now she couldn't quite believe it. Despite the sleeplessness and the recent hints of nausea, it was hard to get her head around the idea that this baby was real.

'I'm glad to know you want to be involved.' Even if it did complicate matters for her. 'That you're thinking of our child's best interests. But families come in all shapes and sizes. We don't have to marry for the baby's sake.'

Slowly he shook his head, his gaze never leaving hers. 'The girl I knew would never have hesitated to say yes. We'd planned to spend our lives together, remember?'

'Oh, I remember.' She suspected she'd carried the remnants of those hopes longer than he had. Sometimes even now she woke from dreams of them together, only to discover the life they'd built was imaginary, not real. 'But that was a long time ago, Lex. Things have changed. We're different people.'

He shrugged. 'And yet we're about to become parents.'

In the folds of his encompassing coat she crossed her fingers.

'We're still strangers.' Seeing him raise one disbelieving eyebrow she clarified. 'You know we are, Lex. A decade is a long time and a tumble or two in bed isn't the same as real intimacy. It's no basis for marriage. What if we married and found we couldn't get on? What would that do to our child? Far better to live apart but cooperate to raise our baby than to make a terrible mistake.'

'You've changed. I don't recall the Portia I knew being so negative.'

'Not negative. Cautious. I'm not an impulsive teenager anymore. I've learnt life isn't as simple as I once believed. Sometimes hoping just isn't enough.'

His dark eyebrows arrowed down, his mouth turning grim, and she knew he too was thinking about how their dream of a life together had shattered.

At seventeen she hadn't believed it possible that anything short of death would keep them apart. The naïveté of youth!

'So you're not opposed to marriage as such?'

Portia stared. 'How did we even get onto this? Shouldn't we be talking about the baby?'

'That's what I'm trying to do.'

She heard an undercurrent of impatience and realised how unfamiliar it was now. She hadn't heard that since they'd met in London. As a teenager he couldn't wait to leave, his impatience like an electrical charge humming through him.

'By pushing me into a wedding?'

His head jerked back. 'Not pushing. Just raising the most obvious option. We might not be in love and, yes, we don't know each other as well as we used to, but we share enough to know we're compatible. A lot of marriages begin with less.'

His voice took on a husky burr as he said *compatible*, and she felt it brush across her skin, making her flesh pebble and her nipples bead.

The glint in his eyes told her she wasn't the only one thinking about sexual compatibility.

They had weighty matters to decide. They were in a public place and she had to return to work soon. Yet all she could think of was Lex taking her hand and leading her to a nearby luxury hotel. There'd be a huge, comfortable bed and they'd find such delight together that it would obliterate, for a short time, her anxiety about the future.

Portia licked dry lips and saw his eyelids flicker. A thread of excitement wound through her abdomen, drawing her insides tight.

'Or are you trying to tell me you're no longer attracted to me, Portia?'

Damn the man. Did he have no sensitivity?

Not when it comes to getting his own way, said that voice in her head.

Even with the backing of his wealthy father, Lex would never have become a billionaire in his own right without a ruthless streak. And phenomenal determination.

She saw both ruthlessness and determination now in the forward thrust of his chin and the searing intensity of his calculating stare.

Portia wanted to feel disgusted. Instead, rising to her feet to face him, she experienced a rush of energy that warmed her body as even his cashmere coat hadn't.

Instead of the tiredness and anxiety that had weighed her down, she felt more alive. More like herself.

'Our baby's future *won't* be decided by whether or not we're attracted.' She made a slicing gesture with one hand. 'Attraction is fleeting. Like our teenage love affair. We need to make decisions that will stand the test of time.'

For a second she thought Lex looked taken aback. Had she punctured his ego by not admitting she was still drawn to him? Had he hoped she still yearned for him?

He folded his hands across his chest. 'Okay then, what did *you* have in mind for our baby?'

His words deflated her. That rush of indignant adrenaline faded, leaving her flat. That was the problem. She didn't know.

'At this stage all I wanted to do was tell you the news and find out if you want to be involved.'

His eyes widened as if surprised she had to ask. 'I *want* to be involved.'

'Good.' She paused, swallowing. 'There's time enough to discuss the details later.'

'Why not now?'

Because she was still struggling to absorb the news.

'There are so many variables for a start.'

Keen eyes surveyed her. Lex's taut expression eased and he gestured to the bench seat. 'Shall we sit for a while?'

She looked at the time but knew she was searching for excuses to end this conversation.

Surely he didn't intimidate her so much? She should be thankful he wanted an active role. Thankful too that he'd accepted her word that the baby was his. From what she heard, some men wouldn't.

Maybe Lex hadn't changed so much after all.

Portia sat. He took a seat beside her, but with a telling distance between them.

She should be glad, because being too close to Lex interfered with her thought processes. Yet an insubordinate part of her brain longed for the time when they'd have automatically snuggled up together, his arm around her, her head at his collarbone.

'What sort of variables are you thinking about, Portia?'

She turned to see the martial light in his eyes had died. He looked approachable rather than intimidating. Nevertheless it was easier to stare out at the people crossing the green space.

'If you want a role in our baby's life for one thing.'

'We've established I do.'

Portia drew a slow breath. 'Well, that will be good for the baby. It just makes things a little complicated.'

It would have been a struggle raising a child alone, but at least she wouldn't have had to negotiate decisions around custody and so on.

'You really imagined I wouldn't want anything to do with my child?'

She turned back to him. 'I didn't like to assume. I don't really know anything about your life. For all I know you might be planning to marry some nice Greek woman. Raising a child might get in the way of that.'

'No child of mine would ever be *in the way*.' He spoke through gritted teeth. 'And for the record, I wasn't planning marriage.'

'Because you're a committed bachelor? Not everyone is cut out to have a family and children.'

There was stir of emotion in Lex's expression but she couldn't read it. 'I'm not against marriage.'

'Yet you haven't married.' Because what he'd once shared with her had been so special? Or because he'd outgrown the idea of romance?

Or maybe his single status has nothing to do with you.

'I've been busy, building my business and a relationship with my family. That takes most of my time.'

'Of course. I understand.'

His expression suggested he thought she didn't, but it was a dead-end subject.

'So the question really is how we parent between us. How involved you want to be.'

'Totally. This is my child. I want total involvement. I would be there every step of the way.'

'That may not be possible. We live in different countries and—'

'It would be easy enough if we married.'

Portia breathed out through her nose, counting a slow breath before inhaling again. 'Parents can raise a child jointly without living together.'

Those sardonic eyebrows lifted. 'You envisaged freighting our child between England and Greece every week?'

'I didn't envisage anything! I didn't *know*! That's what I

wanted to discuss.' She wrapped her arms around herself, trying to hold in frustration and nerves.

'It would be easier if you moved to Greece.'

'Or if you moved to London.'

He stared straight back at her, not bothering to voice the fact that his business was based in Greece. 'I want to be there every day for our child. I don't want what happened between my father and me. We were wrenched apart and missed all those years when we could have been together.'

Aghast, Portia stared. 'I'd never deliberately keep you apart!' She knew how that separation had blighted Lex's early life. 'I'm not like your mother.'

A brief smile teased the corners of his mouth. 'I know. And for the record, I'm not like your father. If you're hesitating because you don't trust my character—'

'It's not that, Lex. It's just that I don't know how it will work between us.'

He sat back, shoving a hand through his hair, leaving it ruffled. The sight reminded her of the sensual, earthy lover who made her forget everything but him. Her heart jolted.

'At least we've got a starting point now you've listed all your variables.' He must have read something in her face because his eyes narrowed. 'There's more?'

Portia shrugged a shoulder and turned to watch a woman in a scarlet coat walk down the path. She breathed deeply, intent on keeping her voice steady. 'Only the obvious one. The pregnancy might not go to term.'

Lex felt her words like a boulder smashing into his belly. He stiffened, muscles screaming with tension.

It was confounding. He'd known about the baby for half an hour yet it already was real to him. He imagined holding their child in his arms. Being a father.

Having his own family. His flesh and blood.

Could he do it? Could he get past the taint of early experience and learn how to raise a child? He shoved aside the doubts. He *would* do it.

Emotion seared him. The possibility of their child not surviving hadn't even occurred to him. The idea wrenched at something deep in his chest.

His gaze traced Portia's profile, lingering on soft lips held too tight and the upward thrust of her chin, as if defying fate to play such a cruel trick.

The anxiety she strove to hide was tangible, as real as the baby she carried. That drained away his indignation at her prickly stubbornness.

It struck him now that however real their unborn child was to him, his perception was nothing compared with that of the woman beside him whose body was even now changing to accommodate and protect that new life.

Lex felt awed, the gravity and true wonder of the situation swamping him.

How could he be annoyed at Portia's caution? At her need to proceed carefully?

He reached out and covered her clenched fist. It was cold and he gently rubbed it between his palms.

'The chance of that happening is slim.'

'Yes,' she said at last. 'You're right. There's no point anticipating the worst.'

'None at all.' Yet he didn't move his hands from hers. He liked the feel of it, her flesh warm now and soft beneath his calloused fingers. 'Let's take it one step at a time. Okay?'

Her head swung around and for the first time a genuine smile flitted across her lips. 'Okay.'

'One thing I can do is make sure you get the best medical care.'

'There's no need. The NHS—'

'Is a wonderful institution, but the public health system

is stretched and I have money. I can at least get you an early appointment with a top obstetrician.' He paused. 'Just so you know everything's normal. It might put your mind at ease.'

Portia hesitated for a moment before inclining her head. 'Thank you. That's kind.'

Kind? It was the least he could do. Portia and their baby were his responsibility, the need to protect them a compulsion. But he knew now wasn't the time to press her. He'd bide his time and find a way to persuade her around to his way of thinking.

'When do you have to be back in the office?'

'Now. We're busy. As it is I'll be working late.'

Lex wanted to protest that she needed to get plenty of rest, not work long hours. But he bit his tongue. She wouldn't thank him for fussing. Instead he stood and held out his hand. 'Shall we?'

Portia blinked as if the change of subject caught her off guard then rose, starting to shrug out of his coat. 'You must be freezing.'

His hand on her shoulder stopped her. 'Keep it on. I'm warm enough. Though perhaps you can share your body heat as we go.'

He used that excuse to step near and draw her arm through his. He wanted to scoop her into his arms like some precious, breakable objet d'art. He wanted to cosset her. But he knew she'd resist.

Lex tucked her close as they turned back the way they'd come. Walking like this ignited so many memories of them together. It reinforced too, how well they fit together.

'No matter what happens, Portia, I'll do everything I can to support you. You're not alone in this pregnancy.'

He felt a shiver pass through her and he pulled her closer to his side. 'Thank you, Lex. I appreciate that. There's nothing you can do, but I'd be grateful for that appointment.'

'I'll get the details to you tonight.'

'When do you go back to Greece? Tonight?'

He hesitated. He'd planned to return to Athens, but after hearing her news that was on hold. 'No, not straight away. I've got some outstanding business.'

No need to mention he'd completed his meetings. That *she* was his outstanding business.

He let the silence lengthen as they walked. Despite his calm demeanour, Lex was buffeted by a chaotic tumble of feelings.

Awe, excitement and nerves at the news of the baby.

Did he have what it took to be a good dad? A good husband? Surely his abysmal childhood would drive him to do better for his child and its mother?

He was determined to try. The thought of their baby made him feel…different. Not just protective but proud. Determined to provide all that he'd lacked in his own childhood.

But mixed with the excitement and determination was a deep pang of regret and indignation. When he'd suggested marriage, Portia hadn't seen it as he had. She'd described what they'd shared as a mere 'tumble in bed', not intimacy.

Amazingly Lex had felt pain shear through him at her words.

True, their liaison was founded on sexual attraction. True, he'd told himself giving in to their lust would finally wear it out. Yet there'd been a spark of something, surely. Something positive they could build on for the sake of their baby.

Given their history he understood her reticence. But part of him had hoped she still felt *something* for him. Was that pride or the last remnant of the lovesick kid he thought he'd shed years ago?

It saddened him too, when she said she wasn't impulsive anymore, that life wasn't simple and hoping for good things wasn't enough. It was all true, as any adult knew. Yet he found himself mourning the loss of the optimistic, sometimes impulsive girl who'd meant so much to him.

He realised that if it hadn't been for Portia, believing in him, caring for him as no one else seemed to, his life might have taken a different path. She'd softened his rough edges. Living up to her expectations had probably prevented him becoming the sort of lout her father had accused him of being.

That Lex had been partly responsible for that change in her, because he'd believed her father's lies and left without her, sat like a dead weight of rusty iron in his belly. The metallic taste of it coated his tongue.

He *owed* her. He'd let her down once. He wouldn't do it again. Somehow he'd find a way to make this work between them.

He was concerned for her. She'd been wan and fretful. He knew she was alone with no one to care for her. No one to turn to if something went wrong.

'I have a proposition,' he said as they turned out of the park and onto the street. 'I want you to come to Greece.'

She stiffened and shook her head. 'I already said no to marriage.'

'This is a different proposition.' He paused, conjuring his most persuasive voice. 'Work is stressful and you're tired. You're worried about the pregnancy and the future too. Why not take a short holiday, a week or two, and come to Greece? You can relax, do absolutely nothing but recharge your batteries and soak up the spring sunshine.'

'I can't just take a holiday at the drop of a hat. I told you we're busy.'

'I'm not talking about leaving tomorrow. But consider it.' If necessary he knew he could persuade her manager to give her leave. 'Sunshine and relaxation, doesn't that sound good? You'd be my guest. I'll arrange the travel so you won't have to do anything but pack a bag, and you'd stay at my villa.' He paused. 'In your own suite.'

He'd prefer to have her in his, but knew he had to give her space if he wanted any chance she'd come around his way of thinking.

Portia sent him a knowing, sideways look. 'You think spending time there will persuade me to marry you?'

He allowed himself a rueful smile. 'Well, it can't hurt. Greece in spring is beautiful. The countryside is full of wild-flowers. I can imagine you there.'

The images in his head were so vivid they might have been memories. Portia calf deep in flowers, bending to pick scarlet poppies. Portia laughing as she bobbed to the surface of the sparkling aquamarine shallows off his private beach.

Portia beckoning him to her as she lay sprawled on his wide bed.

They turned down another street and a chill wind buffeted them.

'Have you ever been to Greece?'

'I've never left the UK apart from a school trip to Paris.'

Did she realise how wistful she sounded?

'There are some wonderful art galleries in Athens.'

She laughed, her amusement making his heart lift. 'You don't give up, do you?'

'Not when something is important. You're important to me, Portia. So is our child,' he continued quickly. 'Think about it. A short trip with no strings attached. At least you'll find out what the place is like. Then when you come back to London you'll feel better.'

She regarded him as if sifting his words for hidden traps. Then she inclined her head. 'Thank you. I'll think about it.'

Portia felt a weight rise from her shoulders as she emerged from her obstetrician's appointment.

She was still amazed at how fast Lex had secured the appointment, and that the doctor seemed to have all the time in the world for the consultation.

The woman had been thorough, patient and encouraging, allaying the most urgent of Portia's concerns.

It turned out the slight spotting of blood several days previously wasn't uncommon. She was to report it if it happened again but it wasn't necessarily a sign of impending miscarriage. All seemed well for now.

'You look like you've had good news.'

Portia looked up to find Lex waiting for her on the pavement.

She should have expected him, even though she'd declined his offer to drive her to the appointment.

Reading his expression, a mix of excitement—and was that nerves?—she didn't have the heart to protest. It was good that he was concerned about the baby's welfare.

'I have. Everything seems on track so far.' It was only now that she realised how incredibly tense she'd been, nervous about the baby and the future.

'That's fantastic! Shall we celebrate? There's an excellent restaurant just around the corner.'

His delight made her silly heart flutter. As if he were excited to be with her, not just because the baby was okay.

'I'm sorry, I have to get back to work.'

His enthusiastic expression faded as he turned to walk beside her but he didn't protest.

A man like her father would have complained that a lunch date was the least she could do, since he'd pulled strings to get the early appointment with a top specialist.

It was ridiculous to make comparisons between Lex and her dad. Lex had never been like her horrible father.

But nor had he been the fairytale hero she'd believed in her youth. His belief in her hadn't been as unwavering as hers in him. She'd trusted him but it had been one-sided.

'Thanks again for getting the appointment.'

'It was nothing.' He turned, his gaze catching hers. 'You know I want to help. Apart from the fact it's my child too, it's important you have someone to care for you. Someone to look out for you.'

'You do know I've been looking after myself for over a decade? I'm quite capable.'

His smile was a rueful twist of the lips that only made him more approachable, for it reminded her of years gone by when they'd shared secrets no one else knew.

'I'm fully aware of that, Portia. I've never met a woman so completely determined *not* to ask anything of me.'

She couldn't help it. Immediately she began to wonder about the women who'd wanted his support. Were they friends, workmates, lovers? What had he felt for them?

'I'm not trying to make you dependent, or clip your wings. But sometimes it's good to know you're not alone. To have someone to back you up. Is that so hard to accept?'

Strangely, it *was*.

Portia had friends but none as close as she'd once been to Lex. There were friends who'd do a favour if they saw her struggling or if she asked. But none who'd be there for her and her baby no matter what. None as close as family.

Her breath was a shocked snatch of air.

Lex was the closest thing she had now to family.

She blinked and fixed her eyes on the pavement as they walked side-by-side. She'd never met the distant cousin who'd taken over Cropley Hall.

Lex was no relative and his suggestion of marriage brought with it so many unresolved feelings that she couldn't imagine ever agreeing to it.

But he was related to her baby.

Of course he wants to be there if you need him. He's ex-

cited by the idea of fatherhood. If he looks after you, he's also looking after his child.

Portia didn't know whether to be relieved or disappointed.

But the woman who'd made her own way as a teenager with nothing but a small backpack, a meagre amount of hard-won pounds and a determination never to look back, told her not to be stupid. His offer of support was genuine. She didn't have the luxury to be disappointed that his focus was the child, not her.

She'd be foolish to want that. Lex's 'love' for her had been unreliable, dying at the first test. But she knew his commitment to their baby was different. A neglected child himself, he'd do everything to ensure their baby had all he'd lacked.

She remembered the doctor's advice. That she needed plenty of rest and sleep. That she should accept help when it was offered if it meant reducing her stress.

Her lips twisted in a grimace. Surely there was stress involved in accepting Lex's help?

But she didn't want to wear herself out then find she'd endangered her child.

He might have read her mind. Or perhaps he'd been biding his time, not wanting to rush her straight away. 'Have you thought anymore about coming to Greece?'

Portia drew a deep breath. 'Actually, I think that would be good. *Just* for a week or two. *If* I can get time off.'

His sudden grin and the feel of his hand grasping hers made her heart leap and a rush of longing course through her. 'You won't regret it. I think you'll enjoy it there. And if nothing else, you'll come back refreshed.'

She told herself he was right. This was the sensible thing to do.

But deep within stirred a premonition that she'd taken an unwary step, setting in motion things over which she had no control.

CHAPTER NINE

LEX TOOK PORTIA'S HAND, helping her from the helicopter, enjoying her look of dazzled delight.

He'd wondered if the flight to Athens would tire her. There were still smudges of shadow beneath her eyes, but her pleasure as the chopper took them over Athens then across the Saronic Gulf had eased his concern.

'I never realised the sea could be so blue. And to see the Parthenon from the air...' She smiled at him and his fingers tightened reflexively around hers. That smile. 'It's brilliant. Thank you, Lex.'

She'd said she'd never been in a helicopter before. He was glad to be able to give her that experience.

Gladder still to be the recipient of that stunning smile. He reminded himself that his focus was getting her to relax and, in time, agree to his proposal. *That* was why her happiness made him feel good.

'I'm pleased you like it.'

In her pale trousers and vivid red top she looked like the vivacious girl he'd fallen for all those years ago. In this moment there were no doubts or boundaries, just pure joy.

It was a rare thing. Even in the short time they'd been reunited and become lovers again, he'd sensed hidden constraint. They'd given themselves to each other with physical abandon. Yet Portia kept back part of herself.

He'd done the same. Neither were those naïve youngsters

who'd believed love conquered all, ready to lay hearts and souls completely bare.

Seeing her now, her pleasure unfettered, Lex realised how much he'd missed. How much more there was to Portia than the sexy woman capable of satisfying, even outstripping his erotic fantasies.

He wanted to hoard her joy like a miser hoarded gold.

He wanted her to look at him like that every day.

He'd missed her, he acknowledged.

'This is yours?'

Her sweeping gaze took in this end of the island, the forest to their left and to the right his villa with its informal garden that meandered down to the beach.

'It's a very small island.'

She frowned. 'You own your *own* island?'

'There's an old monastery on the far side of the hill but it's deserted now.'

He didn't explain that the church had let him buy the property for a sizeable sum. Some people were awed by his money, but Portia wasn't one. He remembered her comments about some of her father's guests. She was used to mixing with wealthy people. But she'd never been impressed by people who flaunted their money, or expected it to excuse rudeness or a sense of entitlement.

Is that how she saw him? Arrogantly flaunting his wealth? He wasn't going to apologise for his success.

'I was living and working in Athens but wanted somewhere quiet to come home to.' He gestured to the far side of the garden that gave way to a grove of twisted, venerable olive trees surrounded by a froth of wildflowers. 'It's peaceful. I do some of my best thinking here.'

She nodded, her smile returning as she took in the view. 'The scenery is totally different but it reminds me of the field below the woodland at Cropley.'

Lex remembered the tranquil place with its rich scent of growing things. Sheltered by forest on three sides, it had an otherworldly air. It had been one of her favourite places to escape when her bombastic father made life difficult. 'I remember—'

'Do you commute by helicopter every day?' she said quickly, making him wonder if she felt she'd revealed too much. Her expression now was unreadable and he sensed she'd shut a door on him. Or was it on her past?

'Not usually. It's a short trip by boat to Piraeus, Athens' port. I brought you by air because it's quicker from the airport than travelling by road to the port then making the crossing. I wanted the trip as fast and easy as possible for you.'

'That's kind. Thank you.'

Lex led her towards the house. He wanted to protest it wasn't kind. It was what a man did for his…

What? Lover? Fiancée? She hasn't agreed to marry you yet.

But she would. He'd make it happen. He was determined to look after her and their child.

Portia stopped at a curve on the path, the sun turning her dark honey hair to old gold. The spring breeze was cool, ruffling her hair, but the sun was warm. The English drizzle was a distant memory. 'Thanks for offering this holiday, Lex. A fortnight taking time out from work is what I need.'

Her tone wasn't that of a lover. Her gratitude was genuine he knew, but she sounded like she spoke to a stranger. Her voice was polite but edging towards brisk, like someone determined to be upbeat. It struck a discordant note after her unfettered enthusiasm moments ago.

She was putting up barriers.

Why had he thought that coming here would make everything easier?

'It's the least I can do.' He caught her eye and held it, willing her to see how invested he was. 'You know I want what's best for you and the baby.'

'I know.' She paused. 'And you know that in coming here I'm not agreeing to anything else.'

There it was. Not just a barrier but a solid wall topped with razor wire. She was warning him off, keeping him at a distance.

As if what they'd shared, and the future they'd face together, didn't matter. He understood her caution. Their ill-fated affair had scarred them both. Yet it frustrated him that she couldn't see the obvious, that creating a family for their child was the best way forward. He was willing to put aside his doubts about a permanent relationship and embrace the future. Surely she could do the same.

'Don't worry, Portia. You made it clear what you thought of my marriage proposal.' That still smarted. He'd never suggested marriage to anyone else and her vehement rejection had been an unpleasant shock. He was only trying to do right by all of them. 'My housekeeper has prepared a separate suite for you.'

Colour rose in Portia's cheeks, yet she held his gaze steadily as she nodded.

Damn it! He didn't need to be reminded that it was *her* choice whether she slept with him. Or whether she accepted his proposal. He *knew* that. He'd just hoped she'd changed her mind.

Hoped or assumed?

Perhaps his business success had made him complacent. He was used to setting goals and achieving them. To winning over wary collaborators and investors. To getting his own way. Of course there'd been failures along the way. He'd learnt from them and built his business better as a result.

But he'd grown used to success.

'I just don't want there to be any misunderstanding between us, Lex.'

He heard it then, the exhaustion that had dogged her in London and that her enthusiasm for the flight had hidden.

The sound was like a bucket of ice water dumped on his head, or more precisely, his ego. What did anything matter besides her well-being and the baby's? He had plenty of time to win her round.

Lex unlocked his jaw and made himself smile. 'You're right. It's better to have these things out in the open.' He turned and gestured for her to walk with him. 'Now we've got that sorted, let me show you the house. I hope you like it. If there's anything you want at any time, just ask.'

Portia heard a buzzing and drowsily opened her eyes. Nearby a bee emerged from a pink flower and flew unsteadily past her. Drunk on pollen and sunshine, she thought. Much like herself. She felt lazy and relaxed. Even the burgeoning nausea had evaporated. There'd been no more spotting either, which eased her stress levels enormously.

The book she'd been reading lay open beside her, pages riffling in the slight breeze. The old olive tree above her rustled, silver green leaves moving against the bright blue sky. The scents of nectar and some pungent herb, oregano maybe, filled her nostrils. And the sea too. She lifted her head, propping it on her arm, to survey the sickle of white sand against the clear water at the bottom of the slope.

This place really was paradise, incredibly beautiful and perfectly peaceful. How foolish she'd been to resist coming here. Every day she'd felt her tension ease, her worries erode under the Greek sun. Good food and lots of rest had worked magic this last week.

When Lex had announced he was staying on the island,

Portia had assumed he'd try to press his case for marriage. Or tempt her into bed. She'd tensed, ready to repel him.

Her huff of laughter held a self-derisory note.

Clearly she'd overestimated her allure. He'd turned off his passion as easily as water in a tap.

Lex had told her he respected her decision and, instead of cajoling or pressing her, he'd treated her simply like a welcome guest. As if they'd never been intimate. As if his desire for her had died.

And as if it didn't matter to him one way or another.

It was what you wanted.

But perversely his ability to regard her with easy friendship and no hint of attraction left her feeling flat. He seemed to find a platonic relationship *easy*. That unsettled her.

Portia had wanted not to be crowded. She'd needed space to think. She couldn't do that when she and Lex were physically intimate because he clouded her thinking, and now more than ever she needed to think clearly. Their affair had been amazing, sexually fulfilling yet at the same time it had left her perpetually yearning for more.

She needed physical distance to keep her perspective.

What she hadn't realised was that *not* having Lex, yet sharing a house with him, even one as vast as this, would be so distracting.

Distracting! She thought of him all the time. She *felt* his presence. Her skin prickled whenever he was near, just waiting for him to reach out and caress her. A caress that never came.

He filled her days and nights, even though he spent most of his days working. He respected her privacy, usually seeing her only at mealtimes when he proved to be a perfect host, thoughtful, cheerful and engaging.

Portia enjoyed their conversations, loved the way he challenged her intellectually yet laughed easily. He made it easy to forget he was a now self-made billionaire. He'd done his best to help her enjoy her stay and put aside some of her anxieties about the future.

But there was a price to pay for all that.

She looked forward to being with him. The way his deep blue eyes lit with laughter. The occasional wordless understanding that she supposed came from sharing so much in the past. There was a lot they didn't know about each other these days, yet she knew Lex better than she knew anybody else in the world.

Knew him and wanted him.

Abruptly she sat up, leaning back against the tree and wrapping her arms around her knees.

How had she got into this situation?

She should be making decisions for the future, for the baby. Yet whenever she tried she found herself dwelling on Lex's suggestion that they marry.

It was an outrageous idea. He'd taken her heart and stomped on it. While she was a stronger woman now, the notion of sharing her life with him scared her. Did she trust her emotions not to lead her astray again?

Madness to think of them trying to sustain a long-term relationship with no basis other than sex and a shared child. But the idea kept creeping back into her head.

Something moved on the other side of the olive grove. She turned her head and there he was, walking towards her.

Her breath snagged in her lungs. Lex was such a *physical* man with his leanly muscled torso and long, strong legs. He moved with a fluidity that reminded her how easy he'd always been in his own skin. How athletic.

Portia's gaze skated across his black polo shirt and long khaki shorts, drinking in the proud set of his shoulders and the outline of powerful thighs.

She released a shuddering exhalation, the pungent scent

of wild herbs intensifying as her hands curled into the plants beside her.

Each day it grew harder to resist him.

If he even wants you anymore! Maybe you did him a favour saying you wanted separate beds. He seems happy sleeping alone now.

'Portia.' He smiled but she couldn't read his eyes behind his sunglasses. 'I thought you'd like a drink.'

He hunkered beside her, unpacking the picnic basket his housekeeper, Aspasia, must've packed. As well as the promised drink there were grapes, fragrant little cheese pies wrapped in thin, papery pastry and walnut biscuits dripping with honey syrup. Her mouth watered.

It was easier to focus on the goodies in the basket than on Lex. He smelt so good that her nostrils flared, trying to absorb more of that tantalising male scent.

'You mind if I join you?'

It would be churlish to refuse. She held out her hand in invitation. 'Please.'

'How's the work going?' she asked when the picnic was unpacked and he lounged nearby, looking at the view and munching on one of Aspasia's cheese pies.

'Good. Very good. We've had a bit of a breakthrough in our discussions with the British research team.'

Portia and Lex hadn't discussed their work. In England they'd been too busy assuaging the storm of passion that had engulfed them. Here on the island their conversations had been carefully general. Portia had steered clear of anything too personal and had deliberately reined in her curiosity about Lex's world beyond the island. He, the perfect host, had followed her lead.

But what was the harm in discovering more? Whatever decisions they made, Lex would remain in her life, father to her child.

Her deliberate decision in London, *not* to discover more about Lex's business and family—as if that would cement the distance between them and keep her safe—seemed farcical now. The more she knew, the better she'd understand him. Better for herself and their baby.

Besides, she *wanted* to know more. 'These are the discussions you were having on your visits to London?'

'That's right. My time there has paid off.'

He bit into the pastry and she watched him chew.

Since when had the everyday sight of a man eating become so fascinating?

It was ludicrous, yet she had to tear her attention away instead of reaching out to brush a crumb of pastry off his lips. Already she imagined the feel of those lips against her fingers.

'They're hard negotiators, these researchers?'

He shrugged, apparently unsurprised by her curiosity. 'They have specific criteria they want locked in before they decide to partner with any production company.'

'Really? I thought researchers would be glad to find investors who'd manufacture their product.'

His gaze snared hers. 'That's just it. To what extent does it remain their product once they partner with a company that will turn their concept into a commercial product? There are questions about how their ideas will be used.'

Portia frowned. 'They think you'll misuse their inventions?'

'Not me personally, or my company. But they've learnt to be wary, with good reason. We produce medical devices and technology. Most medical researchers are motivated by the desire to help people. They see themselves making the world a better place. But there are cases where companies acquired breakthroughs, commercialised them and only those with plenty of money benefited from them.'

She sat straighter. 'That's not right.'

'I agree. Our business model is different. We establish strong partnerships with research teams, and we're serious about their desire to make life-changing inventions widely available. We're still driven by the need to make profits, but make specific commitments to our research partners. For instance, a percentage of all our products is either available at cost or donated to communities around the world that couldn't otherwise afford them.'

Portia felt a glow deep inside. 'That's wonderful!'

He shrugged. 'The interesting thing is that our ethical stance has attracted a flood of innovators and investors. Our profits have soared and new opportunities keep beckoning.'

'And you're making a difference to people's lives. You must be proud.'

'I am. It was a hard road to success, but we've built a great team and we're going from strength to strength.'

She saw the glitter in his eyes, heard the enthusiasm in his voice and felt a thrill of pride at what he'd achieved. What he was still achieving.

'How did you get into that? You mentioned working in a restaurant in Athens, not in medical research.'

He laughed. 'I'm a businessman, not an inventor or tech expert. My forte is identifying opportunities, bringing the right resources together and making it happen.'

Portia suspected that 'making it happen' was nowhere near as easy as he made it sound. It sounded complex and challenging, especially for a start-up company.

When he saw her waiting for more information he went on. 'I had a lot of jobs. Working on building sites. In the restaurant. Cleaning. You name it. I usually had at least three jobs. One was as a cleaner at a university. Late one night I got talking to a researcher about joints.'

'Joints?'

'He'd designed a new artificial joint that he hoped would last longer than the ones in use at the time. We got talking about recuperating from injuries and I chipped in with questions based on what I'd seen with horses. Not that I knew anything about artificial joints, but I was interested.'

Of course he was. He'd always had an inquiring mind.

Portia remembered him with the animals on the estate. She'd once thought that in other circumstances he might have become a vet. He had an affinity with horses and his care was second to none. It was the one area in which her father could never fault him.

'His field was fascinating and he was happy to talk about his work.' Lex paused. 'Later, when I met my father and we got to know each other, he offered me a place in his firm. My two older half-brothers worked there but I thought it would be better for me to do something different.'

'Because you felt you didn't fit in? Didn't they make you welcome?' The words escaped before Portia thought about them. 'Sorry. That's none of my business.'

Yet she was curious. The more she learnt, the more she wanted to know.

'I don't mind talking about it.' He paused as if gathering his thoughts. 'They all made me welcome. My father, half-brothers and half-sister. They wanted me to join the shipping business my great-grandfather started. But I felt…' He lifted one shoulder as if uncomfortable. 'I wanted to make my own mark. Build my own success. I suppose that sounds ungrateful but—'

'It doesn't.' Portia remembered Lex's pride and determination. And his hard work. Maybe too, he'd felt he had to prove himself, not least to the wealthy family he'd discovered. Had his siblings thought him a freeloader at first? That would have spurred him on to succeed independently. 'Your father must be proud of you for standing on your own two feet.'

He nodded. 'You're right. For all his protests I think he was pleased. He offered me the money to start my own enterprise. *That's* how I began. I didn't do it alone. I had help. *We* had help. The company wouldn't have got anywhere without that initial funding. But I paid back the start-up funds with interest.'

'Let me guess? You started with your friend's artificial joint?'

'I wish. The university took a deal with a large company. No, we started small and learnt a lot along the way and we've been more successful than I'd dared hope. We work with top-class teams around the world with exciting new technologies.'

Lex's enthusiasm was catching. He loved what he did and she was glad for him.

She hoped she'd find similar fulfilment when she had a chance to pursue her dreams. Her smile faded as she considered the complications ahead. She'd finally got to the point of being able to undertake the study she'd wanted for so long but she couldn't imagine studying with a baby. Maybe in a few more years.

'Is something wrong, Portia?'

'Nothing at all. So you're close to your family?'

How strange it must have felt to acquire siblings and a parent so late in life. She almost envied him the experience. Her mother had died years ago yet Portia still missed her.

'Yes,' he said after a moment's consideration. 'It took a while. That was my fault. I suppose I wondered if they felt obliged to be nice to me. But they're a patient lot and we get on well.'

He took a long draught from his glass. 'That's something I want to discuss with you. Seeing my family.'

Portia snatched a breath.

Was that why he'd been so forthcoming, answering her questions? They'd strayed into personal territory, discussing his relationship with his Greek relatives. Yet Lex had answered every query, letting her into his private life in a way she suspected few others were allowed.

Had he been softening her up to meet them? As part of his plan to convince her to marry and stay in Greece?

Predictably her muscles tensed.

Portia shook her head. It was one thing to have a quiet holiday here in private. It was another to meet his family. Her world was already out of kilter with the news Lex wanted to be a permanent part of it. She wasn't ready to get so involved in his life. Keeping her distance protected her from hurt. Meeting his relatives would complicate things.

'Hear me out before you say no,' he urged.

'You promised privacy. Peace and quiet.'

'I did and I'll keep my promise.' After a moment he continued. 'It's my father's birthday next week. My sister, Zoe, rang soon after we arrived on the island to check when I was coming to Athens. I was swimming and when she couldn't raise me she rang my housekeeper.' He shook his head. 'Aspasia let slip that I had a female guest and Zoe's been threatening to visit ever since.'

Portia stared. 'Surely she knows if you've got a woman here you want privacy, not a visit from your sister.'

Heat climbed her throat. Because she was imagining him here making love with another woman? Or because, despite her caution, she wanted to be that woman?

What a tangled mess!

'Of course she knows. But you have to understand Zoe has spent years trying to find me a long-term partner.'

'Oh.'

Portia's stomach plummeted. It shouldn't be a surprise. She'd wondered if Lex had a woman in the wings.

'She also knows I've never brought a woman here.'

'Really?'

Lex removed his sunglasses, his gaze meeting hers with a warmth she felt all the way to her curling toes. 'Really. This is my private place, my retreat.

'I've fended Zoe off for the last week but she's threatening to turn up anyway if I don't bring you to Athens. My sister is warm and goodhearted but bossy. For some reason she thinks I need taking in hand.' He smiled ruefully. 'I was already going to invite you to my father's birthday dinner. I'd like you to be there.'

'But I'm an outsider.'

Those denim eyes held hers and her blood sizzled. Sometimes it felt like a losing battle, trying to stave off her desire for this man.

Was that weakness? Was she fighting the inevitable? The idea scared her.

'You're not an outsider, Portia. We share so much. Even if you don't want to marry me, you're my oldest friend.

'Friends *trust* each other, Lex. They don't believe the worst then cut them off without a hearing.'

Portia's chest tightened as emotion welled from deep inside. Emotion she'd suppressed too long. Because she'd tried to move past the bitterness of disappointment, not wanting to dwell there. 'You *discarded* me.'

He nodded, his face grave.

'I let you down badly.' His words, slow and deep, had the resonance of a tolling bell. 'I'm ashamed of what I did. I was a stupid kid and couldn't quite believe my luck in having won you. I was proud and selfish but my confidence was a veneer. When it cracked I saw it as proof I'd been fooling myself.' He raised his hand. 'That's no excuse. There *is* no excuse. But it's an explanation.'

He paused, his gaze holding hers. 'I'm sorry, Portia. If I could undo the past I would. But I'll make it up to you now. I want to look after you.'

His expression made her chest squeeze. He could still make her feel too much.

'You're going to be the mother of my child. You're carrying the next Tomaras in your womb. Let me share the responsibility.'

It was on the tip of her tongue to say her baby would be born an Oakhurst. But that was quibbling.

She wanted to tell him she could look after herself. Instead she exhaled slowly, trying to release the tension gripping her.

'I know you're trying to do what you think is right.'

But was it right for her?

'Come to Athens with me next week. I can show you some wonderful galleries and you'll still have plenty of time to rest. You can meet my family and get a better feel for my life in Greece. One way or another they and I are going to be in your life from now on. This way you get to meet them with no pressure on you. Surely that's a good thing.'

'They don't know about the baby?'

'I haven't told a soul. I'd simply introduce you as a friend, visiting from London. Time to tell them about the baby later, when we've made some decisions.'

Decisions she was putting off.

Portia plucked at the herb growing beside her hip, releasing a rich, savoury scent into the fresh sea air.

He sighed. 'If you don't want to go I can't force your hand. But don't be surprised if my sister turns up next week. She often sails from the mainland and is quite capable of arriving unannounced. You could stay in your room and avoid her, but it might be stressful hiding out instead of meeting her.'

Portia stiffened. She wasn't hiding. She just wanted quiet time to unwind and decide what she was going to do.

You're hiding. You've had a week of quiet but you're no closer to sorting out a compromise with Lex.

What are you going to do if his sister comes? Lock yourself in your room?

Lex was right. His family was important to her, because they'd have a role in her child's life. Maybe meeting them would help her decide what to do for the future.

Are you really thinking about migrating to Greece? Even marriage?

She wasn't thinking about anything but making good choices for herself and her baby, which meant being well informed. Besides she was curious about Lex's family. Curious about his new life and the man he'd become.

'Thank you for the invitation. I'll come to Athens and meet your family.'

CHAPTER TEN

LEX WATCHED PORTIA survey the icon, hands clasped and head tilted, totally enraptured by the old painting.

He couldn't take his gaze off her.

It had been an inspired choice, bringing her to this small but impressive museum. Art really was her thing.

'It's magnificent,' she whispered.

'Some people find icons too stylised, a little stern.'

The painting of mother and child, several hundred years old, was both those things.

'Doesn't that just show a reverence for the subject?' she countered. 'Anyway, the formality only makes her tenderness more moving. You can see it in her eyes and the way she's holding him. You can *feel* the love.'

He surveyed the icon and nodded, surprised. In the past he'd barely noticed. Now he registered the emotion both in the image and himself.

Because the bond between parent and child had never felt so personal to him? His relationship with his own mother had been problematic.

Is that why Portia was so fascinated by it? Because of the way it portrayed motherly love?

Lex had a vision of Portia holding their baby in just the same way, nestled in the crook of her arm. She'd smile down at it, her expression tender and beguiling and he...

What would *he* be doing?

His pleasure faded, replaced by an unsteady churning in his belly.

If she had her way he'd be in another country, getting updates on the child's progress from afar.

His mouth tightened. He wouldn't let that happen. One way or another, he'd persuade Portia that their futures were so entwined separation wasn't an option.

His son or daughter wasn't going to be raised far away from him. His child would know the security of a mother *and* father. It wouldn't have a life marred by secrets or relationships broken by distance. These last years he'd experienced familial love and he wanted that for this baby. With his father as role model he'd learn to be a good dad.

Lex rarely let himself think of the years he and his father had missed out on, or the siblings he hadn't known until his twenties, because to do so brought bitterness and regret. But that knowledge made him absolutely determined to convince Portia to his way of thinking.

Instinct urged him to move swiftly and secure what he wanted. But his knowledge of Portia told him to take his time. Ordering her about, as her father had, only provoked obstinacy. He needed to be persuasive. Yet patient.

After ten days on his island she looked better, with more colour in her cheeks and the shadows almost banished from beneath her eyes.

Whereas he wouldn't relax till he had a ring on her finger and her promise to build the sort of family he'd never had. But it was more than that. Having her under his roof, forced to play the mild-mannered host, was torture. He'd spent his nights imagining her back in his bed.

It was a wonder she hadn't noticed the tension riding him, the brittle shell cloaking his visceral hunger.

His gaze skated hungrily over her. She looked fantastic in

a cinnamon-coloured dress with cream polka dots. Chic but casual. Incredibly alluring.

She shifted and he was so close that her scent teased him. The faintest fragrance, like bluebells, fresh and beguiling, stirred his senses in an altogether earthy way. Years ago he'd thought it was a perfume she wore. Now he wondered if it didn't come from a bottle but was intrinsic to Portia.

Lex's flesh tightened and that ever-present urgency notched higher.

You've never responded this way to any other woman. Just a drift of scent or the hint of a smile or the fleeting brush of satin-soft skin...

He wanted to take her to bed. Now.

He had a one track mind where Portia was concerned. Pregnancy hadn't altered that. In fact, it made him want her more. He wanted to protect her and bed her and persuade her.

Lex shoved his hands into his jeans pockets, rocking back on his heels. He was locked in a continual battle between mind and body. The urgent need for intimacy and the knowledge that this relationship, fractured and full of pitfalls, was too important not to get right.

'Are you ready for lunch?'

Finally she transferred her attention from the painting to him. Was that why he'd interrupted her reverie—because he wanted her attention back on *himself*?

'I *am* hungry.'

She sounded surprised but he knew how little she ate for breakfast. She'd explained about morning nausea and there'd been a few days where even at lunchtime she'd barely nibbled at her food. It was a relief to see her looking forward to a meal.

'No morning sickness?'

'Not today. It hasn't been quite as bad in the last couple of days.'

'Then we need to make the most of it. Come on, I know just the place.'

He led her through the building but instead of exiting through the main door, ushered her up to roof level.

Her eyes widened as they stepped out onto the flagstone roof terrace. The building was an elegant old villa. But the space here was modern with its café, potted plants and wonderful view over the centre of Athens.

'It's not peak tourist season so it's quiet. It's not a proper restaurant but I thought you'd like somewhere casual.'

It was a good place to avoid the paparazzi too. Soon word would get out that he was in Athens and wasn't alone. He wanted to shield Portia from that attention. He'd arranged discreet security for them and was grateful that for now the protection detail could give them space. He suspected she hadn't even noticed their minders.

'Casual is perfect.' She drifted to the parapet, taking in the view of the botanical gardens and the parliament building, with the Acropolis rising above the city. 'Thank you, Lex.'

That smile.

Something inside unknotted and pleasure sighed through his veins.

She mightn't be ready to marry yet but that unfettered smile had to mean something. It was almost like the way she'd looked at him years before. When they'd been everything to each other.

His pulse skipped.

What would have happened if they'd carried through their original plan to elope? Would they still have been together? Or would the passion of first love have petered out?

They'd been too young. The fact he'd been able to move on and build a new life proved it wouldn't have worked between them.

He thought of all the good that had come from his move

to Greece. Finding his family, his roots. Finding his way professionally. If he and Portia hadn't been ripped apart he'd probably not have made it to Greece. How much he'd have missed. His family meant so much.

Except Portia hadn't betrayed him. She'd been a victim, even more than he. *He'd* been the one to betray her by believing her father's lies.

Lex watched her settle at a table and pick up a menu. With her blonde hair loose around her shoulders, she barely looked older than the teenager he'd known at Cropley.

Something punched him in the belly. A writhing ball of emotion that seared his gut.

Portia still made him feel so much.

It wasn't just the baby he wanted to look after, but her. He cared about her. He'd let her down once; he wouldn't do it again. He owed her his protection.

She was alone with no one to support her if anything went wrong.

Except him. He'd be there, he vowed.

'Lex?' She frowned up at him. 'Are you going to eat or stand there brooding?'

Half an hour later, replete, he sat back as she finished her juice. Funny how he could happily just watch her. Usually his mind buzzed with business plans and priorities. He'd always had a lot of energy to expend. But around Portia it was easy to let go of the busyness of his life and just be.

Lex smothered a grimace. He'd never been one for just sitting. He'd be meditating next.

'Why art history?'

He'd held back from asking since she shied from discussing herself. But it was time to chip away more of those barriers.

'You find it a strange choice? But you're an art lover. I've seen the pieces you have in your home.'

His eyes narrowed as she channelled attention back to him. 'Why are you afraid to talk to me about it?'

'I'm not *afraid*. I just… It's personal. I'm not used to sharing my hopes and plans.'

He stiffened. Having a baby together wasn't personal?

Was she reminding him their renewed relationship had been based on sex alone?

His mood dipped. The bright, sunny girl he'd known had altered. Once she'd have shared her plans, excited to discuss them. Was it just their broken relationship that stopped her?

Or something more elemental? She'd changed, withdrawing into herself. What had happened in those intervening years?

Something stark pulled his skin tight.

Portia focused on the straw she used to stir her drink. As if the fresh juice were more interesting than her future. 'If you must know, I want a career in the art world.'

'So you're still sketching?'

He'd remembered her love of art but now, suddenly, he recalled the sketchbook she'd often carried. The deft drawings she'd done while she waited for him to finish his chores. Of spring flowers. Of the horses. Of Cropley through the changing seasons.

Anything but portraits. She'd said she couldn't get faces right, though to his eyes her attempts had been outstanding.

Why hadn't he thought of that sooner?

Because you decided years ago to chop her from your life.

Because lingering on the past was no way to get on with the future. How much else had he deliberately forgotten?

'No, not an artist. I don't have enough talent. But I love art.' Her voice lowered. 'It can bring such solace, don't you think?'

Lex met her earnest gaze and felt something shift between them. At last she was letting him in. When had she needed solace? Just when he left? He wanted to press for details but was wary of pushing too hard.

'I totally agree.'

His appreciation of art had begun after meeting his father and being exposed to his private collection. Though they had differing tastes, Lex had enjoyed accompanying his *baba* to exhibitions and auctions, over the years developing a particular interest in sculpture.

'So if you don't want to create your own art...?'

She abandoned her stirring, her expression guarded. 'Eventually I want to work in an auction house or museum. Once I'd imagined being an art restorer but now I've set my sights on curation and maybe valuation.'

'That's very specialised.'

Her lips curved in a smile that looked more like a grimace. 'Is that a polite way of saying my chances of getting work are slim? I already know that.'

'It was just an observation, though I imagine it's a small jobs pool. Lots of competition.' It surely wasn't the easiest of careers.

'You think that should put me off?'

Portia's expression was assessing.

'Because it's not easy?' Lex shook his head. 'I'm a believer in following your dreams.'

Already he was reviewing his contacts in the art world, wondering how he could help.

She sat back, nodding as if he'd given the right answer. 'Is that why you started your business, because it was your dream?'

Once more she turned the subject away from herself. Lex itched to know more. But answering her frankly, helping her know him better, could only bring them closer.

'I didn't have a long-held dream to work in medical technology. I saw the opportunity and I was interested, very interested in the concept. But it was more that I wanted to shape my own destiny, not work for someone else.'

He'd had enough of taking orders in his youth, working long hours for little pay or thanks. He didn't mind long hours. He'd never worked harder than in setting up his own business. But now he got to make the decisions.

'Not even for your father.'

It wasn't a question and normally he'd have left it there. But he was determined to bring Portia closer.

'I considered it. The thought of contributing to an enterprise founded by my family and continued through the generations…' For a guy who hadn't even known he had a family, it was heady stuff.

Lex looked into pansy-brown eyes and decided to share something he never had before. It felt almost too intimate but the stakes were high and if opening up to her pushed through her spiky defences, it was worth it.

'I care for my family deeply and that's reciprocated.' Their warmth had been remarkable. 'I was too young when I left Greece to remember them, but my half-siblings are older and remembered me. They'd all been concerned when my mother took me and vanished. Apparently my sister had nightmares about it for years. My father spent years searching for us but in the wrong places.'

'It must have been terrible for him, for all of them.'

Lex picked up an olive and munched on it. Once upon a time he'd wondered if his father were a brutal man who'd scared Lex's mother into leaving. Now he believed some of her mental health issues had been exacerbated by pregnancy and the stress of adapting to a new culture and language in Greece.

He frowned. Was he asking too much of Portia, suggesting she make her life here with him? But it was the only good solution. He *had* to make her see that.

'Lex?'

'We were talking about the family business and why I

didn't join.' Anything was preferable to discussing his mother. 'I felt I had something to prove. To myself as much as anyone else. I didn't want to be a freeloader.'

Portia's snort startled him. 'As if you'd ever be that. You've always worked hard, especially when your great-uncle grew frail. You were basically the breadwinner for three people.'

He was pleased she respected his work ethic at least.

'I'm sorry my father took such a set against you, and that others took their lead from him. To have everyone about you so negative, it must have been—'

'That was a long time ago.'

No need to agree that he'd carried a chip on his shoulder. It had put fire in his belly and given him a mutinous determination to prove everyone wrong.

Had his planned elopement with Portia grown as much from the need to thumb his nose at her father as the way Lex had felt about her?

Shock rippled through him. Could that be true? Surely not! How callow had he been at nineteen?

He forced himself to smile despite his roiling gut. 'That's something else we have in common, not opting for the easy road. I can see this art course is important to you.'

She twisted her now empty glass. 'I've dreamt of it for a long time. I know it will be tough and perhaps I won't get the career I'd hoped afterwards, but it's important to have dreams, don't you think? Sometimes…'

'Sometimes what?'

Portia shook her head, her mouth turning down. 'Nothing. I was rambling. Tell me about this party tomorrow.'

What had she been going to say? Why were dreams so important? Because they were better than the life she'd led?

Again he felt that steely thrust of shame that he'd fallen for her father's deceit and left her when she needed him. It stifled the question on his lips.

'The party.' He dragged his thoughts from the past. 'It will be at my father's home in Athens. My two brothers and their wives and my sister and her husband will be there along with their children.'

'Quite a few then.'

Lex watched her smooth down her skirt. A nervous gesture?

'They're all very nice and eager to meet you.'

'How much do they know about me?' Her voice rose a notch.

'Only that you're a friend from England.'

Portia sighed. 'They're bound to be curious about us.'

'Naturally. But they're too well-mannered to give you the third degree.' They'd save that for him. His sister in particular would be eager for details. 'After the family dinner the other guests, wider family and close friends, will arrive for the party.'

Her eyes widened. 'Just how formal is it going to be? I packed for a quiet island holiday, not for dressing up.'

Of course Lex had a solution to her lack of suitable clothes for a billionaire's birthday bash. He organised a personal shopper to bring a selection of items to the penthouse.

Portia bit her lip, surveying the racks of expensive clothes filling her spacious bedroom.

Instead of feeling excited, she found it daunting.

It was one thing to let Lex pay for her outfit, since her budget didn't run to glamorous party clothes. But it was yet another reminder that his world bent to his whim. Where shops came to you and no expense was too much if it saved you time and effort.

Her family had been wealthy, at least in the beginning, but Lex's money was on a whole different level. It reinforced how unequal their relationship was.

How could they ever be real partners? If they married would she always be the wife he had to have in order to get his child? Her spirit rebelled at the idea.

'Where would you like to start, Ms Oakhurst?'

'Portia, please.'

'Thank you. And I'm Angeliki.' The personal shopper smiled, suddenly looking much younger, and the jittery feeling in Portia's stomach eased. 'I know you want something for an evening party. But what do you like?'

Portia looked at the huge array, from trousers and tops to full-length formal gowns and everything in between. There were sequins and satins, linens, beading, ruffles and lace.

'Something simple.' She drew a slow breath, then added, 'But something stunning.'

Not because she'd be mixing with well-heeled guests. But because she wanted Lex to see her through new eyes.

The baby had motivated his proposal. But she was more than the person carrying his child. She wanted him to see *her* and to be bowled over.

How appealing it would be to nudge him out of his comfort zone, even just a little.

Portia was tired of him being so reasonable and effortlessly considerate, the perfect host, as if keeping his distance was easy while she found it almost impossible.

She wanted to see the heat of desire in his eyes again and know he missed their intimacy as much as she did.

It was contrary, she knew. *She'd* insisted on physical distance. She should be delighted that he respected her enough not to press her.

But she missed his urgent desire. Missed the affirmation that at least sexually, they shared something.

Instead of appreciating his easy charm and the space he gave her she'd grown fretful and needy.

Blame it on pregnancy hormones.

Easier to do that than investigate why it matters so much.

'Simple and stunning.' Angeliki grinned. 'We can do that!'

It turned out to be fun, shopping without any thought for the cost. Trying on things she'd never have considered, egged on by Angeliki who did have a wonderful eye. Laughing with her over some over-the-top couture creations.

Then they found it. Portia knew it as soon as the silk settled over her hips and she heard Angeliki's sigh.

Turning to face the mirror, Portia froze, eyes widening.

It *was* simple. A sheath that loosely moulded her body to just below the knee. She didn't have a name for the colour. It wasn't purple nor scarlet nor russet but somewhere between them. The deep, rich hue did wonderful things for her complexion and made her eyes glow.

The narrow shoulder straps consisted of a narrow band of deep gold that also ran around the neckline. The band consisted of tiny beads, stitched in an intricate scroll design.

'That one,' whispered Angeliki.

Portia smoothed her hands over the fragile material. 'Yes.'

She'd worn pretty dresses at Cropley but never anything like this. She felt...

Seductive.

Powerful, she added as movement in the mirror caught her eye. The door had opened and Lex stood there, one hand still on the handle.

His gaze was fixed on her with an intensity that scorched. His eyes were dark, colour streaked those high cheekbones and his nostrils flared as if he worked to drag in oxygen.

Fire raced through Portia's blood and her senses hummed.

She lifted her chin, holding his stare. Revelling in his expression. It was the look of a man undone. The look of a man who wanted, more than wanted. A man who craved...

Her.

CHAPTER ELEVEN

'I'VE NEVER SEEN my brother so fixated on a woman.' Zoe smiled conspiratorially as they watched Lex at the centre of a group of guests, all resplendent in evening dress. 'I like it. But do take pity on him soon.'

There was so much to unpack in that. Portia liked that Zoe called him her brother rather than half-brother. For Lex's sake she was glad he really *was* part of the family.

She couldn't help enjoying the other woman's approval. Through the family meal Zoe's positivity and humour had drawn Portia. All the family had been welcoming but she felt most at ease with his sister.

But as for Lex being fixated on her...

'You're mistaken. I've never known a man more self-contained.' If he was focused on anything, it wasn't *her*, but getting her to agree to his plan.

That moment yesterday when their gazes meshed in the mirror was long gone. It had lasted only until Portia swung around to face him, silk swirling around her legs.

His heated expression had vanished. He'd complimented her on her dress choice but there'd been nothing effusive in his manner.

Tonight Lex had taken her to the family home. He'd been solicitous, the perfect escort. For all his response she could have been an aged great-aunt, not a woman he'd asked to marry him.

That single sizzling look might never have been.

He'd as good as said he wanted to marry her to atone for his past actions and to protect his child. But Portia didn't want atonement. Or a protector. She wanted to *matter* to him, and not because of duty.

At least her disappointment had an upside. It had stirred her pride, feeding a vivacity she hadn't felt in ages.

Portia hadn't blinked twice at being with so many billionaires, meeting the guests' curiosity easily. She refused to feel sorry for herself and refused to let Lex see any trace of hurt. Instead she'd mingled, smiled and enjoyed herself.

'You can't see it?' Zoe leaned closer. 'But then he doesn't stare except when you're not looking.'

'Stare?'

'You haven't noticed? He looks at you like a hungry dog eyeing a juicy bone.'

Despite herself, Portia laughed, rotating the bangle on her wrist. 'You've got some imagination, Zoe.'

Lex had said his sister wanted him to settle down. She was seeing things that weren't there.

'If you think I have your brother on a leash, you're mistaken.' Half to herself she added, 'I can't imagine him dependent on anyone. He's so self-assured.'

'If you mean he knows what he wants and goes out to get it, then yes. He does listen to advice, particularly from our father, but even when he first came here, he had confidence in his own decisions.'

'That sounds like Lex.'

He'd always been that way. When her mother died and her father's temper became even more erratic, Lex's reliability and confidence had appealed more than ever. But in those days he'd let her in. He'd loved her.

Or so she'd thought.

Portia's mouth tightened.

She missed that. There'd been something affirming and wonderful about being the one special person in his life. Believing she *mattered* to him.

'You may not see it,' Zoe murmured. 'But I can. You're important to him, Portia. Don't keep him waiting too long.'

Portia stiffened. 'What has he said to you?'

He'd promised not to tell anyone about their situation. She didn't need more pressure to marry and besides, it was too early to tell people about the baby. Especially as she knew that, if the worst happened, there'd be no marriage. Lex had only proposed for the baby's sake.

Zoe tilted her head, expression thoughtful, looking uncannily familiar. Lex did the same when considering a problem, the angle of his head exactly like that.

'He's said nothing. Just that you're a friend having a break on his island.'

Portia exhaled, relieved.

'But he's never taken any woman there. Ever.' Zoe's knowing gaze pinioned her. 'And he's gone out of his way to specify we shouldn't pry about your relationship while you're here.'

'He asked the whole family? Or just you, Zoe?'

'*Touché*.' The Greek woman laughed and Portia couldn't help smiling. 'It's true, I'm the nosy one. No one else would dream of asking what's going on between the pair of you. And I haven't done that, have I?'

Portia held up her hands in mock surrender. 'No, you haven't asked. You've just drawn assumptions.'

'Assumptions? Look to your right, next to the stout man and the woman in red.'

Portia already knew where Lex was. Her internal compass was always attuned to him.

She shot a glance to her right. Lex stood with the couple,

apparently listening to something the man said. But his gaze was on *her* and the look in his eyes…

Instantly she felt the heat of it, like petrol poured on a bonfire. She could almost hear the whump of ignition then the sizzle and crackle as flames shot through her bloodstream.

For a second their gazes held then, abruptly, Lex turned his head, speaking to his companions.

Portia rocked back on her heels, equilibrium blasted to smithereens.

Now he was laughing and so were his companions, more guests clustering close. That searing shared moment might never have happened. Except she *felt* its aftermath in her racing pulse, the febrile heat swamping her, and the tell-tale signs of arousal, her tightening breasts and the melting sensation between her legs.

'See? It's not my imagination. My brother's locked onto you like a heat seeking missile.'

Portia's nipples budded against her bra. That look had been unmistakable. It wasn't the stare of a man obsessed with his unborn child. It was the look of a man obsessed with a woman.

'Lex would say I shouldn't interfere. But my brother's been through a lot. I don't know how much you know about his early life, but it was difficult.'

For the first time Zoe sounded completely serious, subdued even. Portia was about to explain she *did* know about that period in Lex's life when the other woman spoke.

'Let's just say he doesn't trust easily. Nor does he wear his heart on his sleeve. It took a long time for him to relax with us and believe he was welcome. Sometimes I wonder if he still feels he has to prove himself.'

Portia's heart squeezed. That made so much sense. Lex's early life was filled with rejection, even from his mother who was too self-absorbed to care for her child. More often it had been Lex looking after her.

Zoe hesitated for a moment. 'With a past like his, there's a lot for him to move past. Belonging is important to him. *Family* is important.'

She wasn't saying anything Portia didn't already know. She'd witnessed Lex's curiosity about his unknown father and the shadow it cast over him. Yet hearing Zoe spell it out, Portia felt the weight of that shadow. Did it still haunt Lex? Did he still crave family and belonging?

If so it made his ironclad determination to raise their child together poignant rather than selfish.

'Lex is a strong man and proud. I know some people find that intimidating, but he has a good heart. I'd hate to see him yearning for someone who doesn't reciprocate his feelings.'

Portia started. *His* feelings? For her? *She* was the one who had feelings. Feelings for Lex that time and the brutal voice of logic couldn't eradicate. She felt too much for him and he saw her only as the mother of his child.

But did he? The expression on his face moments ago…

It's just sex. You can't build castles in the air on that.

And yet… Was there a chance he *did* feel more? Was it possible that over time their relationship might develop?

Was she willing to take that risk?

Her younger self wouldn't have hesitated. She'd have jumped in, confident and unafraid.

Portia liked to think she still had courage, but it was of a different sort now. Bravery was more often about endurance, about keeping going through tough times rather than taking a single, bold step.

But Lex's look just now made her want to be bold again. To take a chance and see where it led.

She rubbed her arm, feeling the comforting weight of her wide bangle.

'I love that piece. It's antique isn't it? It looks very special.'

Portia met Zoe's bright eyes, then looked down at the wide bangle on her left wrist.

Lex had presented it to her before they left his apartment. Despite every effort to hold back, she'd found herself breathlessly accepting the gift.

She'd assuaged her conscience earlier when she accepted his generosity, telling herself that the trip to Greece was a wise move for her own health and the baby's. And it made sense to accept the sumptuous dress she wore tonight, rather than stand out in her budget-priced cotton sundress amongst the haute couture.

The solid gold bangle was completely different. Even though he said he'd bought it on a whim because it matched the dress perfectly.

It was studded with deep red rubies that formed a series of flowers embedded in the old gold. The engraved scrollwork around the edges almost perfectly matched the embroidered detail in her dress.

Portia had fallen in love with it instantly and hadn't found the strength to deny herself this pleasure, though she'd told herself she should.

Zoe's reaction confirmed her own. This gift wasn't a meaningless frippery purchased by a man with too much money. Maybe that was why she'd been touching it all evening, as if the contact would confirm that Lex *did* feel something for her again. Something more than guilt and protectiveness because she carried this baby.

What did Zoe see? A statement of intent?

'Yes, I believe it's antique. I love it.'

The other woman nodded. 'A gift from Lex?'

Portia straightened her shoulders. 'It was, as it happens. My budget doesn't stretch that far.'

She refused to pretend to be someone she wasn't.

Zoe didn't even blink. Nor did she narrow her eyes as if wondering whether Portia were a gold-digger, after Lex's money. 'Fair enough.' Then that irrepressible grin appeared. 'That makes gift choices easy for Lex. Men have such difficulty choosing presents, don't you think?'

'Actually, I disagree.' The weekend escape to a luxurious country house hotel had been perfect. But even in their youth, before he had money, Lex had surprised her with small but thoughtful gifts that had made her feel special. 'Some of the nicest presents I ever received were from—'

'From Lex? So you *are* very old friends?'

Portia hurried to set things straight. 'Our relationship isn't what you think. Until recently I hadn't seen your brother in a very long time.' Quickly she changed the subject. 'You're not afraid your brother's hanging out with someone who just wants his money?'

The Greek woman huffed out a laugh. 'I can't see you in that role and he's too canny for that.' Her expression turned serious. 'I trust his judgement. I trust *him*. Maybe you should do the same.'

Trust him? But at what cost to herself?

Portia wondered that all the way back to his penthouse.

She was torn, tempted to take a leap of faith and admit Lex's plan for their child had merit. Yet her instinct for self-preservation held her back. Life was safer when she relied only on herself.

But was it time to stop playing safe?

'You're quiet, Portia. Was this evening too much for you?'

'No, I enjoyed myself.' She'd been surprised to find herself liking most of the people she'd met. 'And your family are lovely.'

'I'm glad you feel that way. They clearly like you too.'

The warm resonance in his voice reminded her of Zoe's words. How much family and belonging meant to him.

She and Lex had more in common than she'd let herself believe. Sometimes the sense of something vital missing from her life, the sense of loneliness, was incredibly strong. Perhaps he'd struggled with that too.

'I like your sister.'

'You do?' He took his attention off the road for a second to shoot a glance her way. 'I saw you two with your heads together. I was going to rescue you then you laughed and I assumed everything was okay.'

'There was no need for rescue. And if there had been I'd have done it myself.'

'I know. You've made that clear.'

She frowned, trying to pinpoint his tone since it was too dark to read his features properly. It wasn't disapproval she'd heard, but could it be disappointment? Did he want her to turn to him for help?

It wasn't like Lex to want her vulnerable.

Maybe her rejection of his plan wasn't just inconvenient. Was it possible he felt *hurt*?

The idea lodged hard beneath her ribs, making it difficult to breathe. That would imply a level of emotional engagement she'd thought impossible.

'Thank you for inviting me to meet them. It was a privilege.' She paused. 'It's good to know our child will have uncles, aunts and a grandfather, even cousins to play with.'

'Believe me, they'll be thrilled when they hear our news. That's something we both missed out on, isn't it? No siblings growing up. I'm glad our child will have a wider family.'

Portia's throat closed. That realisation brought peace of mind. Imagine if Lex hadn't been interested in fatherhood. If he'd turned his back on the baby. If there'd been no one to raise her child if something happened to her.

Her blood ran cold and she curved her palms protectively around her belly.

Somehow he picked up on her distress. A warm hand closed around hers. 'It will be okay, I promise.'

The knot of emotion in her throat tightened. He couldn't make such a promise. No one could. But she appreciated the reassurance, found herself clinging to his hand for a fraction longer.

Enough! There was no need to get maudlin.

She relinquished his hand, enjoying the slide of hard fingers against her skin far too much. 'Both hands on the wheel, please.'

'Yes, ma'am!'

He laughed and just like that, everything changed. Her careful control splintered, leaving her wide open.

His laugh was like sunshine and rich velvet. Like joy after grief. Like hot chocolate on a cold night.

Like a hand stroking her sex, making her hum with need.

All night she'd been attuned to him, body primed as if expecting far more than conversation.

Because you want more from Lex than conversation and consideration.

You want him. You never stopped wanting him.

Instead of celibacy allowing her space to gather her thoughts, it had the opposite effect. It was driving her to distraction.

Now, with just a laugh—a sexy, irresistible laugh—he undid her, leaving her prey to raw desire.

Portia shifted, trying to ease the ache between her legs. But the slide of skin on skin, and silk on skin, made her more aware of her arousal.

The dark intimacy of the luxury car felt claustrophobic. All her senses were centred on Lex, the breadth of his shoulders, the length of his legs, the easy way he controlled the car, his hand so close to her thigh when he changed gears. That fresh beach and man scent, making her nostrils quiver. How it had felt when his hand covered hers.

She drew a shuddery breath as they turned off the street into the secure basement car park. Soon the evening would be over and she'd be safe in her own room.

She didn't want to be safe.

Minutes later he ushered her into his private lift. That's when she saw it again, reflected in the mirrored wall before her. That ardent, dark-as-night stare that shot fire to her pelvis and drew a line of silken heat from her breasts to her clitoris.

Portia spun around.

She'd almost missed it. Lex was already composing his features into an expressionless mask.

Her breath tightened in her chest. 'You want me,' she accused, relief surging.

His eyes widened, as if in surprise at being caught out. Then his chin came up.

'Why make it sound like news? You know I do. But—' he shifted back from her '—don't worry. I gave my word to keep my distance. I always keep my word.'

All this time she'd fretted that he found celibacy easy! Lex had just been good at hiding his feelings.

It was unreasonable to feel angry, but she felt such a fool. She'd worried that he didn't want her anymore, worried about her own unrequited desire. Letting it distract her from the serious issue of deciding her child's future.

Because you're scared you already know the most sensible solution?

Because you don't want to take that step without love?

The doors slid open, straight into the foyer of Lex's apartment, but Lex didn't move. He stared down at her, black eyebrows furrowing. 'After all this, you still don't trust me, Portia?'

She drew a deep breath.

Once upon a time she'd trusted him more than anyone. She'd *believed* in him. But he hadn't believed in her and his desertion had broken her heart. Her world had shattered and the injury to her confidence and optimism had taken a long time to heal. His recent, heartfelt apology had helped.

Now she was recovered, happy with who she was. But his appearance in her life had scared her. She didn't want to be that dependent person again, vulnerable to heartbreak. She *refused* to be that vulnerable person.

But it was too late to corral her feelings for Lex into some tiny, safe box. They were too big. Too real.

There was a hiss as the doors closed. He ignored the movement as if nothing mattered but her answer. Gradually hurt replaced his expression of challenge.

Immediately she reached out, her hand settling on his pristine shirt, between the lapels of his formal jacket. Heat saturated her palm and she detected the heavy thud of his heart.

Her own heart tripped then settled to the same beat.

'I *do* trust you, Lex. I wouldn't be here otherwise.'

His eyes held hers. 'And?'

She trembled. He wanted her complete capitulation.

Yet even now, ensnared by this enormous truth, marriage was a step too far. The shadows of doubt and fear still hovered. Instead she admitted the easy truth.

'I trust you, Lex, and I want you. I want to share your bed again. Can we—?'

His mouth cut off her words.

Not with a gentle kiss but with the deep passion that shot them both to the edge of desperation. Lex knew her body, her desires. He knew how to kiss her till she was mindless with pleasure and frantic for him.

She felt that same passion resonate through him. His hold was firm, yet a tremor of arousal coursed through his strong body.

When he lifted his head enough to look into her eyes, Portia was amazed she could still stand. Surely her bones had liquefied. But of course he supported her, strong arms wrapped around her. They pressed together from breast to thigh, her body moulding to his.

Their breaths came in short gasps and her pulse thrummed out of control.

'You really doubted that I wanted you?'

With his erection solid against her, that seemed laughable. 'I did. I thought you'd lost interest in me as a woman.'

Bewilderment showed in his darkened gaze for a moment, then a laugh exploded from his lips. A glorious laugh that made her mouth curl.

'Lost interest? Lost interest! *Chrysi mou*, how could you think for a moment…?'

'Okay. Maybe I wasn't thinking clearly. Maybe pregnancy temporarily addled my brain.' And worry and her own distracting desire.

His arms wrapped more firmly around her so she stood between his thighs, her neck arched and his face tilted down to hers. Slowly his amusement drained.

'I can't imagine a world in which I don't want you.'

The words went straight to Portia's heart. She had to remind herself they were talking about physical desire, not love. But the way he looked at her, and the way she felt, that was enough for now.

'Show me.'

'With pleasure.'

His hand on the button made the doors swish open then he was drawing her into the apartment, across the white marble of the foyer and into the first reception room. Another swipe of his hand and a couple of lamps illuminated.

Long fingers around hers, Lex guided her deeper into the apartment. But her need was too great, the distance to the bedrooms too far.

She halted. 'I don't want to wait.'

Portia saw something flit across his face, edging his taut features with a hint of wildness. Her heart beat faster as he smiled. It was the look of a hungry man sighting a banquet.

She shivered and even that, the slight friction of silk against skin, aroused her further.

Without a word, Lex led her to a long sofa upholstered in soft, pale suede.

'I don't want to wait either.'

Still holding her hand, he sat in the middle of the sofa, his hand going to his belt, drawing it open. She watched, her chest rising on a stymied breath, as he undid the fastening of his trousers, then moved to the zip.

Interior muscles clenched while other parts of her loosened and liquefied. She wanted Lex so badly.

The taste of him was in her mouth and she needed him in her body, as if it had been years since they'd been together instead of weeks.

This, her need for him, had never altered.

'Portia.'

The invitation was half command, half plea. She lifted her gaze to his and what she saw there planted a kernel of hope in her breast.

Whatever happened between them, they were equally bound by this.

Holding his eyes, she gathered the fragile fabric of her skirt, bunching it up to reach beneath and drag down the damp scrap of lace and silk that she wore beneath it.

Lex's hissed breath was loud even over the thrumming in

her ears. His expression exalted her. She felt invincible under that heated, mesmerised stare.

Still holding her skirt up, she moved closer, putting one knee on the seat beside him. Automatically he steadied her until she found her balance, straddling his lap.

His breath cocooned her, the heat of his long limbs and the lambent glow of anticipation in his desire-hooded eyes.

'Portia,' he said again.

Just that, but in a voice so hoarse and deep, it touched her heart.

She shuffled closer, holding herself above his lap as he positioned himself beneath her. She couldn't wait, the tension inside was wound to breaking point.

Portia sank a little and felt the hard velvet head of his erection. A shiver erupted, running from her core, along her limbs and up her spine. Her dress fell as she reached to clutch his shoulders, offering her lips as she lowered herself, finally coming to rest as they locked together.

This kiss was ineffably tender. It seemed to hold a whole world of promise and recognition. As if all that had gone before were merely a prelude.

Lex's hands swept her back, stroked her bare nape, then slipped beneath her dress to her hips.

Urgency reignited, that stunning moment of stillness obliterated by mutual need.

Portia rose, friction stoking the fire between them. When she sank again Lex lifted to meet her, his hands tugging her down. There was no faltering, just a smooth, urgent synergy that bordered on the miraculous.

Surely such pleasure *was* a miracle. Not just the building physical bliss, the urgency rushing through her towards inevitable climax, but what she saw in Lex's eyes. What she felt deep, deep inside as she looked back and gave herself to him.

Her doubts fled as rapture rose.

She couldn't think. All that mattered was this, him and her together, greater than anything that had gone before. She opened her mouth to gasp his name as the tide of climax engulfed her. But her whisper was drowned by his honey and whisky voice.

'Now, *Chrysi mou*. Now!'

Ecstasy took her, piercing pleasure, the myriad sensations and purest joy. Portia surrendered to the inevitable. She was Lex's and he was hers. That was her last thought before the world exploded in shards of gold.

CHAPTER TWELVE

LEX WHISTLED AS he prepared a breakfast tray next morning. Portia had slept late, and who could blame her after they'd spent so many hours awake, making love?

He, on the other hand, had woken at his usual early hour, full of vigour and optimism. As well as the satisfaction of terrific sex, he felt anticipation. Surely Portia's decision to enjoy a physical relationship again meant things were on the right track.

Last night had felt momentous. It had felt like far more than sex.

He'd been stunned by the depth of his feelings when she said she trusted him. When she declared she wanted him. When she held his gaze as they lost themselves in each other.

A shiver tightened the skin of his neck and shoulders, shooting down his backbone before coiling into his belly.

Every instinct told him that what he wanted was within his grasp. He and Portia raising their baby together. Their own family. And if it took more time to convince her, Lex was happy to use his body to persuade her.

He pushed open the bedroom door to see her emerging from his bathroom, wearing nothing but one of his business shirts and an expression of flushed well-being that made him want to tumble her onto the bed.

'I hope you don't mind. I wanted to shower and didn't want to put on last night's dress.'

Lex put the tray on the end of the bed and strode across to her, gathering her hands and planting a possessive kiss on her mouth. That was better. The taste of her lips was more delicious than any morning coffee.

With difficulty he resisted the urge to trawl her bare thighs with his fingertips then pull her hard against him. Instead, on a shaky breath, he kissed her hands.

'Help yourself to anything in my wardrobe. You wear it much better than I do. In fact,' he purred, leaning in to nuzzle her scented throat, 'let's get rid of your clothes and you can wear mine all the time.'

Her laughter sank inside him, making the day shine brighter.

'Come on, Ms Oakhurst. I got you a piece of freshly made *tyropita* from your favourite bakery. You can eat it while it's hot.'

Portia had developed a taste for the flaky cheese pie, finding savoury food worked better at staving off incipient nausea.

But instead of moving to the bed, her fingers curled around his, gripping tight. 'Lex, I've been thinking.'

He froze, searching her face. His buoyant mood dipped at the gravity of her expression.

'You're right. Marriage will give our baby a good start.'

'Not just a good start, it means...' Lex felt his eyes bulge. 'You agree? You'll marry me?'

He knew last night had been a breakthrough but he hadn't expected this.

'Yes, Lex. I'll marry you.'

Yes! He wanted to fist pump the air. But her tentative expression said she wasn't so elated. He hated that she'd had doubts about this and still looked wary. His fault because he'd once let her down. But now that she'd agreed he'd do everything to show her it was the right decision.

They'd build a relationship based on respect and common purpose, and attraction, of course.

Gently he kissed her, filling it with all the reverence and tenderness he felt. He cupped her face, thumbs gently brushing the fine skin of her cheeks.

She kissed him back, arms wrapping around him and he felt the last of his tension slide away, even though his heart was hammering fit to burst.

Lifting his mouth he bent his forehead to hers.

'Thank you, Portia. You honour me with your trust.' They weren't mere empty words. He knew how she valued her independence. This decision hadn't come lightly. 'You won't regret it, I promise. I'll do everything I can to make you happy and to build a good life for us. For our *family*.'

Their *family*.

He'd give their child the love he'd never had when he was young. Though he had a lot to learn, he'd be the best father, the best husband.

Jubilation filled him. 'I know you only met them last night but my family like you. They'll be thrilled with our news.'

But not as thrilled as he was. Lex wanted to shout the news to the whole of Athens. He wanted to gather the family together and announce it today.

'About that.' Portia paused, her forehead wrinkling. 'I want to wait.'

'Wait? What for?'

The sooner they married the better as far as he was concerned. He wouldn't feel completely at ease, he realised, till he had his ring on her finger and their marriage certificate in his hand.

'Let's sit.'

She led him towards the bed and sat down. The movement opened his partly buttoned shirt to reveal one slender thigh and an intriguing hint of shadow between her legs that threatened to distract him.

'Good idea.' As if the idea of delay didn't bother him, or

the temptation of her nearly naked body mess with his head. Deliberately he released her hand and moved away to grab a small table to put beside her, then placed the tray on it. 'You can have your breakfast while we talk.'

Though he'd much rather ignore breakfast and her idea of delaying and simply make love to her again.

Lex gritted his teeth. He was a civilised man. Wasn't he?

He waited until she'd taken a sip of tea and a bite of *tyropita*, forcing himself not to watch the way she slipped her tongue along her lips to catch an elusive crumb of filo pastry. Instead he looked towards the window and the view of the white city beyond.

'Why delay, Portia? There's nothing to stop us moving ahead now.'

She put the plate down and lifted one shoulder. Instead of an insouciant shrug, the gesture looked defensive. Her eyes met his and he sensed something there, something he couldn't read.

'Give me another six weeks before we share our news.'

'Six weeks?' That seemed like an inordinate amount of time. She was already two months pregnant.

Portia nodded. 'In the meantime I'll go back to London, to work.'

Lex scowled. 'You don't want to be with me?' He'd thought everything had changed after last night and her announcement just now. 'I'm going to be your husband. I want to be with you, look after you and the baby.'

Did he imagine she stiffened? He didn't understand. What was wrong with him caring for their child and her?

'Those are my conditions, Lex. I want to carry on my normal life until then. If everything is all right in six weeks' time I'll come to Athens or your island, wherever you're living, and we'll tell your family.

Flummoxed, Lex stared as she picked up her breakfast.

Watching her eat, those neat bites and those lush lips, he was reminded of the way she'd used her mouth on him last night. She'd undone him in so many ways. Yet here she was, munching away as if unmoved by the intimacies they'd shared or the bond he was so sure they'd forged.

Then it struck him. The need for secrecy. The desire to keep her job when clearly he could support her.

She was thinking about the possibility of miscarriage. If there were no baby there'd be no need to marry and she'd want to keep her job.

It was a sucker punch to his belly, winding him and making every muscle spasm. He breathed through the pain, telling himself it wouldn't happen.

His joy dimmed.

'You're young, fit and healthy. The doctor was pleased with you. There's no need to imagine—'

'There are no guarantees with pregnancy, Lex.' Portia spoke softly but her unsteady voice revealed anxiety. It curdled his belly because he knew there was nothing he could do to assuage it. 'No one, not even the doctor, can be completely sure. So let's take our time. There's no need to rush.'

Lex exhaled slowly. 'Okay. In a month's time you'll be twelve weeks through the pregnancy. Everything I've read says that's when it's most likely something could go wrong.'

'You've been reading about pregnancies?'

He frowned. 'Of course. This is important to me too.' He'd even started dipping into parenting books.

She nodded then turned away to pour more tea. 'Even so, I want six weeks. Then, all being well, you can tell whoever you like.'

He looked at her determined profile and knew there'd be no budging her. He understood her determination hid nervousness. The last thing he wanted to do was stress her more.

'All right, though I have conditions of my own.'

She looked at him over the rim of her cup, brown eyes wide. For all Portia's inner strength he saw her fragility. It made him more than ever determined.

'First, if you're going back to work in London, take one more week's holiday first. You said you were owed leave. Take it now in Greece and have a good rest before returning to work. We can fly back to my island and you can relax there.'

After a second she nodded. There was even a tiny smile playing around her lips as she said, 'That's a condition I'm happy to accept.'

'Good. And I'll be there to make sure you're okay.'

'And that I get plenty of *rest*?'

He knew by the glint in her eyes she too was thinking of the night they'd just spent together.

How much better to see that than her hunched tension thinking about the pregnancy going wrong. He'd do whatever he could to take her mind off the possibility.

He waggled his eyebrows 'You can count on me, Portia.'

'And your other conditions?'

'Just one. I'll come with you to London and we'll live together.'

'But I share a tiny flat and—'

'But now we're a couple.' Lex paused to let that sink in. 'We're in this together.'

He understood her caution about telling the world she was pregnant. But he refused to be set aside for the next six weeks, coming back into her life again only when she passed the fourteen week mark. His child *would* survive. Portia would carry it to term. They'd marry and raise it together, perhaps have several children. He refused to countenance the alternative.

'But your work is based in Athens.'

'I have a great team. I can work from virtually anywhere

with a bit of planning. Anyway I've got interests in the UK as you know. So I propose this. I'll rent somewhere for the pair of us. Somewhere convenient to your work. We'll spend next week on my island and then five weeks in London. Together.

'In that time you can talk to your obstetrician about any concerns. If any issues arise, or if you've got any worries at all, we'll stay in London through the whole pregnancy. I can arrange excellent support for you here but I want you to be comfortable and confident in your care.'

Portia put down her cup and twisted to face him fully. 'You'd do that? Work out of London all that time?'

Lex reached for her hand, curling his fingers around it and stroking his thumb across the soft skin.

'I'll do whatever it takes, Portia. Trust me. I won't let you down again. Ever.'

He felt a tiny shudder pass through her and caught a glimpse of emotion flit across her face. She'd already agreed to marry him yet somehow *this* felt more momentous. Knowing he had her trust.

At last she spoke. 'Good. I'll hold you to that.'

He heard the gravity in her voice but he also saw the warm glint in her eyes.

'Excellent. Now we've agreed to terms we need to seal the bargain.'

She arched an eyebrow. 'With a handshake?'

'In the circumstances I believe a kiss is more suitable.'

Clearly Portia agreed. As he leaned towards her she lay back. He found himself leaning over her looking into bright eyes. Her expression made his heart sing.

This was going to work. Everything was going to be okay.

Everything was okay. Far more than okay. The past five weeks had passed in a haze of well-being and comfort.

That final week on Lex's island had been paradise. Lex

had been attentive, tender and passionate and Portia had felt blissfully alive, optimistic and convinced she'd made the right decision to marry him.

That had continued in London. Miraculously Lex had found a stunning Mayfair home with its own private garden less than ten minutes' walk from the auction house.

He finished work early enough to spend the evenings with her, sometimes taking her to fabulous restaurants or galleries. Their nights were filled with such passion she felt almost as if she were sixteen again and wildly in love.

The obstetrician was happy with the baby's progress too. Even Portia's morning sickness had subsided.

Thirteen weeks and two days into her pregnancy and all was well.

Yet her mind raced and the tension that had settled between her shoulder blades lately had turned into a constant ache.

At the end of this week Lex would jubilantly announce her pregnancy to his family. He'd already talked about an engagement ring. Would she prefer modern or antique? Diamonds or something different?

Portia rolled one shoulder, feeling the stiffness there as she stirred bechamel sauce for the moussaka. She checked the clock. She'd left work early to attend her obstetrician's appointment and there was still plenty of time before Lex got back from his meeting. It would be a nice surprise to share a home-cooked meal instead of dining out or ordering in something prepared by a professional chef.

Maybe she'd make dessert. It would keep her busy.

The sauce was ready. She turned it off and poured it over the moussaka. Then bit her lip when her unsteady hold resulted in a massive splat of hot sauce across the countertop and her hand.

Maybe more cooking wasn't a good idea. Maybe she should have a relaxing bath instead.

But Portia preferred to do something that kept her mind occupied.

Thirteen weeks and two days.

Another five days until they were engaged.

It would be all right. Of course it would be all right. The wheels had fallen off her life before but this time was different.

What if it's not? How will you cope?

The tension in her shoulders swept down her back and around, making the muscles in her abdomen spasm. She gasped and put her hand to her belly. One slow breath then another. On the third she tottered to a stool by the island bench, subsiding there while she caught her breath. The spasms stopped.

Heat prickled her hairline even as a chill enveloped her. Her heart hammered too fast and she felt tremors racking her body.

She needed to be calm. She was worrying unnecessarily. Everything would be fine.

'Portia? You're home?'

Lex had rung her at work to see if she'd like to go out tonight, only to be told she'd left early for some appointment. She hadn't mentioned leaving early and he'd been surprised. These last weeks they'd shared everything.

He shook his head as he strode down the hall. She'd probably gone to get a haircut or something equally ordinary.

But his sixth sense stirred with a warning. Lately she'd had something on her mind. He hadn't probed, not wanting to push her. But despite her sweet lovemaking and passionate kisses, he sensed moments of distraction, even tension.

Was she regretting her decision to marry him?

The idea carved a hollow through him.

They were so good together. Surely she saw that? Weeks ago he wouldn't have questioned it but lately he'd begun to wonder. Her recent determination to fill every hour seemed almost frenetic. If it had been later in the pregnancy he'd have wondered about the nesting instinct he'd read about kicking in. But surely it was too early for that. She didn't even look pregnant.

Apart from her lusher than usual breasts that filled his hands so perfectly.

Lex walked into the kitchen and slammed to a halt. She was perched on a high stool, a white-knuckled hand grasping the edge of the countertop and her other hand cradling her almost flat abdomen.

He was there in seconds, an arm around her back, his other hand on hers where it rested over their child. His heart was in his mouth, his words urgent.

'What is it, *Chrysi mou*? Are you sick? Light-headed?'

'No, I'm fine. Maybe I just did a bit too much.'

With one glance he took in the cooking utensils and the large baking dish of food, but he was more concerned about the way she shivered.

'Come and sit somewhere more comfortable.'

'You need to put the moussaka in the oven. It's already preheated and—'

'We'll worry about that later. First let's get you settled.'

He gathered her into his arms, comforted by her warm weight against him, and carried her out towards the stairs.

'I don't need to go to bed.' Her voice was sharp. 'Just take me to the sitting room. Please.'

He took her there, planning to lower her onto a comfortable armchair. But at the last minute he changed his mind and sank down with her on his lap instead, still cradled in his arms.

Something had been wrong for days. He stood a better chance of finding out what with her here in his arms.

She didn't try to wriggle out of his hold and his disquiet eased a little as she leaned against him. That was one thing the past weeks had cemented, their physical relationship was all he could wish for.

But it worried him that she had something on her mind, something that made her white with worry, yet didn't share it with him.

Didn't she yet realise he was here to support her? He'd promised to be the best husband he could.

'Are you going to tell me what's wrong?'

She drew a shuddering breath and shook her head, her soft hair tickling his chin. 'It's nothing.'

Lex shuffled in his seat, moving her slightly so he could see her face better. 'We've been honest with each other haven't we, *Chrysi mou*? But now you're shutting me out. Obviously something's wrong.' He paused, not wanting to go on, yet needing to know. 'Is it me? Something I've done?'

'No.' The single syllable sounded choked. 'It's not you.'

His stomach dropped. 'Is it the baby?'

She stiffened, a shudder ripping through her, confirming his fears.

'What is it?' He fought to keep the urgency from his voice, to sound calm, though his pulse had skyrocketed. 'Are you in pain? Are there contractions?'

Portia shook her head. 'Nothing like that. I think the baby's fine. The doctor said it was, just hours ago.'

She'd seen the doctor and hadn't mentioned the appointment? His gut knotted. What did he not know?

Lex held her close, moving one hand against her in concentric circles designed to soothe. She'd stopped shivering and she leaned into his touch in a way that told him she needed comforting.

'Are you going to tell me what's going on?'

'I'm sorry.' She sat straighter, no longer leaning close, and he missed the contact. 'It's just me worrying over nothing.'

The hitch in her breath told him it wasn't nothing. 'All the more reason to tell me.'

He stroked his hand along her chin then lifted it so he could meet her eyes. They were huge in her pale face. Haunted. He wanted to cuddle her close and tell her everything would be okay. But he needed to understand.

'Talk to me, Portia. Help me understand.'

For a moment it seemed she wasn't going to say anything. Finally she gave a jerky nod.

'Everything's been going well and I keep telling myself things will turn out okay. But I'm scared. Today is thirteen weeks and two days into the pregnancy.' She gulped in a breath that sounded like a muffled sob. 'That's when I lost our first child.'

CHAPTER THIRTEEN

AT FIRST THE words made no sense. Lex's brain refused to process them.

Portia had lost a baby?

Lost *their* baby?

For the longest time, frozen, he could only stare into her grief-stricken features.

Finally his body made sense of the words though his brain still reeled. Gently he pulled her to him, wrapping his arm more closely around her back, threading his fingers through hers as if he could ward off the chill enveloping her.

His own body felt like it had been dipped in ice. Parts of him felt numb. But his chest started to prickle painfully like when blood began to flow into frostbitten extremities.

'You were pregnant—' he cleared his throat '—before?'

She nodded, the movement jerky.

'When you were seventeen? You were pregnant then?'

He heard himself asking obvious questions even though her meaning was already clear. It was as if he couldn't grasp it. It was too momentous. Too shocking.

But the truth was there in her distress.

'You miscarried as a teenager.'

At least this time he managed to make a statement rather than the question.

Something spasmed in his chest. 'Our baby.'

Portia's bottom lip trembled and she bit it, nodding.

'*Chrysi mou.*' He leaned in and kissed her hair, cuddling her to him. 'I'm so sorry.'

Words weren't enough. He could barely comprehend the enormity of what had happened. They'd made a baby but it had died. *Their* baby. It might have been a happy ten-year-old now, maybe with Portia's big brown eyes and determination.

The thaw was complete now, numbness replaced by searing pain, so sharp it stole his breath.

He pulled back just enough to look into her face. 'What happened?'

She paused before answering. 'It came out of the blue. There was no warning. I was feeling well and then suddenly...' She shook her head. 'The doctor said sometimes these things just happen, but I...'

Lex watched emotions race across her features. 'What is it, Portia?'

Another pause. He felt her tremble. 'I was working multiple jobs, trying to support myself. Knowing there'd be more expenses when the baby came.'

The jab of pain in his chest became an enveloping ache as he imagined teenaged Portia facing that alone.

'I was working as a stablehand. Long hours of physical work.' Her eyes met his. 'But I stopped riding as soon as I found out I was pregnant. I was trying to be careful.' Her mouth twisted. 'At night I worked stocking supermarket shelves. I didn't have qualifications and I couldn't go back home. I didn't trust my father.'

The ice was back, enveloping Lex, yet somehow the pain was there too. At the thought of a teenaged Portia trying to support herself and care for her unborn child, afraid her father would force her into a termination.

And where were you, Lex? You'd fallen for his lies and left her to carry this burden alone.

Lex was a proud man who took satisfaction in doing the right thing. He felt anything but proud now.

'Maybe I was working too much. I tried to be careful but maybe—'

'No! It's not your fault.' He cupped her chin and turned her face towards him, capturing her gaze, willing her to believe him. 'You can't blame yourself. You were doing your best to look after our baby.'

His breath stopped on the word *baby* and for a second panic struck at the thought of another miscarriage with *this* baby, until he forced the idea away.

'But if—'

'The medical professionals said it was just one of those things. Sometimes miscarriages happen. It's no one's fault.'

He'd read about it in the pregnancy books but had never thought it would apply to them. Even so many years after the event it felt like a wound he'd carry permanently. How much worse for Portia? No wonder she'd been stressed about this pregnancy.

So many things took a new meaning now. Portia's insistence that they not tell anyone about the pregnancy. Her insistence on returning to work, rather than marrying him straight away. Because she had a real fear the baby might die. That they wouldn't marry and have a family.

Pain ground through him, crushing his certainties.

Thirteen weeks and two days. *That was* why she'd specified fourteen weeks before they told anyone.

That was why she hadn't been herself these last few days. Why she trembled in his arms. She was afraid for their baby.

'Oh, Portia. I wish I'd known. You've been fretting all this time. What did the doctor say today?'

'That she saw no indications of a problem. Everything seems to be on track. The baby's heartbeat is good.'

Relief engulfed him. 'There you are. You have a good medical report. The doctor isn't worried.'

'But that doesn't guarantee…'

No, there were no guarantees. The realisation terrified him as nothing ever had.

'True.' He made himself say it. 'But if there's no sign of trouble all we can do is look after you both and take each day as it comes.'

How trite did that sound? Lecturing to a woman who'd lost a baby about being positive. But he couldn't bear to see her so panicked. Nor could he bear to think about the possibility of another miscarriage.

'I know. I'm trying.'

'Of course you are, *Chrysi mou*. But from now on I'll be here at your side. Remember that. You're not doing this alone.'

He thought of her in her teens, pregnant and alone, then losing the child with no one there to support her.

His skin crawled with horror. His belly cramped. He should have been there. He should have been by her side, even if there'd been nothing he could do to save their baby.

Regret, guilt and something close to despair overwhelmed him. He needed to be strong for Portia and this child but for a moment all he could do was lock her in his arms and weather the emotional storm.

She turned her head into his shoulder and he welcomed that sign of her trust. He held her tight, wishing there was more he could do to ease her pain.

Finally he found his voice. 'Why didn't you tell me, Portia?'

It would probably sound ridiculous, admitting to a superstitious fear that by voicing the possibility she might jinx this pregnancy. Portia wasn't normally superstitious.

'I didn't want to think about it. Besides, why worry you when I'm doing enough worrying for the pair of us?'

The steady hand stroking her back faltered for a moment before continuing. 'We're a couple now, Portia. I can't promise I can fix everything, but surely it's better not to bottle up your worries.'

She couldn't imagine Lex afraid of anything. If so, would he share with her?

But she'd seen his devastation at her news. There was no doubt he cared about this baby she carried, and the one she lost.

You always knew he cared about the baby. Everything he's doing is to protect his child.

Portia stifled regret. It was churlish to worry that she'd always be a lesser priority to him than his children. She'd accepted that when she'd agreed to marry him. She had no false hope that he loved her now as he once had.

Yet she felt a little better for blurting out her deepest anxiety. Seeing Lex's response to her news, knowing he felt some of the same emotions, eased something inside her. Even just burrowing into his body, letting his strength and heat act like balm to her wounded soul made a difference.

Her mother used to say a problem shared was a problem halved. Yet Portia had spent so long reliant only on herself, she'd got out of the habit of opening up.

She doubted anything would ever completely take away the pain of losing her baby, but it seemed her mum was right. Maybe talking about this was part of a healing process.

'Thanks, Lex. You're right. Talking about it does help.'

'I wish I'd known about our child all those years ago.'

She stiffened, sitting straighter and putting some distance between them, though he still embraced her.

Would he have stayed by her if he'd known about the baby?

Of course he would.

But his words brought back the terror she'd felt, so young and facing an unexpected pregnancy on her own.

'I never did get my phone back. But I tried to call you later. You didn't pick up, remember?'

Lex looked uncomfortable. 'I'm not blaming you. I know I let you down.'

Did he have any idea how much it hurt that he'd been so ready to believe the worst of her?

He read her distress. 'I'm sorry, Portia. I was young, proud and hurting. I was an idiot, believing that lie even for a second.'

Whereas she, even younger than he'd been, had taken far too long to realise the man she adored and for whom she'd given up everything, hadn't believed in her.

That had been the crucial difference between them. Portia had loved him with her whole heart. Had pined for him for years, despite his desertion. But Lex…maybe he'd thought himself in love but it couldn't have been real. Liking and lust maybe.

'I hate that I abandoned you. It makes me sick to the stomach, thinking of all you endured alone because I let pride blind me to what I should have known.' He paused. 'You were the first person I really believed in. I think that's why I reacted so badly when I thought you'd just amused yourself with me. I behaved appallingly. I'm surprised you had anything to do with me when we met again.'

'So was I.' She'd tried, heaven help her. But she hadn't been able to resist the deep-seated yearning. 'It wasn't what I'd intended.'

Because she knew having anything to do with Lex was bound to hurt her.

Because even after all she'd been through, she'd never quite shaken her weakness for him.

Call it what it is! You've been hiding from it too long.

Love. You love him.

He only had to sweep back into your life to have you sharing his bed. And when you discovered you were pregnant you went to him. Not because you couldn't cope alone but because, no matter what lies you told yourself, you wanted another chance with him.

Even though it's the baby he loves, not you. You can't walk away from him, can you?

You're going to marry him and make the best of this convenient marriage.

He's a good man. Caring. Honourable. Passionate.

You can't let it matter that he'll never love you.

Portia looked down to where one large masculine hand gripped hers, needing to hide the hot tears welling behind her lashes.

'Chrysi mou.' To her amazement his voice was unsteady.

She blinked furiously and raised her head. He looked… ravaged. Not like the powerhouse billionaire and confident lover she knew. He looked as upset as she felt.

'Please don't look like that, Portia. I've learnt my lesson. I promise I'll never give you reason to regret being with me. I'll do everything I can to make you happy. You and our child. I'll look after you both.'

There it was. Their child. His real priority.

Yet how could she fault him for caring about their baby? He was going to make a wonderful, dedicated father.

So what that she didn't need someone to look after her? That what she wanted was a partner. An equal. Someone to share with. Someone who felt for her what she did for him.

She was going to be sensible and pragmatic.

'Let me make it up to you, Portia.'

She inclined her head. It might be a lopsided relationship but they'd make it work. She'd learnt not to reach for the stars, expecting love. She'd settle for an imperfect marriage because she'd be with the man she loved. And their child would have a secure, supportive family.

'Yes,' she said, striving for a smile. 'You can start by putting that meal in the oven.'

His crack of laughter wound like a golden thread around her heart.

'Yes, ma'am. Meanwhile how about I run you a bath? Let me pamper you a little.'

His smile was teasing but she read concern in those denim blue eyes.

See, he really does care.

'That sounds perfect.'

But she steadfastly turned her thoughts away from what would really be perfect. To have Lex love her.

CHAPTER FOURTEEN

PORTIA LET HERSELF into the Mayfair house, dropping her keys on a table in the entrance and toeing off her shoes.

That was better. She rolled her shoulders, stiff after a day at work. Lex was right, reducing her hours from next week would make a welcome change.

He'd been as good as his word since that day two months ago when she'd shared her fears for the baby. Nothing had been too much trouble for him. He'd changed his plans so they could stay in London through the pregnancy because the city was familiar to her and she trusted her doctor.

They'd agreed to move to Greece after the baby was born and though she had some trepidation about moving to a new country and learning the language fluently, she knew it was the right thing. In Greece their child would have family, more than just Portia and Lex. She wanted their baby to grow up as part of a large, loving network.

She padded down the black-and-white-tiled hallway to the vast kitchen and family room that looked out onto the garden. Flicking on the kettle, she got out the tea, settling on a stool while the water boiled.

To her surprise Lex hadn't tried to persuade her to stop work as the weeks passed and her fears of miscarriage abated.

Portia couldn't fully explain why she clung to her job. It wasn't as if her modest wage made a difference to their income and she didn't plan to return to the job after the birth. She still hoped, one day, to pursue her studies.

Maybe it was just a way to keep her mind off those occasional doubts.

She shook her head and got up to make the tea.

Surely it was ungrateful, that niggle of disappointment she still felt as the date for their wedding approached.

Lex's family was flying out from Greece next week. She had the dress. They had a venue. Marrying Lex was the right thing. Solicitous, he'd even suggested they wait a couple of extra months before marrying so she didn't feel rushed.

Her husband-to-be was considerate, generous and thoughtful. Their sex life was phenomenal. Any impartial observer would declare her a lucky woman. And she was. The fact that he didn't love her shouldn't matter.

She remembered his heartfelt declaration at nineteen, and how easy it had been to tell him she loved him too.

But that man had gone. Despite Lex's physical passion and solicitude, it was love for their *child* that motivated him. He'd made it clear that was his priority, agreeing more than once that they'd moved beyond romance.

That had stopped her blurting out her own feelings. She didn't want his pity.

She firmed her lips and carried the steaming mug across to a comfortable sofa.

Life isn't a fairytale. Better to have the man you love, his thoughtfulness, generosity and passion, than not have him at all.

Yet despite the glow of pregnancy and Lex's passionate lovemaking, she felt restless. As if the walls were closing in around her.

Instinct warned her not to go ahead with the wedding. Didn't she want more for herself? Didn't she want love?

Annoyed at the direction of her thoughts, Portia sipped her tea, only to spill it at the sound of the doorbell.

Lex! Had he returned early from America? She was on her feet, pulse quickening, when she realised her mistake. He wouldn't use the bell because he had a key. Besides, he wasn't due back for two days.

She opened the door to find their neighbour on the doorstep.

'Mrs Buscot!' One look told Portia something was wrong. The elderly lady was trembling and pale, one hand at her throat in a gesture of anxiety. 'Please, won't you come in?'

'Thank heaven you're here. I need your help.'

Lex told himself Portia had probably gone to bed early, yet he couldn't stifle disappointment that the house was dark. He'd tried phoning and texting to tell her of his changed travel plans but couldn't raise her.

That had sent unease shooting along his spine. Had something happened to her? To the baby?

He turned on the light and strode through the house, finding only empty rooms.

Maybe she'd gone out for the evening. But he didn't believe it. He hadn't missed her tiredness and knew it was only partly due to their lovemaking. Something had interfered with her sleep and lately she preferred to stay home at night.

Just when he thought she'd begun to believe everything would be okay with the baby.

Something was worrying her but she hadn't confided in him. He tried not to let that bother him, telling himself to be patient, that she'd share with him eventually just as she'd done about the miscarriage.

He took the stairs two at a time, driven by the need to see her, hold her. The whole time he'd been in the States he hadn't been able to settle—a first when it came to business. The hotel bed had been too empty. He'd missed Portia in his arms, missed talking with her over breakfast, relaxing with her in the evening, and in meetings his attention kept wandering.

He found the bedroom deserted, the bed neatly made.

Lex glanced at his watch, his nape prickling.

She wasn't expecting you. Maybe she went out to see a late film.

But he didn't believe it.

The bathroom was empty too, except a door in the vanity unit was open. Lex stared, trying to remember what had stood on the now empty shelf.

Portia's toiletries bag.

Swiftly he opened every drawer and door. It wasn't there.

He crossed the bedroom, flicking on the light switch as he entered the dressing room.

A set of Portia's work clothes lay discarded on the velvet couch. A couple of other garments spilled across them as if hastily dropped. That was unlike Portia. He strode to the vast cupboard that held their luggage. The new pieces he'd bought her were all there but there was a gap beside them where her small case had stood.

Something sliced through his abdomen like a butcher's knife carving meat. He rocked back on his heels and would have stumbled but for his grab at the door.

There's a sensible explanation. Portia wouldn't just walk out on you. She's not that sort of woman.

Yet panic bubbled inside him.

A nasty little voice in his head reminded him that he'd once walked out on her. Valiantly he tried to ignore it and not jump to conclusions.

He'd known something wasn't right. Despite Portia's smiles, the phenomenal sex they shared and her changed attitude to Greece and marriage, lately there'd been an undercurrent of… Something he couldn't put a name to. He couldn't shake the idea that something was missing between them.

He spun around, surveying the dressing room. In one corner hung the long bag containing her wedding dress. The box with her bridal shoes was beside it. But there was a gap where her favourite flat shoes normally rested and a few other empty spaces here and there.

He swallowed a knot of fear.

Portia wasn't answering her phone. She'd taken a bag and some of her clothes and left without a message.

Lex sprinted from the room and down the stairs. Maybe she'd left a note and he'd missed it.

But the search proved fruitless.

Sweat beaded his hairline as fear gripped him. Two horrible options lodged in his brain, curdling his stomach. That she or the baby had taken ill and Portia had gone to the hospital. Or she'd decided not to go through with the wedding. Maybe she'd left him. Both ideas were untenable.

He pulled out his phone to begin ringing hospitals.

Fatigue bowed Portia's shoulders as she trudged up the steps, her small case in her hand. It had been a long day and she couldn't wait to put her feet up.

She fumbled with the key in the front door, finally fitting it properly, only to have it jerk open so quickly she teetered on the brink of falling over the threshold.

A huge figure loomed before her, backlit by the hall light. Her heart thudded high in her throat but in an instant relief rushed in. She'd know that sexy, tousled hair anywhere, the silhouette of a powerful, familiar figure.

'Chrysi mou.'

His arms encircled her, hauling her in against his tall frame, his mouth brushing her hair as he murmured a stream of incoherent words.

Portia dropped her bag and slid her arms around his waist. It felt so good to be in his arms again. *This* was the homecoming she wanted, not returning to the empty house as she'd envisaged.

'What are you doing here? You're supposed to be in America.'

Not that she minded. This fervent embrace had her heart skipping and her silly brain reading more into his welcome than it should.

'I came back early to surprise you. Where have you *been*?'

There was a discordant note in his deep voice and she finally registered the tremor running through his big frame.

'Lex, are you all right? Is something wrong?'

A huff of laughter brushed warm air across her forehead then he turned, one arm still around her back, and drew her inside, grabbing her bag on the way. It was only then that she saw the blaze of light inside. She'd been so tired she hadn't even noticed from the street.

'You disappear for at least twenty-four hours and ask if something's wrong? I've been out of my mind with worry.'

The door shut behind them and in the spill of light she saw his face properly for the first time. He looked strung too tight, the planes of his face more pronounced. Lines furrowed his brow and grooved deep beside his mouth. The pulse at his temple hammered.

She'd seen Lex annoyed, thrilled by the news of their child, lost to a world of sexual pleasure, or warmly smiling, but never like this. Instantly she knew what he'd feared.

She grabbed his upper arms, holding his gaze. 'It's okay, Lex. Nothing's happened to the baby. It's perfectly fine.'

He sucked in a deep breath that made his chest rise. He nodded then exhaled. Yet instead of looking relieved, his features remained tense, like a man on the edge.

That didn't make sense. She was here now and he knew the baby was okay.

'Why did you go away, Portia? And why didn't you tell me?'

'It's a long story.' And it had been a trying twenty-four hours. She felt completely done in. 'I had no idea you were worried about me. But right now I need the bathroom and a cup of tea in that order. I'll tell you all about it in the kitchen.'

Instead of stepping back, his grip on her remained firm, almost as if he didn't want to release her. 'I'll carry your case upstairs while you freshen up. Then I'll make tea and some supper for you while you talk.'

He kept his arm around her all the way up the stairs into the bedroom. Was it fanciful to think him reluctant to let her go? Of course it was. He'd had a fright, thinking something had happened to the baby, that was all.

Yet she was aware of him watching her every step of the way as she walked into the bathroom. Her skin prickled, heating under that intense stare.

It felt like the very air sparked with electricity. Like when an enormous thunderstorm was about to break.

Portia longed to take a shower or a long soak in the bath but didn't have the heart to keep Lex waiting.

As soon as she entered the kitchen he swung around. Was that relief on his features? She was so tired she was probably seeing things. She'd already assured him about the baby so there was nothing left for him to worry about.

Her bones seemed to melt as she sank onto a stool beside the gleaming counter. 'I didn't expect you back here yet. Was there some problem with your meetings? I thought—'

'Why did you leave, Portia? And why didn't you answer my calls?'

Lex put a steaming mug of tea in front of her but didn't move away. He stood with one hip propped against the counter, ankles crossed. But his tightly folded arms belied his casual pose. He looked just as tense as when he'd ripped the front door out of her hand. Like a man on the edge.

* * *

Lex looked down into her wary eyes and tried to tell himself he was worrying about nothing. One of the traits that made him an excellent businessman was his ability to remain calm and think quickly under pressure. To adapt and turn problems into solvable opportunities.

That facility deserted him now. For a night and a day he'd been frantic with worry and he couldn't seem to switch off. Even the news that their baby was all right didn't diminish his fear.

Portia had returned but not necessarily to him. She hadn't expected him home. He should still be in the US, except his need to be with her had surpassed all his other priorities.

Was she back for good? Or had she returned temporarily, not expecting to see him?

Gut instinct told him something was wrong. Something she'd tried to hide these past weeks.

She sighed and lifted the mug, cradling it in both hands. 'I didn't answer your calls because my phone was dead. I left in a rush and forgot to take my charger so the phone went flat. I didn't think you'd worry. We'd already spoken yesterday afternoon and I was returning today.'

'But the couple of times I've been away overnight, I always ring in the evening too.'

To check she was okay.

Because she was precious to him.

The terror he'd felt since yesterday, not knowing where she was or *how* she was, had undone him. And proved beyond all doubt the true depth of his feelings.

It amazed him he hadn't realised before. But then he'd spent years telling himself he was done with such feelings. What a time to discover the truth!

The immense resources he'd put into the search for her

hadn't turned up any viable clues and he'd been mindless with worry.

Portia surveyed him over the rim of her mug as she sipped. 'I know. I'm sorry. I have your number on speed dial but I never memorised it. When the phone died I told myself one night wouldn't matter.'

It had mattered to him. His blood had run cold at the idea she was either sick or had left him.

'I'm sorry I worried you. But truly the baby is fine.'

He nodded. That had allayed some of his fears, but not all.

He'd imagined Portia finding a new place to live, without him, because she'd decided marriage would be a mistake. She'd given up her old flat and her friends hadn't heard from her. Had she been scoping out a new home, returning only to tell him she was leaving?

In her unexplained absence, Lex had finally worked out what had made her so edgy lately. Their upcoming wedding. It had to be. Which meant she was working up to jilting him.

Because she didn't feel the same way about him that he did about her. Despite the sex, despite the friendship, despite the baby, Portia kept a part of herself separate.

Because she didn't trust him enough or care for him enough. That realisation had gutted him.

But he had to hear her say it.

Then persuade her not to leave him.

'Where were you, Portia? What were you doing?'

'You should sit down, Lex. You don't look good.'

She *really* didn't want to tell him what she'd been doing. His heart plummeted.

When he didn't move, she frowned. 'I was helping Mrs Buscot.'

The name was familiar but he couldn't place it. 'Mrs Buscot?'

'Our elderly neighbour.'

Finally recognition dawned. The spry, grey-haired woman who'd befriended Portia, or vice versa. Lex had only seen her to wave to. 'Go on.'

'She'd had bad news. Her daughter in Cornwall was rushed to hospital after a car accident. She's got three young children and her husband is on an overseas work trip. Mrs Buscot had to get down there as quickly as possible to see her and take care of the children. But she was so upset she didn't trust herself to drive yet she needed the car in Cornwall because her daughter's car was written off.'

Lex drew a steadying breath, his racing pulse easing a little. 'So you drove her then stayed overnight.'

She nodded. 'I helped with the children a little today while she went to the hospital again to see her daughter. I caught an afternoon train but there were delays on the line so it took forever to get back.'

He planted his hand on the countertop as relief weakened his knees.

Portia hadn't been running away. The invisible chains weighting his body fell away.

After long moments his brain started processing the rest of what Portia had said. 'How's her daughter? And how's an elderly lady going to look after three young children?'

'Her daughter is doing well. She'll be released in a day or two and her husband will return by the end of the week.'

'I can arrange home help in the meantime. Three little children might be too much for an old lady who's probably still in shock.'

'That's a lovely idea. I'm sure they'd appreciate it.' An expression he couldn't read flitted across Portia's features. 'You really are good at thinking of practicalities and getting things organised.'

Lex narrowed his eyes, trying to identify something in

her tone that made his nape prickle. Ostensibly it had been a compliment. It felt more like a double-edged blade.

'You don't like me being organised?'

'That would be stupid. It's a valuable trait.' Portia sipped her tea. 'It's what you do. You see a problem and you fix it.'

He waited but she said nothing else.

'What is it you've seen me fix?'

But he had a good idea.

She lifted one shoulder. 'Our situation. Our baby.'

'You think I've been *fixing our situation*?' Something lurched in his belly at the idea she thought he was so cold-blooded. She *knew* how he felt about their child.

But she doesn't know how you feel about her.

Lex met guarded dark eyes and felt the rush of blood, the adrenaline surge he sometimes experienced, on the cusp of a major breakthrough.

Could that be it?

He'd avoided confronting his feelings for Portia because of the atavistic fear they might undo him once and for all. He'd told her he'd put her behind him years before but the truth was that had been impossible. It was one of the reasons he hadn't found a permanent partner in the years since they'd separated.

She looked down at her tea. 'I wouldn't put it quite like that. I know the baby means everything to you.' She looked up again, her gaze challenging. 'I admire you for going to so much trouble to create a family for our child.'

Not just for our child.

The words hovered on his tongue, eager to burst free.

But how will she respond if you tell her?

What does Portia feel for you?

Fear, like a lump of ice, skittered down his spine to lodge in his belly.

Still her eyes met his. He couldn't bear the doubt he read

there, couldn't bear that he'd hurt her, in the past and it seemed, now.

'I'm not acting just for the baby's sake, Portia.' He cleared his throat over jagged shards. 'I love you. I fell for you all those years ago and despite everything I told myself, I never stopped loving you. It wasn't just a youthful infatuation. It was something far more profound and still is.'

Portia's mug slammed onto the countertop. He heard the noise as if from a distance. All his senses focused on the woman before him, her eyes growing wide, her beautiful mouth sagging as if in shock.

'You don't have to do this, Lex. We promised honesty, remember?'

He nodded, the movement jerky, and stepped closer, into her space. He lifted an unsteady hand to stroke her cheek, needing the physical contact. His breath expelled in a rush as he touched her warm skin.

'I remember. And I confess I haven't been completely honest.'

Portia started back, jerking away from his hand as if scalded.

He was making a mess of this but he'd lost all his finesse. He was left with only the bare truth.

'I told myself for ages that what we shared was only sexual desire and the remnants of old friendship. That was enough to go on with. And when I learnt about the baby, I told myself the thrill I felt was all about being a father.

'I was a coward. At first it was unintentional, a way of keeping my emotions in check so I wouldn't be hurt again. And there was shame too, that I'd left you to cope alone because I didn't see through your father's lies. I wondered if I were more like my mother than I realised, sabotaging anything like an intimate relationship.'

He raked a hand through his hair, hating what his actions

said about him. 'I let you down, Portia, and at the most fundamental level I knew I didn't deserve you.'

'Oh, Lex.' Warmth encircled his left wrist and he looked down to see she'd grabbed it. Swiftly he covered her hand with his right hand, holding it in place. 'We were both so young. You'd faced prejudice all your life. I'm not surprised you fell for that lie.'

'But you still held it against me when we met again.'

She nodded. 'It took me a long time to trust again. Especially to trust my feelings—'

'Give me a chance, Portia. If you want to put off the wedding, or not marry at all, I'll accept that. I just want to be with you. I love you. I know you've been having second thoughts but I'll do whatever it takes to make you happy. To win your trust back.'

To his horror, she blinked, her eyes overbright.

'Ah, *Chrysi mou*, please don't cry. I—'

'They're happy tears.' She sniffed and her chin wobbled. 'I've loved you all this time. I tried not to but never quite succeeded.'

His heart leapt. 'You love me?'

Her other hand joined his so they gripped each other tight. They both trembled and he saw in her face the dawning wonder and excitement that spilled through him.

She inclined her head. 'That's why I've worried about the wedding. I know it's the best thing for the baby, but marrying someone who doesn't love me back—'

'But I do. With all my heart I do.' Lex lifted her hands, pressing kisses to her fingers.

He dropped to his knee, still holding her hands. 'Portia. *Chrysi mou*. Will you marry me? Not because of our child, but because my life would be hollow without you. I don't think I could go on.' He took a breath so deep his lungs ached. 'I promise to be upfront about my feelings in future.

And if you'll have me, I promise you my trust, my devotion and my love. Always.'

If he lived to be a hundred he'd never forget her expression. So open and loving he felt like he'd swallowed pure sunlight.

'Just try and stop me.' Her sudden laughter was joyous. 'I promise to trust you and love you too, Lex, and share how *I* feel. You're the only man for me. No one has ever made me so happy.' She tugged at his hands. 'Now, get up and kiss me before I really do start crying.'

Lex closed her in his arms and finally believed it was real. She loved him and no man in the world could be happier.

Ages later she murmured, 'What does *Chrysi mou* mean? I tried to look it up but can't spell Greek.'

Lex's hand was supporting the back of her head. He let his fingers comb her beautiful blonde locks.

'It means my golden one. I've always thought of you that way.' He met her dazzled eyes and smiled. He felt dazzled too by his tremendous good fortune. 'You light up my life, Portia.'

'My Lex.' This time her eyes didn't fill with tears. 'We're going to be so happy together.'

EPILOGUE

'*CHRYSI MOU*, is everything okay?'

Portia swung around, smiling. Her handsome husband still took her breath away. Not merely because of how scrumptious he looked in faded jeans and a pale shirt, sleeves rolled up to the elbows.

But because of the familiar light in Lex's eyes as he approached and wrapped his arms around her. That glow of love she saw every day.

'Everything is absolutely wonderful.'

She reached up to curl her arms around his neck, borrowing her fingers in those lustrous curls and tilting his head towards her.

His lips met hers unerringly and she opened her mouth, inviting him in as he pulled her close. Their kiss was slow and full of promise as if they had all the time the world.

Until the sound of someone clearing their throat interrupted and Lex lifted his head.

'Sorry to disturb you lovebirds but the children are getting hungry. Would you like me to get their snacks instead?'

Lex's laughing eyes met Portia's. 'Sisters, eh? Someone needs to talk to her about her timing.'

'My timing's perfect,' Zoe said as Portia turned in Lex's arms to see her stepping through the open bi-fold doors from the terrace into the sitting room. 'If they don't get food soon there'll be a riot.'

'Georgia is too young to riot,' Lex protested. 'She's only a toddler. But if your hooligans are on the rampage I'd better go and get them something.'

Lex pressed a swift kiss on Portia's cheek and loped off towards the kitchen.

'Sorry, Zoe,' Portia said. 'I came in to get the platter of food Aspasia is preparing but got distracted.'

Her sister-in-law laughed. 'You two are always distracting each other. You're like honeymooners.'

It was true, so Portia didn't bother explaining that it had been a painting, not her beloved Lex that had initially distracted her.

'Oh, I like that.' Zoe stopped beside her, looking past her to the very same painting Lex had moved from their London home just this week. 'The place looks enchanted, drowsing in the sunlight, surrounded by roses.'

Portia turned to survey the painting she'd always loved. The one that had brought Lex back into her life. 'That's what distracted me. I love it but I was wondering if it belongs on the wall of a Greek house.'

'If you love it, it belongs. It's your home.' Zoe looped her arm through Portia's. 'I'm so glad you're back in Greece. I'm looking forward to spending lots of time together this summer.'

Lex and Portia had agreed that they'd live here on the island for a while, returning to London when Portia's studies began. For the next several years, probably until Georgia started school, they'd move between the UK and Greece.

'I'm looking forward to it too, Zoe. You're the best sister-in-law a woman could have.'

Zoe hugged her close, smiling. 'Sister,' she corrected. 'I think of you as my sister. And I count myself lucky my brother convinced you to marry him.' She led the way outside where the sound of whoops and splashing reached them from the seashore. 'I hope you held out for lots of special gifts before you said yes.'

Portia laughed and caught Lex's eyes as he appeared on the terrace with a massive tray of food.

She thought of the presents he'd given her, not because she'd asked, but because he knew how much they'd mean to her. Her mother's jewellery. And the exquisite portable writing desk with its secret drawer that had been her mother's grandmother's. Portia and her mum had left each other secret notes and drawings there right until her mum's death.

How Lex had tracked them down, she didn't know. But it felt good having them, knowing she could share them with Georgia and any other children they had.

'Oh, please! There you both go again.' Zoe marched across and grabbed the tray from Lex, her grin belying her mock scornful tone. 'I'll go ahead with the food but be warned, if you're not down at the beach in five minutes I'll send the children up to find you.'

Lex roped his arm around Portia as they watched Zoe head down the path to where eight children, supervised by parents, aunts, uncles and a venerable grandfather, splashed in the shallows.

'No regrets about marrying me and my family?'

'I love your family,' she said as she leaned in, resting her head on his shoulder and flattening her palm to his chest. 'And I love you, Lex.'

His hand tightened on her hip, scrunching her purple sundress. He spun her round to face him and she saw the laughter had fled his face, replaced by intense emotion.

'*S'agapo*, Portia. I love you with all my heart. I can't bear to think what my life would have been if I hadn't seen your painting in that auction.'

She pressed her fingers to his mouth. 'But you did. After

all we've been through it's time to put the past aside and concentrate on what we have now.'

'You're a wise woman, Portia Tomaras. No wonder I adore you.'

He took her hand in his and together they walked down the hill and into a future as bright as the sunlight glittering on the sea ahead.

* * * * *

If you just couldn't get enough of Ring for an Heir, *then be sure to check out these other passion-fuelled stories by Annie West!*

Nine Months to Save Their Marriage
His Last-Minute Desert Queen
A Pregnancy Bombshell to Bind Them
Signed, Sealed, Married
Unknown Royal Baby

Available now!

MILLS & BOON ®

Coming next month

ACCIDENTAL ONE-NIGHT BABY
Julia James

Siena took a breath, short, sharp, and summoning up her courage, stepped into the lift that would take her to the one man in the world she did not want to see again.

Vincenzo Giansante.

'He'll think you're chasing him – and he's made it clear he's done with you.'

Siena's mouth tightened. Vincenzo Giansante had, indeed, made it crystal clear he was done with her – had walked out in the briefest way possible in the bleak light of the morning after the night before.

Well, now she was walking back into his life – to tell him what she still could scarcely believe herself, ever since seeing that thin blue line form on the test stick.

He has a right to know – any man does – whether I want him to or not.

The lift jerked to a stop, the metal doors sliding open. For a moment she just wanted to be a coward, and jab the down button again. Then, steeling herself, she walked forward.

Continue reading

ACCIDENTAL ONE-NIGHT BABY
Julia James

Available next month
millsandboon.co.uk

COMING SOON!

We really hope you enjoyed reading this book.
If you're looking for more romance
be sure to head to the shops when
new books are available on

Thursday 27th February

MILLS & BOON

LET'S TALK

Romance

For exclusive extracts, competitions and special offers, find us online:

⬤ MillsandBoon

𝕏 @MillsandBoon

⬤ @MillsandBoonUK

♪ @MillsandBoonUK

Get in touch on 01413 063 232

For all the latest titles coming soon, visit
millsandboon.co.uk/nextmonth

Afterglow Books is a trend-led, trope-filled list of books with diverse, authentic and relatable characters, a wide array of voices and representations, plus real world trials and tribulations. Featuring all the tropes you could possibly want (think small-town settings, fake relationships, grumpy vs sunshine, enemies to lovers) and all with a generous dose of spice in every story.

♪ @millsandboonuk
⊙ @millsandboonuk
afterglowbooks.co.uk

#AfterglowBooks

For all the latest book news, exclusive content and giveaways scan the QR code below to sign up to the Afterglow newsletter:

SCAN ME

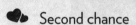